The
Hidden Dance

The
Hidden Dance

Susan Wooldridge

First published in Great Britain in 2009 by
Allison & Busby Limited
13 Charlotte Mews
London W1T 4EJ
www.allisonandbusby.com

Extract on page 307 from *The House at Pooh Corner*
by A.A. Milne © The Trustees of the Pooh Properties.
Published by Egmont UK Ltd, London,
and used with permission.

A CIP catalogue record for this book is available from
the British Library.

10 9 8 7 6 5 4 3 2 1

13-ISBN 978-0-7490-0741-6

Typeset in 12/16 pt Adobe Garamond Pro by
Allison & Busby Ltd.

The paper used for this Allison & Busby publication
has been produced from trees that have been legally sourced
from well-managed and credibly certified forests.

PEFC
PEFC/16-33-111
CATG-PEFC-052
www.pefc.org

Printed and bound in Great Britain by
MPG Books Ltd, Bodmin, Cornwall

Susan Wooldridge is probably best known to the public for her role as Daphne Manners in the award-winning *The Jewel in the Crown*, for which she was BAFTA-nominated and won the ALVA (Asian Listeners and Viewers of Great Britain Award) for Best Actress.

Having trained at the Central School of Speech and Drama and École Jacques Lecoq in Paris, Susan followed in the footsteps of her mother, the actress Margaretta Scott, and worked extensively on the stage both in London and around the country in repertory theatre.

She went on to become a well-known face on both television and film, winning the BAFTA award for Best Supporting Actress for her role in John Boorman's *Hope and Glory*.

Having appeared in the award-winning BBC drama *Bad Company*, about the Bridgewater Four, Susan became actively involved in the campaign to overturn this terrible miscarriage of justice.

Susan lives in London with her partner, writer and theatre director Andy de la Tour.

For Andy,

without whom this book couldn't have been written.

Prologue

Clear as clear she hears whispers from behind the half-open door.

'Wait, the hat's not straight. Now!'

With hands obediently over her eyes, she glimpses the drawing-room door swing wide and a small pair of feet comes pattering in.

'Now, Mummy, now. Open your eyes!'

Clear as clear she sees... A little clown. White pointy hat, red pom-poms the size of dahlias, baggy white suit, a gleaming face. Up to this point the memory is perfect. But a new voice, a man's voice, spoils it all and she freezes. Even in the memory.

'Stop hiding behind closed doors.'

Mother and child stand very still. The man arrives in the doorway. She moves in front of the child to shield him.

The man speaks. Quietly. Almost a whisper. Seductive. 'You can't seriously be thinking of dressing the boy like that.'

She tucks her hand behind to the boy. He clutches it.

The man turns to leave the room.

She cries out without thinking, 'But it's his party—'

She stops. The man is turning back.

'Get those clothes off him,' he whispers. 'I won't say it again.'

The boy runs. The door slams.

The man roars after him, 'Nicholas!' Then he turns slowly back to her. 'You bitch! My God, you'll pay for this!'

Her cry is cut off by the first slap, the sound cracking through the stillness of the day. She gasps, winded. Tries to keep the terror from her face, doesn't want to anger him further.

He stands swaying slightly. She struggles for breath and sees his hand swing back a second time. 'Oh no! Please, don't—'

He delivers the second slap to the side of her head, catching her ear. The pain is precise, crystal clear. All is silent except for the ringing, singing pain – and a far-away knocking.

'My lady, my lady, open the door! Oh, my lady!'

The man leans over her, slowly raising his hand. He doesn't strike. 'Get rid of her!'

She opens the door.

Her maid's face is white, tears in her eyes.

'Go away, Mary. *Please!*'

From behind, the man shoves her and slams the door shut.

'You've made the child a pansy-boy!' She feels the spray of his spit on her face, smells the drink on his breath.

He pushes her to the ground.

'You revolt me!' There is extraordinary loathing in his voice.

He leaves, banging across the hall, slamming the front door.

She lies still, huddled on the carpet, ashamed, terrified at the enormous anger she has provoked.

Everything is quiet.

PART ONE

CHAPTER ONE

SS *Etoile*. Friday morning, 3rd March 1933

Across the third-class day room the children tore back and forth, skipping and hopping, thrilled with their new outfits of limp velvet and torn taffeta. As she watched them, Lily thought, *It's the smell of camphor that's always so extraordinarily intoxicating.*

Mothballs and camphor, the scent of dressing up.

Into her mind came Nickie and clearly she saw her son, her darling Nicholas – the only child she really wanted to see playing and dressing up. Her darling boy, dressed as a little clown. *How happily he would have joined in with these children here*, she thought. *These children who play so freely. How he would have loved to dress up with them...*

As she sat on the ship crossing the Atlantic, such a long time since Nickie's Pierrot fancy-dress party, Lily suddenly felt overwhelmingly sick, her imagination painting pictures that left her trembling. Always the memory of him dressed as a little clown brought a fear that grew and grew and flooded her entire being.

Enough. She turned away from the children.

Slowly the nausea ebbed.

She stretched. She'd been momentarily distracted by the bustle created by the arrival of two huge wicker dressing-up baskets. She'd attempted to focus on a large woman, a tumble of skirts and shawl, at the centre of the room, trying to tempt a pale plump little girl into a frowzy frock and bonnet. *Dear Lord, what a dreadfully unappealing child – what must its mother feed it on? Mind, the fat woman herself can hardly move.*

She turned away. These thoughts didn't hold her; she was too restless to concentrate. Since the previous evening a storm had been threatening. Ropes had been rigged to imprison wooden benches and trestle tables; tablecloths dampened to hold sliding cutlery and tea-urns. But the storm had not arrived. Now a trio of sailors on the edge of the large communal room stood ravelling up the storm ropes, skillfully flipping and coiling them to avoid the excited children, all pulling out shirts, skirts, bonnets and caps from the big old baskets. Through the portholes, Lily saw the lumpy clouds unroll and slip away, and the weather, as if to apologise for its former bad behaviour, suddenly beamed bright and clear, the sunlight dancing through the swirls of dust that heralded each newly discovered costume.

She felt removed and out of place in this sea of clatter and banter, and having chosen a bench in the far corner, she clung here to the vestiges of quiet. All she wanted was to be left in peace, to be completely unnoticed. Leaning back against the wall, she closed her eyes. Her apricot hair, she knew, caught attention, but for this trip she'd decided to keep her so-called crowning glory discreetly hidden, the curling waves pulled back into a bun of puritan severity. *Nothing otherwise*, she prayed, *distinguishes me. I'm just a tired middle-aged woman in an old tweed skirt and beige cardigan.*

She stared down at the acres of dreary linoleum upon which so many feet were drumming, drumming…and caught sight of her shoes. Chocolate suede lace-ups with a small heel. They were old but expensive and hand-made, thin leather ties neatly threading through the eyelets, and in some ways the shoes were even more elegant in their battered state. All her maid's clothes had fitted her, the tweed skirt and the coat, Mary's dusty-pink crepe blouse – a bit on the big size but better that than the other way around. No, it was Lily's large feet that had let her down; she'd had to resort to an old pair of her own shoes. Mr Mancini's – and she suddenly had an image of her wooden lasts lined up with dozens of others in the backroom of the smart shoe shop in Bruton Street. So, so far away.

Perhaps, she thought, *they are the one item that will give me away: my shoes. Some eagle-eyed snooper will catch sight of them and, putting two and two together, report me to the captain.* She tucked her feet hastily under the bench as the absurd thought made her heart beat irrationally, a sudden skim of sweat breaking out on her forehead. She pulled her hanky from her sleeve, held it to her brow and, making herself breathe evenly, stared on, unseeing, at the sallow green linoleum.

Three days at sea and already the trip seemed interminable. Oh, how she longed for the hush of first class high above her. Down here, the constant mayhem was proving such a terrible torment after the many sleepless nights that had preceded her trip. Though she had to admit, steerage was not quite as tiresome as she'd feared. Having always hitherto travelled first class, she'd wandered through the third-class smoking rooms and day rooms, surprised to find them open and spacious.

No, it was the cabin itself that was proving such a trial. Not that the spartan berth was uncomfortable, just so tiny. And always the endless heavy churning of the engines making any sleep or rest impossible, so that however much she longed to be away from these rowdy crowds and their endlessly drumming feet, the claustrophobia of her cabin was, today, much worse than this boisterous chaos. She had survived two days cooped up but the need for space and distraction had driven her into this, the third-class day room.

And then, as if in answer to her prayers, the noise in the large room fell into a lull and the most wonderful peace descended. With a sigh of relief, Lily stirred herself upright and turned with resolve to the journal on her lap. But the relief was short-lived for all at once there started into life the whine and hum of a pair of bagpipes.

Oh Lord, this is too much – it must be stopped! She spun round.

Instantly any word of complaint died on her lips. Beside her, hitherto unnoticed, sat a group of people tightly huddled round a table, concentrating on the whining noise spooling from a hidden centre. As the pipes warmed up, the huddle uncoiled, revealing a dozen people, their faces gnarled and tanned; citizens of a far-away life. At their heart sat a large square blond man swathed in a tartan shawl. The player of the bagpipes, chief of his tribe, his cheeks were full-blown as he massaged the bag of sound.

A whoop, a cheer, clapping hands.

Lily stared, caught by the unexpected sight and sound, the chief's muscular hands drawing forth the trembling haunted music of mountains. Now, from the midst of the shawled group, an old woman rose up and, cupping a hand to her ear, turned her tanned beaten face to the ceiling and started to ululate the meandering cry of minarets. The mystical sound coiled round and round the room. On and on. Lily sat entwined.

'You like our music, lady?'

The music had stopped and, on a whine, the swollen bag was deflating.

'You smile, you like our music?'

Lily, stung into life, found the blond man looking straight at her. Expecting a Scottish voice to go with the bagpipes, she was instantly thrown into confusion – not so much by the man's rough incomprehensible accent but by his jet-black eyes, glittering, full of life… She scrabbled for something to say, unsettled by the sensual power of his gaze.

'I beg your pardon?' (Oh heavens, I sound such a stuck-up fool!)

Unable to think of anything more, she was left smiling helplessly like a child as, around their chief, the women chirruped a spiral of chattering sounds. *Perhaps from the Balkans*, she thought, all their dark eyes now upon her.

'Our music, lady. You like?'

He held the tangle of pipes high above his head. Trusting the pipes were the subject under discussion, she nodded eagerly. 'Very good.' With a faltering smile, all she could muster under the circumstances, she lifted her hands, gesturing a clapping motion, childishly eager to please these new acquaintances.

The shawled heads of the women danced and bowed in gusts of laughter and, in her confusion, Lily found herself laughing along as well. Then, just as suddenly, their attention left her. With much relief, she realised she no longer held any interest for them; the man had started singing and all eyes turned in on him once more.

Agitated, she glanced to and fro to see who had witnessed this embarrassing interlude and her subsequent abandonment. Then the fear caught her again. Had she been seen? Had someone glanced across, alerted by the music, and recognised her sitting there, so that even now a purser was being told of her presence on board? She tentatively scanned the vast room.

But no one was looking at her; no one was in the least bit interested. She was alone again.

In the middle of the vast room, Mrs Webb's spirits were seriously flagging. Having polished off cock-a-leekie soup, a couple of grilled mutton chops and apple meringue for her midday meal, all the large woman really wanted was a nice little nap on the comfy bunk in her cabin. But ever game – especially under testing circumstances (that apple pudding was sitting very heavy) – Mrs Webb rallied herself. 'Keep going, lass, this boat trip's nearest thing to 'oliday that family's gonna get.'

And, everything considered, she had to admit it was turning out to be a right good 'do' – fresh air, free food a-plenty, a champion tug-of-war on deck that morning and tomorrow's fancy-dress parade to look forward to.

She felt a feeble tug at her skirts and looked down. 'I'll not tell thee again, our Anthea,' she snapped, 'stop thy pulling.'

'But I'm tired, Gran,' wheedled the child, her pasty face hidden by a fat little fist, the thumb buried deep in her mouth. 'I want to go 'ome.' The thumb popped out and popped in again. The child was dressed in a faded lemon-yellow cotton dress. Once her best – it had been smocked by Mrs Webb herself – it now strained tight over the puffy little girl, its colour sour and unforgiving.

Mrs Webb chose to ignore her grandchild. She knew Anthea wanted nothing to do with any fancy-dress competition but she was determined not to let the child slump into yet another sulky fit. Aye but to that end, she feared, it'd take a deal more than fresh air and free food.

'Get cracking, me duck,' she admonished, gesturing towards the big old wicker baskets, 'else all big boys and girls'll take best fancy dress.' And wiping her face with a sparkling white handkerchief the size of a picnic cloth, she sank gratefully onto a large wooden chair that creaked loudly as it received her.

'Gran?'

Mrs Webb looked down. The little girl was holding up a battered straw bonnet trailing a mould-spotted ribbon.

'Go on, me lovely, that'll be Bo-Peep.'

'But Gran—'

'Come on now, let's see what else we can find.'

Aware that all Anthea wanted was to run away and hide every inch of her wobbly body, as the two of them searched through the mounds of musty material, Mrs Webb tried to shield the child from view by means of her own corpulence.

Ten years old and she should be such a pretty little girl, she thought. *Her mam was right bonny at that age.* And, of course, Mrs Webb knew that that was the real reason for the child's despair – five empty years without her mother. Poor little mite, no wonder the girl was sullen and fractious; her mam's shocking death was enough to smack away any child's pep and charm. No, little Anthea had never really had a chance.

'Gran, where's me sheep?' asked the child in a tiny voice

and, sinking onto the floor, tears very near, she sat utterly defeated by her struggle to become a shepherdess.

Her grandmother looked at the miserable girl. *A new start's what this child needs if she's to survive: a new start to make her forget. Make us all forget.*

'Nay, lass, you're right,' she said, shaking her head. 'It won't do, it won't do a' all.'

And never one to be brought down by Fate's travails, the large woman levered herself back onto her feet and started to rummage in the wicker basket as though her life depended on it.

Ten years later, sitting in a garden, Anthea would say, 'And that was the beginning, that day on the boat. The beginning of what I can remember of my life. I'd been asleep, like, since my mam'd died, five years before, and I couldn't remember anything – still can't, not from those five years. And then that day on the boat, I woke up – I s'pose from when me and Gran met you. It was the start of the adventure. And now I have memories. From our trip all together.'

And Lily had smiled.

Lily looked down at her journal. At the top of the page she had written the day's date. Friday, 3rd March 1933. But besides that, what was there to write after all?

She screwed up her eyes in an effort to drown out the screams and the endless banging noise of the children, and tried to compose her thoughts. At her side her neighbour's insistent singing vied with the whirl of childish cries. She put pen to paper.

Nothing appeared; her fountain pen had dried up.

For heaven's sake. Lily shook it. Still nothing. She tried the little lever on the side only to be rewarded by a large inky blob swelling from the nib, which hovered over the snowy-white page and then firmly plopped onto her tweed skirt.

'Oh no, this wretched pen.'

'A tomato's what you need for that.'

Surprised not only by the proximity of the voice but also at the eccentricity of the suggestion, Lily swung round to find the large dressing-up woman at her elbow. If she had hoped to make a reply of some kind, it was now washed aside in a torrent of advice from the large woman, who settled herself comfortably on the bench next to her.

'A tomato. Rub it well into the wet ink-mark then rinse it out wi' water. Never fails. Mind, they say if you put red ink over black ink, it dissolves the iron in your black ink so that when you wash it, it's gone – t' stain, I mean. But I don't think it's as – efficacious.' Lily caught the echo of an 'h' before the word. 'Anyway, love, where we gonna find red ink down 'ere?'

The big face was creased and smiling. Lily, stunned by this ebullient volley of information, managed only to mutter, 'Quite,' before the lecture was confidently concluded: 'Then there's milk, o'course. Aye, that might be best.'

Swiftly rising, gathering the layers of shawl about her, the woman called out to the tubby child still half-heartedly looking into the wicker basket. 'Now, Anthea, where's milk bottle?' No doubt fully expecting the child to stay put, she crossed herself to one of the trestle tables – for a portly woman, she had an impressive turn of speed – and collected a small half-full milk bottle with a straw. 'Milk takes up stain,' she said pouring a tiny amount of milk onto the ink-mark, which immediately darkened the white liquid.

Lily sat dumbstruck. She was vaguely aware that, in her present state of tension, there was a luxury in being ministered to by this stranger who conveyed her advice not only with confidence but also with warm kindness. She stared down at the woman as more liquid was dribbled with all the precision of a scientist, and her eye was caught by the most beautifully starched blouse, a little cameo brooch nestling amidst the folds of shawl and jowl. At such close quarters, Lily noted that the harshness of the woman's iron-grey hair pulled back, seal-sleek atop the vast tumble of clothes, detracted from an open wise face. *How often bulk is wrongly equated with stupidity*, she thought, and saw that although the woman's face was battered and lined, a high unhealthy colour on each cheek, the eyes, grey-blue, held a sweet softness and the fleeting glimpse of a once-pretty girl.

'Now, let's go and rinse it off in't cloakroom. We'll finish with a little more milk if needs be.'

The woman set off at her impressive speed and, like a good girl, Lily ran to catch up only to find, walking beside the short stout woman, she felt absurdly tall, her limbs all sharp-angles. Added to which, her new companion's ceaseless chatter in a dense North Country accent, meant Lily lurched along, bent sideways, in an attempt to catch what was being said. Behind them, silently, padded the dour fat child.

It was this circus-like trio that stared back from the wide mirror in the cloakroom where, sure enough, after a judicious dab of water, the dark mark on the tweed skirt vanished. 'There,' said the woman triumphantly.

Lily stared. It was a magic trick.

'I'm Mrs Nellie Webb. How'd you do?' With a big red

hand, the woman clasped Lily's and shook vigorously.

'Oh...um...Lily Valley. Hello.' She managed to say the name in a hurried mumble but saw the woman, unsure as to what she'd heard, about to question her. Lily sped on. 'I can't thank you enough, you've saved my skirt. That was very impressive.'

'Should be, my love. Run me own laundry this last thirty years, I have. Haven't I, Anthea? This is me granddaughter,' she introduced proudly.

Lily stared at the gormless child in the mirror and saw, with a shock, the child's heavy little face was aged, the eyes vacant and dull. 'Hello,' she said and held out her hand. But the child wasn't having any of it; she backed away and dawdled out of the cloakroom.

The two women followed and Lily found herself hoping to bring matters to a close. But the other woman took control. 'So, where've you been hiding yourself then?' With a job well done, it was all the excuse the woman needed to nestle into a nice chat.

Lily hesitated. A new acquaintance and a lot of dangerous questions were the last thing she wanted. 'Oh...um...I'm afraid my husband and I have rather fallen victim to seasickness. It's my first day up.'

'Yes, well, you look pale enough but it should pass, 'specially since last night's storm never 'appened.' The woman appeared to wink. 'Mind yer, I've known the calmest waters cause the greatest problems but don't tell yer 'usband, eh?'

At that moment, Lily was distracted by a tall man appearing on the other side of the room, a huddle of people moving aside to let him through. Involuntarily she flinched and then saw, to her horror, Mrs Webb turning to see what had caused her reaction. 'Here is my husband,' she said quickly and was surprised to hear her voice sounded unstrained, almost calm. *Please, God, protect us*, she prayed.

The man made his way towards them and although middle-aged, his hair thinning on top, as he cut across the room, there was almost a buccaneer dash about him.

'Everything all right, darling?' Lily asked as he arrived. Again her voice sounded light and easy.

'Fine, fine.' The man smiled comfortably. 'Just felt like a spot of lunch. Do you think I'm too late?' He put a light hand on her shoulder.

'Well, that's a good sign; appetite back. Any more trouble and a little Mothersill's Remedy should do't trick.' Mrs Webb beamed at him; a bemused expression crossed the man's face. 'Your wife's told me all about it,' she concluded.

Hastily, Lily took the man's arm. 'Darling, this is Mrs Webb. I told her all about our seasickness.'

'Oh, I see. Johnnie Valley. Hello there.' He leant forward and cheerfully shook the woman's hand. This time Lily knew she'd heard the name.

'Enjoying your trip otherwise?' asked Mrs Webb.

'Very much, thanks,' Johnnie replied.

'Mrs Webb's been extraordinarily clever with a milk bottle and some water, and saved my skirt.' She could hear her manner social and gracious as she smoothed the damp tweed material for him to inspect. A moment hung in the air. Nothing was said.

'Well, very nice to meet you both. But that's enough from us, in't it, Anthea?' Mrs Webb gustily gathered her grandchild to her. 'See you later, Mrs Valley.'

The relief Lily felt was enormous; the ordeal was nearly

over. She heard Johnnie take his cue. 'And we'd better go and find some lunch, darling. Before it's all finished. Cheerio for now, Mrs Webb.'

Putting an arm round her, he started to steer her away but she hesitated, looking back over her shoulder. 'Bye bye, Anthea,' she called. For a second, the little girl glanced at her. Lily felt their eyes lock – an instant flicker of recognition between them, a joint compact of pain – and then, as quickly, the child looked down at her sandals. They were old, brown and scuffed almost grey as she stood wiggling her toe into a point on the lino.

'Come along now, our Anthea, let's go and find that brother of yours. We'll sort y' fancy dress out later.'

Lily and Johnnie watched as the large woman drew the reluctant child through the knots of people and vanished between the swing doors.

'She wouldn't stop talking. Nosey old boot.' Lily sank down onto the bench; she felt wretchedly tired. '*And* she saw my face when you came towards me. I was just so worried something had happened—'

'Hush, darling. We knew we'd have to talk to someone eventually. And she seems harmless enough.'

Lily shrugged; the constant terror made her want to sleep and sleep...

'Hello, "Mrs Valley",' he said.

The sound of the new name almost made her smile. She looked up at him.

He pointed to the bench beside her – 'May I?'- and holding her eye, grinned so that, despite herself, she was forced to chorus with him, 'No hat there!'

He sat and wrapped his arm through hers.

Momentarily, the shared memory of the hat that Johnnie had once so fortuitously sat on stilled her anxiety. She felt an echo of contentment and put her head on his shoulder. She knew what they must look like, a tired middle-aged couple. But she was glad. They were of no interest to anyone. Nobody was taking any notice of them.

Melsham, England. 1931

The hat sat on the marble-topped hall table. Robin-red, made of felt, it had a small bunch of cherries pinned to the side of the crown. Alongside the hat lay a pair of delicate red suede gloves and a small red and black clutch bag. Lily lifted the hat and, looking in the hall mirror, put it on. She adjusted it to the right angle with no delight nor particular interest in her appearance but out of a sense of duty and good manners for the day to come. Against her wan skin she knew the robust red material was too strident, the cherries too frivolous, serving somehow to emphasise her thin face, making it seem longer. She caught herself staring warily back, her tired eyes gleaming glassily, their honey colour unnaturally bright, her so-called aristocratic nose, boney and shiny. Why was it when she was unhappy her nose went sore and red? She pulled a powder puff across it but it made no difference. Her lipstick, also, was too stern a shade but she continued dutifully to paint it on and, with a final attempt at softness, fluffed the short waves peeping from the side of her hat. The little rolls of copper hair chose to remain as stiff as brandy snaps. Damn it, it would have to do. She stood very, very still.

The thick silence filled the high wide hall. *If Nickie were here now*, she thought, *there'd be so much noise. We'd run up the little wooden backstairs and get Mary to make bread-dipped-in-egg, and then we'd rig up a ghost's house in my bedroom and...*

She stopped. Such daydreams only made her heart feel emptier, empty. She stood trying to untangle the pain. It's the first Saturday of term and I'm only allowed to visit him on the second Saturday. Seven whole days more. And anyway, Mary's no longer here; today she's getting married – and I have someone new to train. A new maid after all this time—

For goodness sake, Lily, stop. Don't think; do.

She set off across the wide black-and-white tiled hall and, without allowing herself to hesitate, opened the study door.

Her husband sat as usual at the big heavy desk. The curtains half drawn, a lop-sided standard lamp supplemented the morning light which, despite the heavy curtains, fell across numerous papers scattered untidily over the desk's surface. A whisky and soda by him, the amber-coloured liquid twinkled as his large hand slowly rotated the cut-glass tumbler.

'Charles, you're not even changed and we're going to be late enough as it is.' She started pulling on her gloves in an attempt to hide her fear. Even in the half-light she could see how unnaturally ruddy the man's skin had become, his nose taking on a pitted coarseness. And although his brown-black hair was still thick, the shine had gone, the texture now emphasised by the flicker of grey around his temple and ears and the ever-stern white parting.

'I won't be coming.' Without looking at his wife, the thickset man took up his fountain pen and started to write.

She knew to all intents and purposes the subject was closed

but for once she was not prepared to abandon it. 'But Mary will be so disappointed—'

'For goodness sake, Lily, don't be so sentimental. The way you've been fussing on, getting all dressed up, you'd think it was the Princess Royal and not some servant's wedding.' He graced her with a cursory glance and took a swallow from his glass.

She tried to keep her voice calm and even. 'Mary is not *some* servant. I need hardly remind you she has been with us for over fifteen years, indeed, all our married life. I would have thought you of all people would have had the decency to realise that it is simply not done to ignore her on her wedding day.'

Charles looked up and coolly asked, 'Have you quite finished?'

She remained silent.

'Frankly, I shall be glad to see the back of her – the two of you gossiping in corners like a couple of washer-women.' He returned to his document.

Though ever vigilant to the unstable electricity of his temper, she could feel her own anger steadily rising. 'It would have been courteous if you could have told me earlier.' With right on her side, she felt impelled to add, 'I think it's extraordinarily unkind of you not to put in an appearance.'

'Don't be so pompous; it doesn't suit you.' He smoothed a blotter over the page. 'And I've decided to go up to Town later. I'll be staying the night. Tell Benton I wish to catch the midday train.'

She knew this to be his final word and she stood impotent with rage. But, although motionless, she held herself alert; she knew from experience that the heavy man, if he chose to move upon her, possessed a whiplash speed.

Charles looked up. She held her breath but all he said was, 'You'd better run along, Lily, or you'll be very late.'

She didn't slam the door, she closed it; fifteen years of their marriage had taught her to submit. She stood once more in the vast hall, in a fury and yet so relieved to have escaped. A small figure, all alone.

Through the open doors she heard the stable clock chime eleven. She shot forward into the bright day and, dazzled by the sudden loud sunshine, blinked as she looked across the drive to where a chauffeur was standing by a gleaming Daimler. At the sight of his mistress, George Benton's polishing cloth hastily disappeared into the pocket of his uniform.

'George, Sir Charles has decided to catch the midday train up to Town so I'm afraid that means you and Mrs Benton will have to miss the actual wedding service. But once you've dropped him off at the station, why don't you use the Daimler to get you both to the reception. I can drive myself in my car.'

'Thank you, my lady.'

'I'm sorry for the inconvenience.' She moved off towards a smaller car, a Standard, becoming aware of the chauffeur scampering after her.

'Tell Mrs Benton I'll only need something cold for this evening.'

Benton arrived at her side with a puff, handed her in and, as she went to turn on the petrol, remarked, 'May I say, my lady, that's a very fine hat.'

Lily looked up, surprised. 'Oh, thank you, George.' Fury at her husband now conflicting with unexpected delight at the compliment, to cover her confusion she found herself checking the clock on the instrument board. 'Now I *am* going to be late.'

It was all the excuse she needed to drive very fast along the little lanes away from Melsham House. Repeatedly hitting the steering wheel, she struggled with tears as her anger at Charles welled–up again. 'Bastard, don't you dare make me cry. You selfish bastard! And that's right, run away up to Town to your prissy little mistress and her prissy little dress shop.'

Not that in a calmer frame of mind she cared about the presence of a mistress in her husband's life, a mistress whose arrival two years previously had proved a blessed distraction. However, although Mrs Thelma Duttine had followed in the footsteps of many others, this time the telephone line had hummed.

'Lily, my dear, that Duttine woman whom Charles has chosen to take up with has been seen purchasing the entire contents of the lingerie department! And in Sutton's of all places – Charles's own department store. It's too vulgar. *And* such a common-looking woman. How could Charles let you down so?'

But Lily didn't care. Charles could give Thelma Duttine the run of his department store; he could set her up in a discreet dress shop off Bond Street, then they could *both* play at shopkeepers. What did it matter? All she felt now was unbelievable relief that his violent temper was directed elsewhere and that their sexual forays, however sporadic, Charles often so unbelievably drunk, had stopped.

Had he always got so drunk? She couldn't remember. She thought back to the young bride dazzled by his sporting prowess and boundless energy, and saw herself as a distant figure, inhabiting another life, a life full of hope and playfulness.

Charles and Lily. This match, this joyful union, the envy of all her girlfriends. Sir Charles Sutton. He'd been the pick of the bunch, glorious in his uniform. Not much conversation but rugged and handsome. A different class maybe, family money made in trade, but he had wooed Mother and drunk with Father. And how she had secretly anticipated an all-enveloping response on her wedding night, a response to quite what though, she hadn't been sure.

As she drove, she found herself unexpectedly smiling at the memory of her innocence and wedding-day fears. Woozy from no breakfast, she'd been escorted up the aisle by her father, exuding elderly brandy fumes – the stale alcohol vying with the strongly perfumed lilies and drifts of elegant roses that wreathed the church, the floral wealth of Father's precious greenhouses. After all, the sacrificial lamb had to be seen to be properly served upon the altar of convention – with decorum and good taste, of course.

And Mother's contribution? Even now Lily laughed. Her mother stoutly sitting on her eiderdown the night before the wedding and shouldering her duty, in a hush, as Mother of the Bride. 'I must warn you, Lily, of the great gulf between a lady and a prostitute.' She had spat out the last word. 'Let me tell you that a prostitute feels passionate about a man; a lady does not.' Lily had sat frozen, suffused in embarrassment at the mention of such matters. That Mother, of all people, should know about these things! But, oh, if her mother ever guessed her delicious dreams, her *passionate* desires. To be held at last in Charles's arms, to allow him… But Mother was steaming on relentlessly. 'And anyway, I have it on good medical authority, my girl, that no woman is capable of feeling passion.'

And then the wedding night was over, a bafflement of drunkenness, and in so little time the delicious desires had dissolved into confusion and disappointment, feelings that slowly metamorphosed further into dread and then terror...

Now, thank God, with the arrival of Thelma Duttine, there appeared to be the permanent sanctuary of separate beds in separate rooms. *A separate room to make a ghost's house for Nickie and me. A separate bed to make a pirate's galleon to set us out to sea... Oh, my Nickie, my love, my joy, why aren't you here with me now on our way to Mary's Big Wedding Day? Why do you have to be away at rotten old school? It was always so perfect, wasn't it, you, me and Mary? Your father away in London – and Melsham all ours to play in.* But even through this sweet memory, Lily felt the perpetual fear, the dread of Charles's unexpected return from London at any minute – and with the memory came a sudden gust of sickness.

She pushed the memories from her mind and concentrated on driving fast. The lanes curled away before her unseen; the sunny spring light that glanced through the high hedgerows unnoticed. Long years of surviving had taught her to numb her mind, make it blank, but even so, today, the trick wouldn't work. She pushed her mind on and on, in search of solace. *I suppose, in the end, I must concede that boarding school has protected the child from Charles's insane rages, I must take comfort in that.*

But what spare comfort she found brought no glimpse of joy. For with Nickie so far from her, her loneliness was now hounded by despair; her despair, a terrible private secret, imprisoned by the rigours of her upbringing. 'It's not done, Lily, to reveal one's feelings. It is, frankly, bad manners.' Though one person did know. Mary, her maid and her true friend.

Mary, the keeper of all secrets; Mary, the confidante; Mary, who had watched the carefree bride turn into a sad despairing middle-aged woman whose only passions now were anger and disappointment. And today Mary was getting married. Lily felt dazed by the abyss of loneliness that yawned before her, she felt sick and frightened.

She stopped the car and got out. She lit a cigarette and, inhaling deeply, leant back, one foot on the running board, and looked across the string of open fields towards Melsham Woods.

She tried to think back to a more contented moment in her marriage. Had it ever been? She tried to remember the Charles of her wooing, her wedding. Charles before he had hit her that first time, when she had finally known the marriage was over. Five years before. The terrible memory, old and wretched, hovered, ever ready to rear into life...

She made herself breathe in the lovely young spring air and forced all thoughts of Charles from her mind. And watching the golden light, bright against the dark sturdy trees, the green wheat, frisky as it danced in a playground of breezes, she slowly felt the fear and fierce chaotic anger leave her. It was the perfect day for a wedding. *Dearest Mary, you have won the heart of your Sam, your prayers have been answered.*

She thought of Nickie, laughing, lying in the long grass, buttercups tickling him, glinting under his chin. 'Nickie loves butter, Nickie loves butter.' And she caught the moment her breath came at a calmer pace. She got into the car and, very sedately, drove into the town of Freston.

The bustle of market day pulled her from her thoughts and she became aware that, up ahead, the road was crammed. A delivery van trying to overtake a wide bullock cart filled with a flock of beige woolly sheep had resulted in both vehicles becoming wedged amidst the Saturday-morning shoppers. Lily sat waiting, her engine ticking over.

Everywhere people thronged the little pavements, ambling and chatting. On this bright sunny day all along the High Street, striped awnings, flapping and cracking in the sharp breeze, were pulled down over the shop windows. At the far end, she could see the market place equally teeming: pens packed with cattle and pigs, an auctioneer's bidding rising on the air. And high above the roofs stood the stone turret of the Norman church, square and sturdy. With no hope of moving further towards it, Lily pulled across to the pavement and parked.

Suddenly with so many people around, she became aware of her tear-stained face and, looking in the tiny car mirror, encountered her rather extravagant hat. She removed it and realised to her relief she was parked opposite the Crown Hotel. Collecting her hat, gloves and bag, she quickly crossed the road.

A hush greeted her as she entered the elderly inn, a strong scent of dusty tobacco enveloping the low-beamed rooms of the bar. She looked around for help, placed her things on a chair and became aware of the only sound: the stately ticking of a grandfather clock. Half past eleven. Damn, now she was too early.

'May I get you something, madam?'

She jumped. 'Um…yes, why not? A gin and French, please. Oh, and where's the ladies' room?'

It was while she was repairing her face that she suddenly realised she'd left her hat and gloves in the bar. Returning, she was greeted by an anguished cry and the sight of a smartly dressed man holding her squashed hat, an aghast expression on his face.

'I'm most terribly sorry – I didn't know it was there – and I'm afraid I must have sat on it.'

He looked so stricken, holding the damaged hat as if it had just done him the most terrible injury, that Lily burst out laughing.

'It's all right. Very little harm done.' She took the hat from him and, with a quick smooth movement, remoulded the crown. 'Look, see? Good as new.'

'I'm so sorry. You see I was so busy ordering a drink—'

The waiter appeared, a glass on his tray.

'I think you'll need that now, rather more than ever.' Lily grinned at him.

The man sank down into the chair. 'I'm very glad I ordered a large one.' Despite himself, he was smiling. 'Rather a shock – oh, I'm sorry, forgive me.' He pointed to a drink already on the table. 'Is this yours?'

'Yes, I'd completely forgotten— Oh, my goodness – what time is it?'

'Twenty to.'

'I must be going.' She gathered her handbag and hat. 'I'm actually on my way to a wedding.'

'St Joseph's?'

She nodded.

'Well, perhaps I might escort you. I'm on my way there too.' He waved at the waiter. 'And please, as reparation for nearly ruining your beautiful hat, may I stand you that drink?'

'Done.'

Lily crossed to the mirror and, putting on the hat, caught the man watching her. Tall and slender, perhaps in his early forties, he was dressed in a dark blue double-breasted suit, which he wore with casual ease. *An elegant man*, she thought, and had an image of an Elizabethan courtier in doublet and hose. Beneath the brown thinning hair, cut short, she saw his face was tired and lined, and she would have thought his expression cynical, weary of life, had not deep creases served to emphasise his eyes. It was these eyes that made her glance a second time. Soft laughter eyes, eyes that made you want to smile back. *(Dear God, I had such a hangover that morning, Johnnie told her much, much later.)*

Turning to him, she questioned her appearance with a look.

'Despite my best efforts,' he said, 'you look delightfully damage free.'

Walking up the High Street, she said, 'I'm Lily Sutton, by the way.'

He stopped. 'Of course! I knew I recognised you. I met you and Sir Charles at the County Fair; two years ago I think it must be now – a memorable occasion for me as my piglets won the Blue Ribbon. Probably not such a memorable occasion for you.'

The memory, like a dancing wave, rippled across her mind and came to rest. 'But I know exactly who you are! You're a friend of Dolly Barton. And the piglets, if I remember rightly, were enchanting. Are they well?'

'Adorable. Though I'll be the first to admit I'm biased, having witnessed their birth and the progress of their somewhat undramatic lives. Is Sir Charles not with you?'

'No, he was suddenly called up to London. Why have we not met more often?'

'I'm a miserable old recluse, I'm afraid. Happy only when

I'm immersed in my books and talking to my pigs.'

'And what has got you away from such pleasures today?'

'My good friend, Sam. I've been roped in as his Best Man.'

'*Mary's* Sam?' She stopped.

'Of course, how stupid of me,' said Johnnie, stopping also. 'Mary works for you and Sir Charles, doesn't she?'

'Though sadly not after today – and oh, I'm going to miss her so terribly, she's been such a good friend. But,' she said to distract herself from the dark shadow wilfully hovering at the side of her mind, 'she does seem to be wonderfully happy, don't you think?'

A large woman dipped out of a shop door backwards and nudged into them, sending up a flurry of apologies. Johnnie tipped his hat. They moved on.

'And how do you know Sam?' Lily asked.

'We farm together.'

'Well, as they say, what a small world! Of course, Mary's told me all about your farm. She's brought Sam over to us quite often, with Melsham being just down the road.'

They flattened dutifully against a shop-front as a lingering line of boy scouts passed in front of them, the scout master obsequious in his bobbing manner. Waiting, Lily carried on, 'How do you and Sam come to farm together?'

'Do everything together – *have* done. The war, y'know. Sam was in my Company. Then after Armistice, we were both at a loose end, so we joined forces, read a few books and, bingo, we became pig farmers! Though truth be known, Sam's the expert.'

'They're going to live in one of your estate cottages, aren't they?'

Johnnie nodded.

'Mary doesn't want me to come over just yet. Not until it's quite finished.'

'It was a bit spartan but she's cheering the place up no end. I'm sure you'll be invited to tea very soon.'

They crossed the road, Johnnie skirting behind her to take the outside edge. The church and a small crowd came into view.

'I have to confide I'm rather nervous.' He smiled awkwardly and her attention was caught by a pair of front-teeth, crooked, a tiny chip in one. He looked like a schoolboy and the wearied look had vanished. 'I've got to do a bit of a speech later on and, to be quite honest, at this moment I'd rather be in the thick of battle, about to go over the top.'

'Oh dear,' she said. 'And there was I going to slip away after the service. Now I shall have to stay and see how you do.'

'Just keep wearing that hat and fingers crossed, I might even get through it in one piece.'

They arrived at the cluster of people and immediately Johnnie greeted an elderly gentleman distinguished by a gleaming pair of brown gaiters and a bright yellow stock.

'Hello, how nice to see you again. Lady Sutton, may I introduce the father of the groom?'

'How do you do,' said Lily. 'Isn't it a lovely day?' And suddenly she realised she meant it.

CHAPTER TWO

Kent. 31st December 1914

The dark room was sliced in half by a shaft of pale orange light shining through from Nanny's sitting room. It did nothing to dispel the gloom as Nanny still insisted on gas-lamps, not wanting anything to do with electricity and its 'new-fangled habits'.

'I knew I'd find you here,' said Lily.

Her brother stirred in the gloom of the empty nursery. He was dressed in evening clothes though his white tie was still loose and his black jacket slung over the brass bedstead. She stood and watched him from the doorway.

Hugh sat, a tall lanky form, untidily hunched on a little stool, his knees almost to his ears. He was stirring a small enamel saucepan on a Primus stove and, without looking up, he invited, 'Bovril. Come and join me.'

'Nanny asleep?' She nodded towards the open door.

'No fear. She's up to her eyes in khaki wool. Talk about knitting for England.'

Lily stepped into the nursery – even in the darkness she knew every inch of the room – and made for the old armchair at her brother's side. She sank into it. Her evening skirt billowed up and a childhood memory of a similar nest of fluffy chiffon, her feet encased in bronze dancing pumps with elastic crossed over her ankles, stirred at the back of her mind.

Through the open door, she caught sight of Nanny, a shiny-black bombazine bun. The old woman sat with her eyes half-closed, needles smoothly clicking, her stumpy veined fingers moving with swift delicacy; cocooned in her deafness, she was unaware of Lily's arrival. On a small table beside the old woman there were neatly stacked piles of newly knitted balaclavas and socks.

'Ears and feet, always Nanny's prime areas of concern.' Earmuffs and gloves on elastic and thick woollen stockings. Now grown-up, there was no longer the cheering comfort of being bossed and tucked into layers of scratchy mufflers and bonnets, the treacherous cold, in Nanny's opinion, always there ready to kill and maim.

She turned back to her brother and saw him staring intently at the little saucepan. In the half-light his young face was as stern and aquiline as a church carving, his fair hair strictly greased, parted and combed, at odds with his dishevelled evening suit and tie.

He poured some Bovril into an enamel mug. 'Want some?' The salty aroma wafted towards her.

'Mmm, don't think it really goes with Moselle cup.'

'So Father's serving the guests German wine this year. Well, good for him.'

Lily nodded. 'Dinner's in twenty minutes. Are you coming down?'

'You been sent to find me?'

'No, course not.'

The window rattled; the wind was up.

Lily looked round the room. Here, all the familiar shapes of childhood were wrapped in a cosy orange glow from Nanny's room, so that in the half-light, she could only just glimpse the large world map commanding one whole wall, the British Empire gleaming, vast and rose-pink. Endless lessons… 'Where is Timbuctoo? Who is the king of Siam?'

Across the window, black against the purple night sky, the old rocking horse, ears cocked, nostrils flared, stood sentinel between the two single beds, neatly made. On hers, Baz, an old furry owl; on Hugh's, a tangle of legs and arms: Koko, his over-stuffed monkey.

And in the furthest corner, the faint ghostly outline of her doll's house, its front-door firmly closed on what she knew to be a tiny world of Georgian chaos.

'Why does Nanny keep all these things?'

'She's not done yet,' said Hugh. 'She may be eighty-one but she's determined to bring up at least one more generation of brats.'

Far below, a faint gust of laughter rose up from the party, followed by a ripple of bright curt piano music.

'Mendelssohn, eh.' Hugh nodded down at the music. 'So the old man's decided to turn a blind eye to German music *and* German wine.' Lily caught the acid bitterness in her brother's voice; it was a new tone. If she'd hoped for a glimpse of fun away from the guests assembling downstairs, she knew, tonight, Hughie wasn't going to provide it. But if she was honest she'd known the minute she'd picked him up the day before from the station that nothing was the same. A serious

Hugh, gaunt, changed, had climbed up into the pony-trap beside her and as they turned up the drive towards the house he'd jumped down again, saying, 'You go ahead, Lil. Need a bit of fresh air. I'll walk from here.' They hadn't seen him for hours and when at last he arrived, just as they'd sat down to dinner, his smart uniform was rumpled and his face dirty. He had proceeded to get spectacularly drunk and then pass out. Mother and Father, of course, had pretended nothing was amiss – only asking Bowler to 'put the young master to bed'. Later, when Lily had gone to see how he was, she'd discovered his bed empty. Climbing the stairs she'd found him up here with Nanny, the nursery landing reeking of tobacco. The smell had brought back a long-forgotten memory. Nanny at harvest one year – *ancient even then and I must have been all of five* – a clay-pipe between her lips, knitting needles a-dance, sitting atop a bale of hay, bantering with the farmer-boys.

'Do you remember Nanny's pipe?'

'She still smokes it – when she thinks no one's looking.' Hugh gave a short dry laugh. 'That old baccy of hers. It's what she sends me. I've told her, "that's what'll get me in the end, not some old whizz-bang."'

'Oh, Hughie, don't – not even as a joke.'

Since last night she'd been torn between the desire to make her brother laugh, to make everything normal, and the frantic need to ask him questions. As to the latter, she knew any direct approach would yield nothing.

'You'll never guess,' she began. 'Some man came down from London and asked Father if we'd turn the house into a nursing home.'

'Good God, Mother must have had a fit.' Hugh pulled himself upright and swung towards her.

'We were saved by the plumbing. Apparently our drains don't come up to scratch, not modern enough.' She managed a grin. 'As you can imagine, Mother was immensely relieved.'

Hugh rubbed his hands and turned the lever on the side of the stove; the little blue flame flared. 'So I hear you've got a young man on the go.'

'Oh, Hughie, don't you start! Why does everyone keep teasing me?' She smoothed her pale pink skirt, her hands felt hot and clammy. She tried to sit silent but the need to know more proved irresistible. 'Who told you?'

'Nanny. She says he's very nicely put together, by the by – *and* that he knows it.' In a softer tone, he added, 'And you look very nicely put together this evening as well.'

'It took hours.' She groaned. 'Martha tonged my hair.' She turned her profile to let him admire the two hours' work. 'It feels like a great big puff-ball's settled on my head. Anyway, I'm luckier than Lettie and Harriet; with my wavy hair I don't have the misery of curling rags every night. Can you imagine what a bore! And this is my Christmas present from Mother and Father.' She bounced out of the chair and twirled for him to see her gown. 'The belt's made of moiré with a diamanté buckle and the sleeves are ecru lace. Mother and I bought it in Gooch's and,' she lowered her voice, 'it was 7½ guineas – I saw the price!' She grinned at him, an enormous wave of happiness engulfed her; Hughie knew about Charles at last.

'So where did you meet this young man?'

'Oh, don't be such a pompous ass – you sound like Father. Charles is only a couple of years older than us.'

'Oh yes?'

'He's twenty-three, if you must know.' She perched on

the edge of the armchair. 'And I met him in the summer, in London, when I was staying at Lettie's. We met at one of the Sunday concerts at the Albert Hall. Or rather, he wasn't at the concert, just there collecting his sister, Adele. And then he took us across the Park in his motor car, and we all went and had ices at Gunter's.' She longed to tell him everything but sensed this evening wasn't the moment. To date, she'd only really told Lettie, her best friend, not getting very far as she'd been met with the abrupt response, 'Well, dear, don't let him get a pea of his greens!' After that Lily had clammed up completely. She realised she might be jumping the gun; she and Charles had only met a few times and nearly always in company, but it was a start – of that she felt sure. She wanted – oh, with all her heart! – her friendship with Charles to be the start of a glorious romance. She wanted to be Charles's sweetheart not some floozy to be trifled with – even now she still felt disturbed by Lettie's allusions to a sordid liaison. Not that she'd have known how to conduct a sordid liaison, and as far as she could see, neither would Charles, who always insisted on treating her like a china doll. 'You're my little girl,' he'd whispered into her ear that one time they had been alone together, at the theatre.

'You've gone all moony,' said Hugh. 'Everything all right, old girl?'

She looked at her brother's tired, thin face and put a hand on his arm. 'Father won't let me or Mother read the newspapers; he considers it far too morbid and upsetting for us to follow the war. So please tell me, I want to know. Is it bad in France?'

'It's worse,' he said. He shifted and wrapped his long arms

around his thin frame; her hand fell away from him.

'Oh Hughie.'

He sat staring into his mug. 'What's so damnable is that the powers-that-be don't have the faintest notion what's going on, of what the conditions are like for the men. They're living in another century. They were prepared for cavalry charges, would you believe it? And sword fighting. Some of the officers even told their batmen to pack evening clothes for Berlin.' Wrapped round himself, he started to gently rock back and forth. 'They said it'd be over by this Christmas – well, it's New Year's Eve and they're still pumping millions of munitions and men into France. And what for? Slaughter.' He looked across at her, his face in shadow. 'Did you know Toddy's copped it? I heard yesterday when I went for my walk. One of the other gardeners told me.'

She nodded mutely but sat frozen, not daring to move. She must let Hughie speak. Since his arrival home, he had been silent.

'Our generation, Lil, all the young men, are going to be destroyed. Ignorantly and thoroughly.'

She flinched and looked down. 'I knew it must be pretty awful when you wouldn't answer Father's questions at breakfast.'

'No point. If you're not there you simply wouldn't believe it.' She heard again the strange new flatness in his voice. 'Anyway no one really wants to know the truth. All this "everyone's got to do their bit". Ye gods, no one even begins to understand.' His voice faded and he took a swallow from his mug. Even in the half-light she could see how much thinner his face had become in his three months away.

Next door, Nanny heaved herself onto her feet. They listened as she moved slowly about her room making encouraging little clucks and talking to herself.

'Actually, that's not true,' Hugh sat up. 'Nanny understands. Do you know what she told me last night? It was five of her brothers and not four she lost in the Crimea. The littlest, Walter, was a drummer boy but he was so young – twelve – his name never made dispatches.'

The loss of one brother for Lily was too terrible to contemplate but five... 'Oh Hughie, how could she bear it?' She closed her eyes.

'Don't know. But I think it's one of the reasons she's so furious about this war, God bless her – *and* she doesn't mind who knows it. Bowler came in with her coal bucket just now and she let him have it, poor man. "It'll be another pointless bloodbath, Mr Bowler, you mark my words." Hugh caught Nanny's muscular Norfolk burr. '"The Kaiser, he held Queen Victoria in his arms as she lay dyin', and now they've gone and got us into this stoopid mess!" Poor old Bowler didn't dare say a word in defence of King and Country – scuttled off with his tail between his legs.'

As if on cue, everything went dark and Nanny arrived in the doorway. At eighty-one, she still stood upright – as tall as she was wide, most of the light was blocked out of the room.

'Lily Robinson, get up this instant. Look how you've creased your dress!' Lily jumped to her feet, ten years old again. Nanny toddled towards her and started to pat and flounce her skirts. 'Lovely silk tulle like that and I find you sitting about like a scullery maid. And you, my manny, you're no better. What're you doing still sitting up here – and in the dark? I thought you'd gone down an age ago.' Hugh slowly unfolded and got to his feet. 'Your mother and father have spent good money on this New Year party and you're hiding away up here. Now get downstairs the pair of you, dinner will be served shortly.'

'Yes, Nanny.' Meekly Hugh started for the door and then, swooping back, he gathered the old lady into his arms. 'What would I do without you, dearest Nanny!'

'Ooo, get on with you,' cried the old lady, scolding and slapping away the boy's advances.

They clattered down the wooden back-stairs and then ground to a halt on the first landing, the noise from their feet instantly soaked up by thick oriental carpets. As a child Lily had always loved the mystery of noisily emerging from the nursery into this soft fragrant world, but tonight Hugh's bitter reluctance at joining the bubbling fray below overshadowed any possible enjoyment.

'We're only twelve sitting down to dinner – it won't be that bad.'

'I can see that Monks man,' muttered Hugh, leaning over the banisters. 'And God, there's Sir John and Lady Padget.' He sank down onto the top stair. Sprigs of holly had been threaded through the iron filigree of the banisters.

'Their Billy's joined up,' said Lily.

'Good for him.'

They stared down at the wide square hallway below. A Christmas tree stood huge, the warmth from its myriad little candles throwing off a haunting scent of pine and, so tall was the tree, the guests appeared dwarfed as they sauntered past into the drawing room. Beside it, so as not to impose upon the chatter in the drawing room, a string quartet sat playing a chunky gavotte, the frivolous music contributing an unexpected sense of fun to the rather staid interior.

From her high vantage point, Lily had often mused how the interior of the house reflected her grandfather's lack of imagination and strong practicality, a Victorian sturdiness prevailing throughout. Standing now at the top of the staircase, she was struck by how the stairs straightforwardly descended and then turned back on themselves rather than lusciously curving, as in other houses of a similar size and age. Arranged round this first-floor landing, glum family portraits were interspersed with classical hunting scenes; her grandfather's vain attempt to prove himself more than a businessman, though the pictures held no interest for him at all. Off this first floor ran a passageway of bedrooms at each of the four corners, each corridor disappearing into the darkness. Even on New Year's Eve, Lily's father maintained the newly installed electricity to be a foolish expense unless publicly enjoyed by one and all.

And outside, the house, though enfolded in glorious English countryside, stood sturdy in its design rather than imaginative, having been built by Lily's grandfather in the 1840s. An early investor in the railway, he had chosen the crest of a Kentish hill, not so much for its rolling beauty as its proximity to two newly constructed branch lines taking the adventurous passenger not only south but also west into London in under an hour.

'Come on, we'd better go down,' said Lily.

Hugh reluctantly got to his feet.

'Oh, for goodness sake, you dumbo, you're half undressed!' She pulled him towards her and he suffered her to knot his evening tie.

'I hope your young man won't come and duff me up – for detaining you, m'lady.'

'Don't be such an ass.' A glowing heat flowered in her chest at the thought of Charles. She looked down, frowning at the knot between her fingers. 'Anyway, Father snaffled Charles up the minute he came through the front door. Dragged him into the morning room "to discuss a couple of matters". I haven't even seen him to say hello.'

She'd been desperate to talk to him but had been left hovering like a fool at the top of the staircase. She'd watched through the banisters as the butler divested Charles of his heavy topcoat, and gazed as he'd been revealed: tall and broad and muscled. His thick sporting figure, tonight, appeared to be tautly packed into his evening suit, the stiff white collar and tie serving to emphasise his shiny black-brown hair, the high gloss achieved, no doubt, by prolonged and disciplined double-brushing. Under the light of the hall chandelier, she could see his razor-sharp parting etched ash-white against the dark lustre of his hair. His face was square, shaped by big bones over which the skin was healthy and ruddy, the even features divided by a carefully trimmed moustache and strong immovable eyebrows. But it was his nose that brought unpredictability; it had been broken, the central bone weaving a course through an otherwise sensuous profile giving it a clownish tilt. He was already too heavy-set a man to be elegant, his movements constantly reminding one of the muscle and sinew working beneath the clothing, but for Lily, having been acquainted with Charles just six months, his appearance every time they met struck her with surprise and a kind of awe. He had, to her, an almost god-like warrior quality; she was reminded of the vast Achilles statue in Hyde Park, fierce, helmeted and naked. It was a secret she had not even confided to her diary.

Now it was a whole week since that divine day they'd had together in London, Christmas shopping with his sister, Adele. He'd taken them to the new American soda fountain in Sutton's – the three of them treated like royalty – and they had indulged in a sublime concoction of ice and cream and raspberry sauce. Ice cream and Christmas carols! But the most exciting moment had been when they'd given Adele the slip and so, unchaperoned for the first time, they'd gone to a matinee of *Hullo, Ragtime!* Later, looking back, she couldn't remember a thing about the show; it was a blank. All she'd been aware of was Charles holding her hand and his breath on her neck when he had turned and whispered in her ear...

'You've gone all moony again!' Hugh dug her in the ribs.

'Don't!'

'This serious, Sis?'

'Um...think so... Oh, I don't know.' Despite herself she couldn't help grinning; it was all so marvellous. Charles, handsome, beautiful Sir Charles St John Sutton of 39 Hay Hill, London W was sweet on her!

'Does he know about Fritzie?'

The unexpected question instantly crushed every ounce of happiness in her heart. 'Oh don't, Hugh.' She stared helplessly at him. 'Why mention that now?'

'Because Nanny let slip she's very worried about Fritz and Lally, that's why. And I think you and I should talk about it, seeing as Mother and Father have decided to cut them out of the family.'

'Oh Hughie, you know it's not like that—'

'Well, what is it like then? Blind disloyalty, I call it.' He turned away from her.

'Now you're being unreasonable. You must see it's pretty

awkward, the fact that most of Mother's side of the family are German—'

'Yes, but it's Lally and Fritzie, for goodness sake. Are we supposed to ignore the fact that you and I are a quarter German!' His voice had risen; she looked nervously down into the hall.

'Sorry, Girlie. It's just that it makes my blood boil.'

She almost smiled; she knew he'd used her pet name as an act of contrition. 'I know, I do feel the same.'

'Have you heard from them?'

She shook her head. 'All my letters have been returned unopened.'

'Nanny's still got their photograph in pride of place on her bedside table even though they've become *persona non grata* in this house. Bless her.'

'How do you think they are?'

'I expect Fritz is at the Front and Lally is nursing,' he said evenly.

She dropped her head; she couldn't bear the thought that her beloved German cousins, Fritz and Lally, were now on 'the other side', the four of them facing each other as enemies across the new world order. 'I do miss them most dreadfully.'

'Oh, Lil, you don't still—'

'Love him?'

Hughie nodded awkwardly, emotional matters always a treacherous terrain for him.

'For goodness sake, I was sixteen.'

The firmness of this reply seemed to satisfy him. In a lighter voice he remarked, 'Well, Fritzie may be the devilish Hun but Nanny still thinks you should marry him. When the war's over, obviously!'

She ignored the comment.

He slipped a hand into his trouser pocket and drew out a slim silver cigarette case. 'Does Charles know about them, that we spent every summer with our German relations?'

For a moment, Lily was torn between the delight at hearing Charles's name and the dread at having to tell him about this forbidden side of the family.

'No, there hasn't exactly been the right moment.' She pulled a face and for the first time Hugh laughed. He struck a match on the sole of his shoe.

'Sorry, old girl, didn't mean to put a damper on things. So, come on, tell me, what does this Charles do? Has he joined up?'

'No, not yet.' She smiled despite herself. 'Actually, he works in his family's shop.'

'Good lord, does Father know he's "in trade"? He'll have a fit!' Grinning at her, Lily saw how absurdly young her brother looked.

'No, stupid, not a shop like Mr Blacks the Ironmongers. Sutton's, the department store in Oxford Street. You know.'

'By gum, he must be worth a pretty penny. Well done, old girl!'

Lily punched his arm. 'Pig!'

'Ow! And will I like him?'

'Yes,' she said firmly, patting the finished bow tie. 'Because he's very handsome and he likes me!'

'Well,' he said, 'I suppose I'd better go down and meet him.'

In the large drawing room, the guests, having travelled through an icy starry night, had been met, here indoors, by a heat that was fierce. The ladies, mostly in sturdy evening dresses, sat, frothy fans waving, trying to counteract the unexpected warmth whilst the gentlemen stood stuffed into their evening suits surreptitiously dabbing at brow and upper lip.

As the brother and sister entered the drawing room, a small compact bald-headed man in heavy spectacles made it his business to cross the carpet to greet them, a hand extended expectantly. Lily saw in an instant that Charles and her father were not of the party.

'Oh lor, who's this?' Hugh muttered.

'Good evening, Mr Potter,' said Lily clearly. 'How are you? I do hope you have had a pleasant Christmas.' She turned to her brother. 'Hugh, you remember Mr Potter, chairman of our local Conservative Association.'

'Yes, yes, indeed,' interjected the little man and, throwing her an abrupt greeting, 'Good evening to you, Miss Robinson,' turned greedily to Hugh. 'Doing your bit for King and Country, I hear. How's it going out there?' He started to pump her brother's hand as if to extract the information he required.

'Well, sir, strictly speaking we're under orders not to talk about it.'

'Oh come, my boy – man to man.'

A butler appeared. 'Moselle cup, Miss Lily?'

'Thank you, Watkins. Hughie?' Turning, she saw her brother had gone very pale, thin beads of sweat breaking out along his neatly combed brow. 'Bring Mr Hugh a brandy and soda would you, please?'

'And bring me a refill while you're about it,' the Tory chairman cut in.

The butler slid away and a stout woman, dressed in a swooping gown of chocolate-brown velvet, took his place.

'Hello, Hugh dear, nice to see you. Still in one piece, I see.' She leant up towards the young man and proffered a heavily powdered cheek.

'Aunt Violet,' he muttered and, ignoring the cheek, stood stock-still.

'We were just saying, weren't we, Frank,' said Aunt Violet, not noticing the snub, 'that things seem to be going all our way out there in France.' She looked with child-like eagerness towards the young man to confirm the point.

'Giving these Boche what-for, eh,' concurred Mr Potter, removing his spectacles and polishing them vigorously. 'Teaching the cowardly blighters a lesson.' He popped the glasses back on his nose and blinked.

Lily saw Hugh reach into his pocket and, drawing out a handkerchief, pass it over his brow. Watkins arrived with the drinks. Not waiting to be handed his, Hugh swept up the brandy, downed it in one and replaced the glass on the tray.

Lily looked round the little group. Nobody seemed to have noticed; there were more important things on their agenda.

'Too big for their boots, if you ask me,' Aunt Violet was lustily continuing. 'I've always maintained the Germans are a greedy lot. They'll be wanting our Empire next.'

'I have it on very good authority,' Mr Potter dropped his voice. 'The Hun is a monster. Incapable of human feeling.'

'Have you heard the vicar's dog has been stoned?' Mrs Henfrey, a small quiet woman, had joined the group. She was decked out in a yellow dress, the shade of which reminded Lily of very strong mustard; it was an unfortunate colour.

'Good Lord, Majorie, why?' demanded Mr Potter.

The little woman suddenly looked uncomfortable; all eyes

had swung towards her. 'It's a sausage dog,' she muttered by way of explanation.

'And what on earth's wrong with that?' boomed Aunt Violet.

'Oh, my dear, you know – it's a "dachshund".' Mrs Henfrey's voice was now barely audible, the danger of contamination from the German word too terrible to contemplate.

At Lily's side, Hugh started to laugh. Vastly relieved, she turned, only to realise the laughter was empty of all merriment as he stood, head thrown back, hands on hips, his face a caricature of amusement. But it was the noise escaping from him that shocked her – an ugly insistent rasping.

'Hughie – oh Hughie, don't—' Horrified, she saw tears spring into his eyes.

Around them, their chattering group silently melted away as all over the drawing room conversation drizzled to a halt; Hugh's wretched barking laughter commanding attention, the harsh sound growing ever more coarse, more alien.

As one, the assembly now standing stock-still, stared. The young man flung himself backwards and then recoiled, his body doubling up as though shot. Slowly, very slowly, he sank to his knees, his arms knotted into himself for protection. No more laughter now.

In the hallway, the music had stopped.

A sickening silence followed.

Helpless, Lily dropped to her brother's side and tried quickly to gather his lanky frame into her arms. But there was a new problem, for the boy was sobbing. She lay across him attempting to muffle the pitiful sound. 'Shhh, oh Hughie, shhh.'

Looking frantically round for help – where was Mother? – she saw the door to the morning room open and her father and Charles swing into the room. And strangely, for all that was happening, she was aware at once that the two men had been drinking. They stood at a loss, hovering in the doorway, both grinning inanely at the assembled company. It was at this point Charles saw her, instantly his expression changing. Horrified, he started forwards and then as abruptly drew back, glancing from side to side to see who had noticed his move. But the company continued to stare solely at the brother and sister, everyone frozen in embarrassment.

Gently Lily started to rock back and forth, her brother's head cradled in her lap, a nest of pink tulle, willing his sobs to subside. 'Quiet now, Hughie,' she whispered, completely lost as to how to help him further.

Frantically she looked up once more but all avoided her eye until suddenly there was a commotion at the back of the room and guests shuffled to one side. Through the gap, the round black figure of Nanny toddled towards them.

'Oh, thank goodness. I don't know what to do,' she whispered hoarsely.

But the old woman ignored her and instead, standing at the boy's head, commanded quietly, 'Come on, my manny, up you get.' Her aged voice was strong and firm.

At the sound, Hugh seemed to awaken. His whimpering died and a perplexed expression settled on his face. 'Nanny?' Lying there, his head in Lily's lap, he reached his hand up towards the old woman's face.

'That's right, child, up you get now.' She caught the outstretched hand and the boy made to rise, his body a tangle of unfocused limbs.

Nanny turned and commanded, 'Thank you, Mr Watkins.'

From the back of the drawing room, the butler now also appeared. 'Here you are, Mr Hugh, lean on me.' He slung the boy's arm round his shoulders, and heaving pulled him to his feet.

The two of them stood swaying for a moment, getting their balance, and then, following Nanny, who led the way, sweeping party guests from their path with a wave of the hand, Mr Watkins half-carried the boy from the room.

As one, the assembled company had the good grace to silently look away from the dragging boy. However, with the trio's departure, a burst of greedy conversation broke out all around the room. Finding herself alone and stranded, still on her knees, Lily quickly turned to Charles. But he was not attending her. Instead he stood, caught in the doorway, staring at where Hugh had just left the room. And now as she looked, Lily saw that Charles's handsome face was all but unrecognisable, distorted by an ugly expression, an expression created by a mixture of fear and revulsion. She couldn't believe her eyes.

Years later, she would realise, in that moment, two things had been made clear – and both involved Charles. She had seen in Charles's reaction to her brother, in his disgust at the young man's collapse, the capacity to loathe any such vulnerability, never allowing himself to understand. For to understand was to appear to collude in such 'weak' behaviour. Such weakness, to Charles, was beyond compassion. And so now the two young men stood ranged, one against the other. Never, ever to get along.

But perhaps, even more importantly, the cold white-light of reality had cut through her dreams and shone its beam, albeit briefly, on Charles Sutton himself, the true man. Glimpsed but revealed. Hard and unforgiving.

If Lily had chosen to see.

But for whatever reason, that night she had neither wanted to see nor wanted to comprehend such revelations.

SS *Etoile*. Early afternoon

'Come on, old girl, we can't sit around here all day.'

Johnnie, jumping to his feet, scooped up Lily's bag and journal. 'Let's go and get some grub. It's about time we found out what this boat has to offer.'

'I'm not really hungry—'

'Listen, if we stay here that nosey woman and her granddaughter might come back and ask a lot more questions.'

Reluctantly, Lily got to her feet. She followed Johnnie to the swing doors of the third-class day room, the two of them edging between groups of people.

Having come on board three days earlier, the terrible possibility of discovery had kept them confined to the cabin. They had made do firstly with a variety of sandwiches cut by Mary, wrapped in greaseproof and all lovingly labelled – and then with endless snacks of potato crisps, Jacobs assorted biscuits, a tin of Sharp's Super-Kreem Toffees plus a couple of bottles of whisky. But today Lily had had enough; she'd had to escape. Not that she was hungry, just tormented by the cabin's safe but sickening claustrophobia; suddenly the thought of the fresh air and freedom in the public areas had seemed wonderful. But after sitting for an hour in the crowded third-class day room, she had to confess her release from the cabin had brought little relief.

Now, as they pushed through the double doors away from the communal room, Johnnie and Lily found themselves in an equally busy corridor, a sign pointing them towards the canteen – although no indication was necessary; the air was suddenly filled with great wafts of food. 'Good Lord, I'm ravenous!' announced Johnnie.

The canteen was a large hall not dissimilar to a school refectory. Long wooden benches stood on either side of long wooden tables and the shafts of afternoon sunlight flooding through a row of portholes bounced off the polished surfaces. Although the design was simple, Lily was struck by how bright and clean everything appeared to be. At the far end, a row of sailors stood doling out steaming food from big steel urns and pots, and although the place was only half-full – most third-class passengers having already eaten their midday meal – the noise was tremendous.

Slowly, over the last three days, she'd become aware that, more with an eye to hard business than an inclination to democratic goodwill, the Silver Star Line had made sure that the steerage quarters, although not in any way luxurious, did possess a certain degree of practical comfort. As with other shipping lines, Silver Star had been badly affected by the Wall Street Crash and the Depression that followed. Now Lily could see the owners were realising survival of their line was as dependent on steerage passengers, many travelling in the hope of fresh starts and new lives, as on the wealthier clientele who crossed and re-crossed the Atlantic often solely in search of fun and amusement.

'Must be "help yourself",' said Johnnie leaning into the wall and starting to read a menu. 'Oh, I say.' He turned and grinned at her. 'It's Lyons Corner House.'

Although she had no appetite, she was surprised to see the choice of meals on offer for that day. Porridge, kippers or tripe and onions for breakfast; soup (cock-a-Leekie or Mulligatawny), rabbit stew or bacon and cabbage for lunch with, of course, a pudding (apple meringue or Spotted Dick), and brawn, beef, cheese and pickles plus jam, tea and buns at teatime. She remembered recently reading a magazine article about shipping lines that had described the tiny galley for steerage compared to the vast kitchens for first class. She stared anew at the menu and marvelled at its promise of plenty.

'Well, I think it's a bit of rabbit stew for me with an apple meringue for afters! What about you, old girl?'

Lily could see the prospect of food had cheered him considerably and although not in the slightest bit hungry, not to spoil his mood, she said, 'I wonder if they could do me a hot Bovril – and some buttered toast?'

'Take a pew – I'll see what's what.'

Down the end of the room stood a group of empty tables. She made towards them – always the instinct to keep apart from the crowds – and, seated, looked about her. People were eating enthusiastically, vigorously scraping bowls and plates squeaky-clean, the food demanding attention through the chatter. A sudden memory of Nanny flashed into her mind. 'Lily Robinson, what on earth are you doing licking your plate clean in such a fashion! The King'll never invite you to tea if you carry on like that.'

A whooping at the far end of the room by the food counter distracted her. She looked up to see a surge of people stepping up to queue – the men in shiny black suits and caps joyfully jostling a group of women, also dressed in black. Surely not funeral weeds? As if to refute this, a wave of laughter rose up followed by a prolonged babble of chatter, and Lily caught the unaffected enthusiasm with which the group were queuing for such ordinary fare – after all, it was hardly the Savoy Grill, a bit of boiled bacon and cabbage. But with this thought came a startling realisation; it was probably more food than most people down here had ever seen.

She sat feeling strangely foolish. And unworldly. Her brother would have realised, of course. He'd actually been to the soup kitchens when he helped those miners' families. She recalled the day Hughie had tried to tell her about his trip up North – funny, they'd actually been having lunch at Lyons – and he'd leant across the table and, as he'd spoken, his expression grave, she'd been struck how his long crooked face with its big bony nose, to her mind as old-fashioned and beautiful as a medieval knight's, had been so absurdly at odds with the candy-coloured table-tops and the waitresses, the black-and-white 'nippies'.

'You know when I went on that walking tour, Lil,' he'd explained, unexpectedly placing his hands over hers. 'Summer of '25 and I did Hadrian's Wall?' And she had nodded, enjoying the comfort of her brother's hands through the suede of her gloves. 'Well, one evening I walked into a village – Brighthorpe – and there were a group of miners waiting to go on shift, squatting on their haunches playing Pitch and Toss. What struck me about these men was that were playing with buttons – they didn't even have a ha'penny to venture, you see.' The discomfort of the thought had made Lily awkward; she'd gone to move her hands but Hugh'd held firmly on to them. 'No, listen, Lil. If you're brought up, as we were, to think the working man cares only about his beer and tobacco – that he gets drunk every Friday and gambles away his money while his dozen ill-conceived children run around filthy and barefoot – then it's quite a shock to discover that, after clawing out coal for seven hours in his own sweat and sewage, he doesn't even have a farthing to play a child's game. And when he *is* allowed to go home, exhausted at the end of the day, the journey from shaft to face, sometimes several miles long, is not even counted as part of his shift!' His voice had risen and, flustered, Lily's eyes had flicked to the adjoining table.

'That's right, Lily, be ashamed.'

'Oh Hugh, I'm not.' She'd felt slapped. 'It's just – I didn't know.'

'No, nor do most people. And nor do they want to.'

And had she wanted to know? Not really. Her own life at that time, the time before she'd met Johnnie, had seemed too full of its own distress. She'd dutifully glance from time to time at Charles's newspaper and get the general gist but, truth be told, these people's problems seemed a universe away from her and her son's life.

'Penny for them!'

'What?' Lily looked up, startled; Johnnie was standing with a tray. She could see dollops of hot food steaming on the plates.

'You looked miles away. *Voilà!*' He handed over her toast and a mug; the nostalgic aroma of Bovril rose up.

'I was just thinking about Hughie – and his good works.' She smiled to dismiss the subject.

The thick white china mug made the soft brown liquid look even darker as the steam gently spooled up from it. She blew and, without thinking, started to cut up pieces of toast and dunk them in. They were soft, sloppy and buttery. She drank and dunked – perhaps she was hungrier than she realised? – and looking up, caught Johnnie ladling stew into his mouth. 'Mmm, very tasty,' he mumbled. 'And excellent mashed potato – no lumps.'

'Praise indeed, coming from you. I can see my first cooking

lesson will have to be rabbit stew. Only as long as I don't have to shoot the damn thing first!'

The bubbling group of gentlemen in black with their womenfolk arrived at the next table and, with much nodding and laughter, wide soft bottoms nestled onto hard wooden benches. '*Buon giorno, signora.*' '*Permesso, signor?*' '*Grazie tante.*' Plates and cups, bags and shawls spilled onto Johnnie and Lily's table as people arranged themselves and finally settled to their meal. Out of the merry chatter, a song rose up. '*O sole Mio*'. There was an instant ripple of sunshine and warmth.

But the effect of so many people so close caused Lily to tense instantly; she felt unexpected terror claw back up her spine. She put down her mug. Johnnie reached across and took her hand. 'They're Italian, darling,' he said softly.

'I know, so stupid of me. It's just that—'

'It's just that you think the world is spying on us.'

She nodded dumbly, the fear of discovery so sharp and raw. At their side the singing gently rose and fell, but Lily sat unhearing. 'I don't think I can take another two days of this. I knew it was going to be risky but I thought the excitement of escaping would somehow – oh, I don't know – compensate?'

'I know, my love. But remember – there is absolutely no likelihood of anyone recognising us down here.' He chucked his head towards the group. 'Unless one of these *signoras* ran a pensione that you and Charles stayed in?'

She almost smiled. 'We never went to Italy.'

'So there you are.' He scraped his plate clean and put his knife and fork together. 'Bet the food up top isn't half as good as this.' He reached for his bowl of apple meringue.

'We had *Parfait de Foie Gras à la Gelée de Porto* on our

trip to New York in '23.' She pulled a face; Johnnie laughed. 'Charles, as I recall, wolfed it down and then got very sniffy and English when he realised what it actually was. I kept the menu for years, it was our last night on board and we were invited to the captain's table – everyone signed it.'

Johnnie rested his chin on his hands. 'Tell me more.'

'About the high life?'

He nodded but she hesitated.

'Go on – especially as it looks as if I'm never going to get up there.'

'Well, all I can remember is forever changing my clothes; it was such a palaver. And if you dined at the captain's table – fortunes having usually changed hands to get a place, as far as I could make out – you had to turn out in full fig, jewels – and the chaps in medals. It was like a constant cocktail party – and as exhausting because, of course, you knew everyone. The first thing you did when you got on board was read the passenger list – it had been shoved under your door – so you always had a good old look at that. But the most important thing – according to Charles, anyway – was to make friends with your steward and then for the rest of the trip your pink gin or whatever turned up without being ordered. However, on the way home we made the mistake of booking our passage on a "dry" boat. Charles was not best pleased. Even so we got round it as a friend told Charles to go to the ship's doctor before we sailed with the list of drinks we wanted on the voyage. He then wrote us out the order in the form of a prescription and all these bottles were sent to our cabin—'

She stopped mid-sentence – the memory of Charles, dreadfully drunk at the cards table, arguing violently, swearing obscenely, heads turning...

'What?' asked Johnnie.

She shook her head. 'Nothing, just remembering.' To squash the image, she said, 'Charles got "done" by a card-shark. He reported him to the captain and the next morning, in his office, the three of them had a surreal conversation – Charles and this shady character on one side of the desk, the captain on the other, and the captain's enormous pistol in the middle. I don't think Charles ever got his money back though. No proof.'

'Well, you see what a quiet life we're having down here. And what's more, that's the most you've said in days – and it was delightfully refreshing!'

'The Bovril obviously did the trick.'

'Come on, let's go back. We've been out long enough for one day.'

She smiled at him. 'Nanny,' she said but her heart was sinking. She dreaded the thought of the tiny cabin.

CHAPTER THREE

SS *Etoile*. Early afternoon

As Mrs Webb reached her cabin – Anthea insisting on skipping one-potato, two-potato down every passage – she was surprised to be greeted by a very smart bellboy, who jumped to attention by her open doorway. 'Billy Bottle, ma'am,' he announced. 'At your service.'

Before she could reply, another voice called from inside the cabin. 'Gran, where's me jersey?'

She entered to the sight of her grandson's grey-cloth bottom, his head being stuck under a bunk. With a great deal of shoving and banging, the boy was trying to pull out a battered tin-trunk. Mrs Webb heaved herself down onto her knees beside him.

'What y'doing down here, Freddie? I thought yer were supposed to be at work up in them kennels.'

'Don't worry, ma'am,' said Billy Bottle, peering round the door. 'We're using Fred's dinner break to get him kitted up. You want a hand with that?' and he, too, dropped to his knees.

'The kennel master says he needs warmer clothes. For walking the dogs on deck, like.' All three tugged at the trunk, which popped free, and Mrs Webb rummaging quickly through its contents, drew out a small grey jersey. Fred pulled it on and made for the door, his hair standing up like a hedgehog. 'Bye, Gran.'

'No, you don't, young man.' The woman's hand shot out and caught the boy. 'I'm not having you walking round 'mongst't ladies and gentlemen upstairs looking such a scruff.' She started to brush his hair vigorously.

'Awww, Gran – that 'urts,' squawked Fred.

'Stand still, young man.'

'Your gran's right, Fred me lad,' remarked Billy. 'Doesn't hurt to be smart.' And he buffed his buttons with the back of a gloved hand.

Mrs Webb gave the bellboy an old-fashioned look but said nothing. Truth be told, she was pleased to see her grandson had made a friend. After only a couple of days, the two lads were obviously getting along.

'One potato, two potato, three potato, four,' sang Anthea, up and down the corridor outside.

'Now, let me 'ave a look at yer.' Turning her grandson round, she stood him next to his new friend and, despite herself, smiled. The two boys couldn't have been more different. There was Billy, tall and gangly, though band-box smart in his mulberry uniform, pill-box hat dipping to the left ear and a gleaming trail of tiny brass buttons down the front of a neatly fitting jacket. (Only a rather spotty face detracted from this otherwise polished appearance.) Beside him, Freddie looked wider, smaller and scruffier, his face round and soft, though Mrs Webb was pleased to see a touch of colour in those chubby cheeks, the sea air doing the child some good. But, as ever, she was only too aware of the boy's shabby clothes. His short grey trousers were too tight – at twelve years old, the lad was growing fast, though outward rather than upward, she feared. His plimsolls were grubby but at least his rumpled green aertex shirt was hidden by the grey jumper he'd just pulled on. But even this, knitted by herself, she knew to sport a large neat darn on each elbow.

'Have you two had some hot food?' she asked.

'Just on our way there now, ma'am.' The bellboy gave Mrs Webb a little bow.

'Get along, pair o' yer,' chucked the woman, seemingly unimpressed by the lad's courtesy.

In the vast crew's Mess room the noise was enormous, swollen by a medley of languages and the constant steam-whistle of a giant tea-urn. Freddie stood frozen in the doorway and stared. Sailors trooped back forth, plates piled high with shiny food, the air ripe with the aroma of sardines, fried eggs, black pudding and sausages.

'Come on, my son,' shouted Billy over his shoulder, 'we haven't got all day.'

They found themselves a seat in the midst of the bustle and, side by side, proceeded to demolish a mound of tripe and onions followed by a large plate of bread, butter and strawberry jam. Fred munched and stared about him but not a word was exchanged, eating being the matter in hand. And to that end Billy was content. He liked his new pal. In young Fred Webb he recognised a kindred spirit, and as the older of the two, Billy being fourteen and Fred twelve, he knew enough of life to spot a 'bit of a loner' like himself. What's more, only the day before, knowing the value of a few coins, he'd been able to put his new friend in the way of a job – that of ship's kennel-hand and apprentice dog-handler, an opportunity young Fred had jumped at.

Their meal finished, Billy took a final slurp of tea and pushed back his stool. 'Come on, Fred, no more skiving; back to work. We'll go back to the kennels by way of the printing room on E deck.' He waved a piece of paper. 'Got these boxing-match details to deliver.' And before Freddie could say anything, the bellboy was off, setting a sharp pace.

'I know it's a bit of a round-about – along to E deck and then up to the kennels – but it's as good a way as any for you to see something of the old tug.' A gangling youth, Billy was cantilevered for the moment between man and boy. Ill at ease with himself, his face slowly erupting into a nest of spots, when he talked of 'the old tug', he felt different; his heart melted and his face stopped itching. He cast a loving eye about him. More than anything, he wanted his new pal to share his passion.

'The SS *Etoile*'s not a superliner, Fred my son, not like the *Europa* or the *Bremen*, but she's got class. She was painted grey in the war and could carry up to two thousand men, and then she was put over to oil in 1923 but they had to make her funnels longer 'cos all the passengers got covered in smuts!' Speeding along, he rattled out the facts.

Billy had been brought up in a little house overlooking Southampton Docks which, down the years, echoed to tales of the sea, Grandfather Bottle being a seaman also. All through his childhood, he'd wander all over the docks and into the Ocean Terminal to see the great big liners. And on Sailing Day, scampering between towers of luggage, he'd tuck himself away and watch these majestic worlds slowly depart for all corners of the earth. He had a dream – though he'd never dared believe it would come true – one day he'd sail away on one of 'em…

'But my dream did come true! Three years, a bellboy, me.' He grinned down at Freddie puffing along beside him. 'I can tell you the tonnage, length and weight of the *Etoile*, and I loves every inch of her. You know, in this job,' he put a hand to his pill-box hat, 'I can be, one minute, climbing through the boiler casings, and then I push open a hatch and I'm there in the middle of all them swanky passengers. Best of both worlds.'

As if to illustrate this he unlinked a chain across their path and led them up an outer gangway. 'Here we are,' he announced, 'the print shop. Now, when we go inside, leave me to handle matters.'

But Freddie had other things on his mind. 'What time is it? Me dinner break's near over—'

'Don't you worry. We'll deliver these fight details and get you along to the kennels, all in good time.'

They ducked out of the wind and entered a tiny dusty office cluttered with ledgers, printing blocks and old newspapers. The ship's print shop, it was responsible for turning out hundreds of daily items: menu cards and posters, notices and news-sheets. Amid this paper bedlam, however, there was a concentrated silence, the two occupants huddling over a large old desk, scanning sheets of newspaper, the only sound the *rat-tat-tat* of the ship's wireless tapping away from an inner room. The boys hovered in the doorway.

The younger of the two men looked up and – much to Billy's surprise – declared, 'Hello, young Fred.'

'This is m'Uncle Barney,' swallowed the chubby boy. 'He works here.'

'How do,' said Billy.

Beaky and boney, Barney Webb now unfolded himself from the reading desk and stood up, tall and exceptionally thin. 'Come to see my office, lad?' But before Freddie could answer, the older man had snapped, 'Let's have a bit of quiet, we're trying to work in here!' Barney swiftly folded himself down again.

'That's Al, the editor,' Billy whispered.

'What they doing?' asked Freddie, staring only at his uncle.

'Sorting through stuff for tomorrow's *Poseidon Post*.'

'What's that?'

'Ship's newspaper. For the first-class passengers.'

'I can hear you, boy!' cried Al the editor. A dedicated newspaperman, he was wearing a green visor and had a cigar-butt clamped between his lips. 'Speak up or hold your tongue, some of us are trying to work. Read out what you've spotted so far, Barney.'

'Well, boss, *Daily Express*' front page has a couple of headlines we could use. And there's an eyewitness account of the fire in Germany—'

'Read that out. See if it stands up.'

Barney Webb straightened the newspaper and cleared his throat. Billy nodded at Freddie and put a finger to his lips.

'"The fire broke out at 9.45 tonight in the Assembly Hall of the Reichstag. After twenty minutes of fascinated watching, I suddenly saw the famous black motor car of Adolf Hitler slide past. I rushed after them and was just in time to attach myself to the fringe of Hitler's party as they entered the Reichstag."'

Al stood listening carefully, chewing on his cigar. The smell of old tobacco was heavy in the little office.

'"We stride across the lobby filled with smoke. Hitler watched the firemen for a few minutes, a savage fury burning from his blue eyes. It was then he turned to me. 'God grant,' he said, 'that this is the work of the Communists. You are witnessing the beginning of a great new epoch in German history. This fire is the beginning.'"

Barney stopped. 'That's it, boss.' He checked down the bottom of the page. 'Says here, D Sefton Delmer's the journalist.'

'Mm.' Al pulled heavily on the butt, his face revealing neither enjoyment nor displeasure. 'Well, it's colourful, nice bit of detail even though it's a couple of days old. Might go down well.' The editor swung round. 'Now, what can I do for you two young men?'

Billy got out his piece of paper. 'Details of tomorrow night's boxing match. The trainer says, if you're generous, can he have twenty posters?'

'Cheek,' muttered the editor and turned back to his newspapers.

Barney Webb twitched the details out of Billy's hand. 'Let's have a look, then.'

'There's a 50 guinea purse an' all,' said Billy, grinning at Freddie. The boy pulled at his sock.

'I remember the first boxing match I saw,' murmured the editor. 'Kid Lewis and that Georges Carpentier. Olympia, 1922. Cracking, it was.' In his reverie, he tugged on his cigar but it had gone out; he turned in irritation to the boys. 'You two, get along. Take those menu cards up to Mr Doyle on D deck. If he wants any more printing up, I'm on a tea break.

And you can deliver the lunchtime editions up to first class while you're at it.'

'Aye, aye, mate,' said Billy cheerfully, scooping up the menu cards, a hessian sack of newspapers and his new companion.

'See you later, young Fred,' Barney Webb shouted after his nephew.

The boys climbed to D deck, delivered the cards and, scooting up the outside companionway, clambered back on deck. Despite the force of the wind and their streaming eyes, the two raced each other only to find themselves caught up in a feeble attempt at an egg-and-spoon race. Passengers battled wayward winds that whipped hats and scarves in front of faces, and for a full five minutes the boys hurtled here and there returning spilt eggs to grumpy contestants.

With the race over, they ran the remainder of the quarter mile deck, arriving alongside a giant funnel which housed the kennels. As they turned into the entrance, with just two minutes left of Freddie's dinner break, the air was suddenly filled with the sound of barking dogs. They stood holding their sides, laughing and gasping for breath.

The inside of the kennels had all the circular airiness of a circus tent, the medley of barks and yelps rising high into the funnel. Light danced at eye-level through a ring of portholes, beneath which separate stalls housed a variety of dogs, this fine day all in loud and boisterous form.

It was not, however, the insistent barking of the inmates but a harsh booming human voice that brought the young lads up short and finally stifled their laughter. Before them stood a hill of a woman carrying an elderly fur, a library book and a large gentleman's umbrella. But it was by her voice alone that Billy recognised the woman; often to be heard at full tilt in the first-class quarters, it rang out with the bark of Empire.

Lady Lavinia Slocombe was dressed this lunchtime in a purple wool day-costume, and though only in her mid-forties, so heavy was her make-up – a pale mask relieved by a severe gash of lipstick the colour of her suit – it made her appear several years older. Her face was further framed by a bright pink cloche hat, the whimsical colour of which was somewhat at odds with the haughty heaviness of her bulldog features.

'That's the culprit!' The woman's hand flailed out towards Freddie Webb. The boy stood stunned.

Billy would have run but such was his loyalty to his new friend, he decided to remain manfully at his side. Young Freddie, however, was having none of it. Instantly recovering his senses, he turned tail and ran blindly into the unseen figure of a tall thin woman standing behind him. There was a soft 'poof' of pain as the boy's head thumped into the woman's middle and both staggered apart with a moan.

Ignoring this mewl of pain, Lady Slocombe grabbed the nearest bit of the gasping Fred, his left ear, causing the lad to let out a further singing yell of pain. A quick to-do followed, he trying to yank away from the big woman whilst Billy bobbed helplessly at his side.

'Enough now, *s'il vous plait*. Enough!' Mr Degas, the kennel master, had spoken.

All stopped and all was momentarily still; except for Freddie, who stood wriggling helplessly.

Lady Slocombe drew herself together and, ignoring the boy held disdainfully between her fingertips, snorted, 'I expected my beautiful little Gainsborough to be in your exclusive care,

Mr Degas. Not abandoned to be walked by some common little urchin.' Gainsborough, the 'beautiful little dog' in question, was snapping round and round her feet on a smart leather lead.

Billy looked from the dog to Mr Degas. What would the kennel master do next? A small neat Frenchman, though possessing a great knowledge and enjoyment of all things canine, he had an intense dislike of one thing – the large bossy owners of spoilt little dogs. But for the moment Billy saw the man had no expression on his face – a face which sported a little waxed moustache, an ornately stiff affair somewhat at odds with his floppy morose features.

Suddenly the man made his move. He bent forward at speed, gathered up the 'beautiful Gainsborough' and popped him into her ladyship's arms. Such was Lady Slocombe's surprise, she let go of Freddie's ear and her mouth clamped shut. With the boy released and the woman successfully silenced, the kennel master started to speak very quickly.

'My lady, let me assure you your beautiful animal is constantly in my thoughts. As for Monsieur Freddie here,' the boy was tenderly rubbing a very scarlet ear, 'he has a particularly gentle touch when dealing with animals as sensitive as your ladyship's. For that reason, I have chosen him as little Gainsborough's walker.'

The small dog in question now let out a piercing yap and, flustered, Lady Slocombe turned swiftly and dumped the animal unceremoniously into the arms of the thin woman at her side. With the arrival of the dog, the woman was forced to stop rubbing her sore middle.

'Monsieur Degas.' Lady Slocombe turned back majestically to the kennel master and bathed him in a frosty look. 'If you

think you can blind me with your so-called Gallic charm,'
she stared first at his spotty bow tie and then at his stiff little
moustache, 'you are very much mistaken. My maid, Timms
here,' she waved towards the thin woman, 'informs me that
this' – here she paused to search for an adequate description
of Freddie – '*lout*' – she landed heavily and triumphantly on
the word – 'is nothing more than a "steerage passenger".'

'Just so, my lady,' agreed Mr Degas. 'And an eager and
bright one with a natural talent whom, I'm sure you will
agree, should be given a chance.'

Her ladyship's eyebrows curled up. 'I trust you are not a
Communist, Mr Degas.'

She paused. No one spoke.

The dog yapped into the silence and her ladyship took up
the cudgels anew.

'Unless there is not more vigilant attention employed
whilst caring for the superior breeds, I will take the matter
up with the captain himself.' Mr Degas remained silent, his
face a blank. 'Although I have the sensitivity to realise' – her
ladyship's voice grew louder – 'that the captain has much on his
mind during the day, I will await a suitable moment at dinner
this evening.' And catching sight of her maid holding the by
now constantly barking dog, she finally snapped, 'Timms,
do stop holding Gainsborough as if he were an explosive
device!'

'Oh, my lady,' wailed the pained Miss Timms.

But 'my lady' had had more than enough. She motioned
her maid to return the dog to the kennel master and, with
that, the two women swept away.

Mr Degas bowed low.

When he stood upright, the Frenchman's melancholy

features had vanished; he was all smiles. But Freddie was having none of it.

'She gives that dog nowt; she don't want him!' He scooped Gainsborough into his arms. 'I tell thee, first bit o' love the dog gets, he fair curls up happy like, but wi' that frosty female, he does nowt but cry. *And* that – that – Timms one, she's a right nosey parker an' all. You can have your job, mister; I don't want no more to do wi' the likes of them.' Throughout this speech, he'd been stroking the little dog, who now stopped barking and began to whimper softly.

'Enough!' commanded Mr Degas. 'It's very important, even if we may know better, we make the customer think they know best. *C'est très important.* Monsieur Bottle here knows of what I speak.'

'First rule, mate,' Billy agreed.

Mr Degas rested his hands on Freddie's shoulders. 'I mean what I say, you are *très sympathetique* with the dogs. I hope you do not leave this job so soon?'

Freddie looked down at his gym shoes. He liked Mr Degas – only yesterday he'd told Billy he was the first grown-up person not to treat him like a kiddie. And he liked the dogs, he'd had a right old run-around with them all. After a bit, he spoke. 'All right, mister. I'll stay.'

'Thank you, my friend. Now take Gainsborough, give him water. And I must eat; this little contretemps has made me hungry. I return in an hour.'

'And I've got these newspapers to deliver,' said Billy Bottle. 'See you later, Fred old son.'

The first-class Paris Lounge was sturdy and stuffy, the designer of the room having been heavily influenced by the seventeenth-century English manor house, here reproduced in the creamy moulded ceiling and walnut panelled walls. At the centre of one of these walls, opposite the long windows through which the sunshine now streamed, stood a vast carved wooden fireplace in which logs were stacked high, their crackle and fizz the only sounds punctuating the sedate murmurings of the lounge's few passengers. There was an atmosphere of desultory anticipation; the room seemed to be holding its breath, afternoon tea the next big event.

The insolence of the kennel master had put Lady Lavinia Slocombe into a decidedly ill humour. She sat in the middle of the Paris Lounge in an armchair, glowering at all who came near her, bad-tempered and bored.

Looking across the room she hailed a waiter; she was hungry. Although it had been less than an hour since she had consumed a large luncheon, she fancied something a little sweet to put her into a more cheerful frame of mind. However, when the man arrived at her side, after a momentary struggle of conscience, she ordered a slimming Brand's Essence and water, and glanced back towards the copy of *Vogue* magazine she had just been reading.

It instructed, 'We shall be smart but not hard, we shall gird our loins, there will only be one silhouette this season – the youthful one.' Lady Slocombe's heart sunk at the prospect.

For a woman of ample proportion, the contest with her shape had become more than a challenge; it had become an obsession. In pursuit of a lither outline, she had travelled far and wide from one health spa to the next – Denglers to Brides, Baden-Baden to Orsier – though in reality she was having to rely more and more upon the sadistic strictures of her foundation garments. She had thus been briefly heartened to read that morning that 'the bosom was making a gentle reappearance', though disheartened to note that 'the jersey belted over pleats' was this season to be '*de rigeur*'. No, whatever the magazines commanded, she would remain loyal to her dressmaker's 'youthful' designs, designs that she felt disguised and flattered her shape so well.

Out of the corner of her eye she saw her friend and companion Dora Carroll bustling her way across the room towards her. Although Lady Slocombe would have preferred to travel with her husband, Sir Charteris, in recent years various business engagements appeared to coincide each time she had wished to journey abroad. Hence, not wishing to travel alone – her maid, Timms, obviously did not count as any kind of companion – Lavinia had asked her friend, Dora Carroll, to accompany her. Dora was no fool. A middle-aged woman of no private means, she was practical in her acceptance of the unspoken arrangement, acquiescing in the wayward mood and manner of her friend in exchange for a glimpse of the world she would hitherto have only dreamt about.

'Here we are, Lavinia, the lunchtime edition of the ship's newspaper has just been delivered.' Dora placed a folded copy in front of Lady Slocombe. Her ladyship grimaced.

'Are you not well, Lavinia dear?' Seemingly all concern, Dora was well used to Lavinia's wily ways; she knew better than to ignore any expression of displeasure.

'I fear the food is not to the standard it once was,' her ladyship exhorted. 'I have been kept awake most of the night and I still have the most dreadful dyspepsia.'

Dora chose not to mention the hearty meal her friend had consumed the night before, nor the recent four-course luncheon. Instead she dropped her voice and suggested with some solicitude, 'Perhaps a small brandy and soda might settle things.'

'Oh, Dora, do stop fussing. Just read me the headlines.'

Anything for a quiet life, thought Dora, and unfolding the paper, glanced down the front page. 'That Mr Hitler seems to be making a mark for himself in Germany,' and she looked brightly at her friend, checking whether to continue or not.

'No politics, thank you – and certainly no foreign politics.'

Dora looked back again. 'Oh, listen to this, Lavinia dear! The Americans have made a moving picture about a giant gorilla who climbs the Empire State building.' She looked up gaily. 'I do hope we won't be meeting him on our shopping expedition down Fifth Avenue!'

'Don't be patently absurd,' snapped her ladyship, instantly squashing any attempt at levity. 'Let me have that – I don't know why you can't find anything of interest. Now, where are my spectacles?'

As Lady Slocombe lent towards the commodious handbag at her feet, Dora, despite herself, let out a gasp. 'Oh, my goodness!'

Lavinia's head came up instantly. 'What?' she demanded.

'Oh nothing, Lavinia, just – erm—' She awkwardly shuffled the newspaper and folded back the front page.

'Please don't fib, Dora. Will you do me the courtesy of reading out whatever it is you have spotted.'

'Oh no, Lavinia, it's really nothing—'

Lady Slocombe was silent; she held her friend's eye.

'Oh, very well,' said Dora reluctantly, and read out, her voice soft, '"Aristocrat's Wife Vanishes."'

'Please speak up, we are not in church.'

Dora cleared her throat. "'Lady Lily Sutton, 39, wife of wealthy business tycoon Sir Charles Sutton, has mysteriously disappeared. Sources close to her husband, who owns the fashionable department store, Sutton's, in London's West End, said he was very concerned for his wife's safety, fearing she may have suffered some kind of memory loss. Scotland Yard has been notified. Until the last election Sir Charles was Conservative MP for Freston North, when he stepped down in order to pursue his business career full time—'" Dora hesitated. 'There's more, shall I read on?'

But for once Lavinia Slocombe was without words. She sat like a monument, very still, her face pale as stone.

Chapter Four

SS *Etoile*. Mid-afternoon

Four decks below, Lily, swiftly leaving the cabin, was brought up short by the unexpected darkness of the passage. The lights dismal, each bulb throwing a custard-yellow glow that held no brightness, she stood leaning against the wall, her body throbbing from the incessant thundering boom of the engines below her.

'I'll just stand on deck for a couple of minutes,' she'd told Johnnie. 'Get a mouthful of fresh air.' Quickly leaving the cabin, she'd ignored his look, reasoning that after his rabbit stew and apple pud he was quite happy to stay put with his pipe and his book. Anyway, she'd be much better company after a walk on deck alone...

Up ahead a pair of doors banged open and two children raced down the drab corridor, their cheeks red as apples from the outdoor air. Dressed in leather bootees, sturdy coats and woolly pixie hoods, they were both about six years old.

'*Bang bang*, missus!' The boy pointed a silver toy gun at

her. She dutifully raised her hands. He ran on unimpressed.

'We're scaring big people,' confided his little sister huskily, hopping from foot to foot.

At that moment, a steward appeared at the far end carrying a trouser-press.

'There's one, let's shoot him,' yelled the little boy. 'Joyce, come on!' and before Joyce could refuse, she was dragged towards the steward. '*Bang bang!* You're dead!'

Ignoring the death threat, the man sashayed past and away down the corridor.

Both children hollered happily through the far swing door, leaving Lily listening to their wild yells echoing back along the passage.

Nickie, she thought, *joyfully playing. Cowboys and Indians...*

'For Christ's sake, silence that child or I'll do it myself!' And once again her husband's hated voice slashes through the gentle memory. She hears, sees, feels Charles roaring insanely over the banisters at Melsham, his hefty face sweating and purple. She's rushing from the drawing room in time to see Nickie scrambling from his wig-wam under the stairs, a game indoors for a rainy day, the wretched child standing, frail and white, frozen under his father's glare.

She looks up. Charles is starting to descend, heavily, slowly; there is excitement in this chase. And Lily catches the menacing oily gleam, the look she knows only too well, the look that presages terrible danger. Frantically, she pushes Nickie down the kitchen passageway...

'Are you all right, ma'am?'

In the dark bleak passage of the ship, a sailor was standing at her side, his hand hovering to prevent her faint or fall. Shaking, a numb impotence suffusing her, she leant on the sailor's outstretched arm, unable to speak. She focused on the beefy red hand, streaked with petrol, and wretchedly dumb, found she could only raise her eyes and nod at the man.

My God, she thought, *to think I let him near Nickie. Why could we never get away from him? Why were we so endlessly in his thrall?*

'Ma'am, I'll call the doc, shall I? You're very pale.' She caught the stern steady tone of the man's voice, as if talking to a child or invalid – and with every ounce of strength, she closed her mind and forced herself to smile.

'Thank you, I'll be fine. Just a touch of sea-sickness.'

The man looked unconvinced.

'Really I'll be fine.'

'Well, if you're sure—'

Lily nodded and released his arm. She walked slowly away from him along the ill-lit passage. Away from the sounds of the children, away from the terror of the memory, and pushed through the swing doors.

For God's sake, Lily, breathe... The old family training... Breathe... No feeling... Absent yourself...

She stood, staring at nothing, until at last her mind was a blank.

Eventually, she became aware of a strange whirring sound. Looking about her, she realised she was standing in a small lobby facing an electric lift. Somewhere, high up the shaft, the noise stopped abruptly and she heard the iron-clanging of a pair of gates opening and closing, and then the whirr steadily started again. Focusing, she saw she was staring at a panel of buttons.

AFT 'E' DECK ELEVATOR (Not for use of steerage passengers)

C deck 'Shelter' (2nd Class Library, Gymnasium, sheltered promenade)

   D deck 'Saloon' (Squash Court)

   E deck 'Upper' (2nd and 3rd class open public areas)

   F deck 'Middle'(3rd class passenger General Room)

   G deck 'Lower' (Swimming pool, Turkish baths)

Where would she go if she had the chance? The gymnasium, the library? Down here in steerage, there were only two places to 'escape' to – the third-class general room and the poop deck.

She turned quickly away from any temptation to call the lift and pushed through a further pair of doors onto the poop deck. In her hurry, a brace at the base of the door caught her heel and she almost fell.

'Oi, oi, missus, you'll take a pearler!'

She found a brawny pair of arms around her. Once again a member of crew had come to her rescue and she was all but lifted onto the deck. 'There now, catch yer breath and you'll be right as rain.'

'Thank you,' she called after the sailor's retreating back and stood, foolish from her tumble, tears very near.

Dear God, please don't let me cry. Not here... She pulled Mary's tweed coat round her and the scent of her maid's talcum powder, the smell of dusty roses, filled her with unbelievable longing for her friend. *Oh, Mary, I need you so much at this moment. How could I even think of doing this without you?* She hugged the coat to her, the one shred of comfort knowing Mary was at home, thinking of her and, no doubt, frantic for news.

Taking a deep breath, Lily looked around – if she was on deck, she'd better get that mouthful of fresh air – and was shocked to discover she'd arrived in a small alien city. Whichever way she turned the view was obscured by large heavy machinery, vast hooded air vents, ropes of thick chains and the iron-tangle of a mighty crane rising high into the sky. All over the dull metal, people were leaning and lounging, giving the stern landscape a strange impression of comfort.

But where was the sea? It had completely disappeared from view. She started forward, this absence of the ocean making her feel stranded and lost. She had to get her bearings. Edging past an untidy group straddling a lifeboat, she glimpsed the horizon, then the sea – grey on grey – and pushed with all her might against the hauling swell to reach the railings. She was alone here, free of the crowd, winds wildly tugging at her clothes, and she stood, one hand holding the smooth wooden railing, the other windmilling about trying to button her flapping coat.

And there just beneath her was the sea. She stared down, her heart beating. It was so much nearer than she was used to up in first class. Raw, alive. Mesmerised by the rolling motion, enthralled by so much danger, so much power, she cradled the rail as the huge ship swayed its way through the heavy pewter waters, a great grey train skirting the ship's bulk, foamily trailing away, away...

Facing into the winds, she closed her eyes. She let the spray spit her face, relief in the tiny needles of pain, the roar of the ocean filling her head; tremendous, ear-numbing. She tried to let her mind fly away and, with her eyes and nose streaming, she felt at last the pain ease, the anxiety lulled for a moment.

She turned her back on the hauling winds, leant against the railing and reached for her hankie. And saw ahead of her, in the middle of the deck, a crowd whooping round a blindfolded man. On his knees, children were nudging and knocking him as he crawled about desperately trying to scratch a tail onto a chalked pig's porky rump. The laughter of the crowd was ear-splitting and, unexpectedly, Lily felt buoyed by this hard squealing energy.

She staggered and swayed on her way, fighting the wind and climbing against the swell of the ocean, but before long, found her path blocked by a lifeboat. She leant towards it and held on, catching her breath, giving herself totally to the sway of the waves.

Through the booming roar she became aware of a child's tight tinny cries and, looking down, was stunned to see at her feet a tiny baby in a wooden vegetable box. Yelling its head off, the baby's fat little fists were banging against the side of the rough cot. The mother, however – a fat woman never drawing breath – was ignoring it as she hung out her washing, an equally fat neighbour silently handing across pegs. Damp nappy-cloths flapped on a line slung between two lifeboats.

Lily dropped to her knees. She must soothe the child; its squalling face was plum, the angry-red gums toothless. Poor little mite, it was teething.

'Hey, what d'you think you're doing?' Lily felt a scuff on her shoulder and rose to find the fat mother, hand on hip, four-square in front of her.

'Well?' the woman demanded.

'I thought I might—'

'Might what, indeed?'

'Oh, excuse me.' Lily rapidly turned from the woman; she couldn't cope.

'Toffee-nosed bitch!'

The insult trailed after her, the momentary hurt cutting unexpectedly deep and, hurrying on down the deck, Lily found herself praying the big woman wouldn't follow, calling out further insults, urging her to turn and fight.

That's what Charles would have done. Urged a fight. Added insults and taunts, challenging her. And as ever, she found herself blaming her lack of stamina, her lack of gumption to stand her ground. *Oh, dear God, why have I never been able to defend myself?* She knew the answer. From the very first battle of their marriage, even before Charles had hit her the first time, she had taught herself to submit, to absorb the horrors. Never to answer back.

Perhaps if I had fought back? But then, she thought, *everything would have been so different and I wouldn't be here on this boat in the middle of the Atlantic...*

In the distance, her eye was caught by a rough, furious tug-of-war. The contestants were kicking and shoving and Lily pushed forward, grateful for the distraction. The shouts and ripe swearing were fierce – hooligans' yells rising on the air – and it was only as she got nearer that Lily realised the 'hooligan' contestants were all women.

Hurling themselves apart, straining along the rope, the women were screaming and alive, free of any modesty. Lily stared. All the women were bare-headed, their coats loose; the men, on the other hand, though mostly tie-less, wore cloth-caps. She thought of first class and how passengers would be smartly gloved and hatted and was equally struck by the zest with which these crowds were making the best of the fickle

March winds. Up top, few would be braving the elements. Here, children were whooping and shouting, their elders making only a little less noise.

She pulled off her headscarf and shook her hair free; she was sick of the tight pins. And suddenly sunlight flooded the decks, the bright fresh air bringing laughter and an unspoken sense of comradeship. Standing at the edge of the tug-of-war, Lily felt her spirits lift and she started to cheer on both teams.

Instantly, she shrank back. Amongst the raw, ripe voices of the crowd, her voice sounded absurd; reedy and fastidious. People turned and looked at her and although the stares weren't unfriendly, she felt exposed; a fraud and a fool. *Dear God, do I always sound so wretchedly toffee-nosed?* Ducking down her head, she slipped her scarf back on and pushed away from the crowd. She walked quickly on.

The sun shot behind a cloud and the deck instantly presented itself hard and unfriendly. In a single moment, all had become cloud-drab and chilly. Lily shivered and pulled Mary's coat around her. She must go back in, Johnnie would be waiting.

London. May, 1926

Again, the quiet. Just like yesterday.

She lay listening, trying to catch the comfort of the early-morning sounds. Even tucked away here in Bryanston Square, she could usually hear the faint rumble of buses and trams trundling comfortably round Marble Arch. Perhaps it was still too early. She leant across and held her little clock into the stripe of early spring light that fell across her bed. No. Ten past six. Even so, still too early to telephone Melsham.

She lay in the quiet, her heart heavy and weary. Where was Charles? Surely he couldn't still be at the House at six o'clock in the morning. Anyway, he's such a junior MP, even if they are all still working, what use could he be to any of them? This mad-cap notion – Charles, a Member of Parliament, it was utterly laughable... No, perhaps he'd left the House late and gone back to his department store; perhaps there had been some business matter? But in the middle of the night? Had he gone to meet someone?

Where was he? Blast him. On and on her mind coiled, the unending jealousy tugging at her heart. And now she was stuck in London because those wretched men from the North of England were making all this unnecessary trouble...

''Morning, my lady.'

'Oh lord, what time is it?'

'Half past eight.'

'I must have dozed off. I have to telephone Melsham.' She sat up and immediately felt sick and dizzy. 'Oh, drat.'

The maid set down the tray and was at her side, pulling the blanket back up over her. 'Now, don't you get cold. It's a bright morning but there's still a crispness in the air.'

'I feel so sick again, Mary. No, don't open the curtains yet—'

'Stay still. Here's your hot lemon drink. That'll settle things.' She sipped slowly but the lemon-water was sharp; Mary hovered over her encouragingly. Lily pulled a face but the maid pointedly ignored her and started tucking and clucking around the room. Eventually finishing the drink, she allowed herself to be propped back up against the large full pillows. 'Is Sir Charles in his dressing room?' She felt unbelievably tired.

'No, my lady, not that I'm aware of.'

'The House must have sat late. Not surprisingly, I suppose. You can open the curtains now, Mary.' Sunlight flooded the bedroom. Lily flinched.

She lay listening, the house silent with no Charles. 'So quiet,' she said.

'Not over by the Park. Cook says it's a sight to behold.' Mary bent and picked up her dressing gown. She placed it on a hanger. 'Says it's like some small city. Seems every railway company's got its own office and that, with gas and light and even a telephone.'

'Good heavens.' Lily could feel the nausea gently, gently slipping away. 'Thank goodness.'

'What, mum?'

'The sickness, it's passing.' She leant back and closed her eyes.

'And the roses are coming back into your cheeks.'

'Tell me more about Hyde Park. I'll put a call through to Melsham at nine when I feel a bit brighter. Don't want Nickie to hear me all dreary.'

She watched as Mary clipped about the room, adjusting her brushes and hand-mirror on the dressing table then opening drawers and carefully laying out her clothes. 'I thought,' said Mary, 'the grey and blue pleated for Doctor Mallard.' She gave Lily a little wink.

'What time's my appointment?'

'Three o'clock.'

Lily closed her eyes, the tiredness was extraordinary. 'I

wonder how Doctor Mallard will get to Harley Street from Ascot.'

'Cook says after them traffic jams yesterday, people started earlier today. She says when she went for the milk, she saw a pony and trap as well as all them bikes. And even a couple of gents on horseback. And that was around five-thirty this morning.'

'I can't imagine Doctor Mallard on horseback.' Lily closed her eyes again and curled away from Mary.

She must have dozed off for the next thing she knew Charles was banging into the room and Mary had gone. He crossed to the dressing table, without acknowledging her, and opened a drawer.

She quickly raised herself upright and pushed her hair back into some semblance of order; Charles hated to see her in disarray.

However, he never glanced in her direction but strode about the room as he replaced his wing-collar, a tricky job achieved with nimble dexterity, only then starting to talk, in a loud voice, as though addressing the House. All early morning calm was shattered.

'Winston's asked me to raise funds. Rustle up St John and Astor. Some kind of fighting fund. He's coming up with some tremendous "whack 'em on the snout" policies.' He dipped to check his handiwork in the mirror. 'His wife, Clementine, is a great fan of the store, by the by.' A skip and hop in his mood; a rare occurrence these days. Lily felt her heart lift. She knew better than to speak.

'Winston's got the right idea. Propaganda sheet. He's not sitting around Downing Street poring over fine print while these common little men in their blue serge suits walk all over him.' He opened an adjoining door and disappeared from sight. There was the sound of him urinating. 'Propaganda, that's what it's all about. Baldwin met John Reith at the club yesterday, emphasised the importance of the wireless.'

She quickly and quietly dropped from the bed and crossed to the dressing table mirror. Lord, she was pale. Pinching her cheeks hard with one hand, she pulled a comb through her hair and then she was back in bed, placing her bed-jacket about her; she now reclined. She listened to Charles, gargling and spitting.

His ablutions done, he re-entered and picked up his two hairbrushes. He brushed with vigour, checking his image in the mirror with a more than passing interest.

He's not so handsome, she thought, this tiny criticism almost a balm to her aching heart. *And his face is now always so ruddy. But I want him*, the other insistent jealous voice shouted back inside her head. *Notice me, love me, desire me again. Is his waist so much thicker? I've not seen him without his clothes for such a long time. And when, long ago, he stood naked before me, why had I not known how to please him... And now? In these recent times. Only that once, he came to me, in the dead of night, in darkness, and so drunk.*

The marriage is over, in all but name. The reality of this thought, for the first time confronted, shook her. It came unbidden and left her confused and sickened.

She looked away, suddenly ashamed, from this powerful and virile man who still she didn't really know after nine years.

On the other side of the room, Charles pulled on his jacket. 'So Reith said, assuming the BBC is for the people and the Government is for the people, it follows that the BBC must be for the Government. I'm glad to say that settled that.'

The scent of his cologne filled the air.

'And Lily,' the sound of her name made her jump. 'I hope you're not foolish enough to think of going back down to Melsham today; the railwaymen are supporting these damn miners and being thoroughly difficult. I certainly don't want any wife of mine haring round the countryside.' He finished knotting his tie. 'Dear God, these working-class men and their sentimental loyalties.'

Lily sat up. 'But Charles, I telephoned Melsham last night and told Nickie I'm getting the ten past six—'

'Don't be absurd, the child is three years old and has no need to be so ridiculously tied to his mother's apron strings.'

'But I haven't seen him for over two weeks—'

'Oh, do stop whining, woman. And can't that fool of a doctor prescribe you some sort of tonic? We pay him enough. You look so damned peaky.' With a final glance in the mirror, he left the room.

I hold no interest for him whatsoever, she thought. *But, I suppose, who can blame him, I feel so dim and dreary. Well, this time, at least, he's fallen for Winston and his cronies, and not some little floozy at the department store.*

The telephone rang on her bedside table.

'Darling, just reporting in.' Sabine Ambrose and a social bulletin. Lily could see Saby sitting up in bed girlishly wrapped in a lacy bed-jacket, the fluffiness of this night attire only serving to emphasise her strong manly features. *Well, I suppose I'll only have to listen*, she thought. Though even at this hour of the day, Saby's baying tones could be quite challenging.

'Now, Lily dear, we've got tickets for *The Ringer* tonight and I know it's jolly short notice but Polly Charter has let us down because of this ghastly strike business – Tubby has forbidden her to come up to Town, can you imagine – and I wondered if you fancied taking in a show?'

Lily heard her reply come smoothly. 'Darling, thank you so much but I'm afraid Charles and I are busy.'

'Right-ho.' Mrs Ambrose sounded unconvinced. 'Feeling better?'

'Fine,' said Lily, shovelling away her friend's concern. 'How was the Royal Academy?'

'Darling, practically empty. The first time I've ever actually had to look at all those wretched paintings. Can you believe it? These ghastly little men are frightening everybody out of Town. Bill says, Why can't they confine this simply frightful business to the North of England, where it belongs? I mean, why do we all have to be made to suffer down here? Anyway, Edwina's got the right idea; she's got herself a job manning the switchboard at the *Daily Express*. Such fun, she says. She asked if I wanted to cut along one evening but I said, what with the arrangements for Tolly's coming-out "do" on Wednesday and Hurlingham at the end of the week – apparently Bunny Austin's going to down his tennis racquet and drive a bus, isn't it heaven? – I haven't a moment to call my own.'

'No, of course not,' said Lily, while thinking, *Maybe Charles is walking out with some floozy. But which one could it be? Mind you, there are always so many new staff and I haven't been to the Store for such ages.*

'Lily, are you still there?'

'Sorry?'

'You went awfully quiet—'

'Oh, yes, Saby…um…I'm so sorry, Mary just came in to take away my breakfast tray.'

Undeterred, Mrs Ambrose drove on. 'Well, if you can't

make tonight, come and watch some tennis later in the week. It's such fun to have you in Town and I want to make the best of it. Anyway, Bim says we've all got to go out and show 'em. Though, between you and me, he'll be the first one to cut and run if there's going to be some ghastly revolution.'

Mrs Ambrose laughed; a surprisingly girlish sound for one who prided herself on the jagged sophistication of her ways. The laughter stopped; the woman no doubt aware that her friend was not joining in the fun of this new adventure. 'So, how are you bearing up, darling? Thinking of taxiing people around in that gorgeous car of yours?'

'Oh, Saby darling, I really wouldn't know one way or the other. Though to be honest, I can't say I feel personally any animosity towards these men. Just as long as they let me get back and forth to Melsham.'

'For goodness sake, Lily.'

Too late, she realised that this whimsically-held viewpoint had the potential to agitate Sabine's disapproval into an alarmingly long telephone conversation. Firmly, she cut off her friend's next remark. 'Charles says Winston is coming up with some splendid "whack 'em on the snout" policies. And now, my dear, I really must dash; Mary has run my bath. Can't wait for Tolly's on Wednesday; I'll be able to come now, now I'm stuck up in Town. One of the bonuses,' she added. And her heart sank as she put the telephone back on its cradle.

The deadening silence returned within. But outside she could hear the world marching on. Without her. She didn't care; she felt bored and so, so tired.

The telephone rang again.

'Girlie?'

'Hugh!' The surprise of the call made her ask, 'Are you all right?'

'Never better, old girl. Listen, come out to lunch. There's lots to tell you.'

'And is my little brother treating me?'

'Yes, of course. There's something I want to show you. Let's say Speaker's Corner, one o'clock?'

'Oh goody, how exciting. But, Hugh, why aren't you in Oxford? I thought it was still term-time—' But the line had gone dead.

Lunch with her little brother, what fun! She would take some crusts so that they could feed the ducks on the Serpentine and then they could pretend they were coming back to the nursery for tea… She almost skipped into the bathroom and, dressing in the grey and blue pleated as ordered by Mary, she finished her make-up and was on her way down to the kitchen for a bag of crusts just ten minutes later.

Descending the dark back staircase to the basement, she saw through the kitchen-door's frosted glass Mary and Cook, alone and chatting, Mrs Benton, as ever, her elbows deep in dough. 'Mistress's still not herself. Pale as pale,' Mary was saying.

Lily froze. Fearful of making any sound yet fascinated to hear what would be said, she flattened herself against the wall where the unlit stairs were darkest.

'What that doctor's thinking of when it's plain as plain my lady's missing Master Nickie,' Cook exhorted. 'You could charge me a fortune and I'd be more than happy to tell Sir Charles. Give him a piece of my mind—'

'Ooh! Hush, Mrs Benton—'

'Well really, I ask you. Master's worse than useless now

he's this Member of Parliament. At least when he was just in charge of his shop he didn't leave her all alone in London. Pining for Melsham she is, and the child.' A fist was raised and thumped into the dough. 'He should know better. He should be here at her side, not hiding away in Westminster. Whatever the state of the country.'

Lily could see Mary hopping nervously back and forth, checking the area-steps through the window for any soul who might hear. 'Mrs Benton, don't.'

But Cook was not to be deterred as she warmed to her theme, the dough now hauled onto the wooden board. 'I said to Mr Benton, England may be in this trouble, the country not knowing whether it's coming or going. But if a so-called Member of Parliament can't even look after his own wife – whilst all the while carrying on with some fancy piece – then he's not going to get my vote.'

Lily clutched at the stair-rail, a dreary sickness flooding through her. What fancy piece? She stood unable to move, her heart sullen. *That will teach you, Lily Robinson, snooping about behind closed doors.* She could hear Nanny's voice...

There was the sound of footsteps descending the area-steps and the dark shadow of George Benton entered. Carefully wiping his boots on the brushes by the door, his presence caused his wife to stop kneading – the dough heaved into a bowl, thump against china – and turn to a large brown teapot.

'What news, Mr Benton?'

'Price of milk's being raised to 2d a quart.'

'And how's that going to help these here miners, I'd like to know.'

Even through her wretchedness, Lily heard the chauffeur's

sturdy Cornish voice. George Benton, he and his wife had been part of the household, hers and Charles's, since their marriage. A sickening thought rose up. *Benton must know, he must know this fancy piece. They* all *must know.* Lily was filled with a desire to rush into the kitchen and shake the name out of them. She wanted to cry out, 'Who is she? What's she called?' How was it they knew about this fancy piece and she didn't? She felt utterly, utterly foolish; the last to know. She'd almost known about others but never dared pin Charles down. Nor any of their friends.

'It's all "stop" out there, I can tell you.' Through the frosted glass she saw the chauffeur pull off his leather gauntlets and settle back into a large wooden chair. 'Furnaces stopped and factories shut down. Though the master and them in the Government don't want people to know. I could kill a rasher, Mrs Benton.'

There was a clang as a big black iron frying pan was swung down onto the range. Within seconds, the pungent smell of bacon fat filled the air and Lily felt the nagging sickness bubble up once again.

'What else, Mr Benton? Mistress wants to know.'

Lily hesitated; despite the nausea she must know more.

'Traffic from Marble Arch to Piccadilly only moved a few yards in an hour.'

'No!'

'Sir Charles was steaming. Wouldn't give nobody a lift, neither. Even though they're saying it's our duty. Some motors have signs with, "Ask for a lift if you want one".' Through the glass, Lily could see the two women gazing at the driver with all the concentration of a silent picture-show.

'Took a back route. Cavendish Square through to Hay Hill.

Got the master back to Westminster in twenty minutes.'

'No!' The women chorused again, and Mr Benton, with his professional skill acknowledged, sank back into his chair and supped his tea, his tale at an end.

Quickly Lily re-mounted the stairs; there was the lavatory in the hall – she was going to be sick.

She crouched on the floor and placed her sweaty forehead against the cold linoleum. *Dear Lord, what would Charles say if he knew the servants were talking like that...* She felt a sudden jolt of nausea; she straightened up and retched into the china pan. *Oh, no, the servants mustn't hear... no more gossip...* Tears streamed down her face.

Slowly, the sickness passed. She dragged herself to her feet and climbed back up the silent house to her bedroom. She'd wash her face. *Come on, Lily, get a move on, it's lunch with Hughie.* She felt a hundred years old.

When she turned out of Cumberland Place and into Oxford Street, the first thing that struck her was the crowds; the all-encompassing quiet of her bedroom had been deceptive. Mary had been right, the roads were a pickle of carts and bicycles.

She made to cross into Hyde Park. It was quarter past twelve, still three quarters of an hour to kill. Perhaps she'd go and look at the ducks even though she had no crusts. She plunged into the traffic slowly progressing round Marble Arch and ducked between two sturdy lorries, one with its tailgate down holding a cluster of office girls, grinning and waving like Queens of the May. Lily found herself waving back.

'Come along now, miss, we're not at the Races.' Her arm firmly taken, she was swept along out of the way of an oncoming motor car. 'Thanks, thanks so much.' But her protector was away, turning back only to tip his cap.

She found herself on the pavement amidst a sea of lunchtime workers. Passing sandwiches and Thermos flasks, there was a high buzz of chatter as, bunched together, they stood staring through the iron railings into the Park. With such a sense of festivity in the air, Lily realised she, too, wanted to join in the fun, to forget. And on this pale spring day, in the midst of strangers, she suddenly succumbed to the gaiety and allowed herself to fully absorb the bright holiday atmosphere. She felt her mood shift and realised how profoundly weary she was of the endless emotional nagging, all that was left of her fading marriage…

'Get a move on, some of us've got work to do.'

The crowd as one moved to the side, allowing through a horse-drawn cart, 'Milk Deliveries' emblazoned on its side. In its wake, Lily was drawn through the gates. She stood on the edge of the Park, unsure how to fill the next half an hour. She didn't really want to cross into the solitary quiet of Mayfair; she found these crowds, with their curious bonhomie, comforting and a distraction. Strange, from what Charles had said she'd expected ugliness and turmoil.

She stopped and looked towards Speaker's Corner and a small crowd of people.

'…the spectre of famine will walk every street and reside in every house…' A voice leaked through the general hub-bub and caught her attention. Where? Where had it come from? She turned towards it then turned away, intimidated by the small intent crowd.

'Our men and their families are eking out their days in semi-starvation on wages of under £2.10s a week…'

Again that voice. She stopped.

'Britain's civilisation is founded on coal...'

No, surely not? It sounded like Hughie. Hughie? My God, it is. But for goodness sake, he's standing on a trestle table, addressing a crowd. When did he take up public speaking?

'...hewing coal for seven hours at a stretch steeped in their own sweat and sewage...'

She crossed to the huddle of people, excusing her way through to the middle. And stopped, her eyes locking onto a banner that danced above Hughie's head: 'OXFORD STRIKE COMMITTEE: Not a penny off pay. Not a minute on the day.'

She turned quickly to leave but found herself trapped, wedged into the very heart of the crowd, her escape barred by people, all of whom appeared to be much taller than her. She strained upwards and peered over a man's shoulder. To her horror, she saw a bobbing line of policemen's helmets heading towards them and then, in the next minute, the helmets were inexorably closing in a circle all around them.

She ducked back down. She stood, head bowed, terrified that her brother would instinctively know she was there and call her forward to voice her opinions in front of the crowd.

'...Do you know, ladies and gentlemen, on average five miners are killed every working day. Five families of orphans left with no breadwinner...'

The people stirred. As they listened, some with a disinterested air, some with informed passion, the miners' plight swelled and became ugly in the dainty springtime park.

'...Every single working hour thirty-two miners are injured...'

She felt instant terror as a ripple of suppressed violence ran through the knot of people listening and she saw the police armed and waiting, truncheons and the weight of the State ready to crack the skull of this ragged cry for Justice.

With all her strength she started to push to the edge of the group; she must escape this trap. But it was too late. The message heard, the embers ignited and the fire took light, the ferocious energy erupting and sweeping through the small crowd.

'Shame!' 'Blacklegs are traitors!'

A howl, and arms punched up and out, shoulders barged. Lily felt a blinding kick to her shin. She reeled sideways, her fall stopped by frantically clutching at the mackintosh of a thickset neighbour who roughly turned, shrugging her off. There was nowhere to escape; the group pushed and shoved as one and Lily found herself trapped at the centre, her face mashed up against rough material, her hat knocked skew-whiff.

'Bolshevik scum!'

A thin voice of dissent wailed up; an opposing gang had taken shape out of nowhere.

'You and them fucking miners'll bleed our Empire dry!' 'Commie shites!'

But the challenge was not picked up for all around the anger had started to flicker and fade, the power evaporating, and Lily saw the brief violent energy die as policemen pulled and separated the ragged crowd, which instantly fell apart.

Hobbling to the railings, her shin bleeding, her stocking torn, she hung on as nausea rose up again, a cold dreary sweat breaking out all down her back. She closed her eyes, trying to control the queasiness. The thought of being sick here in front of all these people was too awful. She must get away. What had possessed her to stay amongst this common wretched crowd? She had enough problems of her own and here she was in the middle of Hyde Park looking like a tramp, having almost been arrested! She straightened her hat and, limping, started to move hastily from the Park.

A few men were being rounded up. She skirted past the police van, keeping her head down. But dear God, where was Hughie? Was he being rounded up?

She swung and swung about but couldn't make out anyone in the wandering crowds, people now moving freely again. She hobbled towards the little stage. A young woman with her hair severely plaited into headphones, shook a bucket under her nose making her jump. 'A penny for our men.' Lily found herself digging into her handbag, flustered and unsure as to her duty in the paying of this donation.

'Girlie!'

Hughie's voice. Thank God! Her big tall brother, her younger protector from all the ills of the world. Except now there were too many ills. For both of them, it seemed.

'Girlie, you're here. Terrific.' Turning to Headphones, he announced, 'This is my sister.'

The young woman nodded, unsmiling. 'Nice to meet you.' Then continued at once, 'I'm going back to Eccleston Square. Don't forget to relieve me at four. Mr Cook and Mr Smith must be at Number Ten by five.' She turned briefly, acknowledged Lily and hurriedly joined two men dismantling the platform and re-furling the banner.

'Charles let you off the leash.' Hugh grinned at Lily. 'Hey, old girl, you okay?'

'Oh, Hughie.' She buried her face in his coat and hugged him, not wanting to let him go. 'What *are* you doing here?'

'Come on, Sis, don't play dumb.' Before she could say anything, he'd put his arm through hers and was wheeling her towards Marble Arch. 'I'm starving. You can stand me lunch at Lyons.'

Over beef stew and sponge pudding, he carried on talking. It wasn't until he was spooning up great custardy mouthfuls that he caught her expression. 'Not a bite since yesterday breakfast so you needn't look so po-faced, Sis.' He grinned at her.

'Hughie, honestly.' Always the appetite of a gorilla, he'd been a dustbin to which she could turn in their nursery and dispose of any hated food. But as he'd grown taller and taller, his strength had decreased and he'd been ever-prey to childhood ailments. But now, at six foot three, he sat opposite, stooped in his seat, blooming with health and energy, his bony middle-aged face young again.

'And you should have a pud, Girlie, you looked all washed-up.'

'Don't you start!'

Hugh stopped eating. 'Hey, old girl, what's up. All not well?'

'Don't want to talk about it. Go on with what you were saying about Oxford.'

She watched him as he spoke. He'd returned from the war a stranger, his eyes turned within, never once talking of the horrors he'd witnessed nor his endless dreams of despair. And in the years since he had aged, become a solitary man, an academic, escaping into books, eschewing crowds, keeping to himself, spending his spare time out of doors, walking. Usually alone. But now, here in Lyons Corner House, Lily saw the energetic, wilful playmate of her childhood. Alive again.

'It's the mobilisation of a ruthless provocative State intent on total victory over the labour movement. The wretched Government knows the strike can only be broken with the use of troops – and volunteer labour, of course. My students are bicycling all over Oxford from one Government agency to the next, frantic to be engine drivers and tram drivers. Not a thought to the actual cause of this bloody strike. Just *Hurrah Patriotismus!* Fun, fun, fun!'

His meal finished, Hugh sat back and lit his pipe. Lily got out her cigarette case.

'But Charles said this morning that all the buses and trams were still running—'

'Don't be so dim, Girlie, of course he did. That's the official Government line to keep up so-called public morale. But the strike's rock solid. No buses, no trams.' He looked triumphant. 'All the factories that depend on electricity have shut their doors. At last we're going to right this terrible wrong.'

'But, Hughie, really, how can any of us make it better?' Her head was hurting horribly and this damned cigarette was making her feel sick again.

Hugh looked at her. 'You really don't have any idea what's going on, do you?'

She stubbed out the cigarette. 'I'm sorry, no, I don't. Charles tends to speak in short sentences at the moment. I don't really know much about any of it.'

'No, nor do most people. And nor do they want to. And if this fat complacent government of puritanical reactionaries has its way nor shall they.'

Lily giggled; it was the unsayable. 'If Charles heard you—'

But Hugh didn't laugh back. 'If only he would.'

She stopped laughing.

'Lily, listen to me. I never realised such appalling poverty existed. The squalor these men and their families live in – and I've seen it – it wouldn't be endured by anyone with sufficient wages to get out of them. Now I must go. Thank you for my lunch.'

He rose, gathered his coat from a nearby stand and wound a scarf round his neck. But at once he sat down again. 'I'm sorry, I didn't mean to preach. It just seems to me the only way I can make sense of the war and what we all went through. Oh Lord, here I go again.' He sat sideways on to her, the coat bunched in his lap, his frame too big.

'It's just that—' He began again, less confident, looking down. 'I wanted to have lunch 'cos it's very important to me that you – you of all people – know what I'm up to.' He looked up at her. 'Which side I'm on.'

'Well…um…yes, of course. But have you thought of what Father—'

'Father would have a fit; I'm fully aware of that. But if I'm arrested—'

'Arrested, good God! Have you done something wrong?'

'No, for goodness sake.'

She sat silent. Family. Duty. Our side. Their side.

Hugh started again. 'Listen. If I'm arrested, I need to know there's someone, someone close to me I can telephone. For help.'

'You absolutely believe in this, don't you.' She had never seen him look so certain.

'More than anything, Girlie. I wish I had more time to talk to you, to explain.' He smiled at her gently. Her little brother always the more grown up.

'So what can I do to help?'

'Dear old Girlie, that's a brave offer. Nothing for the moment. But if I get into hot water, I'll telephone. All right?'

She gave a tiny nod. 'Just try and make it when Charles is at the House.' The thought of her husband's reaction too frightening, she dismissed it by asking, 'Where are you staying while you're in London?'

'You offering a billet?' She pulled a face. He smiled. 'Don't worry. Just joking. Eccleston Square. The Trades Union Headquarters. If you telephone, ask for the Oxford Strike Committee, that'll find me. I'm driving Mr Cook and Mr Smith. I took them to Downing Street yesterday.' His face suddenly registered boyish pride.

'But what if Charles sees you?' Lily burst out.

'Don't worry, old girl, I think he's got more important things on his mind. At least I hope he has.'

He was gone, nearly running through the cafeteria.

And now she, too, should go. She checked her watch; Doctor Mallard mustn't be kept waiting. Back in Oxford Street, there wasn't a taxi to be had for love nor money. She decided to walk and arrived in Harley Street with three minutes to spare.

In the formal waiting room, the clock quietly ticked. She collected a copy of *The Queen* from the large oval table covered in smooth magazines and sat, trying to gather her thoughts for her appointment. But her mind remained in a hateful whirl; her walk hadn't pacified her at all and her shin still throbbed painfully. She crossed her ankles to hide her dirty holey stocking and glanced to see if any of the other people in the room had noticed.

Opposite, a man was hidden behind a copy of *The Times* and, to one side, a child dressed in a smart little blue coat with a dark velvet collar coughed incessantly, a uniformed nanny in attendance. 'I've told you, Winifred, use your handkerchief.' The nanny's whisper was hoarse and loud. She held a hanky in front on the child's face while it coughed, a dense scratchy rumble. As the handkerchief dropped away, Lily caught sight of a wizened little profile, gazing exhaustedly frontwards.

'Ahem, Lady Sutton? The doctor will see you now.' The receptionist intoned her name with all the discreet hauteur of royalty. An elderly woman with a grey helmet of ridged permed hair, she trod carefully along the hushed hallway. Lily followed. Neither woman said a word; they had known each other for over ten years.

Doctor Mallard welcomed her into his consulting rooms. 'Well, Lady Sutton, I'm delighted to see you looking much sprightlier. Do take a seat.' After a few delicate questions, he examined her and, having re-dressed, she sat back down whilst the doctor made his stately way around his immense desk. He bathed her with a courtly smile.

'Well, Lady Sutton, I have some rather good news. I'm very pleased to inform you that you are expecting a baby. I suspected – Oh! Lady Sutton—'

But Lily didn't hear anymore, she was sobbing and sobbing. She was pregnant. Thank God, now Charles would love her again.

Chapter Five

SS *Etoile*. Friday, mid-afternoon

The ship clanged out six bells. It was three o'clock and the afternoon session in the gymnasium was in full swing. Billy Bottle pushed through the double doors, telegram in gloved hand, and called into the big echoing room, 'Lord Henry Clairmont. Message for Lord Henry Clairmont!'

Nobody took any notice; everyone was too busy exercising. Today, in the middle of the floor, half a dozen men were straining and heaving on a variety of machines, rings and clubs, fighting the fear that five days at sea would leave them flabby and unfit. Dressed in a mixture of waistcoats and shirt-sleeves, Billy could see they all looked very hot and bothered. He grinned. No doubt they'd had a good old tuck-in, dinnertime. A chubby gentleman, frantically towelling a salmon-pink face, puffed towards him and Billy, standing to attention, held the door. Then leaning back into the gym, he called out, 'Telegram for Lord Henry Clairmont!'

Sweeping a glance around the room, this time his eye was

caught by a young boxer exercising down the far end under
the eye of his trainer. Kitted out in tight, white sporting
trousers and a dazzling vest, the young fighter was rapidly
and accurately punching a sandbag. Billy stared at the speed;
not a catch in his breath, not a break in his swing, until the
trainer looked up from his stopwatch, gave a command and
instantly the young boxer slowed and dropped down onto
his haunches.

'I say,' said a chirpy voice. Billy turned to find a little man
in plus-fours and a tweed cap at his side. 'And who might
that fine specimen be?'

'"The Bermondsey Bomber", sir,' the young bellboy replied.
'Ship's champion boxer.'

'That the trainer? Chap with the stopwatch?'

'Yes, sir.'

The little man shot off down the gym, and needing to find
Lord Clairmont, Billy moved up behind him.

'This rowing johnny,' the little man announced brightly,
'Thought I might have a go.'

'Certainly, sir,' replied the trainer and the man climbed
awkwardly aboard. He gave half a dozen feeble pulls on the
oars and stopped, wheezing and puffing. 'Well, that's my lot
for today. Try again, tomorrow. Toodle-pip for now.' Struggling
to his feet, he adjusted his tweed cap and pottered away up
the gymnasium.

Billy grinned. 'That should keep him in the pink.'

'More money than sense, half of them,' said the trainer
sourly.

'You seen Lord Clairmont?'

'Been gone half an hour.'

'Right-ho. Thanks, mate.'

With Lord Henry Clairmont being a regular passenger on the SS *Etoile*, known to maintain a daily routine, it was with some certainty Billy set off up to A deck and the Paris Lounge. He ducked into the crew's accommodation and moved through the ship along a curving passageway flanking the portside, cheerfully known for no reason anyone could remember as Scotland Road. Then ascending to the aft second-class companionway, he emerged into the passenger's dining saloon on C deck. The air was warm and smelt of rabbit stew. Billy broke into a trot; he was starving again. He cut across the crowded room – boisterous with people and the sound of cutlery – and on into a quieter smoking room which led through to the ship's library. A smattering of people, having partaken of a large lunch, were ignoring the now-sunny weather and snoozing happily in armchairs. Billy quietened his drumming feet.

Gently, he pushed through the double doors onto an entrance lobby and started to climb the wide grand staircase, the spine of the ship, off which ran the six decks. High above, the afternoon sun shone down through the vast glass dome, the buttery light catching the cut-glass jewels of an enormous chandelier. Little rainbows danced on the carpet. No one around, Billy galloped up and up.

He reached a set of double doors opening onto B deck and pushed through, only to be immediately pushed back by the noise of the great waves and a gust of sea-sprayed wind yanking at his pill-box hat. His hands shot to his head. He stood in the doorway catching his breath.

Capricious March sunshine had lured people from their afternoon naps, a hardy few even ignoring the bracing North Atlantic breezes and reclining swathed in travelling rugs on wooden loungers. All around, the joyous shouts of children rang out, released from the stuffy boredom of indoors. Billy set off along the deck. A quoit skidded towards him, pursued by three young women, all arms, legs and laughter, the bright air releasing them from the strictures of their otherwise elegant attire. He sidestepped it and ducked into a passageway where, at the far end, he pushed through another set of double doors. Crossing a wide foyer, he finally arrived at the Paris Lounge and, collecting a silver tray from his post by the door, placed the telegram squarely upon it.

'Lord Henry Clairmont. Telegram for Lord Henry Clairmont!'

Several heads bobbed up and a pair of lorgnettes were discreetly raised – after all a cable, even in first class, was something of an event – but nobody waved him to their side. He stood surveying the large room.

In the middle of the lounge, set in a sea of little tables and chairs, four sturdy women in tweed were sitting talking quietly and earnestly. Heads tucked together, the brims of their hats seemed to nudge and knock. Billy grinned; the hats looked liked fat birds bobbing on a telegraph wire. Suddenly the birdies flew apart – a stout gentleman had arrived from the bar and jovially joined them.

Billy set off across the room, and passing an elderly woman fluttering a tiny gloved hand at a waiter, cheerily called, 'Afternoon, Comtesse.'

'Garçon, une coupe de champagne,' he heard her order.

'Lord Henry Clairmont. Telegram for Lord Henry Clairmont!'

At last, in the far corner from behind a winged armchair, a hand shot up. The bellboy smartly crossed to its owner, a thin young man with an eager face and an outstanding pair of ears.

'Good morning, Mr Bottle. How goes it?' the young man breezily greeted him.

'Fine, m'lord. A wire's just come through for you.'

His lordship scooped up the telegram but didn't open it. 'Results of the Totaliser in yet, Mr Bottle?'

'Not yet, m'lord. They'll be sorted through by four o'clock and we'll get them around half past.' Billy dropped his voice. 'Word is from the bridge we've averaged 26.9 knots the last few days.'

'Splendid. Ah, Matty, my dear.' M'lord jumped eagerly to his feet and waved at a young woman crossing the lounge towards him. Dressed in a discreet grey suit, the only decoration being dark-blue velvet collar and cuffs, the young woman's serious face broke into a bubbly smile as she drew alongside.

'Hello, you two, what are you plotting? You look up to something.'

'Having a bit of a flutter on the Totaliser, my dear.'

''Afternoon, Miss Grossman,' said Billy, and the young woman smiled back at him.

Although to the bellboy she was nothing out of the ordinary, it was instantly plain m'lord thought her the prettiest girl in the world.

'She's Lord Clairmont's nurse,' Tommy the German barman had told him the day before, and Tommy, as the Paris Lounge's head barman – its eyes and ears, so to speak – could always be trusted to come up with good-quality passenger gossip. So Billy had asked, 'What's he need a nurse for?'

'Just been diagnosed with the diabetes. Very dangerous.'

'And what's that when it's at home?'

'*Es ist sehr schade,*' Tommy had said and disappeared up the bar, leaving Billy none the wiser.

The young nurse now sat in a chair Lord Henry held out for her.

'Thank you for your trouble, Mr Bottle.' A coin changed hands. 'I look forward to receiving the news of our gambling endeavours.'

Billy made a swift bow and set off for his post by the door. He gave the room a quick once-over and was about to leave when he noticed Lord Henry lean quickly in and take the nurse's hand. The girl, however, swivelled away and, glancing from side to side, firmly put her gloved hands back in her lap. It was only then Billy saw she was smiling and, for some reason, the pair burst out laughing.

This is all a bit pally for a nurse and patient, thought Billy. *What's going on here?* He moved in closer.

'Come on, Nurse Matilda, let's have a bottle of fizz,' the young man was saying.

'Oh Henry, really.'

'But I'm thirsty, Mats.'

'You and your thirsts, very convenient.'

'I think I'm allowed a celebratory drink, just this once. Please, Nurse?' And giving a great grin, m'lord clasped the girl's hand once more. This time Billy saw he wasn't going to let it go. 'Oh Matty, oh lor, I didn't know it would be so impossibly difficult. Did you?'

Before Nurse Grossman could respond, a dark shadow fell across the couple and a booming voice shattered the hush of the Paris Lounge. 'Good afternoon to you, Lord Clairmont.'

'Oh – ah – good day, Lady Slocombe.' M'lord scrambled

to his feet and turned reluctantly to face the bulky woman standing squarely before him.

Oh no, here she is again, thought Billy, and dived back to his post where, safely tucked away, he watched.

'Lord Clairmont,' Lady Slocombe began with her customary bark, 'my companion, Dora Carroll, and I are getting up a four for Bridge this evening. We do so hope you will join us.'

The invitation extended, it was only now Billy realised the woman was doing all she could to ignore the young nurse. She stood with her back to the seated girl, her large behind all but in her face. And sadly this rudeness was having the desired effect for jolly Miss Grossman was now sitting hunched sideways in her chair, her head bowed.

Very gently m'lord turned and placed a hand on the girl's shoulder, and though his face remained calm, Billy suspected he was boiling mad. Only yesterday the bellboy'd been told by Tommy, 'Such a furore from that woman each evening when Lord Clairmont arrives to dine with his nurse. She is in a fury at this "nobody" sharing the table. *Schutt!* Frau Slocombe would challenge Herr Hitler himself. But always his lordship so good-mannered.'

As if to confirm this, Lord Clairmont now politely said, 'Thank you, Lady Slocombe, but I'm afraid Miss Grossman and I must decline. Neither of us are very good at Bridge.'

'What a shame,' replied the large woman smoothly. 'And will your little nurse be dining with us again this evening?' At this enquiry she turned and smiled down at the girl, her heavily powdered face creasing like the Nile's delta, her big teeth yellow and gleaming. 'You must be so grateful to Lord Clairmont,' she continued creamily, 'for the enormous privilege of being picked to dine at the captain's table. And every evening, too.'

There was a slight pause and Miss Grossman rose to her feet. Holding her head high, she looked straight at her ladyship. 'Yes, Lady Slocombe. Indeed the whole voyage is turning into quite an education.'

'I'm sure it is, Miss Grossman,' replied her ladyship suavely, holding the girl's look.

A silence hung between them.

Then, much to Billy's surprise, it was the older woman who broke first. 'Where is that wretched barman?' she snapped.

Billy could have cheered – the nurse wasn't going to be bullied, after all – she'd got the old biddy on the hop.

'Your ladyship?' As if by magic, Tommy had appeared at her side.

'And about time too,' the woman grumbled. 'I will have a little soda water before I take another turn around the deck. It has become unpardonably stuffy in here.' So saying she sailed away, creating a little breeze upon which lingered a strong smell of mothballs.

'That woman is a bully,' said Lord Henry quite clearly.

The nurse sank down into her chair and, picking up a little menu card, started to fan herself; Billy saw her face had gone bright red. 'Why is that woman so angry with me?'

'Well, if it's any consolation, you're in fine company. She's always detested Mother. Mainly for being American, I think. Mind you, Mother maintains Lady Lavinia is actually an ox and when she dies she'll be made into Bovril!'

Billy almost laughed but the nurse didn't. Not even a smile. 'Why does she spoil everything, Henry? For everyone. If it wasn't me, I'm sure she'd be horrible to someone else.'

'It's her life's work to make everyone as unhappy as she is. She's just a bitter old boot. Come on, enough of all this. Walk on deck. Fresh air required.'

'But Henry, it's nearly—'

But the young man wasn't listening. Billy watched as he pulled the nurse from her chair and gently led her from the room.

Covent Garden, London. 1904

The two little girls were sitting at the front of the box and as the heavy red velvet curtains swooped together and fell to the stage, they joined in with the rest of the audience and clapped and clapped.

Lily turned to her new friend. She was called Harriet and she was ten years old, too. Together they bounced off their spindly chairs and hung over the velvet ledge. Below, the beautiful people swirled and chatted in the glowing rose and gold theatre, frills and fizzing curls, long white kid gloves, floaty fans waving and fluttering. Shouts and laughter. It was wonderful. Harriet and Lily, the two new friends, grinned at each other.

Behind them, their hostess, Lady Durston, called out, 'Ices all round.' A footman bowed to the old lady and retired.

'Isn't this fun, children?' she beamed, and Lily and Harriet scrambled back over the velvet box-edge.

But despite the fun, they were all aware of a sulky dark presence in the box. Lily turned and looked at the third little girl sitting still and sullen. *Why is Lavinia always such a cross-patch?* she thought. *We're all having such a jolly time and she's been a grumpy pig all evening.* During the first act, she'd even whispered to Harriet, *We're going to ignore Lavinia, aren't we? She's such a spoil-sport.* Nervously she looked see if Lady Durston had heard her but the old lady appeared to be ignoring her granddaughter also. Lily was glad.

Her hair is the colour of doves, she thought, gazing at the old lady. *It's like a great big sailing boat.* Swept high and wide, the old-fashioned hairstyle was held in place by two glinting diamond combs, bobbing swan's feathers tucked into the vast waves. Lily thought she was the most beautiful old lady she'd ever seen, her dress, the palest grey, high at the throat with a frothy jabot of snow-white lace, edged with black velvet.

'Well, my dears, and what do we think of Signor Puccini's opera so far?' asked Lady Durston.

'Harriet and I like the one in the yellow dress best,' announced Lily.

'But we also think she's very sad,' added Harriet.

'Hush, hush, slowly. One at a time. Now then,' smiled Lady Durston. 'You think Mimi is sad?'

They both nodded.

'Mmm,' considered the old lady. 'I think you're probably right. *And* I fear she has chosen the wrong young man into the bargain.'

'Are they in love, Lady Durston?' asked Lily.

'In a manner of speaking, they are. And you, Lavinia child?' The old lady now turned to her granddaughter. 'How are you enjoying your birthday treat?'

The little girl sat up very straight and said in a stiff voice, 'I think, Grandmama, Signor Caruso is very good as Rudolfo.'

She pushed at her party dress but the skirts refused to obey; they kept bobbing up.

'If not a little portly,' her grandmother observed. 'I am told Signor Caruso smokes two packets of cigarettes a day and never takes exercise. That may account for his shape.' She twinkled at the three girls.

But Lavinia was not to be diverted. She continued in a determined little voice, 'I think he is doing Signor Puccini's music full justice.'

'Do you, indeed,' replied her grandmother. 'And how about Madame Melba?'

'I think her voice—' But the child stopped, bewildered; the two other girls had collapsed in giggles.

'And what,' demanded Lady Durston, 'do you young ladies find so amusing?'

'Oh, Lady Durston,' Lily gasped for air. 'When they kissed each other—'

'Their arms – they couldn't reach round—' Harriet gleefully fell against her, her little legs swinging back and forth.

'They are, indeed, a trifle stout,' said her Ladyship and was swept into helpless laughter as well.

It was only after a little while, gasping and laughing, Lily became aware Lavinia wasn't joining in. She sat completely still, her face pinched white, her neck bright red against her ice-pale party dress, slowly twisting round and round her wrist a small pearl bracelet – her grandmother's birthday present.

On the way home, Lily struggled to keep awake...the carriage kept rocking...and she kept sinking against the hard buttoned seats...and her yellow chiffon skirt kept fluffing up...like a nest...her eyes drooped closed...

She forced them open – and saw Lavinia opposite, bolt

upright, staring out of the carriage window. *She's hated the evening. But it's her own fault; the silly old opera was her choice. And she's only jealous 'cos I get on better with Harriet than I get on with her. Anyway, she's always so horrid, serves her right.*

She looked at Lady Durston sitting next to her granddaughter, wrapped in white furs. *She's nice though...*and Lily remembered the kiss and the two big stomachs meeting before the people's lips... And she fell fast asleep.

Next morning she was furious – she'd missed the whole drive home. She'd so wanted to see London – and at night-time – and now she was going back to the boring old country and probably wouldn't be back in London again for years. Well, not until she was at least twelve.

She yawned and, looking round the nursery, saw she was all on her own, the other bed empty. Where was Harriet?

A maid bobbed round the door. 'Get up, miss, otherwise you'll not get breakfast. It's half past eight.'

'Where is everybody?' She scrambled out of bed.

'Bit of a to-do downstairs. Get dressed, quick as you can.'

When Lily appeared in the breakfast room, Lady Durston glanced at her but continued talking. 'For the last time, Lavinia, I will *not* call the police. I will deal with the matter as I – and only I – see fit. Matthews, help Miss Robinson to some eggs. There is no time for anything more elaborate, Lily; I see you have overslept... Thank you, Matthews, that will be all.'

As the door closed, Lady Durston said, 'Lavinia appears to have mislaid her new bracelet—'

'It has been *stolen*, Grandmama!'

'Hush. Please do *not* interrupt when I'm speaking. Now

then. Lily, do you have any idea as to what may have happened
to it?'

'No, Lady Durston. But perhaps Harriet saw it?' So saying,
she realised her new friend wasn't there.

'In that case we will not talk about this any more.' Lavinia
made to speak but her grandmother threw her a severe look.
'You will go to your room, Lavinia, and help Bridie with
your packing.'

Left alone, one glance at Lady Durston and Lily knew to
keep quiet as well. The old lady sat staring out of the long
dining-room windows. She looked much older than the night
before and seemed very sad.

Lily gazed out, too, at the trees of Portman Square. She
could hear a hurdy-gurdy and clopping hooves and a motor
car sputtering along, honking of its horn. This was London!
She wanted so badly to get down from the table and join in
the world outside.

A butler re-entered and attended her ladyship's side with
a silver teapot. He glided away once more.

What had happened to Harriet? Why was everybody so
cross this morning? And why did Lavinia want to see the
police? She longed to ask but knew to keep silent.

The old woman slowly rose from the table and left the
room without a word.

Typical! thought Lily, *I always miss everything. Well, I suppose
I'd better do my packing, too.* Fed up, she started to climb
back up the grand old house.

No one around, the vast staircase hung in deadening silence.
She dawdled over the banister, peering up at a domed glass
ceiling high above. Slowly she let her eye drift back down
the shafts of dusty sunlight that lit the silky walls hung with

long-ago people sitting astride muscly steeds, carelessly stroking their curly lapdogs.

It was as she reached the second floor she heard a sound. A tiny sound; a thin tremble of crying. She stood in the middle of the wide landing and listened hard.

Silence.

Then from somewhere behind a half-open door, there came a stifled hiccup. Quickly tip-toeing over, she peeped through the small gap by the hinges and saw, half-hidden by a sofa, curled up on the floor, Harriet.

'They asked me all these questions, Lily—' Great gulping sobs, the two little girls held each other. 'In front of everyone – all the maids. Everyone – they think I'm a thief.'

For Lily and Harriet, her new friend of a day, all the fun of the night before had vanished.

CHAPTER SIX

SS *Etoile*. Friday, mid-afternoon

Little Anthea was bawling. She stood in the middle of the third-class general room, her head caught half in and half out of a torn jersey which sported a faded 'skull and cross bones'. She resembled a fat little beehive. At her side, her grandmother was trying to divest the little girl of the garment without actually strangling her. It was a tempest-tossed exercise.

For one usually so silent, thought Lily, *it's extraordinary, the enormous sound she can make when the need arises.* She had watched as the child, disappointed by the dismal selection of dressing-up clothes and dizzy from the ensuing storm of tears, now appear to be only comforted by making colossal amounts of noise.

'Yes, well, my love,' her grandmother was attempting to console and hopefully quieten her granddaughter. 'I told you, get a move on. Mind yer, this morning you didn't want to go't fancy dress at all.'

'Did,' choked Anthea.

'No use crying about it now, there's no fancy dress left. Unless you want to go as the invisible fairy, there's nowt you can do about it.'

Lily felt so sorry for them both. For nearly half an hour she'd been completely absorbed in watching Mrs Webb trying to cobble together an outfit. At last, the challenge proving too much, the large woman had pulled the little girl free from the final garment, a pirate's jersey, and given up. Now the child sat abandoned on the floor, leaning against her grandmother's legs, her head buried deep in the woman's skirts, her sobs muffled. Mrs Webb was dejectedly fanning herself with Bo Peep's battered straw hat.

Lily crossed the room. 'Excuse me, I couldn't help overhearing—'

The woman jumped. 'Flippin' 'eck!'

'Oh, I'm so sorry, I didn't mean to startle you. I was just wondering if I could help and…um…forgive me for interfering but—' She dropped down to Anthea's level. 'How about going as a clown?'

The child's head remained buried, tiny bubbles of sound popping out of her.

'Well, our Anthea, how about that then?' said Mrs Webb brightly.

'Don't want to go as a clown,' hiccuped the little girl, her head ducking up and then back down.

Before Mrs Webb could remind the child of 'manners', Lily carried on, 'What a shame, because that's what *I'm* going as.'

The child emerged, and said with huffy authority, 'The dressing up's not for big people.'

'Anthea!' snapped her grandmother.

But Lily had got the little girl's attention. 'And you could have bright red pom-poms. Do you have a bit of wool, Mrs Webb?'

'Aye, in me woolbag—'

'And what about a pointy hat?' Lily asked. 'Do you have a bit of card for a pointy hat?'

'You mean cardboard, like?'

'Yes.'

'In our cabin—'

'I'll get it!' cried her granddaughter, and galloped away out of the general room.

'Well,' said Mrs Webb, 'that's stopped her for a bit.' Adding briskly, 'You mustn't mind her. She dun't like change and this trip's scaring the life out o' her.'

'I know how she feels,' replied Lily, without thinking.

The big woman looked at her for a second, nodded briefly but said nothing.

Lily turned quickly to the job in hand. 'Scissors – I've got some in my cabin.'

'Nay, stay put,' said Mrs Webb. 'Madame will have summat and she's just next door.'

'Madame?'

'Needlework woman, she's in charge of all't sewing and darning and that. She's along corridor. Back in a tick.' She bustled off.

Lily sat down on the bench that ran the length of the wall and glanced quickly to left and right. No sign of Bagpipes Man, thank goodness. And Johnnie knew where she was as she'd put her nose round the cabin door after her walk on deck and he'd suggested, 'Why not go back to the day room? All fine here, just finishing my book. I'll join you in a bit for a cup of tea.'

She sat very still and tried, as always, to confront and control the anxiety. Oh, for the fear to cease...

She focused on a little group immediately in front of her. A wiry terrier of a man was straightening a tiny turban on the bobbing head of a little boy, the man's big square hands surprisingly nimble as he adjusted the whorl of purple and gold. The little boy looked distinctly unhappy.

And the little boy's face, of course, became Nickie's...

Which birthday had he been the little clown? Was it only three years ago?

She closed her eyes. Clear as clear she could hear... Mary. She could hear the maid whispering from behind a half-open door, 'Wait, Nickie! The hat's not straight.' And then, 'All right, now!'

Through her fingers, obediently stretched over her eyes, she'd seen the bottom of the drawing-room door at Melsham swing wide and Nickie's little feet come pattering in.

He'd yelled in excitement, 'Now, Mummy, now. Open your eyes!'

There he stood; tall, almost to the height of her shoulder, his thick fringe pushed down onto his face by a smart pointy white hat, three magnificent pom-poms the size of dahlias adorning it, echoing the four others holding the baggy white suit together. A magnificent little clown.

His face gleamed.

'Tremendous! Oh, Nickie, haven't Mary and I done well.'

The maid's face appeared round the door, laughing. But as suddenly the laughter dropped away, her attention caught by an unseen presence. 'Good morning, Sir Charles.' She gave a bobbed curtsey.

'What's going on in there?'

Lily froze at the sound of her husband's voice and, without thinking, she moved in front of Nickie to shield him.

'Stop hiding about behind closed doors.'

At an unseen command, Mary pushed wide the drawing-room door. Lily saw, coming down the marble staircase, the tall heavy man, preceded by a rambling dog. She watched numbly as the dog skittered away across the black-and-white tiled hall, the call of the outdoors more intoxicating than the trio hovering, lost, in the drawing room.

The man arrived in the doorway. Mother, child and maid stood very still.

Sir Charles surveyed the child up and down. Very quietly, he said, 'You can't seriously be thinking of dressing the boy like that. He looks like a bloody girl. Have you no sense, woman?' Though his voice was quiet and controlled, his look was furious. She tucked her hand behind to Nickie. The little boy clutched it.

Her husband turned to leave the room and without thinking, she cried after him. 'But Charles, it's his party—'

She stopped; the big man was turning back.

Almost in a whisper, he said, 'Get those clothes off him. I won't say it again.'

And then Lily saw the tidal wave of disappointment so overwhelm her son that the boy's terror of his father, for once, was drowned. He ran past the big man, out of the room, pulling the heavy door with all his might. It caused a thundering slam, equalled only by the roar of his father.

'Nicholas!'

'Missus, missus.' Someone was tugging at her sleeve. Lily's eyes shot open. 'Missus, what's matter wi' yer?'

She struggled to catch her breath; Charles's voice was roaring in her ears. She heard herself gasp out loud.

'*Missus?*' the little girl persisted, shaking her arm.

'Stop that, Anthea,' commanded Mrs Webb. 'Put woolbag down on't table and stop thy gawking.'

Lily covered her mouth with her hand and realised she was shaking.

'Hush now, lass. Don't take on so.' Momentarily, she'd felt the woman's hand on her arm.

'Come along, let's pull up this table, Anthea.'

At her side, the large woman started to bustle noisily around, unloading white sheets and all the necessary tools – scissors, pins, needle and thread – collected from Madame.

Lily felt the panic subside. She sat up. Pushing away the wretched memory, she made herself look at the podgy serious child, the child that wasn't Nickie. The little girl was hugging the sturdy table leg with wobbly white arms, heaving fruitlessly. Across the way the wiry little man, noticing the struggle, abandoned his grandson's turban and, with a courtly doff of his cap and an 'allow me, ladies', drew the table alongside. His voice had the lilt and twinkle of Ireland. Mrs Webb granted him a gracious nod and, turning back, winked at Lily. She managed a smile in return and, with the table drawn up and the scissors, needle, card and woolbag at the ready, Lily got to her feet.

'All right, lass? Don't stand before you're able.' Immediately, Mrs Webb was at her side.

'I'll be fine.' She turned to the child. 'So, do you want pom-poms, Anthea?'

'What's pom-poms?'

'I'll show you. Very useful to know about pom-poms.'

Mrs Webb and the child watched as, out of a ravel of wool, Lily proceeded to chop and cut until a wondrous pom-pom emerged. The little arms, so densely freckled, wobbled as Anthea clapped delightedly.

'Madame says we can keep the scissors until after tea,' said Mrs Webb. 'It's ironing of an afternoon next door.'

'Ironing?'

'For all't first-class passengers. You should have a look in there. They've rows and rows of ironing boards set up. Now, what do you want us to do?'

'Firstly, Anthea, what colour do you want your pom-poms?'

The girl stood silent.

'I think they should be blue,' suggested her grandmother.

'Red,' said the little girl.

They all set to and, constantly asking Anthea's opinion with as much care and attention as any Bond Street dressmaker, Lily observed the child slowly come to life. The pale fat cheeks pinkened and, her voice found, the little girl began to chat, wriggling with increasing vigour as the pantaloon suit grew between them.

'I want to show Freddie! I want to show Freddie!'

'Stand still, Anthea, I'll not tell thee again,' said her grandmother sharply. There was a momentary stillness and the jacket was pinned into place.

'Freddie is our Anthea's big brother,' Mrs Webb popped into this bit of quiet. 'And my grandson.' Lily could hear the swell of pride. 'He walks the dogs on this here ship. *And* he's higher up than any of us – ship's kennels is in one of them big funnels.'

'The funnel?' Lily stopped, pins in her mouth.

'Aye, but there's nowt to worry on. They say two are real funnels and third's a dummy.'

'No, what fun!' Lily started pinning again. 'And is Freddie good with dogs?'

'More than like. Barney, that's me youngest son, works in't printing shop along here on E deck. Well, Freddie got this job—'

'Freddie – your grandson?' Lily stopped pinning completely; trying to unravel the Webb family tree demanded full concentration.

'Aye, that's the ticket.' Mrs Webb beamed comfortably and settled into a chat, a mother hen on her nest. 'Well, our Freddie, he's twelve. Never been away from home but the lad seems happy enough with't dogs, bless him. And it brings us in a few coppers. Turn, Anthea, love.'

'And is Barney Freddie and Anthea's father?' asked Lily, pinning completely forgotten.

'Nay, nay.' Mrs Webb laughed. 'He's only twenty-one. He's your uncle, in't he, Anthea?'

The little girl didn't appear to hear.

Mrs Webb said, 'Go and get that bucket over there to put the bits in.'

The child got up and slowly walked away; her grandmother dropped her voice. 'Anthea and Freddie's mam, she that was my eldest daughter, my Em, passed away five year ago. 30th March 1928, it was. A fire in the shop where she worked.'

Shocked, Lily turned and saw that the sweet smiling face had gone still and held no expression at all.

The child arrived back, cradling a big red bucket. 'So, now I'm their gran and their mam. Aren't I, love?' Mrs Webb was smiling down at the little girl and Lily saw the warmth of love for this tubby sullen grandchild.

'And how old are you, Anthea?' Lily asked.

'She's ten and three-quarters, aren't you, my love?'

But Anthea had more important matters on her mind. 'Gran, what about Freddie? Where's his clown?'

'Well, we can't ask Mrs Valley—'

'Oh, yes we can,' said Lily firmly. 'Anyway, I like making things and this time, Anthea, you can cut out the hat-brim like I showed you before, and you can also make Freddie's pom-poms.'

'He's going to have green ones,' said Anthea authoritatively, and set about her new task with great poise.

In the cosy orange light, the noisy dressing-up excitements of earlier were momentarily forgotten as a couple of large tea-urns appeared. There was a clatter of china, and mugs of tea were passed round with wedges of cake and trays of biscuits. Families munched together and Lily could see the tentative steps into new friendships as mugs and plates, piled high, were passed to and fro.

At the two women's feet, Anthea, insisting on wearing her new outfit, created a mound of green woolly pom-poms.

Melsham, England. June 1931

The little church hall was festooned with ribbons and early summer flowers. Clutches of bright daisies and purple anemones, sunny jonquils and sky-blue forget-me-nots, all the result of hard work ploughed into the groom's family allotment; the toil had paid off tenfold.

As Lily cast her eye round the hall, she was touched by the devotion with which heads were turned towards Johnnie, his Best Man speech commanding a hush – all were hanging on his every word. Beside him sat the bride and groom. Today Sam was scrubbed and grinning, surprise and delight constantly breaking through his solid demeanour – and dearest Mary, her round face, the soft pink of sugar mice, her eyes holding a special twinkle that made Lily think of an evening star.

'For five years, ladies and gentlemen, Sam and I have shared a billet at the farm. Very amiably too, I may add. But now we're parting company. He and his lovely bride are setting up home in one of the estate cottages. But I'll miss his cooking, I can tell you. He can turn his hand to a more than tasty rabbit stew. Though I have to admit, I won't miss his dirty socks.'

There was a gust of cheerful laughter. From the beams, amidst flower-swags and paper pennants, a picture of the King gazed down. Along the centre of the small hall stood three long trestle tables, their crisp white linen cloths scattered with crumbs and crockery, the remnants of a hearty meal. Now people sat back, drinking and smoking, passing back big jugs of cider constantly in need of refilling.

'I thought I was well and truly lumbered with those socks until a year ago, one wet November evening to be precise, driving his hay-cart home for tea, this knight if not in exactly shining armour, more like mucky overalls,' Johnnie nodded at Sam, 'offered a bedraggled damsel standing at the village bus stop, a lift. And one year on today, we're here to toast the very happy couple as they start their new life together.'

Casting round at the upturned faces, at that moment, he saw Lily and remained looking at her. She found herself beaming back at him across the village hall.

('Oh, I was longing to talk to you again,' he told her months later. 'I saw your apricot hair and extraordinary golden eyes, and I thought, *Of course that's what I remember from our brief meeting at the County Fair.*')

'So it gives me great pleasure to ask you to raise your glasses to the groom and his very beautiful bride.'

The toast over, people rose, stretching legs and backs, everyone laughing and talking. Lily watched as the groom shook Johnnie's hand mightily – the speech had rounded off the proceedings perfectly – then, turning, he nudged his bride forward. Johnnie kissed Mary's cheek and Lily thought, *I don't think I've ever seen any bride look so happy.*

It was then she saw Johnnie break away from the happy couple and appear to be crossing to join her. She felt enormous delight that he should so immediately seek her out and watched as he moved through the small crowd, accepting pats on the back and the odd handshake. When he arrived, for a moment, he said nothing but grinned at her like a boy.

'What have I done?' Lily felt herself grinning back.

'Nothing, it's just jolly nice to see you again. I mean, with my speech over and done with.' He ground to a halt.

'Well, as my mother used to say, "I piped an eye". Your speech was very touching.'

'Oh dear, you cried.'

'Ah, but I laughed also. A rare event these days.' She looked down. It was absurd to feel sadness on such a moment. She made herself smile and look back up. 'Well done. It was a lovely speech. Perfect.'

'And I meant what I said about the beautiful bride. I hear it was all *your* handiwork.'

'Well, not *all*. Her headdress was my handiwork, the veil was my grandmother's. Isn't Limoges lace lovely?'

'But the headdress was wonderful.' He looked hopelessly impressed.

'I suppose, you could call it my hobby. I make hats, hence my lack of heart-failure earlier.' She touched her hat. 'I knew I could cobble something together out of the wreckage.'

Laughing, they slowly walked through the groups of people to an open doorway. The afternoon sunshine flooded in. They stood looking across a green towards the Saturday market packing up. Stalls were being dismantled and a very red-faced farmer was rounding up a small giddy flock of geese. The air was filled with outraged squawks.

'How very enterprising of you,' Johnnie said. 'To actually make hats.'

'It was Mother. Girls were not allowed to learn anything as useful as cooking and preserving, but we were allowed to learn how to sew and how to sing. I've ended up fairly skilled at the first and simply atrocious at the second.'

'And how about your dancing?'

'Oh no,' she said hurriedly. 'No dancing for me today.' There was the sound of a fiddle and a pipe tuning up. 'In fact, I think this is where I might fade away.' She looked back across the heads of the party to where Sam and Mary stood laughing down at three little children attempting to dance round them. 'I won't say any goodbyes, everyone seems very preoccupied.'

'Well then, let me walk you to your car.'

She felt the lovely sunshine on her face as they stepped out into the warm afternoon. A gust of hope whistled through her heart.

'May I say how mightily relieved I am,' Johnnie said, 'that you don't expect me to glide you elegantly onto the dance floor. Delightful as it would be in theory, in practice I fear it would be disastrous.'

She laughed. 'I can't remember the last time I danced. Though I used to be rather a dab-hand in my day.'

When they arrived at the car, without letting herself think, she said, 'It's such a lovely afternoon I was thinking of having a walk and, um... Do you know the castle ruins?'

'How splendid, a jaunt. Yes, please.'

Wandering round the crumbling castle walls that afternoon, Lily slowly became aware that neither of them were taking in the architecture, the history or the breath-taking view from the ramparts; they were too busy walking and talking. On and on. And as the afternoon turned into dusk, Johnnie suggested a drink and they found themselves sitting on an old pub wall, side by side, amongst the market crowd. Shaded from the setting sun by a big mulberry tree, they sat sipping long glasses of local cider.

Slowly as the evening drew in, the garden emptied and the crowd inside the pub swelled, throwing great bursts of chatter and song into the warm darkness outside. Under their mulberry tree, Johnnie and Lily tucked into wedges of cheese and pickle sandwiches as the evening shadows enfolded them, neither aware of the time.

'I was numb after my wife Sarah and the baby died,' Johnnie said. 'I was so grateful when the war came, I joined up almost immediately. It seemed the answer to so many problems. Suddenly there was lots to do, lots of noise, no time to think. And if there was only room for one emotion, then that was fear. It's funny,' he looked at her, 'we couldn't ever admit that then, us soldiers. Even to ourselves.'

'Couldn't admit what?'

'How scared we were. So scared, all the time.' He shook his head. And Lily thought, *This is a dear, gentle man.* She looked at the thinning hair and lined face and longed to reach towards him, to touch him. Instead, she asked, 'When your wife… when Sarah died in childbirth – and then the baby – well, wasn't there anyone you could talk to, to share what must have been such terrible grief?'

'Not really. Sarah had a mother, nice old stick, but she lived in Scotland. And anyway, in my family it was considered not done to air one's feelings.' Despite the seriousness of what he was saying, Lily nearly smiled; the chord of recognition.

'And yet, my grief was so deep, I couldn't have talked about it. In the end I think I sort of went to war to avenge the senseless death of my wife and child.'

'And did it?'

'In a way. Except by the time it was over, I just felt empty. No job. No wife. No life. The anger and that terrible cutting grief had gone but now there was nothing.'

She thought, *I do so understand, the emptiness.*

With her silence, he paused. 'Forgive me, I've rather got carried away talking about myself—'

'Not at all. It's important.' As if to emphasise this, she remarked, 'Do you know, my mother lived her entire life thinking it was "common" to air one's feelings. I often wonder, how did she survive?'

She thought about this for a moment and then turned to him and grinned. 'She used to say that pain was a suitable matter for discussion with the doctor but to complain of it otherwise was "commonplace".' She could picture her mother sitting upright, rigidly trained to silently suffer her father's drunken infidelities. 'Only nursemaids have pain, Lily.' *Poor Mother*, she thought. *And yet, in so many ways, like mother, like daughter...*

'You've gone quiet,' she heard him say.

'I was thinking about Mother,' she replied. 'Even at my great age, she can still silence me.' And she thought, *How do I put this moment in my pocket so that it's always there to have and to hold? With the sun going down and the moon coming up and cheese sandwiches and cider and this man.*

Later that night, alone at Melsham, Charles, thank God, in London, she sat at her dressing table slowly creaming her face and staring out at the warm starry sky. *Careful, careful, don't rush any detail – keep every moment alive and well.*

She thought of Sam shyly kissing Mary, the wedding service at an end, the rickety old organ warbling the 'Trumpet Voluntary'. She thought of her squashed hat and Johnnie's face. And she closed her eyes remembering the first touch of Johnnie's hand as he pulled her up the final rocky step of the castle rampart.

All that talking – and the laughter! *How long must we have sat on the pub wall? And the cider and sandwiches. And the pub that's always been there between the river and the railway line. How often I've passed it collecting Charles from the station and never really noticed it. The Man In The Moon.*

She felt again the strong evening light slipping away into the warm summer night which never became quite dark as they talked and talked. *They had to throw us out – me in a pub at closing time!* She knew Charles would be appalled but she couldn't be bothered to think of him.

When they'd arrived back at Lily's car for the second time that day, Johnnie had asked, 'There's a new book I've just read, may I send it to you?'

It's not yet to be goodbye, sang Lily's heart.

Two days later at breakfast, a brown paper parcel sat waiting for her. As she unwrapped the contents, even with Charles watching from behind his copy *of The Times*, she started to laugh.

'Who's sending you books?' he asked, as though amazed that she had friends who would do such a thing.

'Dolly Barton.' And at the earliest opportunity, she ran upstairs and read *The House At Pooh Corner* from cover to cover.

It was only much later she realised how easily she had lied.

CHAPTER SEVEN

Freston, England. June 1931

When Johnnie Sturridge had sent Lady Sutton *The House at Pooh Corner*, he had done so only out of courtesy, a promise to be fulfilled. They had spent a pleasant enough day wandering round the castle walls but that would have to be that. After all, the woman was married and he was too set in his ways for any romantic entanglement at this stage in the game. He had been pleased to receive her note of thanks for the book but was immediately distracted by an invitation to tea at Sam and Mary's arriving in the same post.

High tea in their new cottage; speckled eggs and ham, shining tomatoes and Mary's freshly baked bread in a bright white-washed kitchen.

'I can see you're not eating enough, mate, now I'm not there to feed you. Come along, eat up.' And Sam had piled more ham onto his plate as Mary nodded at them, walking away across the garden, looking over the gate and down the lane.

'Missus is coming. Lady Sutton,' said Sam. 'Mary likes to keep an eye on her.'

Johnnie had said nothing. But Lady Sutton had not appeared. In some ways, he'd been relieved; sitting with Sam and Mary had been quite like old times, just the three of them. No talk, the men smoking, the only sound Mary tunelessly whistling under her breath as she cut, turned and stitched some old sheets.

At nine o'clock he stepped off home, walking slowly back down the summer lanes to his farm. The evening air was drenched in dusk-scents, wood-pigeons gently fluting in the woods beyond, the sensual beauty all around, massaging his loneliness back to life.

Alone once more in his cold kitchen, a glass of brandy and, tonight, a copy of Thomas More's *Utopia* his solace, he sat gazing at the unlit range, trying to distract his thoughts from the pain of his boredom, the doors and curtainless windows locked against the beauties of the night. Slowly he drifted asleep…

'Open up!'

Thunderous banging.

He woke. And the banging came again.

A dream.

No, again banging. He sat up. Oh, so stiff and his head… the banging going on and on.

He unlocked the back door. 'What on earth—'

Sam stood in silhouette, the moonlit farmyard behind him. He was carrying a woman, she seemed to be sleeping, her head fallen forwards.

From behind came Mary. 'Get her inside.' The authority in her voice pushed the two men into the kitchen. Johnnie, confused by all this sudden noise and company, stood blinking.

'Come on, mate, give us a hand. Let's get her onto here.' Sam propelled him forward and they lifted the figure onto the old sofa in the corner. There was a mumble of pain.

'Hush, hush now,' said Mary and she turned on a light. Sam was saying, 'Careful, there may be bones broken.' But Johnnie didn't hear, he was staring down at Lily Sutton.

She lay folded up, her face hidden by her two hands, and although the night was warm, she was shivering.

'Bad do,' muttered Sam. Johnnie didn't think he'd ever heard his friend so angry.

Mary appeared with a blanket and, carefully, gently, covered the woman, talking softly as she did so.

Sam whispered, 'We couldn't keep her at ours. If he comes looking, it'd be the first place he'd go. The husband, that is.'

'What about a doctor?'

'She won't hear of it. Doesn't want anyone to know. As always.' He held Johnnie's look of realisation, and simply nodded.

'Take her up to your old room, Sam, she'll be more comfortable up there.' His friend carried the woman upstairs.

Now, he could hear them, the floorboards creaking above. He cleared away the brandy bottle and made a pot of tea.

Sam appeared back down in the kitchen. 'Sorry to land this on you.'

'No, no, not at all—' He stopped and looked at his friend. 'Good God, does this happen often?'

'Not so much recently. Sir Charles is in London most of

the time. With his lady-friend.' Sam could barely contain
his disgust.

The two men said nothing more. They had thought
themselves numbed by the horrors of war but here and now,
this fresh violence left them both wretched and ashamed,
horrified by the raw brutality. And its pitiful outcome.

Mary arrived back down. 'She's asleep at last.' She nodded
at Johnnie. 'I gave her one of your tablets like you said.' She
stopped. 'The state of her. She's covered in bruises—' Unable
to speak further, she bent her head away.

The night crawled into dawn, the lemon-light of day filling
the kitchen, and they made and re-made the pot of tea, the
three of them talking low, braced for any sound of movement
above, all the while Mary planning for 'my lady's safety'.

'The master's gone to London, more than like. He usually
disappears after a "do" like this. But the minute he returns
to Melsham, I'll tell Mrs Benton – the cook – to telephone
here directly and warn us. If before's anything to go by, he'll
stay away in London at least a week. But we can never be
sure. Is it all right if she stays here until she's more herself?
Me and Sam can't think of anywhere else. We'd be the first
place he'd look.'

'Of course, of course.'

'Perhaps then we can persuade her to go and stay with her
brother, Mr Hugh. He's a nice long way away.'

Dawn turned into day and with it came the chatter of
birdsong. At last Johnnie asked, 'Do you know why Charles
Sutton did this?'

'Oh sir,' said Mary. 'You don't know the half of it.' She
looked at her husband, who briefly nodded. 'Seems this time
she was seen with a gentleman in a public house, the day of

our wedding, and someone saw fit to tell Sir Charles. Thank goodness, the sneaky tattle-tale didn't know who the man was.'

Lily Sutton stayed three days in Johnnie's farmhouse.

All the while he had to admit he felt a strange sourness, his privacy ambushed by the presence of this unknown woman under his roof, lying broken by the hand of another man. He wanted to be alone again. He wanted his solitary state. And his books. He needed no woman to be dependent on him. He had been married and he had been found wanting. He wanted no more responsibility.

But Lily demanded none. She remained in her room, eating little from the trays of food he took her. She emerged after the third day, the ashen pallor of her face gone, only a tiny cut through her eyebrow remaining. She demanded no talk, no chatter. But sat on the outer reaches of the orchard, hidden by the apple trees. So minimal were her requirements that he felt discomforted by his own grudging hospitality, though it had been in thought only. He tried to entertain her by talking about the latest books and introducing her to Marie Antoinette, his prize pig. She smiled but never laughed.

When she left at the end of the third day, Sam driving her back to Melsham, she extended her hand, a stranger in her stance. 'Thank you for putting up with me.'

He had replied, 'You mean, surely, "putting you up".'

'Perhaps,' she said and walked away to the waiting car.

Left alone once more, his wish for solitude granted, he found himself talking to the silence, his head and heart filled with unspecified rage, rage at his solitude. Somehow her presence had unlocked the loneliness of years. He stood at the edge of the farmyard and gazed at the empty orchard.

A week later there was a knock at his door and Lily stood there. Her Pre-Raphaelite pallor shone on his doorstep, her beauty saved from perfection, he thought, by the tiny white scar through her eyebrow. 'Forgive me for the interruption but Mary said you liked cherry cake and Mrs Benton is so good at them.' She held up a cake-tin. 'I wanted to thank you for my stay.' No smile but the haunted darkness had gone from her eyes, he saw with relief. 'Come in, come in.'

She glanced round the kitchen, no expression registering the bachelor chaos. 'Can I say hello to Marie Antoinette?'

Later, sitting in the orchard at her request, picking at the cherry cake, she explained to him, 'It's the summer holidays next week so Nickie and I are going to spend it with my brother, Hugh.' No mention of Charles Sutton.

'And where's that?'

'The Trough of Bowland. He has a farm and some horses up there. Do you know it?'

'Yes,' he said, and said no more. 'The Trough of Bowland, it's like the Promised Land,' his young wife, Sarah, had observed on their honeymoon as they looked out at the wide, wide plain that crept up to the hills and beyond into the mists of the high horizons. They had sat, Johnnie and his new bride, gazing out of the tiny inn window, so long ago.

'And Nicholas's summer holidays. How long do they get these days?' he asked Lily.

'Nearly eight weeks,' she replied. 'Until the beginning of September.'

Johnnie waited two weeks before he wrote to her at her brother's farm.

Dear Lily,

I hope you don't mind my writing. Mary thought you wouldn't and gave me your address.

I don't think I mentioned but my wife, Sarah, and I spent our honeymoon around the Forest of Bowland and I remembered we very much enjoyed an outing to a ruined castle at Clitheroe. I also seem to recall visiting an Abbey at Whalley. There are terrific day-trips along the Ribble Valley and to the Hill of Pendle, a favoured haunt of the Lancashire witches. I thought Nicholas might enjoy them. Mary tells me he is becoming a splendid angler.

I hope you are well. Marie Antoinette sends her best, as indeed do I.

Johnnie

Dale Top Farm. 12ᵗʰ August

Dear Johnnie,

Splendid, splendid suggestions. We needed a few excitements and like Mother, like son, Nickie loves old castles. Clitheroe Castle was a great treat. Tomorrow, if the weather continues fine, we are off to make the acquaintance of the Lancashire Witches. If they are in residence at this time of year, that is.

Nickie is thrilled with his new-found angling skills and Hugh has also taught him to play chess. We are both as brown as berries.

We return at the end of next week. May I bring Nickie to tea so we can tell you all about our adventures?

Lily

Well, it had been as good an excuse as any to spring-clean the farmhouse; they hadn't had a party there since before the war. Between Sam, Mary and himself, they rustled up a fine spread. Potted meat and spiced beef, veal and ham pie and little pork sausages, home-cured. Mrs Benton had sent over another cherry cake and Mary baked a sponge-roll and scones bursting with currants. Whipped cream in peaks sat ready in the cool of the larder alongside a large pot of raspberry jam, grown, picked and made courtesy of Mr Samuel Valley. Marie Antoinette sported a large red bow.

'This is Nickie.'

'Hello, young man. I hear you're something of an angler.'

They sat under the shade of the apple trees, wreathed in drifts of blossom, swatting flies and fighting wasps. From behind the big barn came the constant snuffling of pigs.

Tea over, he and Sam took the lad down to the stream to plan a future fishing expedition, wading and mud cakes immediately becoming the order of the day. After a fair while, Johnnie left Sam and the boy to it.

Climbing back up through the orchard, sopping yells and shouts rising up behind him, he stopped on the edge of the farmyard. In the soft peace of the late afternoon, he felt the lonely old farm absorb the clatter of life and he caught the sound of the two women washing up. Crockery clinked, a streak of laughter and the continuous gentle murmur of their chatter.

Goodness, I've missed her. He stood looking across at the kitchen window, willing her to pass by so he could have sight of her. As if in answer to his prayer, she appeared, cloth in hand, head on one side listening to Mary, hidden deep within the room.

Suddenly aware of his presence, she turned and saw him.

Neither looked away.

SS *Etoile*. Friday, teatime

In the third-class general room, the teatime crowd milled round a couple of tea-urns. Out of this scrum, the wiry little Irishman emerged bearing two mugs and a glass of milk in his square fists. His grandson, small and square, followed in his wake wearing his purple turban.

'Refreshments, ladies, if I may be so bold.' And depositing the drinks, without waiting, the man scooped up his grandson and disappeared back into the crowd.

Mrs Webb grinned at Lily. 'Well, one of us has found a dancing partner.' The iron-grey hair pulled severely back only served to emphasise the soft, broad planes of the big woman's face but now, with this expression of dancing mischief, Lily glimpsed the courting girl; a pretty girl innocent of the tragedies to come, tragedies that would coarsen and weather-beat the round open face, leaving only the smile undamaged.

Anthea silently got to her feet and, following the little man into the crowd, re-emerged minutes later carefully carrying a large plate with three biscuits. With the solemnity of a serving maiden in a temple, she offered Lily her gift.

'How very kind. Thank you, Anthea.' The little girl stared down at her sandals.

Lily sat back and drank her tea; she took a bite of biscuit. 'Goodness, these are delicious. Here, Mrs Webb, you must try one. And this third one must be yours, Anthea.' The child whipped up the biscuit and jumped into the gap between the two women. They sat, all three, sipping and munching, watching the room.

Mrs Webb remarked, 'And you, Mrs Valley, you've got children. I can see that.'

The statement kicked into life all Lily's sleeping terror and astonishing fear drenched through her, leaving her body empty and numb. Her mind, however, remained clear and ringing so that she was aware of Mrs Webb at her side looking at her – anxious for an explanation. But she knew that if she spoke she would cry. Staring down, she stayed completely motionless, the only movement her thumb running back and forth, back and forth, over the tweed of her skirt. *Somehow, anyhow*, she thought, *I must be still. Don't speak yet. The fear will pass... Yes, there...* She could feel it ebbing. Like pain.

She raised her head and looked straight at Mrs Webb. 'Yes, one. Nicholas. Nickie. He's with his father—' She tried to regroup her words but faltered – then, despite herself, gabbled, 'I mean, he's at school—' She stopped. It was still too dangerous to speak. No more words. But the strain was as a net held taut which instantly dissolved and tears cascaded down her face, bringing a relief that overwhelmed her.

Mrs Webb was immediately burrowing into the depths of her skirt, taking out a handkerchief and flapping it open. 'Here, lass, have this. Don't worry, it's nice and clean.'

Lily tried to gulp back the tears but found the warmth and comfort of the big woman too much. She felt the overwhelming need to cry surge up again. She buried her face in the hankie.

'That's right, have a good blow. Anthea, stop staring! Take—'

'But, Gran—'

'Take that bucket back where you found it.' The little

clown dawdled away, continually checking progress over her shoulder.

Mrs Webb moved herself in front of Lily. 'No one's looking, all got better things to do. Though they're a load of nosey parkers if you give them half a chance. There now, that's better.'

With little gasps, Lily pulled in her breath and tried to control the crying. 'I'm so sorry – do forgive me.' Mrs Webb patted her hand. Slowly, slowly, the sore need to cry eased then ceased altogether, and a sense of stunned calm filled her. Weakly, she turned and looked at her appearance in the darkening reflection of the port-hole.

She saw her face, all blotchy, her hair worked free of its bun. 'Oh dear, look at me. Have you got a compact, Mrs Webb? I look like a pink blancmange!' She puffed out her cheeks. Both women started to laugh, relief and comfort in the sound.

'There now,' said Mrs Webb, 'in my opinion, you look a great deal better than before.'

'You won't tell Johnnie, will you? My husband. He hates to see me cry.' She gave a faint wobbly smile. 'He says it starts him off.'

Mrs Webb looked dubious. She went to speak but, deciding against it, only nodded. Lily turned to her reflection once more and started to sweep the loose hair back from her face. *How stupid of me to cry*, she thought. *And with a stranger. What would Johnnie say if he knew I'd let the side down so?* At her side, she could see the other woman sitting quietly, keeping her counsel, her large hands folded in her lap. And Lily noticed how red-raw and rough they were but with the most perfectly buffed nails. Such big square hands, strong.

Surely this woman will be discreet, after all, she's had troubles of her own...

A thought hit her.

'Oh, Mrs Webb, I'm so sorry, how inconsiderate of me. With all you've been through, the tragedy of your daughter and—'

The woman touched her arm. 'Mrs Valley, we all have tragedies of our own and, wi' the passing of time, we have to learn to bear them best we can. There's no good to be got comparing; they all hurt whatever they're made of. Oh, hullo. You feeling better, Mr Valley?'

'Much, thanks, Mrs Webb.'

Lily caught her breath; Johnnie once more had appeared from nowhere. She felt the sick terror rise – what was the matter? – and ducked her head to hide her face.

'All's fine,' he said, and placed his hand firmly on her shoulder. She glanced up and saw he was smiling. 'So, ladies, where can you get a cup of tea round here?'

'I'll show you,' said Anthea in a tiny voice and held out her hand.

'And that's a very splendid get-up, if I may say so.'

'I made pom-poms.'

'Did you indeed,' said Johnnie, taking her hand.

But Anthea couldn't delay; she tugged him off into the crowd, by now an old-hand at the tea table.

He's always so friendly, Lily thought and called out after him, 'Another cup for us, darling.'

Left alone together, she realised Mrs Webb was waiting for her to speak. She hesitated. After all, what to tell the woman? Leave it simple, say nothing, that's what she and Johnnie had decided. She pointed to the scissors. 'I'll take those back to

Madame, you've got your little ones to sort out.'

'Bless you, she's on this level. Cabin E213. And by the way, I'm here again this evening, once I've got them off. Doing a bit of sewing for Madame. If you're in need of company.'

'Thank you, I'll bear it in mind.'

'Are you sure everything's all right, Mrs Valley?'

'Quite, thank you.'

She could hear her voice, cool. But it was dangerous to be too chummy. It was a slight, she knew, after the woman's kindness but it couldn't be helped. She looked across the room and saw Johnnie and Anthea making their way back to them.

She caught the woman's sleeve. 'Quick, please. Am I presentable?'

Mrs Webb nodded.

'Just been talking to a steward and there's all sorts of excitement up aloft in first class. Seems there's a Totaliser.' Johnnie put down a tray of mugs.

'And what's that when it's at home?' asked Mrs Webb. Anthea carefully placed a plate piled precariously high with slices of cake on the table.

'Gambling, Mrs Webb.' He sat down between the two women and Lily put her arm through his; it was nice to have him near again. 'Bets are laid on how fast this ship is getting us across the water.'

Mrs Webb gave him a decidedly old-fashioned look and helped herself to a slice of cake.

'Is gambling what sheep do, Gran?' asked Anthea, bobbling her pyramid of pom-poms under the bench.

'Nay, more like a quick way for them that knows better to throw money away,' answered her grandmother stoutly.

'Quite right,' said Johnnie. 'I say, this cake's jolly fine. So what have you ladies been up to?'

'I made Freddie green pom-poms,' said Anthea, standing up to show him. The little woolly balls cascaded everywhere. Lily and Johnnie were immediately on their knees. The child stared down at them.

'And this, I think, is where we take our leave.' Mrs Webb rose to her feet. 'Come along, our Anthea. And take those pom-poms from Mrs Valley.' Lily transferred the little balls into Anthea's chubby arms as Johnnie gave Mrs Webb a solemn bow of farewell. Flustered, the woman managed a fluttering wave, and she and her granddaughter departed.

'I thought they'd never go.' Lily sank down onto the bench.

Johnnie sat beside her once again and snuggled her hand into his pocket. 'You've been crying.'

She turned her face away from him. 'Oh, Johnnie.'

'My love, we're so nearly there—'

She could hear the strain in his voice but even so she cut him off crossly. 'I feel so tired. We must have been mad to think we could pull this off.' The bad temper brought brief, fleeting comfort. 'I don't know if I can go through with this – I mean, what if we're caught?' There, it was said, the unsayable.

She looked at him, suddenly scared. She hadn't meant to voice the terror, she hadn't meant to tempt the Fates...

In a firm even voice Johnnie replied, 'Don't say that, Lily, don't even think it.'

She nodded feebly. Behind him in the dark port-hole, she caught sight of her face. She looked wretched and sad, her hair astray at the neck. She turned away.

After a bit he said, 'I've missed you. It's been all of an hour.'

'I'm sorry I'm so bad-tempered, I don't seem able to stop myself half the time.'

He grinned. '"Mrs Lily Valley."'

'Don't. It sounds so ridiculous. I wish we'd chosen a more convincing name.'

'If it's good enough for Sam and Mary,' he said, 'it's good enough for us.'

She nodded.

They sat watching the toings and froings.

London. May 1926

Lily was picked up in the motor car from the doctor's consulting rooms. She had been sedated after her uncontrollable bout of tears, Doctor Mallard prescribing one of his powders. And now how happy she felt! Speaker's Corner and the memory of a fight drifted through her mind… Police helmets bobbing about in great ladles of custard sauce… Mmm, she was so hungry…

When she got home, Mary tucked her up in bed immediately. Doctor's orders.

'Sing me Nickie's song, Mary.' She patted the eiderdown for Mary to sit beside her. It was lovely; all the fear had gone. Nickie was going to have a little brother or sister.

'Hush a bye baby on the treetop—' crooned Mary softly. The nursery song gave her Nickie. If she closed her eyes, she could see him, she could feel her boy. She looked across at her dressing table to Nickie's photograph. *My darling, soon there will be two of you children and Daddy will love us again.* She caught her reflection in the looking-glass. A woman gazing and gazing, clear sky eyes. Upon the pillow lay sunny marmalade hair. Was that really her? Not a cloud in the sky. Clever Doctor Mallard, her mind lifting away and away.

'Everything's going to be all right, Mary.'

'When the wind blows the cradle will rock—'

'Charles is going to love us again, no more "fancy piece"—'

'Down will come baby, cradle and all.'

'Nickie's going to have a little brother or sister.'

'Oh, mum.' She felt Mary squeeze her hand. But Lily wanted more; she wanted celebration. She opened her arms wide and the maid fell into them and held her tight as tight and rocked her.

'We'll tell Charles at a good moment. Perhaps when this beastly strike is over.' She knew Mary would hug the precious news to herself; she wouldn't even share it with Cook.

'Hurrah! Hurrah!' she sang, and fell asleep.

But now she was awake again, wide awake. All around, she felt the cry of sick alarm. Sitting on the landing in the dark, she stared out at the night sky. London, hushed. She wasn't actually looking at anything, her every sense was focused on any sound rising from two floors below. She sat with her arms wrapped round her legs. And prayed.

As St Mary's, Bryanston Square, had struck two, she'd heard the motor car draw up and Charles thunder into the night-time house. She'd run from her bed, still woozy from Doctor Mallard's powders, and taken up her post on the landing. 'Where is my wife?' She didn't hear Watkin's reply as he held the front door for his master. Nor it seems did Sir Charles. 'For God's sake, speak up, man!' These days she could tell exactly how much he'd drunk by the sound of his step; tonight as she listened, she felt danger rise up through the house.

A heavy door banged shut. Then all was silent.

The house stood primed, electric and alive.

She held her breath, trying to make out Charles's movements below. A door squeaked open above making her leap to her feet. Mary, her head a crown of curlers, was leaning over the banisters.

A door-slam rang up the stairs. Both women flattened themselves into the darkness. The landing light below had been thrown on; Charles was coming up.

'Lily, where are you?' he roared; he was moving at speed.

She raced down the half-flight to her bedroom; she could lock the door against him. She managed to pass through just as he reached the first-floor landing. She scrambled with the handle, but it was too late. He barged through the door, fell back and slammed it shut with his weight.

'You bitch! My God, you'll pay for this!'

She heard herself say, her voice remarkably steady, 'Charles, what is it?'

His face was extraordinary, the rage distorting. A mottled gargoyle, purple, pulsating. Then to her surprise he appeared to ignore her. He turned away to the door. Was he leaving? She heard the key in the lock. He turned back.

Carefully, deliberately, he started to advance towards her. Now the terror fully bloomed within her. She backed away around the bed, the fear, unbelievable, strangling her thoughts, her breath. She tried to keep the terror from her face, she didn't want to inflame him further, but he was still following.

'Your darling brother, a wretched little traitor!'

'Oh Charles—' Her cry was cut off by the first slap, the sound cracking through the stillness of the night.

She gasped, winded – and as she struggled for her breath she saw his hand swing back a second time. 'Oh no! Oh Charles, don't – I'm pregnant!' The revelation spun from her.

Momentarily he stopped and stood swaying slightly, bull-broad. 'You lying cow! I've not been near you—'

'Oh, Charles, please – after the Ambrose party?' Desperately, she tried to keep the pleading from her voice. 'You must remember—'

Another slap the side of her head, her ear; the pain precise, crystal clear.

All was quiet – and then, through the ringing, singing pain, she heard a far-away knocking. 'My lady, my lady, open the door! Oh, my lady, are you all right?'

Charles leant over her and slowly raised his hand. He didn't strike. 'Get rid of her!'

She found herself stumbling round the bed. She looked back over her shoulder, the man nodded. She turned the key in the door and opened it.

Mary's face was white, tears in her eyes.

'Go away, Mary. *Please!*'

From behind he shoved her out of the way and, with his bulk, slammed shut the door.

She prayed, Please look after the child. I know he'll hurt me but please look after my child.

He pulled her round to face him, his voice low and furious. 'There, there, in front of all the world—' She felt the spray of his spit on her face.

'Charles, I can explain. No, please. Oh! Please! Not again!' His fist balled and she felt the pounding thump to her stomach. All the breath left her; she buckled to the floor.

'All right, Lily, my darling treacherous little wife, explain to me.' Though so drunk, the man's fury gave his words speed and lucidity. 'Explain why your pansy brother is standing outside Number Ten, making a monkey of me with his fucking Strike Committee. You and your rotten family—'

She lay crouched on the floor making herself as small as she could. She saw his feet start to move to the door. 'You revolt me!' There was an extraordinary loathing in his voice.

He was gone, banging across the landing, slamming the door of his dressing room.

Everything was quiet.

She lay very still, huddled on the carpet, ashamed and terrified at the enormous anger she had provoked in the man. Slowly the shame and terror waned but only because an extraordinary new pain reared into life and tore relentlessly through her. She hugged the pain to her, trying to make it a friend, trying to bargain with it to let her keep the baby.

All through the night, even though she knew Mary was sitting outside, Lily wouldn't let her in. When in the morning she finally allowed the maid to enter, she was bleeding profusely. At midday, she lost the baby.

Afterwards, the only way she knew how to survive was to speak of that night just once, and that was to Mary. She made the maid swear on the Bible never to tell anyone. Anything. It was a private affair. Anyway, who would have guessed her husband would do such a thing? After all, he had left her face completely unmarked.

CHAPTER EIGHT

SS *Etoile*. Evening

Up in first class, the post-prandial atmosphere of the Savoy Room had been soothingly enhanced by the alluring scents of Cuban cigars and Turkish coffee. Though for many passengers, the biggest pleasure of all was the calmer waters of this evening's ocean.

Far off, the dance-band in the Starlight Room was playing 'Tonight's the Night.'

Out of the corner of her eye, Dora Carroll glanced at Lady Lavinia and saw that such soothing delights were completely lost on her friend. Indeed, Dora understood the large woman well enough to know that, at this moment, she was paying for over-indulgence at the captain's table as she sat torn between returning to the solace of a Bromo-seltzer in her suite or responding to the challenge of a hand or two at cards. As always, the game of Bridge won. Lavinia drained her little coffee cup and attempted to heave herself from the sofa, all the while never ceasing to talk in her booming voice.

'...and, my dear Dora, we are all aware that Grossman is not an entirely English name.'

Throughout dinner, the presence of Nurse Grossman at Lord Clairmont's side had continued to cause Lavinia considerable irritation and, no doubt, had contributed hugely to her subsequent indigestion. The fact that the young couple now sat across the room, looking very happy as they laughed at a game of Snap, did nothing to quell the woman's bile.

'Is it not, Lavinia dear?' answered Dora. She had weathered a potentially explosive dinner at her friend's side and now fervently wished for nothing other than a pleasant game of cards. Well used to Lavinia's contrary ways, Dora was determined to pour all the soothing oil she could on the troubled waters of her friend's liverish behaviour. 'She looks a pleasant enough young woman to me.'

'Dora, do use your eyes,' said Lady Slocombe in an energetic whisper, her jowl dancing; she was not used to being contradicted. 'She is quite obviously Jewish. Even to me. Which means her father is in trade or something a great deal worse.'

'But, Lavinia, you yourself informed me the girl is a nurse.'

'Exactly.' Lady Lavinia cleared her throat. 'And we have all seen how that profession has been used as a cover for quite unmentionable activities of the sort Miss Grossman, if I look closely at her common little face, is not entirely unaware.'

Across the room, Lord Henry and his nurse played on, blissfully ignorant of this tirade.

'Come, Lavinia,' bustled Dora, 'I think they're about to start. Ah yes, there is dear Mrs Wells.' With much relief, Dora spotted the arrival of the last of their Bridge four and the first rubber hove into view. Lady Slocombe, launching herself again from the sofa, this time managing to stand, was, however, not to be distracted.

'In my young day,' her Ladyship's imperious tones swelled as she crossed towards the Bridge tables, 'one could be assured when travelling on such a cruise as this that one's position in life would be respected and indeed reflected by the captain inviting one to dine alongside friends and acquaintances of equal standing.' Lady Slocombe chose to look neither to right nor left, simply presuming all were listening. 'It made life a great deal easier; one was not expected to plunge about in conversation trying to understand and entertain the lower orders. Now I am not only expected to sit beside tradespeople but also Semites.'

During this speech, without pause for breath, the large woman arrived at the Bridge table of her choice, sat herself down and, lifting her hand in a gesture of command, received the playing cards from an orderly. 'I'll cut for first deal,' she announced as Dora puffed to a halt alongside. Across the lounge, Mrs Wells and her husband, a ruby-faced cleric, comfortably chatted their way towards the Bridge table, and in order to assemble these tardy troops, Lady Slocombe raised her voice and instructed sharply, 'Do come along, you two. We really must begin. Just look at the time.' As the players took their places, Lady Slocombe glanced down at her watch and, to everyone's consternation, a trumpet of horror emitted from her ladyship's lips. 'My jewels! They've gone!'

Dora immediately saw that the diamond bracelet, which usually resided beside her ladyship's evening-watch, was not there. Concerned that her somewhat overexcited friend was about to spiral out of control, she swiftly attempted to bring common sense to the proceedings. 'Lavinia dear, try to remember where you have been. Think back.'

Swotting at her companion with a large handkerchief, Lavinia yapped, 'Don't be such a dunderhead, Dora. The two of us have been cheek by jowl all evening!'

'Except when you retired to the ladies' cloakroom,' whispered the eternally-practical Dora. 'Did you take it off, perhaps, to rinse your hands?'

If she had hoped this suggestion would solve the problem she was immediately to realise otherwise, for, triumphant, Lavinia crowed, 'Yes, that's it!' and swinging round, pointed officiously across the room. 'That girl – in the cloakroom – that Grossman girl, she brushed against me. Call the steward!'

There was a swell of interest as all eyes turned towards the young woman who sat laughing at her game of Snap, unaware of the impending trial.

Horrified at the severity of the charge, Dora frantically counselled, 'Lavinia, I really don't think you can—'

But she never completed the sentence, for, as if by magic, a steward arrived at Lady Slocombe's side.

Down in the third-class general room, Lady Slocombe's maid, Miss Enid Timms, was spending the evening doing a little mending. She was not in the best of moods. Her middle still ached from the encounter with the beastly dog-walker earlier in the day and she prayed that an infestation of nits had not jumped from the boy's greasy scalp onto her best cloth coat. Added to which, she had had to spend the evening with a pair of tweezers picking dog hairs from her ladyship's purple angora travelling suit. What had possessed that wretched kennel man to push Gainsborough into her mistress's arms? Had he no idea of the quality of the cloth? Men!

About to return aloft to prepare her ladyship's suite for retiring, her attention was caught by two women walking past her laughing, in what seemed to her to be an unnecessarily vulgar fashion. She stared after them as if she had been personally chosen to suffer such noisy thoughtlessness – and was instantly rewarded by a flash of recognition.

Lady Sutton of all people. And in steerage!

For a moment Miss Timms sat stunned. What on earth was her ladyship doing down here – and, to be frank, looking decidedly peaky? She watched greedily as the women made their way across the room to the far side and sat down at a table covered in what appeared to be laundry. She found herself torn between turning down her mistress's bed and staying to observe this new and exquisitely interesting prey. Was Sir Charles down here with his wife? She peered hopefully about but the gentleman was not to be seen. The lady's maid had a soft spot for Sir Charles – always very properly and nicely turned out, he was; a real English gentleman. Not that she was a close acquaintance of the Suttons or any members of their staff but her faithful perusal of the social columns meant that she was more than *au courant* with their comings and goings – and those of Society in general.

She gazed at Lady Sutton. Mmm, her ladyship's cardigan was well-cut enough but her skirt was very drab; she had always considered m'lady to be an elegant if somewhat timid dresser. And who on earth was that common woman sitting with her? Really, the working classes and their dreary clothes! Though, even at a distance, her professional eye noted the woman's blouse was beautifully pressed.

Miss Timms' long years in service had taught her two

essential rules: to always keep oneself to oneself, never mixing with other staff, but more importantly never to ignore an opportunity to pry. She therefore knew instinctively to keep Lady Sutton within her sights. But should she move closer to hear what was obviously an interesting conversation between the two women or should she remain, unseen, at a distance? No, she should stay where she was; it would be a shame if she were spotted and, for some reason, recognised. She must be content in watching, solely.

And such was her growing excitement at this unexpected turn of events, Miss Timms started to breathe heavily, causing people to turn and look. Hastily, she ducked behind a drunken coat-stand weighed down by shawls and mufflers and scarves, not daring to move. With an experience honed by long years of loyal service, she drew herself upright and made herself breathe deeply and quietly until finally she was able to watch the two women with all the stillness and concentration of a private detective.

Nellie was thoroughly enjoying Mrs Valley's company. She felt pleased that the woman had decided to take up her offer of a bit of company, knowing how gloomy the little cabins could become of an evening. And as the two women sat together under a lamp and sewed, they were much relieved to discover the big communal room a good deal quieter. Supper had come and gone, a clatter of plates and mugs. Now all was calm. And although the light outside had turned to black, the atmosphere indoors was cheerful enough. People played cards and smoked, and there was a cosy hum of chatter. Indeed, the snug warmth was perfect for the sharing of stories.

Nellie Webb was one of life's good listeners. She had

drawn from her new acquaintance the tale of the squashed hat – Mr and Mrs Valley's first meeting, so to speak – and she'd thoroughly enjoyed every moment of it. Now she was hoping for further tales, providing, as they did, glimpses of a life she really only knew about from her magazines. Mind, she could tell Mrs Valley had enjoyed talking, the happy memories bringing comfort, no doubt, as she seemed a good deal calmer than before. And brighter. Her shocking paleness of earlier had gone and this evening there were even roses in her cheeks. No, Nellie had to admit, for all her la-di-dah manner, the woman was a pleasant enough soul.

'Mary must have been that pleased when you started to step out with your Johnnie.' Nellie took off her glasses and rubbed her eyes – by, she were that tired.

'Poor Mary,' said Mrs Valley. 'The day she got back from her honeymoon I went straight over to her cottage and just talked and talked. She never got a word in edgeways!' The woman broke into a bubbling smile. 'Not that there was much to divulge about that first day I'd spent with Johnnie.'

'Get away,' countered Nellie, every detail of the story absorbed. 'You and him'd had your walk round the castle together. And then all that talk in the public house.'

'You are a good listener.' Mrs Valley looked at her. 'You know, Johnnie says it's a sign of true friendship when the listener wants every little detail.'

'Or perhaps they're just a nosey old so and so!'

Mrs Valley smiled.

'Anyway, go on with what you were saying. About you and Mary,' Nellie urged.

'In some ways I didn't dare talk about my day with Johnnie, even to Mary. I was just so fearful that, in speaking about it, it would all disappear in a puff of smoke and become nothing more than a dream.' She closed her eyes. 'Goodness, it seems such a time ago – and yet it's only – let me see, one and a bit years. June 1931.' She sat drifting in the memory.

'Sounds like you both got on like a 'ouse on fire from the off.'

'Do you know, Mrs Webb, it was just such fun having someone to talk to. And someone you didn't have to talk to, if there was no need. I'd never met anyone before who just seemed to understand.'

Nellie leant across to the pile of sewing and picked up a torn pillowcase. 'So tell us about your Nickie, then?'

For a moment, Nellie thought she'd finally asked one question too many. Mrs Valley sat very still, and so pale did she become, Nellie was on her feet asking, 'Shall I get your Johnnie?'

'*No!*' The woman's response came hard and sharp.

Nellie sat back down. She felt well ticked-off.

'Do forgive me,' said Mrs Valley at once. 'My husband's still poorly – this beastly seasickness. Please could you get me a glass of water?'

By the time Nellie had returned, the woman appeared calmer. 'I'm so sorry, Mrs Webb, I don't think I've fully recovered my sea-legs either.' She said nothing more but sat staring at the ground. When she eventually spoke, her voice was quieter than usual and Nellie found herself leaning close.

'Charles, my husband, was so angry when I fell in love with Johnnie, he refused to give me a divorce.' She hesitated, still looking down. 'He was fully aware that if I were to publicly acknowledge Johnnie, I'd be seen as an adulterous woman and therefore an unfit mother. As such, I would never be given custody of my child.' She lifted her eyes and looked at Nellie. 'My husband has made me decide between Johnnie and my son. Having chosen Johnnie, I'm not allowed to see Nickie anymore.' She stopped, the sag of her shoulders completely despairing.

Appalled, Nellie sat unable to think what to say.

Suddenly the woman grabbed her arm. 'But you mustn't tell anyone, Mrs Webb, so much depends on it. No one knows. You see, we're on our way to America but we mustn't be seen – and no one will know us down here in steerage – it's why we're calling ourselves, "Valley". It's Sam and Mary's surname, and— Oh, I can't tell you anymore.' She released her grasp. 'Forgive me but you won't tell anyone, will you?'

'Nay, nay. It's between thee and me, lass.'

'If Charles finds out... My husband's a very angry man.'

'And I'll put good money down, you meant nowt to him until you meant summat to your Johnnie.'

The woman almost smiled, and nodded. Neither said any more.

Nellie picked up the pillowcase once again. As she worked she kept her face down, focusing on her stitching. She tried not to think of what she'd just been told, she tried not to judge. But it was difficult. After all, she knew only too well the unending misery of her two orphaned grandchildren; she'd seen their terrible longing for their dead mam. To actually choose to leave a bairn behind... Nay, but it wasn't for her to judge, it wasn't her business.

They sat silent until the woman asked, 'Has Anthea read *The House at Pooh Corner*?'

Nellie looked up, unsure what she was on about.

'It's a children's book,' explained Mrs Valley.

'Nay, our Anthea's letters are none too good.'

'Well, I must read it to her.' The woman cut her thread and brought her hands to rest in her lap. 'May I ask, Mrs Webb, why you said earlier Anthea was scared and didn't like change?'

'By, you remembered. Well, when her mam died, my Em, Anthea went underground, like. Into herself. While our Freddie, he's 'ere, there and everywhere. Though he's still a lonely one. Mind you, he seems to have made friends with this Billy Bottle.'

'Billy Bottle?'

'One of the young bellboys, they call them. Well, he's got no mam, neither. So, lo and behold, they're two of a pair. And now, of course, our Freddie doesn't know if he wants to be a bellboy or a dog-walker when he gets to America.'

'And where are you going to live when you get there?' Mrs Valley started to fold her sewing.

'My sister's in Minnesota. She's got a big family. It'll be better for the little ones, I reckon.' She sat back in her seat and rubbed her eyes. She were that tired, she could sleep for a week given half a chance. 'Barney, my youngest – son, that is – 'cos he works in't print shop here on the boat, he got us cheaper tickets. Couldn't of come, otherwise. Mind, I've got meself this bit of sewing. And none of us can get over the bread and butter on offer of a mealtime.' She looked down and patted the pillowcase; that was as good a mend as any.

'You'll carry on as a laundress there?'

'Seems more than like. If I can prove after a time we're lawful residents. What with them job quotas an' all.' She looked at Mrs Valley. 'You do remember well.'

'I'm interested. I like to know about people's lives, they always seem so interesting.'

'Well, I don't know about that.' Nellie laughed and shook her head.

'Have you always done that? Laundering?'

'Aye, thirty years, lass. Started in Sheffield General Hospital. Then come the war, I was moved to a Home for Disabled Men. Second year of peace, Davy – my husband that was – got himself killed falling off a steam train, so I started up on me own.'

'Oh no.' Mrs Valley stared at her.

'A wonderful charmer, my Davy, 'specially wi' a drink inside him. I knew from the off he'd leave me in the lurch but even I couldn't o' guessed how.'

'But it must have been so tough for you. How large is your family?'

And there it was, Nellie thought. *The question*. It had to be answered. Always had to be answered. '1915, I had a husband and five bonny bairns. Eight year on, I have no husband and just the one son. My Barney.'

'Oh, my dear.' She felt the woman reach for her hand. 'How? Was it the war?'

'No. Influenza. We get through that bloody war and then three of them, just swept away by the Spanish 'flu. And the twins only sixteen, and then Em in that fire... Except for my Barney and the two grandbabbies, all that's left of me family is five silent birthdays a year. Five days o' nothing.' If only every time she talked of it the pain could get less. She took a deep breath. 'But I've learnt to live wi' it. You've got to look after the living, after all. And that means yourself as well.'

She looked at Mrs Valley. The woman seemed that tired.

Aye, poor lass, now you'll have a silent birthday to bear, she thought. *Your Nickie's.*

Somewhere deep within the ship, a bell rang.

'Good heavens, Mrs Webb, I'd completely forgotten the time.' Without further ado, the woman swiftly got to her feet, crossed the room and disappeared through the swing doors.

Now, what's bitten her? thought Nellie. *There we were having a nice little chat and off she goes without a by-your-leave.* Not that she was bothered. She'd tidy up and then she could turn in. An early night. Lovely.

She moved to put her work-basket off the table and saw, like an egg in a nest amongst the bits of laundry, Mrs Valley's watch. She picked it up by the neat leather strap and held the little gold face to the light. Very nice, very tasteful… Mind, Mrs Valley would be worried sick when she found she'd left it. She'd better get it back to her.

Nellie got to her feet, stowed the sewing into a neat pile, and set off across the general room after her new friend. She made her way quickly along the all but empty passageways, the engines, to her way of thinking, making a companionable chuntering.

E263. Yes, she was sure that's what Mrs Valley had said her cabin number was. She'd hand in the watch – the woman would be that relieved to have it back – and then bye-bye, nighty night.

E263. Aye, there it was.

But having found the cabin, an unusual shyness caught her. She knocked very quietly.

No answer.

With a deep breath, she knocked more firmly. A duty to be done.

Beyond the clanking engines, she thought she heard a scuffle. Then nothing. Suddenly, Mrs Webb was aware of all sorts of reasons for the cabin door to remain closed. The Valleys were a new couple, after all. Flustered, she turned to go.

'Yes?'

Turning back, she saw through the half-open door the centre-panel of Mrs Valley's face. It was ashen – plus the woman seemed to be trembling. Alarmed, Nellie said quickly, 'It's only me, love.' She dangled the watch in the woman's view.

'Oh, Mrs Webb. I'm so sorry, you rather startled us.'

Nellie was about to hand through the watch when from inside the cabin, she heard Mr Valley's voice. 'I think you should invite Mrs Webb in, darling.'

At this, Mrs Valley turned and stared disbelievingly at the unseen man, her back arrow-straight, her white hand clutching the door. Slowly, she stepped aside and held the door for Nellie to enter.

Mr Valley was sitting on the lower bunk, smoking his pipe. 'Good evening, Mrs Webb.' He rose as she entered.

The cabin was very cramped – *Smaller than ours*, thought Nellie – but her eye was drawn to the upper bunk. There, fast asleep, was a little boy clutching a lead soldier.

'Let me introduce my son, Nicholas Sutton,' Mrs Valley said.

Nellie stared.

'Darling, can you?' Mr Valley whispered urgently.

Mrs Valley nodded. 'Mrs Webb, if you don't mind, I think we'd better go back to the general room. Johnnie's only just got Nickie off to sleep.'

England. February 1933

'Nicholas Sutton, headmaster's study, *now.*'

The mathematics teacher, mid-algebraic formula, back turned to the blackboard, stared coldly. Nickie felt his face getting all hot and sticky. He opened his desk-lid and started to put away his books.

'You can clear those away later. Don't keep everyone waiting, boy!'

He ran away down the corridor, a thick belt of boys' laughter following him from the classroom. At an intersection of cold passageways, a teacher unexpectedly hovered, fiddling with a noticeboard. Nickie whisked by.

'*Walk* in the corridors, Sutton. How many more times do I have to tell you?'

The headmaster's door was standing open. 'Ah, Sutton, come in, come in.' Tall and bending, continually flapping at his gown, the headmaster completed a circle of his large desk to reveal Nickie's mother in a chair, smiling across at him.

Nickie stood stock-still. Inside, all his feelings jumbled about. Relief, delight, embarrassment, worry. He managed to squeeze out, 'Hello, Mummy,' his joy at seeing her stifled by the terror that she'd kiss him in front of the headmaster.

'Come in, Sutton, don't just stand there.'

'Yes, sir.' He drew level to his mother's side. She was wearing one of her hats – thank goodness, not the silly red one with the cherries – and he saw at once she had on her no-laughing face. Something important had happened. Over her shoulder, he noticed out of the window Fawcett senior crack a ball with a cricket bat. It flew through the air, fielders' arms reaching to the frosty sky. Even on such a cold day, there was the sound of far-away clapping.

'Now then, Sutton. Attention, please.' Nickie looked back into the room, the field's icy white making him blink.

'Er – Headmaster?' His mother looked at her watch.

'Lady Sutton, of course. I understand; time's of the element. May I advise you put Nicholas in the picture on the way?'

'Thank you, Headmaster. So understanding.' Nickie looked down at his mother. She was 'pretending', her voice was all funny and smooth. She glanced up and caught his query, a whip of understanding shooting between them. *No questions for now.*

'Come on, darling. Sam's outside in the car.'

'But what about tomorrow's practice, sir?' blurted Nickie. 'And there's "Fives" this afternoon—'

A large hand descended on his shoulder. 'All will be taken care of, my boy. Now run along with your mother.'

'But, sir—'

His voice was drowned by the headmaster's. 'I've asked Matron to pack you a small bag, Sutton.'

There was nothing he could do but follow his mother across the large echoing hall, his world all in a muddle as the headmaster himself helped him into his grey school coat and handed him his cap. Matron stood to one side, all smiley, and with an abrupt little bob, gave his mother his small brown case. *She looks like one of Sam's hens laying an egg*, he thought.

On a swell, they all arrived outside at the top of the school steps. There in the middle of the gravel drive, besmattered with grimy snow, stood the Daimler and Sam himself.

He was down the steps and up into Sam's arms. ''Morning, young man. Oi, watch it! You've grown ten feet.'

'I've hit a six, Sam, though it was only inside with a tennis-ball. I did it like you showed me – spring term I might get into the Third Eleven—'

Packed into the car, they crunched away down the drive, none of them looking back at the waving matron and headmaster. And Nickie, tucked into the red-leather back seat, found himself torn between ten hundred million questions and a final look at Fawcett senior streaking towards the winter wicket, a black umbrella stuck into the frosty field. At the main gates, the school motto struggling through iron branches and furbelows, 'Actions Not Words', they left the school grounds. And turned right, not left.

He scrambled forward. 'Aren't we going home?'

'No, darling.'

From the front, Mummy leant back towards him and, at last, he found himself all caught up as she hugged and hugged. He breathed in her special smell – lemons and raspberries – the perfume she kept for best in the little bottle on her dressing table. He just knew she'd put it on especially for him.

But she was saying lots of things to him and all in a rush, '...and we're going on a big, big adventure and it's a huge secret, probably the biggest secret you'll ever have to keep.' She slowed down a bit. 'Which is why I've just had to tell the headmaster a bit of a fib.' Her eyes were all shiny.

Sam drove fast.

'But where are we going?' She had to understand that he had very important things to do; he didn't really have time to go on an adventure. 'I've got practice tomorrow at three o'clock – and there's "Fives" this afternoon—'

'Sorry, darling. Not this afternoon or tomorrow.'

Hopeless. 'But why not?'

'No more questions for now, Nickie.' Not her laughing voice. He sat back in the seat. He saw Sam and Mummy look at each other. Grown-ups, huh.

'How about a bit of grub then, young man?' Sam asked as they entered a small village.

In the teashop, he found some consolation in a plate of steaming steak-and-kidney pie followed by semolina apples. He knew something serious was up when Mummy let him have custard *and* ice-cream. And she wasn't saying anything, just staring out of the window smoking cigarette after cigarette. Usually on Parent's Day, she'd ask so many questions, he couldn't eat a single mouthful.

He eyed Sam's plate; there was a bit of veal and ham pie on it. 'On you go, Nickie me lad,' and the pie followed the semolina apples. Neither Sam nor Mummy spoke. A stick-like waitress all in black put down two cups of very milky coffee and the bill. He watched as she crawled away with a funny pointy-toed walk; a milky-coffee spider.

The church clock chimed one. Sam was on his feet. 'Time to go.'

Snuggled down, watching the wintry countryside flying by from his red-leather world, Mummy turned round to him and began, 'We're going on a big boat.'

Plans for Indoor Nets vanished. But then, instantly, the worst thought: 'Is Father coming?'

'No, darling. Your father is staying in London. It's just you, me—' she paused. 'And Johnnie.'

Looking down at his knees, gently picking at an old scab, he said, 'But I thought Father said I couldn't see Johnnie anymore.'

'No, all that's changed now.' The firmness in her voice

brought his head up. 'It's part of the secret.'

'Are Sam and Mary coming?'

'Can't, old chap,' said Sam. 'Got to stay here and keep an eye on things.'

'But where's Johnnie now?'

'He's meeting us at Southampton.'

'Is that where the boat is?'

'Yes, darling,' smiled Mummy.

They drove swiftly through the cold afternoon. As the frosty darkness crawled across the countryside, he slept. 'Fives' forgotten, scab forgotten, safely wrapped in an old tartan car-rug, the mumble of the two grown-up voices a lullaby.

When he woke it was dark and the car was stopping, the wavering headlights picking out a small wood and brick cottage, and a running figure was calling out, 'Where's my Nickie?' before the headlights were turned off and all was dark once more.

He knew the voice instantly. 'Mary!'

'Whoa, slow down! Let's stop the car first,' grinned Sam.

They all whirled into the cottage, away from the dark and the cold, and into the warmth of a tiny kitchen. 'This is my big sister, Susan,' said Mary. 'Say "how-do".'

'Is this your house?'

'It is,' said Susan.

'Are we staying here?'

'Just stopping the one night.'

He pulled Mary down to him and whispered in her ear. 'Does she know about the big boat?'

'Yes.'

'But does she know it's the biggest secret we ever have to keep?'

'Yes,' nodded Mary.

In a little room at the top of a tiny staircase, Mummy tucked him into a big high bed. She climbed up beside him and lay on the faded floral counterpane; it was covered in swirly commas. There was the sound of crackling and scratching all along the eaves.

'Birds are going to sleep. Snuggle down, darling.' But he didn't. In fact, he sat up again. 'Mummy, are we running away?'

He knew it was her very special wish to keep him safe. Safe from Father. He knew that's why he'd had to go to Big School a year early. But if they ran away, what would happen to his place in the Third Eleven? She was looking at him, her face all wobbly and smiling. 'Yes, darling, we're running away.' And then he knew it was something extra-secret she was going to tell him because her voice went all quiet and little. 'You see, darling, I want to be with the two people I love most in all the world. You and Johnnie. And because I think you and I will be happier if we don't live with your father, it means we must go away for a little while and hide.'

He nodded, all that made sense. To complete the idea in his mind, he said, 'So we must never let Father find us.'

'That's right, darling.'

Satisfied that this seemed to be a most sensible plan, he snuggled down.

There was the murmur of voices through the floorboards and when Mummy got back down to the kitchen, he heard her say, 'I've told him. Thank God, he seems to approve.' He fell asleep.

Next morning, it was so freezing his breath kept huffing out in cloudy puffs. He had to bang his arms round him to keep warm.

'Nickie, stop doing that and stand still,' said Mary.

'But I'm cold.'

'I know you are but the sooner you're dressed the sooner you'll be warm.' He was tired and fed-up at being pulled around and stuffed into strange scratchy clothes.

'Now, come on, come and have a look in our Susan's mirror.' The women pushed and pulled him through to a looking-glass. He stopped and stared, he couldn't believe it. There in the mirror, a small girl in a beret was staring back at him.

But he wasn't having it. He flung off the beret. 'Why do I have to wear this?' *And* he was dressed in some rotten old tartan skirt!

'Now then,' said Mary sternly. 'We don't want no one on this here boat to know who you are. And best way is for you to pretend to be a girl. Anyhow, you're all changing clothes. Look at your mum in my hat and coat.'

It was too much. Even worse, Sam started to laugh the minute he saw Nickie. And though Mary said 'Sam!' in a voice that could've killed an ox, and Sam's face went all serious, Nickie knew his friend was laughing at him.

They all crowded round the kitchen table and Sam explained, 'Here are the tickets. All in my name. So now you're Miss Nickie Valley, aren't you?' He winked at Nicholas but Nickie turned away. He was disgusted at his friend ganging-up with the women.

CHAPTER NINE

SS *Etoile*. Evening

Enid Timms was confused. She had been considering following Lady Sutton and the fat woman from the general room when they had re-appeared arm-in-arm and smiling, settling once more at their original table, still covered in laundry. Unable to hear a word of the conversation and baffled by all the comings and goings, Miss Timms made a decision that, for the moment, she would remain tucked behind her laden coat-stand. Her instinct informed her that Lady Sutton's presence down here in steerage presaged a secret and, having hawkishly watched the conversation between m'lady and the fat woman, the two women's heads tucked together in conspiratorial exchange, Miss Timms' experienced eye told her that this might be a secret of some value. Whether it took coin or guile, Miss Timms was determined to possess it.

While pondering these many sudden new possibilities, her attention was caught by a loud clattering. Peering from her hiding place, she saw two young ruffians dashing across the wide linoleum floor, and was shocked to observe the common-looking boys not only bounce down beside the fat woman but also, upon being introduced to Lady Sutton, be warmly greeted by her.

In the next instant, one of the boys started to tell a tale of great interest, for the two women and the two boys all drew together eagerly. On closer observation, Miss Timms was astonished to realise that the boys were none other than the bellhop and the common little dog-walker whom she had encountered earlier that day. Unconsciously, she began to massage her tender stomach whilst pondering on the situation.

Surely there was much here to unravel. She stood obelisk-like, frozen and silent, gazing from behind her coat-stand. Turning down her mistress's bed would have to wait – this situation was of greater importance; she could feel it in her bones.

She didn't think she had ever been happier.

'... And when the steward arrives,' said Billy, 'the nurse is pulled over. And she looks dead scared. But we all knows she's innocent and that she never took no jewellery.'

Having finished his day's duties, the bellboy was spending the remainder of his evening with young Fred and his gran. He knew they liked his tales from up top, and this evening there was an extra audience. They had been joined by a posh lady called Mrs Valley. Billy was pleased. Sure as eggs was eggs, he knew tonight's story was a right go-er.

'Where's the poor lass now?' Fred's gran wanted to know.

'They dragged her off to the captain's office.'

'And who is this dreadful woman who made the accusation?' asked the posh woman.

'This dreadful woman, mum,' Billy replied stoutly, 'is one Lady Slocombe.'

'Right old busybody an' all,' young Freddie piped up. 'I walks her dog and she—'

'Lady *Lavinia* Slocombe?' The posh woman was staring hard at Billy.

'Do you know this woman?' Fred's gran asked.

'No, not really,' the woman muttered quickly. 'I may have met her once.'

She's fibbing, thought Billy, as the woman, jumping to her feet, quickly swept bits and pieces into her bag any old how. 'Mrs Webb,' she said, 'I have to go but I wonder if you'd call by our cabin. Just for a quick word.' Fred's gran nodded, and without another word the posh woman crossed the room and was gone in a blink.

'What's got into her?' Billy asked.

'Seasickness,' said Fred's gran firmly.

'Anyways,' he said – the story had to be finished. 'Once in the captain's office, the nurse collapses. And everyone's in a right old two and eight. The ship's doctor's called and says she's suffering from shock and—'

Freddie gave a great yawn.

'It's bed for you, young man,' commanded Mrs Webb. 'Come along. We'll finish your story tomorrow, Billy.'

The bellboy escorted them to the double doors. 'Good night, mum. See yer tomorrow, Fred my boy.' And, like the commissionaire he'd seen outside the pictures, he gave Mrs Webb a flourishing bow of farewell.

Everywhere people were stretching and yawning, making

their way to bunks and berths. Billy stood considering the day's earnings and doings, his duties at an end. Suddenly on the other side of the room, his eye was caught by a dark figure slipping from behind a coat-stand. *It's that old biddy from the kennels*, he thought, *the Slocombe maid. What's she slinking about for?* At that moment, the tall thin woman gave a shifty look around and shot off through a pair of double doors. *She's up to something.* Billy was across the room behind her.

He emerged into the passage in time to see the woman look first to left and right then push through a door marked 'Crew Only'. She was now on Scotland Road.

How's she know about this? thought Billy. *It's a shortcut for crew only.*

The long passageway flanked the port-side of the boiler uptakes and ran from the stern of the ship providing access to crew accommodation and the engineer's mess further aft. At this time of night it was empty though hardly silent as, all around, the guts of the ship thundered and clanged.

Billy nudged through the door and saw that the woman had already got some way ahead. Trying to keep a safe distance, he found he had to break into a trot as the woman pushed on very fast. Twice Scotland Road took a bend and twice he was nearly flung into her as he rounded the corner, only to find she'd stopped to take a breath. Both times, she rallied and sped off very fast.

At what he knew was the third and final bend, he moved carefully forward and peered round, but there was no sign of her – only a swing door at the end barely moving. Running forward, he was just in time to see her long navy skirt disappearing up a stairway. She was now back on the passengers' side of the fence. He bolted up the stairs after her.

For four flights he followed as close as he dared until she finally disappeared through a doorway. It led, he knew, to the luxury suites in first-class accommodation. Billy let her get ahead before he followed.

The carpeted first-class corridor was completely quiet. And empty. Had he lost her? He raced to the far end and caught sight of Miss Timms' skirt once again disappearing round a corner. Carefully, he followed – to find her slowing to a more even pace, then, like a clockwork mouse, she slowed, slowed and eventually stopped, sinking onto a small settee set back from the corridor in the depths of a swagged alcove. Placing the basket she was carrying on the seat beside her, she gulped in breaths and began to massage what Billy knew, if she was anything like his gran, to be her corset. Closing her eyes, the thin woman started to rock until, after a few minutes, her breath seemed to come more evenly.

Billy watched carefully. He prided himself on his instinct and he knew, just knew, this one was up to no good. Why had she been hanging around all suspicious-like in the general room? And why had she rushed down Scotland Road like a bullet from a gun?

Quietly he crept towards her and was two alcoves away when she opened her eyes again. Billy jumped back behind a swagged curtain. He made himself count to ten and then very slowly peered out. The woman was checking a watch pinned to her jacket. She glanced quickly about then, peeling back the cotton covering on her basket, took out a small tin box. Even at a distance, Billy could see the word OXO written on the lid. Opening the tin, she withdrew a short length of white chalk and a piece of paper, which she consulted. Rising, she peered to left and right, checking the numbers of each suite until one particular door held her attention and she leant forward to put down the basket. At that moment, a roar of laughter heralded a party of people at the other end of the passage. The woman leapt up as though shot and, without a backward glance, ran away down the corridor, turning a corner. Billy was after her.

He arrived in time to see her hurriedly knock at a suite door and enter it at once. 'It's impossible, my lady,' he caught her saying.

'You stupid woman!' the bellowed reply came whipping through the closing door. 'Do I have to do everything myself?' The door snapped shut.

Billy turned away, only to find himself engulfed by the party of merry-makers.

'Ah, just the chap. We seem to have had a bit of an accident.'

Two young men and a girl locked arms around him and started to pull against each other. It was a harsh ring-a-roses. The girl laughed, rich and fruity. She had the face of an angel and a dress of glinting silver.

'Go on, Milly, show him!'

Billy, jostled, stared at the girl; her hair a dazzling swirl of blonde, her figure a picture in a magazine. *She must be a Motion Picture star.*

Catching the young boy's look, she waggled a silver sandal in front of his nose. A broken heel dangled. She laughed and laughed, the biggest joke in all the world.

'Get it mended, there's a good fellow.' A young man pushed Billy away with a hard shove.

'Suite 1004. And bring us a couple of bottles of fizz while you're about it. Chop, chop.'

The girl swayed dangerously, the two men strapped themselves to her side. They turned as a unit to unlock the door and, pushing and shoving, piled into the suite.

Billy started to move off down the corridor when he heard the girl's giggling suddenly stop, followed by what he thought was a whimper. He rushed back to the open door. It slammed shut in his face.

The hush of the corridor returned.

'There's someone I know on the ship!' Lily almost fell into the cabin in her rush to tell Johnnie. He looked up from his book and asked levelly, 'Who?'

'She's a horrible woman called Slocombe. I can't believe she's here on board! She's poison, Johnnie. If she were to discover—' The thought unbearable, she stood shaking, her face silver-pale in the electric light.

'First things first.' Johnnie took her hand and made her sit on the bunk. He could see she was frantic. 'Is she down here with us in steerage?' he asked, his voice calm.

'No, of course not, she's in first class!' she snapped. 'Billy Bottle saw her tonight. She was causing some sort of scene and—'

'Hush, darling.' Firmly he put his arm around her and was shocked to discover how badly she was trembling. 'I can understand what a fright you've had but you must remember there are a thousand passengers on this ship. Added to which this woman's travelling in another class altogether.'

He was relieved to see her give a tiny nod. 'Sorry,' she said, 'I didn't mean to bite your head off. It's just I got such a fright.'

Johnnie said nothing in reply. He felt the terrible disquiet he'd managed to control over the last three days instantly flare into life. He blamed himself, allowing Lily to go wandering round the boat. He'd recognised her claustrophobia, fearing the consequences if she remained in the tiny cabin, but he had trusted she'd be too scared and preoccupied to talk to another passenger… What a bloody fool! The very thing they'd feared had happened; she'd discovered an old acquaintance. Albeit many decks above.

Quietly he said, 'Tell me about this woman.'

'Her grandmother and mine were friends – old schoolfriends. And because Lavinia was an only child her grandmother was eager for her to meet other children the same age. We really only met if I came to London in the holidays.'

'How old were you?'

'I first met her when I was about eight. I never liked her. Even if she lost at Snakes and Ladders she'd give me a Chinese burn.'

Johnnie couldn't help smiling.

'Oh, I know it sounds pathetic but she's a terrible bully.'

'Go on.'

'Well, one Easter holidays I was told there was going to be an enormous treat. We were going to the opera at Covent Garden for Lavinia's birthday. I didn't really want to go because, even at ten years old, I found Lavinia utterly hateful. But they said her cousin was going to be there – Harriet. And of course she turned out to be adorable.'

'Which is why,' said Johnnie, realising, 'she's still one of your best friends.'

'Exactly. Well, the minute Harriet and I met we got on like a house on fire. And Lavinia, of course, was livid.'

Quickly, Lily recounted the story of the birthday opera and

the discovery that Lavinia's pearl bracelet had been 'stolen'.

'Of course, a maid found the wretched bracelet two weeks later in a drawer in Lavinia's bedroom. Naturally, Lavinia could offer no explanation as to how it had got there.'

'But why?' asked Johnnie. 'Why did she pretend it had been stolen?'

'To get back at Harriet. She was jealous of her, I suppose. Not that Harriet was prettier, she wasn't. Just happier. Until Lavinia accused her – and then the child got ill and for years wouldn't go out or meet people. Her nerves, they said. But I always thought it was Lavinia's doing. Even at ten years of age she could pick her prey – always the most vulnerable, always the ones unable to stand up for themselves. In Harriet's case she was Lavinia's poor cousin – oh, yes, Lavinia was always clever at making her accusations plausible. Harriet was poor therefore she needed to steal.'

'She picked on her because she was poor?'

'Partly but also because she was happy. I don't think Lavinia could cope with anyone being happy.'

'And when the bracelet was found, was Lavinia punished?'

'Not on that occasion as far as I know. But some years later, after a string of petty thefts, she was actually caught red-handed trying to play the same trick at a weekend house party.'

'What happened?'

'Well, let's say she was apprehended before the crime was actually perpetrated.' Lily couldn't help smiling.

'By you, you mean? You were there?'

She nodded. 'I found her going through the jewellery case of a fellow guest.'

'Did you tell anyone?'

'I told the people whose house party it was and they told her father. I made jolly sure Lavinia was seriously rattled. And to that extent, I suppose I retrieved Harriet's honour. Certainly from that day on Lavinia has heartily loathed me. What was so extraordinary, I don't think she even thought she was guilty. That's what makes her so dangerous – she has absolutely no moral sense.' The memory of Lavinia's shocking fury at the moment of squalid discovery came back to her; she sat filled with terrible fear. 'My God, she was angry. I don't think I've ever seen such hatred in anyone's face.'

Johnnie reached for her hand and held it. 'What happened then?'

'Lavinia's father decided his daughter's kleptomaniac tendencies were proving a little inconvenient – by then, you see, she'd been caught elsewhere, reported to the police and managed to get herself a police record – so it was agreed by the family she should be packed off to be "finished" in Germany. As always, the whole thing was swept under the carpet and Lavinia got away with it once again.'

'Well, not quite,' said Johnnie. 'She'd got herself a police record. I wonder how many people in her circle are aware of that?'

He leant forward and, opening a little cupboard between the bunks, got out a bottle of whisky. 'Come on, we need a stiffener.'

'Mrs Webb will be here in a minute—'

'Oh, no, Lily, why?'

'Because I was just telling her about Nickie and these two boys arrived and told us about Lavinia and I really feel she shouldn't be wandering round the boat with only half the story. Mrs Webb, I mean.' She dribbled to a close. 'Sorry.'

'Darling, it's fine. It's just that you need some sleep – you look completely done in.'

'For some reason, Lady Slocombe seems to have got it in for Nurse Grossman, Captain, and as far as I can make out there's no evidence to support her accusation. Added to which the doc seemed quite concerned about the young woman. The poor lass couldn't stop crying.'

In the captain's cabin, First Officer Trinder was reporting the theft of Lady Slocombe's diamond bracelet.

'And Lord Clairmont?'

'Pretty het up, sir. Refuses to even countenance the charges. I managed to reassure him you'd take full control of the matter and said I felt all charges would be dropped?' The first officer flipped the end of the sentence into a question.

Captain Henshaw nodded but said nothing. He didn't like thieving on his ship; it created a shimmer of anarchy. He made a decision. 'Inform his lordship I'll be happy to see him at nine o'clock tomorrow morning as he suggests. I'll see Lady Slocombe an hour later.'

He dismissed his first officer but his peace of mind had been disturbed; reluctantly, he closed his book. He'd been enjoying his pipe and a few chapters of *Ivanhoe* when First Officer Trinder had knocked. Now he sat staring into space, the only movement in the cabin a thin wisp of smoke rising from his pipe.

Although Captain Henshaw had neither the international reputation nor the knighthood of some of his colleagues, he knew himself to be respected and, in some quarters, feared. Having started in sail, rising from a humble bellboy, he was more than able to handle stoker and duke alike, no amount of Millionaire's Gold buying a place at his table if he chose otherwise.

Alone now in his quarters, he mulled over the theft and made a decision.

Tonight he would leave matters be. Tomorrow morning, if there were no further developments, he'd call for Billy Bottle, his most reliable ears and eyes within the ship; a collaboration that both man and boy kept secret. He'd get the lad to watch the various players in the game.

Captain Henshaw relit his pipe. Opening his Walter Scott, he smoothed the page and settled back once more in his chair.

As Mrs Webb and Freddie entered their cabin, Anthea sighed in her sleep and turned to the wall. Lying on an upper bunk, an old knitted monkey squashed up against her soft pink face, the child was making bubbly little snores.

The other occupant, Barney Webb, looked up and, with a chuck of his head, said to his mother, 'She's flat out.' He returned to his paper; he was catching up on a couple of back copies of *The Winning Post*.

Mrs Webb filled the cabin, taking up both space and light. She sank down onto the lower bunk opposite her son. 'You all right, Barn?' Oh, her legs were giving her gyp.

'Aye. That Donald O'Dea's on board,' he said, never taking his eye from the sporting news.

'No! You mean the singer?'

'Aye. On't way to 'ighest-paid concert tour ever.'

'What, in America?'

'Aye.' Barney turned the page. '*And* we 'ad a theft up top.'

'I know, I 'eard.'

'Word is, they've got an idea who the culprit is.' Barney said no more.

Mrs Webb looked at Freddie. The lad stood with his eyes closed, sleep so near. 'Wash your face now, come on.' He suffered a quick wipe of a flannel and then bundled up into his sister's bunk – the children fitted together, two jigsaw pieces – and was out.

'All that fresh air, eh?' Mrs Webb yawned. Her bunk beckoned. Lovely. But first she must pop to the Valleys' cabin, as promised. She was weary but, if she was honest, keen to get the rest of the story.

'Keep an eye on things, Barney. I won't be long.'

Her son grunted; the report on the 2.30 at Aintree held him.

She stepped out into the corridor, her eagerness to be with her new friends overcoming her tiredness and motoring her away from the cabin.

Matty lay in Lord Henry's arms. He was watching over her as she slept. Every so often, she would call out from the depths of her drugged dream until the doctor's sedative would take hold once again and subdue her. Over and over he thought through the terrible business of the evening. What in heaven's name had possessed the Slocombe woman to make such a vicious charge?

He looked down at the young nurse. Her face was chalk-white, her lips slightly grey. And he thought of her face usually so full of life, remembering how he had seen her that very first time in Africa at the embassy picnic, three years ago...

'You've gone very pale,' he'd heard a voice say. 'Would you

mind if I took your pulse?' Opening his eyes, there, dark against the sun, was a girl, a nurse. She proceeded to kneel over him and check his pulse. 'My name's Matilda Grossman by the way. Everyone calls me Matty.'

The last thing he'd wanted was to go on the wretched embassy picnic. All he longed for was to settle down with Mr Evelyn Waugh and his *Decline and Fall*, the book having newly arrived from England. The fact he felt severely out of sorts he chose to ignore. Once by the lake, shaded from the aggressive African sun, he'd been happy enough to leave the others to swim and play. Splashes, screams, laughter...and he'd fallen asleep. Now here she was, what was her name – Maddy? Mary? – commandeering the only car and driving him straight to the native hospital.

There, all he could recall later was the rain tipping down, drumming on the corrugated roof. Drumming in his head. And the steaming heat. And the joy of a cool, damp cloth. And Nurse Grossman – *Matty*, that was it – and an African doctor, and a terrible thirst...

After lots of water, he began to feel better. So, of course, he wasn't going to hang around getting under everyone's feet. And, yes, he promised Nurse Grossman, he'd see the embassy doctor if he felt ill again... And, yes, he'd go straight home.

And he had. Falling again into the deepest sleep...

Monday morning and I'm better, he thought. He jumped on his bicycle, to be met by early morning traffic tangling all the way to Government House. A camel, an overturned bullock cart, people shouting, shouting... And again, the muggy rains blanketing down. He didn't feel so good but he was late and His Excellency would blow a gasket. In his office, his secretary greeted him, 'Good lord, old man, you all right?' And then no more…

Whispers. And the thirst again…

He opened his eyes. A fan was weakly turning above him, waving fetid air across his face. Mulligan and Livingstone were looking down at him. What on earth were his garden boys doing here?

Then a damp cloth on his forehead and a nurse – Nurse Grossman? No, not today. But still the thirst. Worse and worse…

The diagnosis, a couple of weeks later, was quite a relief; a 'cause' for his wretched tiredness and extraordinary thirsts had been found. In fact, he left the consultation quite light-hearted, the Embassy doc skirting round the seriousness of his condition with a fussily jovial approach. 'Diabetes Mellitus, old man. In the eleventh century it would have been diagnosed by "piss-tasters"! These chaps would have drunk your piss to see if it tasted of honey. *Mellitus*, you see, Latin word for honey.' Henry had departed none the wiser except for knowing he had 'the best of the chronic diseases – clean, seldom unsightly and uncontagious.'

'I'm Matilda Grossman, do you remember me? We met at the picnic,' she said when they had met by chance in the hospital corridor.

At a loss for something to say, dazed from his diagnosis, he asked politely, 'Have you come far?'

'Actually, Harrow on the Hill,' and they'd both burst out laughing.

It was this chance meeting that had helped him face his condition and realise it was not going to go away. ('Not so "chance", Henry. I'd been waiting for you, hovering about like an idiot outside the doctor's office.') She had shown him how to deal with his illness, gently explaining away the terrors, strictly keeping him to his diet.

'Well, yes, it may be life-threatening but it's also susceptible to treatment,' she'd counselled. 'Insulin's a new magic potion. And count yourself lucky. Before its discovery you'd only have had five years to live.'

'That's cheered me up,' he'd replied grimly.

'Well, you could be African and then you wouldn't get it at all. It's strictly Whites only.'

But it had done the trick; he'd used his newly acquired knowledge to fend off his fears. And because of her, the seeming imprisonment of diabetes had actually bestowed on him a new-found freedom. She had given him the confidence to break away from the safety of his self-imposed world of books and the stifling social round of Government House, leaving his Embassy colleagues amazed at the new vigour with which he began to lead his life. But with these reactions came also the whispering gossip. 'I believe there's some girl. Not quite *comme il faut*. Harrow-on-the-Hill, if you get my meaning – not really one of us.'

'*And* isn't he spending rather too much time at that native hospital?'

It had been here, one day, he had seen another side of Matty, her face closed, her expression unreadable, tenderly holding the small body of Benjamin Mboweni. 'Five years old, pleurisy brought on by malnutrition.' And he'd seen her fury. 'Even the Bible says there is such a thing as righteous anger, Henry.'

Yes, Matty was right. Righteous anger.

He sat up carefully so as not to wake the young woman from her drugged sleep. Anger, that was what was required.

This evil bloody Slocombe woman must be stopped; the whole vicious mess must be cleared up. Tomorrow he would talk to the captain in no uncertain terms, and Matty would be vindicated.

Very carefully, Henry lay down once again alongside his nurse. He wanted to keep the night-watch so as to be fully awake for when she finally stirred.

CHAPTER TEN

London. November 1921

The small man leant against the gas-lamp, the mournful sounds from his mouth-organ irritating the passers-by. A cap at his feet lay empty; in it, not one coin.

As Johnnie hurried for his train, it wasn't the sound of the mouth-organ that caught his attention but the pathetic tray of matchboxes slung round the man's neck – and the empty cap. He felt a nick at his conscience, dropped a penny and walked on.

Roused, the little man called after him, 'Thanks, mate.'

Johnnie stopped, turned and stared. 'Sam? Sam Valley?'

The two men sat in the dark on a wall behind an all-night coffee stand and watched, unseeing, the traffic sombrely make its way round Hyde Park Corner. The coffee was milky and sweet. There was a queue of taxis parked alongside the stand. On the night air from inside the cabs, wisps of laughter and the murmur of a kiss rose up, the drivers standing apart in the yellow gas-light, ignoring their 'fares', grateful for the paid break.

Johnnie and Sam drank their sweet coffee and talked. They'd not met for three years. Since the Armistice.

'My Flora and a Scottish sapper—'

'Sam, I'm so sorry—'

'Couldn't believe it, all them letters at the Front from Flora, all that time... When I found out about the pair of 'em, I ups and leaves them to it.'

'But your farm?'

'They can have it. They give me a bit but I don't want their charity. For all the good it will do them anyway; farming's a mug's game now, I reckon.'

'That's right enough.' Johnnie knocked his pipe against the wall and carefully started to repack it from an old leather pouch. 'Things not too bright down our way, either. What with Harvey and his team of workers gone.' Harvey, Edge, Larney – a spin bowler, a wicket-keeper and a batsman, stars of the village cricket team. The green not even mowed these last three years, Johnnie realised.

Both men sat silent, locked together in memories.

Larney, a big man, a ploughman, his sobbing pitiable from No Man's Land as, trapped in the glutinous mud, one leg torn off and one arm shattered by a shell, he'd called out to them, 'Haven't you got a bullet for me?' All through the night. Larney the last to survive, crying out, the others stranded beside him in No Man's Land already silenced. When the sky had lightened, Johnnie and Sam, the platoon's only survivors, could see no sign of anything. Man, horse or gun. All had been sucked into the mud, drowned in a sea of churned earth.

'Dear God, they won't be able to make us do it again, will they?'

Sam shook his head. 'I tell 'em, "We weren't at the Front, we were in front of it."'

'Why did we stand for it?'

''Cos we were mugs, mate. We believed the lying bastards. Military breakthrough, my eye. What did they know? We was the ones there while they hid, all snug in their bleedin' quarters, with their brandy and batmen. And then we get back to Blighty and the family start asking questions, and you can't tell 'em, 'cos they'd never believe it. They'd never imagine—'

On his return, Johnnie had steadfastly done his duty as officer of his battalion and master of the estate. In every cottage he visited, he'd found mourning and misery, no one seeming able to rally, a dilatory emptiness left by the release from years of tension waiting for the telegraph boy to knock. Every day he made the rounds. Every day he wrote letters of condolence. And every day it seemed to rain.

At night, holed up in his farmhouse, a man with no family of his own and now few friends, he tried to assuage the dreadful nightmares with a bottle of brandy. And his books. Trying to close down his mind...

His nervous breakdown, when it came, was in London on a tube train. They'd been stuck in a tunnel and suddenly a terrible strangling fear had welled up – he'd thought they were under gas-attack – and he'd passed out. Afterwards, all he could remember was a young woman sitting opposite, panic in her face, offering him a handkerchief and her seat. He'd used the handkerchief without thinking and realised tears were streaming down his face. At the next station the woman had scampered away, relieved to escape.

Neurasthenia, otherwise known as 'shell-shock', the doctor

said, 'an inner migration to madness'. But this diagnosis brought him no comfort, the guilt at having survived calling up only reproach from the spectres in his dreams. He'd somehow escaped the arbitrariness of death, but Johnnie hated his life as a survivor. The dead ruled the living. And concealing his grief, all alone, he found no remedy for it.

The rambling old farmhouse, which before the war had been the hub of the village, teeming with gossip and farming life, now stood silent, the only sound, night after night, the endless drip of water into enamel buckets. No Harvey to mend the roof and lag the pipes. Harvey, his estate manager, his good sergeant, Captain of the Freston First Eleven.

And out on the silent farmland no longer his team of workers – the fields barren, the rush to war having left the crops unsown. Such young boys, all. His entire battalion, except for himself and Sam, drowned in the sucking clay of Passchendaele.

For over a year he attempted to make a go of the farm, but the fields remained unyielding. And at the unveiling of the War Memorial, when the little town of Freston gathered together in its loss, he was finally forced to acknowledge defeat. He could not farm alone. As the Last Post sounded and he dropped his salute, Johnnie looked away from the bright new memorial cross with its twenty-nine names etched proud and raw – lives, he noted from the inscription, 'given' in conflict, not 'taken' – and vowed to a God he now knew for certain wasn't there, *This is the last time I will ever wear this uniform.*

He watched the group of widows and orphans, under their dripping umbrellas, slowly picking their way home. These wives and sweethearts, mothers and children. And where were the homes fit for the memory of these heroes, heroes of a slaughter called a righteous fight for King and Country?

He would have to do something. He had survived; they were his responsibility. And just in the nick of time, on a trip to London, Johnnie heard the mournful tune of Sam Valley's mouth-organ and, for whatever reason, he didn't hurry past.

SS *Etoile*. Friday, midnight

The light in the little cabin seemed suddenly to become temperamental, it flared and flickered. The din from the engines, however, remained constant.

Johnnie could see Lily was definitely calmer, soothed further – it seemed to him – by the arrival of Mrs Webb. He smiled at the sight of the two women perched together on the lower bunk like a pair of mismatched schoolgirls, whilst he sat cramped on a stool, sideways on. There was an almost carnival air between the three of them.

'And while young Nickie was being rescued from his school, where were you, Mr Valley?' asked Mrs Webb. Though no doubt in some discomfort, her bulky frame parked on the edge of the lower bunk, her expression was rapt.

Johnnie was about to reply when, up above, the boy turned in his sleep. Wriggling around in his sheets, he gave a low moan and the three grown-ups held their breath. The mighty engines churned the ship through the strong night seas; it was the only sound in the cabin. The small boy sighed and lay still, deep asleep once more.

Very quietly, Johnnie carried on with the story.

'I was laying a false trail. I drove Lily's car up to the North of England and left it at Preston Station. Her brother has a farm up that way, in the Trough of Bowland.'

'We're hoping,' said Lily, 'that if someone spots the car they'll think Nickie and I are hiding up there with him.'

'A ruddy terrible trip it was too, Mrs Webb. Rain, sleet and snow the whole way. Plus an agonisingly slow milk train for my return journey. Didn't think I'd make the boat in time.'

England. February 1933

Once again came the heaving creak and clunk as the milk train pulled out of the station. Had it said Matlock? Johnnie couldn't see; no moon, no lights.

Chapel-en-le-Frith, Doveholes Tunnel, Peak Forest Station, Miller's Dale, Chee Dale. *Once upon a time I could remember them all*, he thought.

He tried to settle back against the hard seat. Perhaps some sleep now. But he knew it was impossible. The stop-starting of the train at every halt and station made for little continuity of thought, let alone sleep. If only he had thought to buy some sandwiches at Preston Station. Questions kept going round and round his head. Had he put Lily's car in too obvious a place beside the station's ticket office? Would this train stop completely and the ship at Southampton sail without him? And without him, how could Lily and Nickie cope on their own?

He held his watch under the beige glow of the carriage

light. 3.45 a.m. Dear God, this journey was taking forever.

The train wheezed again to a stop. Cromford. A swinging lamp and a station master, his face hidden in a bundle of wool with only the peak of his cap jutting out. The burly man stamped his feet, supervising the rattling milk churns, their clanging thuds muffled by snow. Thick snow now, Johnnie saw, here in Cromford.

Cromford. He knew the name. And not just as part of a list of stations. Ah yes, Sarah and he had spent a night here. Small hotel and a monstrously lumpy bed. The Greyhound, Cromford. That had been it.

A whistle. He peered out of the window in a vain attempt to catch a glimpse of the small town slipping away into the snowy darkness, to catch hold of the memory.

Cromford and Darley Dale. They'd walked all over, Sarah and he. Walked and walked. She nineteen, he twenty-one. All through their honeymoon. And Darley churchyard with its great yew, two thousand years old. They had been so young, felt so young. And the stifling shyness...she'd never lost that.

In his mind's eye, he caught Sarah's face, an unexpected memory. And the clarity of it was so powerful that the rocking carriage was filled with the presence of her. *Sarah. I never really knew you. But I did love you, your pretty shining face so trusting. But, oh, my love, I couldn't save you. And I couldn't save our child. At my side, all the doctor said, over and over, was, 'I'm so sorry, I'm so sorry,' as we stared down at your two sleeping faces. Dead.*

Forgive me, Sarah. Forgive me.

And with Sarah dead these twenty years, he started to cry, as the little train rocked its way round the hills and climbed slowly down onto the wide plain of middle England. Tears, and the recognition of his enormous grief at the sore, sore loss of this, his first love, and their child.

He leant against the leather and horsehair of the railway-seat, finally full of emptiness. *Sarah*, he said, *I have a new love. Is such a thing allowed? Have I abandoned you?*

And Sarah said, No, my dear, you've abandoned no one. You've kept faith with the memory of me and the child all these years. Live no more in sadness. Live with the happy memory of our young lives and not with the sadness of our deaths. And he thought, *Why have I allowed myself to think about our honeymoon now? For the first time since she died.*

Slowly, he pulled back the veil of amnesia. And there, raw and young, lay the sweet innocent joy of their courtship and their married life. So young, so short. Two years only.

If Sarah saw me now, she wouldn't know me.

And I don't know me; this old man of forty-five, with a heart newly beating. My poor old heart locked away these many long years, forced to beat again.

And with Sarah's permission, he thought. *Oh, my darling Lily. Don't let me ever lose you.*

CHAPTER ELEVEN

Mayfair, London. Friday night, March 1933

Thelma Duttine rose from her dressing table and crossed to the long mirror. In the distance a doorbell rang. She smiled; Charles was early. Good.

She studied her image critically, turning backwards and forwards to the mirror. Yes, she had chosen well from her shop's new collection; a black crêpe de Chine sheath with a tantalisingly low back, the flowing skirt tricked out with two exquisitely embroidered birds of paradise. The willowy outline was completed by a long sash tied in a bow at the side and, from one shoulder, dancing black ostrich feathers which she had coated with glycerine to make them appear even more lustrous. And she was proud, so proud of her figure; only she alone knowing the agony of her addiction to 'banting' and its restrictive diet of lean meat, fish and dry toast. But it was all worth it. For, with her short red-blonde hair softly waved, she knew she looked stunning, the ensemble cunningly distracting from any accurate guess as to her age.

Oh! The anticipation for tonight thrilled. Three years of silent waiting and secret planning.

She unlocked a little drawer beside her bed and drew out a small black and red lacquer box. Opening it, she took out a slim silver syringe and three small paper packets, which she held one by one to the light.

There was a discreet tap at the door. 'Sir Charles Sutton has arrived, madam.'

'Tell him I will be down in a moment, Marie.' He could wait; she was not to be rushed now her ambition was so nearly achieved, her patience about to be rewarded.

She crossed back to her dressing table and unstoppered a small decanter, pouring brandy into a tumbler to which she started to add half of one of the packets of cocaine powder.

Not too much, carefully, carefully. No syringe now. Later, perhaps...

She hummed gently as she lovingly measured out the amount, taking pride in her knowledge; she knew exactly what she was doing. For Thelma, ever since she had been a young nurse in the war and seen the spell cast by the drug, had turned its effect to her advantage. With ambition and discipline, she had made herself so acceptable and ultimately indispensable to the rich young set she had hitherto only longingly read about in her magazines. How clever she had been. How strong. When all about lay stupefied, she was the one, clear-headed, who had taken the taxi to Savory and Moore's in St James's, returning with the packets of 'jolly old chlorers'. She was the one who had listened to her new girlfriends as they doped themselves with brandy and sal volatile, and watched the young men, war-bludgeoned, lace their minds with cocaine. By the end of the war Thelma had got what she wanted: the power of many secrets. And an income.

Which was why, although the world was pleased to think Sir Charles Sutton had provided his mistress with her discreet Mayfair dress shop, Thelma knew her vigorously maintained financial independence to be one of the many sources of sexual challenge between them. Charles Sutton had only two things Thelma Duttine wanted: his title, and his country estate of Melsham.

She smiled. Tonight she knew she looked everything Lady Sutton and the mistress of Melsham should look.

Holding the tumbler up to the light, she watched the powder dissolve. She drank the mixture in one and slipped a violet cachou into her mouth. Her breath must be sweet no trace of brandy. Charles could drink himself into oblivion but he hated the smell of liquor on his women.

She felt her blood begin to sing.

The child, Nicholas, might represent the sentimental memory of his marriage, a Gordian knot that tied him to the dreary Lily. But now the woman had vanished – front-page news for no less than three days – *and*, so it seemed, had the boy, though this second fact Charles didn't wish to have trumpeted from the front of every newspaper. Thelma knew how much the man loathed discussion of his private affairs, and if it became known that Lady Sutton had collected the boy from his school before both of them had vanished into thin air, it could lead to a lot of awkward questions. No, for now he wished to play the grieving husband, deluding the world that his wife was suffering from amnesia. The boy's disappearance he wanted kept secret. Except with the police, of course.

But, truth be told, Thelma couldn't have cared less where

the pair had gone or what had happened to them, except that the timing of their disappearance could not have been more delightfully perfect for what she had planned.

She glanced one last time at her image in the long mirror, noting with satisfaction the opaque glitter flooding her eyes. Tonight, she and Charles would dine at the Berkeley but forgo the nightclub. For, as she had counselled him, the grieving husband of a missing wife must not be seen to be indulging in too much pleasure.

Thelma smiled, the cat with a saucer overflowing with cream. Charles and she could return to her flat in Half Moon Street a couple of hours earlier than usual. It suited her plans beautifully.

She dropped the little red and black box into her evening bag.

SS *Etoile*. Friday night

'Pardon me for prying,' said Mrs Webb. 'But d'you think your husband knows you've run away together?'

'Almost certainly, Mrs Webb,' replied Lily.

'And how long has he known about—' The woman ran out of steam on this most delicate subject.

Lily came to her rescue. 'About the two of us?'

The woman nodded. 'Not wishing to appear nosey, like.'

'Mrs Webb, if you only knew the relief of having someone to tell. Don't you agree, darling?' She turned to Johnnie and reached for his hand. *Whoever would have guessed this woman would be our confidante,* he thought. But he could see Lily liked her, and her instinct with people was usually pretty spot-on.

'You bet, Mrs Webb,' he said. 'This cabin's very small when one's trying to remain calm in the face of adversity. We're very pleased to have you on board, so to speak.' The big woman smiled, and Johnnie saw an unexpected youthfulness in the broad battered face.

'To answer your question, Mrs Webb, my husband found out about Johnnie and I last summer.' Lily hesitated. 'It was a very difficult occasion.'

Her head dropped. Johnnie gently stroked her hand. Her openness had surprised him; he knew only too well the painful cost in talking of this. As he stroked her hand, he turned it over and saw the palm with its strange smooth plasticity. The scar of that final meeting, the terrible burn.

For a moment, no one said anything. Much to his relief, Mrs Webb had the sensitivity to ask no questions.

In a brighter voice, Lily said, 'Up until then, Johnnie and I realised we were trapped in a sort of limbo. We knew the minute I asked my husband for a divorce he'd smell a rat.' She gave him a twinkling smile. 'No offence intended, darling.'

'None taken, I assure you.' *And that*, he thought, *is why I love you. Never, ever self-pity.* 'You see, Mrs Webb,' he carried on, feeling permission granted by Lily's candour, 'Lily had gone along with the status quo for so many years, coming to terms with her husband's lady-friends etc, that if, out of the blue, she'd suggested a change of any sort, he'd have instantly become suspicious.'

'His lady-friends?' blurted Mrs Webb, despite herself.

'Oh, yes. In theory, Lily's husband might still be living in the marital abode but in reality he'd all but moved in with his lady-friend of many years' standing. One Mrs Thelma Duttine.' He heard his voice, even and matter-of-fact, as he talked of the man he hated most in all the world.

'But the hypocrisy!' Mrs Webb's voice was shocked; she looked extremely put out. *God bless you*, he thought.

'Ah yes, indeed, Mrs Webb. But Thelma Duttine is very much a fact in Charles Sutton's life, a fact that is well known to the circle in which he moves. But sadly not a fact that can be used in law to obtain Lily her divorce and custody of her child. He's told Lily in no uncertain terms that if she asks for a divorce citing Mrs Duttine, he will drag her through the courts and, because of me, leave her reputation in tatters. Thus ensuring she will never, ever gain custody of Nickie.'

'As I said earlier this evening, Mrs Webb,' continued Lily quietly, 'my husband is making me choose between Johnnie and my son. And he is prepared to spend every penny of his considerable fortune to make sure that, although I may have one, I will never have both.'

'Well,' said Mrs Webb, 'I've never heard the like.' For once silenced by the injustice of it all, the woman sat shaking her head.

Johnnie and Lily sat silent as well, their story told.

Eventually, Mrs Webb looked up. 'I'll do anything and everything I can to 'elp you good people on yer way.' Johnnie could hear the emotion in her voice.

'Thank you,' said Lily. She leant and patted the woman's hand.

Feeling a further gesture of thanks was required, he pulled open the bedside drawer and once again produced the bottle of whisky.

'You'll join us, I hope, Mrs Webb. Only tooth mugs, I'm afraid.'

'Don't mind if I do, Mr— Oh, I'm afraid I don't know yer name now.'

'Actually it's Sturridge but let's stick to "Valley" for the purposes of this trip, eh?' He smiled at the woman, who positively beamed back, and handed her a mug. 'Chin, chin,' he said.

'But what are yer doing for passports and the like?'

He caught Lily's smile. 'All a bit of a palaver but I was in Intelligence during the war and, luckily, kept up a couple of contacts.' He leant forward and whispered, 'Forgery, Mrs Webb.'

The big woman's eyes popped with surprise and delight, and she dipped into her mug.

After a bit, her head bobbed up and she looked at the sleeping child. 'The poor little mite. He must of been bored stiff in here, all day long. And you both poorly.'

'Ah,' grinned Lily, 'seasickness seemed to be the best excuse to keep us tucked out of sight. We're actually as fit as fiddles. But poor old Nickie, he's had a miserable time of it. It's not the best place for a ten-year-old to be cooped up.'

'I don't think he'll be wanting another game of chess in a fair while,' remarked Johnnie.

Mrs Webb shook her head. 'Well I never, what a tale.' He could hear the wonder in her voice and he topped up her mug; she didn't demur. Her face had taken on a not unbecoming flush as she now settled back. 'And talking of tales, Mrs Valley, Billy Bottle had a bit more to tell us after you left. Seems that young nurse who was accused had a bad turn and collapsed. They had to get a doctor to her. Serious, by all accounts.'

'No, please don't say that!' There was a desperation in Lily's voice as she rose to her feet in a sudden movement. 'I knew it, I knew it.' She stood leaning back against the door, her eyes closed.

'My God, Lily, are you all right?'

'No, of course I'm not!' she snapped.

No one spoke. The silence hung awkwardly.

'I'm sorry,' she said after a moment. 'The strain. Oh Gawd.' She pulled a face. 'These things are sent to try us but why *now*?'

'You're talking about Lavinia, aren't you?' he said hesitantly.

Lily sighed.

'I think you'd better explain.' He nodded at Mrs Webb.

Lily sank down onto the bunk again. 'As you guessed earlier, Mrs Webb, I do know this woman, Lavinia Slocombe. She's a particularly nasty piece of work who I've had the misfortune to know for more years than I care to remember.' Johnnie could hear the deep weariness in her voice. 'You can take it from me, if she's picked this young woman as her prey, she won't be satisfied until the girl's reputation is utterly destroyed. She'll ruin her life.'

'No!' gasped Mrs Webb.

Lily turned to the large woman, her face still and serious. 'I'm not exaggerating. This woman takes a delight in destroying people's lives – she seems to relish the challenge in making as much mischief as possible, causing terrible misery and then getting away with it absolutely scot-free.' She looked down. 'I do, however, know something about this woman that would immediately exonerate the nurse.'

'Well, we must tell the girl at once,' burst out Mrs Webb.

'If only it were that simple.'

'Why?'

'Because Johnnie and I are doing everything in our power to remain hidden away down here.'

'You're talking about her police record, aren't you?' Johnnie cut in.

The question remained unanswered for suddenly the little boy, as if to remind them of the importance of secrecy, turned in his bunk and rootled once more in the sheets. After a moment, he settled.

It was when Lily started talking again – a new firmness in her voice – that Johnnie knew she'd made a decision. 'You're right, Mrs Webb, I must talk to this girl. I just need to see her for five minutes, after all.'

'Lily, you must be out of your mind to even consider it!' He put his hands on her shoulders and turned her to him. 'If you go up to first class, it'd be just our luck you'd run into a whole string of people you know.' He was thoroughly exasperated. 'I thought secrecy was what this whole ruddy trip was all about!'

She looked defeated. 'I know, I know.'

Suddenly, Mrs Webb spoke in tiny excited whisper. 'What if we could get you up to first class? And you were invisible!'

They both turned to her.

'After all, what the eye doesn't look for, the eye doesn't see. And no one knows you're aboard. Except for yours truly.'

Lady Lavinia sat at her dressing table softening her hands with a lotion of her own making; glycerine and rose-water in equal parts with four or five drops of benzoin.

She was extremely proud of her hands. For such a big-boned

woman they were surprisingly small and youthful and to make sure they would always remain that way, every night she religiously rubbed into them a little olive oil followed by a soupçon of her fragrant lotion.

Behind her, Timms busied herself softly around the lavish suite. With no outfit to be worn twice on the voyage by her mistress, she efficiently took each of the day's discarded garments and placed those not in need of either dry-cleaning or pressing between sheets of tissue-paper, stuffing each sleeve in readiness for re-packing. Then, pulling out a needle stowed behind the lapel of her navy jacket, she threaded it and carefully started to tack down the pleats of the tea-dress Lady Slocombe had worn earlier that afternoon. She had news but it could wait, her mistress's hand-softening ritual was sacrosanct and never to be interrupted. She watched her Ladyship as, with closed eyes, she lightly rocked back and forth, softening the ridiculous child-like hands. Thirty years in the service of this woman had taught Timms patience and endurance. Oh yes, she could wait.

Silently, the two women went about their nightly rituals, their lives plaited together with secrets, each with an extraordinary hold over the other, each needing the other's silence. Strangely, it gave them a perverse sense of relaxation in the other's company. They didn't have to pretend; they knew each other too well.

Her hand-softening ritual at an end, Lady Slocombe drew on a pair of white cotton gloves and replaced the ornate silver top on the lotion's small cut-glass bottle. She looked at Timms behind her, reflected in the mirror.

Timms raised her head from her sewing and met her mistress's eye. 'If I am not very much mistaken, my lady, I think I have just seen Lady Sutton.'

There was a crash of glass. Lady Slocombe had turned with such speed that the sleeve of her dressing gown had caught the glass powder-dish and sent it scudding across the table-top and onto the floor. The carpet looked as though it had been flour-bombed. Timms leant forward to clear it up.

'Leave it!' hissed her Ladyship. 'Lady *Lily* Sutton?' She had gone very still. She looked unmasked and dangerous.

'Yes, my lady.'

'Where?'

'In steerage, my lady.'

'What on earth—? With Sir Charles?'

'I didn't see him. She spent the evening talking to a loud common-looking fat woman,' stated Miss Timms, who prided herself both on the spareness of her figure and the gentility of her voice, its accent scrubbed clean of a south London childhood. 'I have enquired of a steward if they have a passenger in the name of Sutton and, for the exchange of a coin, he consulted his lists. She appears not to be on it. Not under that name, anyway.'

Lady Slocombe stared at her maid then looked away. 'Well, well, well, what's that nosey little Lily Sutton up to?' Her maid waited. 'Find out what name she's travelling under, Timms, we have to know. And anything else about her, anything else at all.'

'Yes, my lady.'

Lady Slocombe's eyes closed. Miss Timms knew her mistress was thinking, planning. 'Talk to that steward again. Go through those lists with a fine-tooth comb. Money, on this occasion, is no object. But do not make yourself a subject for any loose talk.'

'Yes, my lady.'

'And while you're about it, you had better read this.' Lady Slocombe leant into her capacious handbag and withdrew a folded copy of the day's *Poseidon Post*. 'According to this, Lady Sutton has managed to contract some kind of memory loss.' She handed the newspaper to her maid. 'You have much to do; you'd better get started.'

With a wave of her hand, she dismissed the hovering maid.

CHAPTER TWELVE

SS *Etoile*. Saturday morning, the small hours

Mrs Webb had departed their cabin at one-thirty. A plan of action in place, the two women had arranged to meet in the Webb cabin a few hours later at half-past six. 'Hardly worth going to bed,' Johnnie had muttered but neither woman chose to hear.

This plan bodes ill, he thought, but said nothing. Instead, he poured himself another whisky, removed the pipe from his lips and tapped it on his shoe. He didn't refill it – the space was too confined to smoke more than one – but looked across at Lily trying to compose a letter.

Through the black night, the ship sailed on and slowly he began to realise that, although at first she'd asked his advice as to what to write, for the last half-hour she hadn't spoken. Hunched over her writing case she sat silent, occasionally scribbling a line. Otherwise she was completely motionless, staring into space.

He felt a mounting sense of unease. It was the middle of

the night and he knew she was at her lowest ebb. After the shock of Lady Slocombe's presence on board, he wasn't sure how much more she could take.

Suddenly he sat up. Deep within himself, he'd felt his body turn ice-cold. *Oh Christ, no – not now!*

He waited with mounting panic.

And, sure enough, he recognised all his old symptoms leaping into life, one by one. There – there was the deep sense of unease uncontrollably turning to terror and, in response, his body breaking – immediately – into a wretched drenching sweat. *Damn!* He closed his eyes. His heart was beating terribly – and suddenly behind his eyes, the blinding frightening flashes. *Dear God, after all these years could the neurasthenia still bite so quickly? Then it had been the memory of a bloody battle, triggered by a motor car back-firing, a balloon popping...*

He looked across at Lily and desperately tried to even his breath, terrified she would hear him – or worse, he would call out. His heart was racing out of control and the adrenalin was rushing through his body. He must get out; the cabin walls were beginning to close in on him. *Oh dear God, no!* His heart was starting to pound again. With every bit of effort he could muster, he managed to say quite casually, 'Going for a spot of air.' Lily nodded, her head down in concentration.

He shot into the passageway. Holding onto a bulkhead, he stood, space whirling, lights flashing, trying to catch ragged breaths. The pain was flowering behind his eyes and he willed himself to count. The old training. The old training to counteract the fear. *Breathe. And two and three. Breathe. And two and three.* He could hear Doctor Addenbrooke counting him down, his riding crop slapping time against his army gaiters.

But now Johnnie's heart wouldn't stop racing, he couldn't rein in the terror. Sweat poured down his back. Air. He must reach the air. He stumbled along the passageway and pushed through a door.

On deck, the wind was so cold and hard, so unexpected, it banged the breath from him. He battled with all his remaining strength to the railings and stood holding tight, staring out at the black sea, urging his mind to nothing, fighting the fear, counting the breaths, counting…and felt the peak and the panic start to ebb away down the other side. But now, wretched and wrung out, he began to cry, the despair terrible, monumental. Dear God, what was he doing on this boat? What was he doing with this woman he didn't really know – and her pale cowed son?

Alone, he sobbed into the roaring wind until at last the need to cry left him. But the desolation remained, black, sightless. What was he doing here? Did he need – did he want – all these complications? His life was fine, no emotions. Why tamper with it? Perhaps a bit lonely but he had his books, his pigs. Above all, his life was calm and he'd kept the neurasthenia at bay.

He stared out at the sea. He couldn't face another onset of the illness; the thought terrified and depressed him. The dreary weeks of constant anxiety, the tremors and, worse, the bouts of unstaunchable tears. And Lily didn't know; he'd chosen not to tell her – he'd thought himself free, having suffered no attack for over three years. He felt utterly shocked that he was still so easily in its thrall. 'In my considered opinion,' Addenbrooke had intoned the last time, 'your condition, if it arises again, will be expedited by the removal to a nursing home where worries and too sympathetic friends can be excluded.' Johnnie remembered suppressing an enormous desire to laugh at the pompous old cove – until he remembered he was paying 10 guineas for this 'considered opinion'. 'Complete change, rest and tonics, Captain Sturridge, are the only cure for a sane and manageable life; the only way to escape this inner migration to madness...'

So, what was he doing here on a ship, turning his life upside down? Complete change certainly but hardly rest and tonics.

Lancashire. Christmas 1931

'Uncle Johnnie—'

'Good Lord, don't call me that. It makes me feel ancient.'

'What should I call you then, sir?'

'Certainly not "sir" either. Just Johnnie. How about it?'

'All right. Johnnie.'

He glanced at the boy beside him. They were driving into Preston to get Lily a Christmas present, her son very dismissive of the goods on offer at Uncle Hugh's local village shop.

'Johnnie.' The boy rolled this new grown-up name around, feeling its weight on his tongue, testing it for approval. He sat hunched in his seat, all ears and knobbly knees, freckles and sleepy eyes, unbelievably grown since Johnnie had last seen him – four months ago already – though the boy was still pale and small for his age. Now the Christmas holidays, they were all spending it on Hugh's farm in the Trough of Bowland. Charles Sutton remained far away in London.

'Johnnie?'

'Yes, old man.'

'Can I tell you the biggest secret in all the world?' Johnnie braced himself. 'I don't think there's a Father Christmas.' He could feel the boy staring at him, needing confirmation. Johnnie looked ahead, finding himself torn across this bridge between childhood and beyond.

'Really. What makes you say that?'

'A boy at my school says there isn't. But we've still got to pretend 'cos Mummy thinks there is.'

Late, late that night, Lily and he sat across from one another in a sea of wrapping paper, packing the boy's presents. The log fire cracked and popped. As he tackled the intricacies of string and paper round a Hornby train and engine, he said, 'Thank you for asking me here. It's the nicest Christmas I can remember in years.'

'Well, even such a recluse as my brother rather likes company at this time of year. And Mary and Sam seem more than happy to keep an eye on your farm.'

He watched as she picked up a box of Pop the Beacon and measured it against a sheet of paper awash with snowflakes and reindeer. She looked up and grinned at him. 'What's more, Hugh can talk politics with you to his heart's content.'

She started to cut the paper, her head down, concentrating. 'It's dreadful, I feel such a fool the minute he starts. I get completely tangled in knots.'

'Speaking of knots, would you be good enough to loan me a finger?'

She leant across and placed her finger on the string; he looped the knot. He caught her scent of lemons.

When she looked up at him, he asked, 'May I kiss you?'

'Please, oh please,' she said.

Christmas 1931. The first kiss. And ever after, he never knew how he had lived without her, this woman, the completion of his life.

SS *Etoile*. Saturday, early

The ship dipped and rose. A cluster of clouds tore across the moon and on every surface the sparkle of ice momentarily dulled. Johnnie realised he was shivering, the sweat clammy and cold on his back. But he remained sitting on the bench; he couldn't face the cabin yet.

His empty cold kitchen. And the memory of the dripping pipes in need of lagging those first three winters after the war. That was what he was leaving behind. Even last winter there'd been no kitchen fire going all through the day – and no warmth in his chilly damp bed either, at night. Until Lily had started visiting the farm.

He lifted his face to the wind. His mind had calmed; the attack had been mercifully brief. And now – as ever – it was the thought of Lily that warmed him.

Was he crazy to even think of leaving this woman? What were a farm and pigs – even dear old Marie Antoinette, a sturdy porker in her old age – if there was no reason for one's heart to beat?

No, it wasn't the moment to retire from the battle. The farm was in Sam's good hands and, once in America, he'd tell Lily of the illness. There, there would be time enough for 'rest and tonics'. For now he'd been entrusted with the safety of these two people, this woman and her son. An adventure, no less. Quite unexpectedly, out of the blue, at his ripe old age. And in many ways he knew he was loving it; because of her, God dammit, and her pale cowed child. At last, life had some reason.

Lancashire. New Year 1931

Hugh looked up as the man stepped into the tack-room and stopped in the doorway. Johnnie stood in the dingy light, breathing in. 'Mmm, smell of leather and saddle-soap; nothing to beat it.'

Hugh said, 'Come on in and join us.'

By the light of a hurricane lamp, Nickie and he carried on cleaning a saddle and bridle, heads down. In the corner, a small wood-burning stove clicked and creaked, otherwise there was a completely concentrated silence. It was Twelfth Night.

'Sorry to disturb you two. Nickie, Mummy says its time for tea.'

On the wind, a horse whinnied. Hugh saw the little boy carry on cleaning. Then silent expectancy proving too much, he looked up at Hugh, hope in his eyes; perhaps his uncle could delay the arrival of bath and bedtime.

But all Hugh said was, 'I'll be over in a bit. We'll have a quick chat before Ma tucks you in. Promise.' The boy stood motionless. 'Go on, off you go. And thanks again for all your help today, old man, Whirlwind really enjoyed the exercise.' Still nothing. 'Fun, wasn't it?'

The boy nodded and left, sullen and silent. The two men

listened as his steps dragged across the stable-yard, leaving the noise to comment loudly on the unfairness of his life.

'Cat got his tongue?' asked Johnnie.

'End of hols blues, I fear,' Hugh replied. 'God, though, doesn't it all come back? Last day of the holidays.' He tucked in a leather strap and hung up the bridle.

'Mind if I smoke?' asked Johnnie.

'Go ahead. It's only forbidden in the stables themselves. Hay and all that. Draw up a pew.' He indicated an elderly lop-sided armchair furnished in a sweet floral material of incongruous femininity.

'I think I'll leave them to their boiled eggs for a bit. Lily and Nickie.'

Johnnie began to light his pipe, the exercise seeming to fully absorb his concentration, whilst Hugh turned to a huge old saddle that creaked as he dismantled the girth and started to clean the handsome worn leather on the underside. Both men, silently occupied, waited, fully aware of the complicated conversation to be had, this last day of the holidays.

'I love her, you know,' Johnnie said into the silence. And each man realised the seriousness of his intent, Hugh honouring it by saying, 'I know, old man. To be honest, I am so very pleased. For both of you. I've not seen the old girl look so well in years. And it's a blessing to hear that laugh of hers again.'

An enormous bridge crossed, both men arrived in No Man's Land, unsure as to which way to turn.

'It's not as simple as that, though, is it?' Johnnie spoke first, quickly, as if afraid his nerve would break and he'd turn, running for cover, back into the privacy of his emotions.

''Fraid not. No,' Hugh replied.

The northerly wind battered against the old window, a gale heaving under the frame; the blue flame in the hurricane lamp flickered. Stepping over, Hugh pulled a bright red-and-white check curtain across the glass; it was cheerful and ineffective on this January evening. 'I hated him from the moment I saw him, Charles Sutton. Bloody bully even from the start. I missed the wedding, I was still in France, couldn't get leave. Big fancy affair. Perhaps Lily's told you?'

'No,' said Johnnie. 'Truth be told, by mutual consent we've rather kept her marriage out of bounds.'

Hugh saw the man pause, no doubt, desperate to know more but anxious not to appear nosey. So he said, 'To be honest, Johnnie, it's quite a relief to talk about it. As her brother and guardian, so to speak.' He heaved over the saddle and attacked it with vigour.

He'd taken to Johnnie immediately, as different as could be to Charles Sutton, not only in his physicality – tall, wiry and balding – but also in his humour, which sparked life into the embers of a day's drabness. Twice they'd sat into the night that Christmas, a bottle of Scotch between them, and shared unspoken memories of Ypres and spoken experiences of life. And then three nights ago, Hugh had heard the creak along the old corridor and the joy of his sister's giggling, as the two new lovers disappeared through one bedroom door.

'The first time I saw Sis after her marriage,' he said, 'was a year after the actual wedding. Charles had just bought Melsham and they'd moved down there away from London, though they still had Bryanston Square. Anyway, I was invited down one weekend.' He looked up and stared across the tack-room at the rows of saddles jutting from the walls, their shadows lumpily dancing in the lamplight.

'Sis had, quite simply, changed. Not so much physically; no, she looked more beautiful than ever. But all her gaiety, all the wonderful child-like fun we used to have, it wasn't there. She was so quiet – and I don't want to sound melodramatic but she had a sort of haunted look, her eyes following Charles everywhere. And then one evening Charles and I had the most terrible row. Inevitable, I suppose, given our very different perspectives on life.' He leant on the saddle and looked at Johnnie. 'My fault really, I felt like provoking the man even though he was behaving like a drunken sot. Anyway, next morning I had the most wretched intuition that Lily had been on the receiving end of some pretty hateful stuff from this new husband of hers. Not that I think he actually hit her. Not then anyway.'

Johnnie said nothing.

'I was effectively banned from Melsham, not in so many words but it became obvious that it was torture for Sis, the anticipation of "words" between Charles and myself. And to be honest it wasn't any fun. She was "cowed"- yes, that's the word – and all the while she kept excusing the behaviour of this drunken bully of a husband. Anyway, slowly they took up with a different circle of friends. More his lot, his set.'

As he was talking, Hugh turned to a small wall cupboard and was rummaging through to the back. He produced a bottle of whisky and, opening the stable door, threw the slops of two teacups into the yard. The wind howled into the room, sharp and stinging. He leant his weight against the door and closed it. Crossing back to a sink, he rinsed and refilled the cups with a good measure of whisky and, handing one to Johnnie, continued.

'By now I was up at Oxford so Lily and I would meet in

the Vac, usually in London, on our own. And again, a bit like you, by mutual consent we didn't discuss the marriage. She knew I disapproved of Charles, to say the least, but Lily's a great one for "if you've made your bed, you've jolly well got to lie on it". Anyway, around then, Charles had this madcap scheme to become a Tory MP, God help us all. And dear old Lil discovered she had all the makings of an extremely good MP's wife. So much so that Charles suddenly realised this wife of his was really quite an asset after all.'

'I didn't know any of this. Tell me more.' Johnnie asked casually but Hugh saw the soft gleam in his eye. *Good Lord,* he thought, *this man really does love Sis.*

'Well, she was in fact very good at canvassing. She was really good with people, really interested in their problems. Unlike Charles who was just a "guts and glory" boy flagging up his war record in a particularly vulgar fashion – and if not that, then flogging that wretched shop of his. But Lily would spend hours, you know, discussing people's problems – and trying to sort them out. She'd say to me, "Oh, I don't know anything about politics," but actually she was extremely political in her belief in fairness and justice. So that, ultimately, as the election drew nearer, Charles became torn between Lily helping him to win his seat and him keeping Lily out of the public eye. Because, of course, by now Charles was unbelievably jealous of her – this prize possession of his – as she became more and more popular with all the folk round Melsham. Then one day—'

He stopped. A light had gone on across the yard and there was the sound of soft steps. The tack-room door opened.

'My two best boys getting drunk.' His sister stood swathed in a muffler and woolly hat. 'Can I join in?'

'No, this is men's talk.' Hugh said firmly. Both men grinned at her.

'Well, as long as you don't plan to be out here all evening. I've got rather a splendid Last Night supper on the go – and it will be ready in fifteen minutes.' She turned to leave, flicking her head round to smile back at them both. Life in that moment was good.

In the silence that followed, the horse in the stable across the yard whinnied again, there was the dull chatter of hooves as it turned and turned about, and then all was hushed stillness, here in the heart of Lancashire, beneath an icy black sky dense with stars.

'How long are you allowing for the journey back tomorrow?' Hugh, the first to speak.

'Six hours. Pray God, the snow holds off.'

'Should do. It's bitter but it's dry.'

He opened the stove and prodded the logs; they crackled heartily. 'Final burst of heat before we go across. Outside and in, eh?' He topped up Johnnie's mug.

'Can I talk through a couple of ideas with you, Hugh? Over the past few days, I've been shaping and re-shaping plans in my head. I'd be jolly grateful for a "sounding-board".'

'Go ahead, old man.'

'As you know, Sam and Mary are holding the fort for me this Christmas at the farm. So I'm going to suggest, when we arrive back, Lily and Nickie drop me off first and then Sam takes my place, so to speak, and accompanies them back to Melsham – after all, it's only five miles away – just in case Charles is there.'

Hugh had been in the kitchen when Johnnie had attempted to talk this through with Lily the night before. 'I wondered,' he'd asked carefully, 'if, once you've driven Nickie back to school, you shouldn't return to me at the farm?' To which Lily had only replied, 'We'll see,' and turned from them both in such a way as to make plain she didn't want to discuss the matter further.

Now Johnnie said, 'I know Nickie is her dearest wish and concern—' He stopped then blurted out, 'Hugh, how are we to keep her safe? If Lily remains at Melsham she's in grave danger. Especially if Charles Sutton were to learn of my feelings for Lily.' He stopped, stranded in the midst of these circling fears.

Hugh said nothing.

'Well then.' Johnnie took a deep breath. 'My sense of the matter is that if Lily were, eventually, to separate from Charles, he would continue to find ways to punish her. And the easiest way for him to do that would be through the child.' He looked at his watch and drained his drink. 'What I'm trying to say, forgive me for rambling, is that she'll never consent to marry me because it leaves Nicholas in too much danger from his father. Not that, from the little I know of Charles Sutton, he could ever be persuaded to give Lily a divorce. To make her happy.'

'What you mean is, Charles must never find out about the two of you until Nickie is old enough to look after himself.'

Johnnie nodded bleakly. Hugh could see that the situation spoken was as unrelenting as the situation silently mulled over in the dead hours of the night. The man looked torn between expectancy and anticipated despair.

'Come on.' Johnnie suddenly scrambled to his feet. 'We'd better get in to supper. Thank you for the drink. Most welcome.'

SS *Etoile*. Saturday, early.

'Darling, it's two o'clock,' Johnnie said gently as he came back into the cabin. In the silence of the night, the ship thundered relentlessly. He closed his eyes, determined to survive the closeness of the cabin.

He reached for the tooth mug and quickly poured himself a drink. 'Can I tempt you, one for bed?'

She looked up, her expression dazed and removed. 'The letter's nearly finished.'

Looking at her, he knew at once her mind was no longer on the letter; he recognised immediately this 'absence'. When he'd first known her, he'd been surprised and puzzled by her ability to remove herself, her mind seemingly elsewhere, her thoughts distracted from the task in hand. She appeared often to cocoon herself in a dreaming abstraction from which it was apparent she took no pleasure, her expression becoming distant, all animation dying. But slowly he had begun to understand that this seeming vagueness and distraction was her armour against the brutalities of much of her existence.

'You can finish your letter in the morning. We must get some sleep.' He stood, depriving the dreary cabin of its light.

'It's all right, it's finished.' Lily made to hand the letter to him but before he had a chance to take it, the words spun from her. 'Oh, Johnnie, we should have left Nickie in England! If I hadn't been so selfish in wanting him with me, he'd still be safe at school.'

She rose up from the bunk but, as always, fettered by the lack of space, sank down. Now he saw her guilt, so carefully suppressed, spiral to the surface. 'We've been so unbelievably selfish. If I'm caught, I'll go to gaol and then Nickie—'

'Hush, hush, darling.' He sat down beside her and gently, turned her round to look at him. 'It's the middle of the night and you are understandably exhausted—'

'Don't try and hush me!' He saw with her anger releasing, an anger fed by the constant watchful terror, all her euphoria at the adventure had extinguished. 'You don't understand.' Her nerves were urging a fight. 'You don't begin to know the fear. If Charles finds us… Christ, what am I doing?' He went to hold her.

'No, don't!' She pulled away from his attempted embrace. 'You're a man. You've no idea of – of how terrifying it can be, the constant fear that you'll be hurt. Or worse, that he'll hurt Nickie. And all because I'm too feeble, because I'm a woman I can't protect him—'

He knew that this sense of impotence appalled and frightened her. She stood and, as if to reassure herself of her child's safety, swiftly checked the upper bunk, distractedly smoothing the blanket. In barely a whisper, she said, 'For ten years, ever since Nickie was born, the two of us have hidden. We've tried never to upset Charles, to keep quiet, stifle cries, stifle laughter, praying that he'd never notice us, knowing that our sheer presence infuriated and sickened him.'

The procession of memories caught and spoken seemed to still her. She continued at a calmer pace, a sourness in her voice. 'Charles and I waited five years for me to become pregnant. I thought I was barren, but, thank God, it happened just before my thirtieth birthday and Charles seemed to be as thrilled as I was.' She stopped, closing her eyes. 'From the moment Nickie was born, I could see the child created in him a mixture of jealousy and discomfort. He'd chide and goad the boy—' She stopped again. When she next spoke Johnnie heard the depth of her despair. 'I thought Nicholas's birth, the wonder of it, would mend the marriage. It ended it.'

They sat in silence, apart.

After a while, he said, 'You are extraordinary. Do you know, in all our time together, you've never once talked detrimentally about Charles.'

'I thought it would be disloyal. So stupid! When you think of the pain…' She shook her head. 'You see, I can't believe there will ever come a day when Nickie or I won't cower.'

He put his arm around her and she leant against him. 'You're a brave woman. Here you are setting off into the unknown with a strange man. Just as the Dolly Bartons of this world are settling down to gardening and Canasta.'

'Perish the thought.'

'Exactly. And, dearest one, to answer your question, no, I most definitely don't think you should have left Nickie in England – to all intents and purposes, alone – to stand up to his father.'

'My "strange man",' she said. 'I do so love you.'

Melsham, England. Summer 1932

The telephone rang at a quarter to six. 'Lily, my dear, is that you?'

Lily had risen early, hope and expectation in her heart knowing she was seeing Johnnie later that day. It was Nickie's summer holiday and they were all going on a jaunt to the Cobb at Lyme Regis.

'Good lord, Dolly, it's a bit early in the day for you, isn't it?'

'Well, I wasn't going to ring but I'm afraid there's been a bit of a misunderstanding.' Lily suddenly felt extraordinarily cold. She stood very still, looking through the long windows across the lawn. It promised to be another hot, hot July day.

Dolly Barton was saying, 'Charles telephoned last night and asked to speak to you. He seemed to be under the impression you were dining with us—'

'Dolly, how stupid of me, I get all my days in such a muddle when Nickie's home from school—'

But Dolly was still speaking. 'Lily, please listen. Charles got terribly angry, you know how he gets when he can't have his way. Though, I said to Gerald, often I think Charles's bark is worse than his bite. Anyway, he was extremely short with me, so much so I put Gerald onto him and... Oh Lily, Charles has got it into his head that you must be having an affair!' Dolly gasped out this final sentence.

But Lily wasn't listening. Up the drive, at enormous speed, she could see Charles's car in a swirl of dust heading for the house. She slammed down the telephone.

She was running through the house. 'Mrs Benton! Mrs Benton! Quick, quick!' The cook appeared through the swinging staff-door, flour up to her elbows. 'Telephone Sam Valley. Freston 219. Get him here now!' Lily was taking the stairs two at a time.

'But, my lady—'

'*Now*, Mrs Benton! He'll know why.' The cook disappeared like a startled rabbit.

'Nickie! Nickie, up! Get up!' Despite his size, Lily started to scoop up the sleeping boy from the bed. 'Your father is downstairs.' The boy flung from his bed. Mother and son were off down the nursery corridor, Nickie clutching at his pyjama bottoms.

They reached the back stairs. Both stopped and listened, breathing in gulps.

In the distance on the other side of the house, the Daimler had crunched to a halt and they could hear Charles Sutton mounting the front steps and hurling across the hallway. 'Lily, where are you?' A roar.

Lily and Nickie shot down the little wooden stairs, along the passage and reached the garden door. 'Now, darling, run as quick as you can to the stables and hide in the hayloft. Like Sam showed you.' She was pushing him through the door.

'But, Mummy, I'm not going without you—'

'Do as you're told, Nicholas. I need to talk to your father—'

'Mummy, he'll hurt you!' Nickie was frantically hanging on to her, sobbing.

'No, he won't.'

Suddenly they heard Charles somewhere near, crashing about. Behind them and above. Sweet Lord, he's in the nursery; he's gone straight to find Nickie.

'Don't leave me! I want to stay!' the little boy cried out, clinging to her. With all her strength she shoved him out of the door. He stumbled and nearly fell. Picking himself up, he ran across the yard, turning once at the corner, tears pouring down his face, and disappeared from view.

She turned away and, racing down the passage, tore into the kitchen.

'Out this way, my lady.' Mrs Benton was waiting for her and took hold of her hand, pulling her towards the scullery door. 'I rang Sam, nobody answered—'

But their escape was barred. Into the kitchen slammed Charles Sutton, with all the clumsy power of an enraged bull, red in the face.

'Got you, you whore! And you, Benton, *scram*!' The cook stood solid, fear in equal mix with bravery freezing her to the spot.

Sir Charles lumbered towards her, raising his hand. Mrs Benton shot through the scullery door. Alone, he slowly turned to his wife. There was a kitchen table between them. Behind her, Lily became aware that, even on this summer's morning, the range was beating out heat in preparation for Mrs Benton's baking.

'So, after all these years, my pathetic little wife has taken herself a lover.' His words were smooth but Lily could see his whole frame was pulsing, his eyes electric with rage. He slowly moved round the table. She backed away but was stopped from moving further by the range. Trapped, she made herself stand erect. She would show no fear.

The man advanced upon her and stood an inch away, not yet touching. She could feel the pent-up fury, smell the sweat; within, she held every fibre and muscle in readiness for the first blow.

But instead of striking her, he leant forward and lightly curled his large hand around her wrist, lifting her arm so that he had her clenched hand in front of his face. Then, half-smiling, he carefully prised her hand open, splaying her fingers apart. With a quick twist, he pulled her arm backwards and placed her hand firmly on the hot-plate. His hand over hers, he held her down, leaning his body the length of hers, his mouth hanging open, inches from her face.

The pain was astonishing, almost exquisite in its intensity. She closed her eyes, the sour whisky on his breath the really hateful thing. But the ice-cold of the heat now hurt, no longer pure. Then the first flailing slap came as expected, the promiscuity of his fingers knocking her ear, and the well-known pain started.

'Stop it!'

Her ear banged, throbbed.

'Stop it, I say!' A voice, a little voice. Had she cried out? The great weight of the man lurched off her and, with her view cleared, through her tears, she saw her boy, her little boy on the other side of the kitchen.

She struggled upright. 'Nickie!'

He stood thin in his pyjamas, trembling in the kitchen doorway, his face chalk-white. He was training a shotgun directly at his father. For a moment the man stared at the boy, swaying slightly. Then he crashed down into a chair and started to laugh. A loud harsh sound, it came in braying gusts as he threw his head back.

The boy stood his ground, the gun wavering as it pointed at the man who now drew in his breath and turned on his son. 'So, boy, you're not such a lily-livered little pansy after all.'

But Lily wasn't waiting. She ran round the table and grabbed at the boy, pulling him from the room.

'That's right, you slut,' Charles yelled after her. 'Run away!'

PART TWO

CHAPTER THIRTEEN

London. Saturday morning, 4th March 1933

Superintendent Outwood's office at Scotland Yard was particularly gloomy, even at nine o'clock on a bright March morning. He sat at his large dusty desk, his eyes drooping, exhausted. He'd hardly slept for two nights. It had been four days since the Sutton woman's disappearance and he'd had the boss breathing down his neck at every turn. Added to which, if Outwood was honest, his heart wasn't really in it; there were many more pressing crimes to be solved. Not that he'd ever have let on to the boss but he resented the priority given to the case just because Sir Charles Sutton had some 'high up' friends.

Now the Sutton son, it seemed, had disappeared as well.

At close of play the previous evening, the chief had called him in and announced, 'I've just had Charles Sutton on the telephone. For some reason best known to himself, he's only chosen to tell us now his son's gone missing as well. God knows why he didn't see fit to tell us before.'

'Any details, sir?' Outwood wearily asked.

'Only that the mother collected him from his school five days ago, and the pair of them haven't been seen since. Put on extra men if you have to. Whatever you do, get this wretched man off my back! And get the story off the front pages!'

'Yes, sir.'

'Not only have I got Sir Charles Sutton on the telephone at all hours of the night and day, now he's roped in his pal, the Foreign Secretary.' The chief was pacing in a fury. 'Clear it up, Outwood. That's an order!'

Tired and fed-up, Outwood returned to his gloomy office and read and re-read his notes. Lady Sutton's disappearance had been in the newspapers for three days and they'd still only had a fairish response; no real 'leads'. A Mrs Topham from Reigate, a clairvoyant, had claimed to have seen the woman on 'the other side' and demanded 10 guineas for her pains, receiving a flea in her ear instead.

He flipped over the page. A farmer down Falmouth way had found a pile of bones and some dim-wit had got the experts there. Not surprisingly, the only mystery solved was that of an ancient burial chamber; the scientists were delighted, Superintendent Outwood was not.

He himself had gone through Lady Sutton's address book but nobody interviewed seemed to know anything – or if they did, weren't prepared to talk. In his waters, he had a feeling a discreet silence was being maintained about certain marital matters but Outwood didn't fancy himself as a psychiatrist; it was not his business to enquire into anything beyond the job in hand.

What else? A car found at Preston Station had, indeed, turned out to be Lady Sutton's, but a thorough interviewing of the station staff had yielded nothing. And Lady Sutton's brother, Hugh, who farmed nearby, appeared to be in South Africa anyway. A whole day and night spent travelling north and back on a fool's errand – and Mrs Outwood had been most unforgiving as he'd missed their anniversary supper. Mind you, perhaps that slab of local Lancashire cheese as an anniversary gift had been too racy a choice. The usual bottle of 'Soir de Paris' would have been wiser, bearing in mind Mildred Outwood's somewhat fastidious taste…

He sighed deeply. Where to go next? He was stumped.

SS *Etoile*. Saturday dawn

Although mid-morning in London, it was only dawn at sea. Even so, Enid Timms sat fully clothed on the edge of her third-class bunk and, in the dreary first light, she was thinking, thinking.

She smoothed the copy of yesterday's *Poseidon Post* lying in her lap and read the article concerning Lady Sutton for the umpteenth time. The maid knew that her most valuable ally, her most valuable tool, was her memory. She could hear a piece of gossip and years later bring it to mind, sifting from it the very essence of its importance. So when she had not been able to immediately recall any specific information concerning Lady Lily Sutton in an attempt to unravel the mystery of her presence in steerage, she was extremely annoyed and not a little frustrated.

Coolly and carefully, once again, she began at the beginning and regimented the facts into order. Firstly, it was obvious that Lady Sutton was travelling under an alias as yet to be discovered. But why? And where was her husband, Sir Charles? Secondly, why was Lady Sutton travelling steerage? For financial reasons? Timms knew that only recently the Duchess of Rutland had confided to Lady Slocombe that she had had to resort to a third-class cabin, 'My dear, a bolting-hole of beastliness among the lower barnacles.' No, that couldn't be it; Sir Charles Sutton was a wealthy man. Indeed, Miss Timms herself was a devotee of Sutton's, the department store... Slowly, she picked at the fabric of her memory. Had there not been talk of Sir Charles and a lady-friend? Could there have been a discreet separation? Her mind gathered speed. But wasn't there a child? Yes, a little boy, she was certain. Like a skilled mathematician, with stealth, patience and nerve, she teased away at her mind.

That was it! She had seen a photograph of Lady Sutton and her son, she was sure of it, in her *Sunday Chronicle*. They had been at a children's charity fancy-dress party.

And with that, another thought struck her. A photograph of the boy might be just the sort of bargaining tool needed to show the authorities and lure Lady Sutton from her hiding-place.

Hardly daring to hope, Timms hauled her tin trunk from under the bunk and frantically unpacked her small collection of boots and shoes. One by one, she winkled out the crumpled newspaper stuffed into each and smoothed every sheet.

And there it was.

She put on the pair of wire spectacles she was too vain to wear in company and held the crumpled newspaper article under the feeble light over her bunk. She peered at the photographs. Party guests, children dressed up as little squaws, little cowboys, watched over for the purposes of the *Sunday Chronicle* readership by proud preening mothers, nannies for the moment tucked out of sight, no doubt ready to resume control the moment the camera-bulb had flashed.

But where was the Sutton child? She was sure she had seen the name, Sutton. No picture of Lady Sutton as she had thought but – there he was! In a little group of children around a party table. She had remembered right.

What was his first name again? She looked beneath the picture and counted from left to right. Ah, yes. Nicholas. Nicholas Sutton.

She stared at the child.

'Like a bullet from a gun, the old biddy runs down Scotland Road,' Billy told Freddie over a bowl of porridge. 'And I knows, sure as eggs is eggs, she's up to something. So I reckon we should could keep an eye on her, see which way she dances. You fancy doing a bit of the old Sherlock Holmes, Fred my son?'

Hunkered down in a broom cupboard opposite Miss Timms' cabin, the two lads were now waiting for something to happen. They had been there nearly half-an-hour.

'Me leg's gone to sleep,' Freddie whispered. 'It's killin' me.'

'OK, mate, move sideways again.'

The two boys shuffled and re-adjusted in the tiny dusty space. Billy could see his friend was fed-up, he'd gone all sweaty just trying to keep still.

'Don't worry, Fred, another five minutes. If the old biddy don't move, we'll call it a day. Keep a secret?'

Freddie nodded mutely.

'Captain wants to see me this morning. We talk sometimes,

captain and me.' Billy, feeling very much a man of the world, sharing the secrets of his life with his new pal. 'I'm going to tell him about the old biddy and how she's up to something funny.'

'Will I watch on me own when you go?' asked Freddie unenthusiastically.

'Nah, too difficult. Besides, don't know which way she's going to dance, do we?'

Freddie looked very relieved.

They fell back into silence. With time marching on and both having duties to attend to, they knew pretty soon they'd have to abandon their post.

'Johnnie, you awake? I've been thinking. Why don't we let Nickie go to the fancy-dress parade?'

Lily was whispering, he could only just hear her over the sound of the engines. 'What time is it, Lily?'

She leant across him. 'Um, I think my watch says five to six, I can't really see. Anyway,' she rolled back again, 'I've been thinking and—'

'Lily, it's six o'clock in the morning.'

'I know, I've got to get up and meet Mrs Webb soon. What do you think, darling? About Nickie?'

He managed a mumble; if he kept his eyes closed perhaps he could stay asleep.

'What's that?' Lily unwrapped herself from his arms.

He opened an eye and saw her, all alert, hair corkscrewed by the tiny bunk; she looked twelve years old. 'I was thinking, Nickie could have young Freddie's clown outfit.' She drew up her knees and perched her head on them, all worries ironed away by sound sleep. 'He doesn't want it anymore. Mrs Webb told me last evening he feels his dogs are more important than some children's party game.'

Suddenly Johnnie was wide awake. 'Dear God, Lily, I can't believe what I'm hearing. Have you lost all sense?'

'Keep your voice down, Nickie will hear.'

'I don't care if he hears—'

'Johnnie, listen. Nickie is going crackers in here; we can't expect him to lie low for a fourth day. And now we've got these new friends, Mrs Webb and Anthea, we can hide Nickie amongst them.'

'Are you insane?'

'No, listen, hear me out.' He could see she wasn't going to leave the subject till she'd had her full say. He waited.

'Nickie can wear Freddie's suit and, with some clown make-up, we can make him look like a little girl again. Like we did to get him on board.'

'And his hair? Or is he suppose to wear that wretched beret 'cos I can tell you for one he'll refuse. Cabin fever or not!'

'No, we've made pointy hats. They come down over the ears; you don't notice the hair. Oh, Johnnie, please. Nickie's going to be so thrilled, a fancy-dress party.' She wriggled fully upright. 'And as you yourself pointed out, it's four days since we've sailed and absolutely nobody's taken the slightest notice of us.'

He could feel, against his better judgement, she was winning him over. 'I suppose,' he said carefully, 'there *are* over two hundred people down here—'

'Safety in numbers, exactly. I want to tell him now!'

Nellie lay in her cabin trying to hold on to the dream. As she fully woke, Davy's smiling face fled away from her and hid in the smoky backrooms of her mind. *My love*, she called to him, *Where are you? Come back to me.*

But her husband's face stayed hidden away; she couldn't see him any more. She closed her eyes. Sometimes she could still feel him, still feel the sense of him, the loving of him. *We had some grand times, eh, my lad. Some right grand loving.*

By, but she missed him. All these years along. Even when he'd been a right monkey with the drink inside him.

And when they laid you out on the slab, your body mashed by that train, you were still smiling. Even in death. Smile for me, Davy Webb. Just one more time.

CHAPTER FOURTEEN

SS *Etoile*. Saturday, early morning

Through the long wretched night, Matty had hardly slept, the intermittent tears leaving her eyes swollen and sore. She lay on her side, coiled in a bundle of blankets, suspended in misery.

At eight o'clock that morning there was a knock on the cabin door. Henry answered it.

Returning to Matty's side, he sat gingerly back on the bed. 'That was the steward. The captain has sent a note saying he thinks it might be useful to talk.' Through the tangled blankets, he attempted to find her hand. 'Oh Matty, you'll see, all will be well.'

She lay silent, her face turned to the wall.

'Why don't you have a bath? Then we could have a little walk perhaps?'

Without lifting her head, she said, 'Why do I have to keep saying it? I'm not going anywhere where I'll meet that woman.'

Reassured by the sound of her voice, he urged, 'But you can't stay in the cabin for the rest of the trip, it's absurd.' He waited for her response but there was silence once again. 'I'll do everything I can to make sure you won't meet her.'

'How? Go into every room to check she's not there? Now you're being absurd.'

He found her hand and held on to it tightly. 'Mats, I swear to you, no one believes you're guilty.'

She sat up abruptly, tucking her hand back away from him. 'Then why've I got to talk to the authorities at Pier 90?'

'That was an idiotic suggestion made last night. And now I'm talking to the captain, I won't let it happen. I promise you. I won't have you put through any more humiliation.' He rambled to a close, ineffective.

He shut his eyes. There, still, the raw, rotten moment of accusation. Well-bred heads turning, the rush to judgement, feral inquisitiveness hidden beneath the smug face of rectitude. And at the centre, Matty, the focus of attention, so bewildered, so vulnerable. Innocent until proved guilty. Bah! Through the Paris Lounge the verdict was immediately writ large. *The Grossman girl is not one of us, she is surely guilty.*

He was heartbroken for her and disgusted at himself for failing to resolve the matter. To add to everything else, the ship's doctor, having examined Matty, had pulled him to one side and expressed concern as to her heartbroken anguish. Henry had crept back to her bedside, wanting only to wrap her in his arms, to make it all better, to make the horror vanish. But all through the long night she had lain curled away from him as though he, too, were the enemy.

Now in the grey early morning, still locked in this emotional limbo, Henry didn't know which way to turn. He leant forward and very tentatively stroked her head. 'When we get back to Africa we'll look back on all this and laugh at that – that – rhino of a woman.' It was an inadequate attempt at humour, he knew that, but for the first time she seemed to respond. He looked at her hopefully.

'No, Henry, you don't even begin to understand.' His hope flickered and died.

She pulled away from his touch and said quite steadily, 'From the start I knew, if I married you, I'd need to be brave to face people, to face their snobbery. Me, the girl from Harrow on the Hill. What I didn't know was I'd have to face their hatred also. I think I can deal with being sneered at. But I can't deal with this loathing because I'm a Jew.'

There, at last, she had said it; he felt dazed. But he knew she was right.

Slowly, with Matty at his side, both at the Embassy and on their return to England, he had become aware of the veiled comments. Often so subtly lodged in the form of an enquiry or compliment, 'Is Grossman some sort of foreign name?' '"Grossman". Ah, that would account for her exotic appearance.' He had tried to ignore them. Now, he couldn't.

'Dearest, it will be different once we're back in Africa.'

'Will it?' She looked so pale; her passionate storming tears through the night had given way this morning to a faded distracted air.

'Of course, look how His Excellency admires you. I think he even secretly envied my sudden onslaught of diabetes. Mind you, remember his face when he marched into my office, asking what all the commotion was about and found me slumped over the desk with you in your nurse's uniform, spoon-feeding me from the sugar-bowl!' He knew it was feeble to blot out the horror of the night before with this continuing attempt at humour but he had no other solution; he plunged on. 'And because of you and your knowing ways, I'm now lumbered with no grog, endless potatoes and a needle in my backside twice a day. Though it's a darn sight more interesting way than most to meet the girl of your dreams, even if she does have puffy eyes and a red nose.'

Looking straight at him, Matty said, 'If you hadn't been there last night, I'd have been called a thief and held in some cell or other. It's only you and your wretched title that prevented it.'

'Matty, don't—'

'No, I think it's dishonest. Of *them*.' She lay back down on the pillow, sullen, her case made.

'But what do you want me to do?' He was completely lost. 'Deliver you up to the captain's office for the rest of the trip on a point of principle? Don't be so ridiculous, Matty.' Despite himself he got to his feet and, fraught through lack of sleep, carried on too loudly. 'No one believes that trivial accusation.'

'Then prove I'm innocent!' she cried.

'I can't!'

'It's a slur. Oh, leave me alone.'

'Matty, please listen to me—'

'*Leave me!*' She burrowed back down into the blankets and turned again to the wall. 'I'm sick of the whole bloody thing.'

Completely at a loss, he hovered. 'Um...all right... I'm going to see the captain...'

With a last look at the huddled, silent figure, he went back through the adjoining door to his cabin. He dressed hurriedly and left.

'Turn,' commanded Mrs Webb.

Lily turned and looked down at the black and white maid's uniform, the heavy lisle stockings and the sturdy shoes. She felt like a Lyons Corner House 'nippy'.

'See, what'd I tell yer?' Mrs Webb carried on. 'Dressed like that, none up there in first class will give you second glance. You'll be invisible, mark my words. 'Specially at crack of dawn, when none of the nobs are stirring. Here's yer headband, love.'

Pushing her towards the tiny spotted mirror over the cabin sink, Mrs Webb adjusted the lace and ribbon band, sweeping Lily's waved hair to one side. She stepped back and surveyed her handiwork. 'Well, though I say it meself, our Barney's got a right good eye. That outfit fits a treat. I'd never of thought it of him.' There was a cluck in her voice.

Lily peered at herself. All she could see in the gloomy glass was a severe head atop the neat buttoned collar of a maid's uniform. Oh, it would have to do, and anyway, she was far too nervous to fiddle about with it. 'What time is it?' she asked for the third time in two minutes. 'And where's Barney gone, anyway?'

'Don't you fret, love. He'll be back.'

'But what if we're stopped—'

'Don't you worry. I told yer, Barney's got his pass and he'll drop you up to B deck on his way to work in't print shop. You'll be all 'unky-dory *and* back in time for fancy dress.'

There was a knock at the door. Both women jumped.

'Who is it?' Mrs Webb called out.

'Barney, Ma.'

She opened the door to her grinning son, who stood framed in the doorway holding a fully laid-up breakfast tray. ''Morning again, ladies.'

'Where'd you get that?' fussed his mum. 'You didn't nick it?'

'Keep yer hair on. It's for Mrs Valley. It's her alibi, delivering breakfast, just the job. And I've double-checked. Nurse Grossman is in Suite 1002, next to her patient, Lord Clairmont, in 1003.'

Mrs Webb beamed as wide as the world. 'See, what'd I tell yer? Now get along, the pair o' yer.' She started to steer Lily from the cabin.

'Do I look all right?' Lily hesitated.

'To the manner born, m'lady,' said Mrs Webb and winked.

All over the ship, there was a bright surge of morning energy. Barney led Lily along a long passageway. 'This is Scotland Road,' he informed her and said no more.

Everywhere crew were intent on keeping the ship working at full tilt. Though Lily couldn't look properly at anyone; her full concentration was on steadying the contents of the silver breakfast tray she was carrying.

'Flippin' 'eck.' Barney suddenly stopped. Lily looked up.

Ahead at the crossing of two corridors, a knot of men stood in conference. Barney, with a jerk of the head, nodded her into a doorway just as a tall man in full uniform separated from the group and started to make his way smartly towards them. Lily saw Barney stiffen, stand erect and look straight ahead. She attempted to do the same but found herself juggling the tray, which was jutting out into the path of the oncoming man.

'Good morning to you both.'

''Morning, Captain,' said Barney.

'Name?'

'Webb, printing shop, sir. This 'ere is…er…' There was a tiny hiatus before the young man said with authority, 'Aintree, Captain.'

Lily curtsied, keeping her head down.

She heard Barney clear his throat, and glanced up to discover the captain staring at her. She looked down again quickly, aware that he was about to speak. She braced herself. However, at that moment an officer marched swiftly towards them. 'Machinery spaces ready for inspection, Captain.'

'Very good, Mr Hodder.' She looked up again; he was eyeing her rattling tray. 'And you, Aintree, get that breakfast delivered. Don't want complaints the food is cold.' He strode away, Mr Hodder in his wake.

Up ahead, the group of sailors had disbanded.

The shock of the encounter caused Barney and Lily to shoot from their doorway and set off again at double-speed.

'Thank goodness he didn't try to taste any of that breakfast,' puffed Barney. 'It's been stone-cold these last twenty minutes.'

'What's he doing down here, anyway?' Lids were clinking and sugar lumps bouncing.

'Daily round of inspection. Makes his way through ship.'

They arrived at an electric service lift. 'I thought we was a goner. You all right, missus?' Barney grinned.

Lily nodded. 'But my arms are killing me, this tray weighs a ton.'

'Nearly there.'

As the lift wheezily arrived she asked, 'What kind of a name is Aintree?'

'Count yourself lucky. You could've been Kempton Park.'

The first-class passage was silent, the oak panelling and Axminster carpet soaking up all unnecessary and inconvenient noise. And Mrs Webb was right, no sign of anyone; all passengers appeared to be slumbering in their cabins. The momentary quiet soothed Lily. She took a deep breath as they turned the corner into the corridor of luxury suites.

'Dear God!' The shock of what she saw nearly caused her to drop the tray.

Beside her, Barney uttered in horror, '*Jee-sus!*'

They both stared in disbelief.

On the door of Nurse Grossman's cabin, Suite 1002, gashed in white chalk, was the word JEW, a Star of David tricked out beside it.

'Barney, report this to the purser. But insist Miss Grossman is not to be disturbed, I don't want to be interrupted.' All her fear gone, she put down the tray and started to rub hard at the markings. 'Quick, Barney, get a move on, before anyone else sees this.' But the young man seemed frozen to the spot.

'Barney, for heaven's sake!'

He was off.

Quickly checking she was alone, she lightly tapped on the door. No response. She tried the door; it was unlocked. She picked up the tray and stepped into the cabin.

For a moment she thought it must be empty but then, on the bed, a muddle of blankets moved and a voice weakly said, 'No breakfast, thank you.'

'Please, I'm so sorry to disturb you but I *must* talk to you.'

A tangled head emerged. 'What?'

'I have to talk to you, Miss Grossman. Oh, do you mind if I put this tray down? It's rather heavy.'

No doubt surprised by such brisk authority, the young woman started to crawl from the bed and push the clothes from a low table. She stopped and stared. 'Who are you?'

'I'm a friend,' said Lily. 'In disguise.'

Chapter Fifteen

SS *Etoile*. Saturday early morning

Enid Timms sat alone in her cabin amidst the muddle of her boots and shoes, holding the rumpled page of her *Sunday Chronicle*. She stared down at the photograph of the children's party and, in particular, at the little boy in the cowboy hat.

Nicholas Sutton.

Where was the child now? And why had his mother chosen to flee the country, deserting her young child? Abandoning him...

Already Miss Timms could see the headlines.

She felt a mounting excitement as a plan began to form. She made herself sit on the edge of her bunk and tried to marshal her thoughts clearly.

She knew that Lady Slocombe loathed Lily Sutton and perhaps now, she, Enid Timms, could help her mistress get even with the woman. Although much to her irritation, even after all these years, she had never been able to discover the exact cause of the deep hatred between the two women. But, she reasoned, anything that put her into good odour with her mistress was a thing to be desired.

She thought on. How best could she use this photograph to prove that Lady Sutton was on the run – and therefore not a fit mother?

And then she had an idea. She would go to the newspaper office here on board. Surely it was just the sort of picture to lend 'meat' to the story. She might even be early enough to get it included in today's edition.

Unable to contain her excitement any longer, Enid Timms rushed from her cabin, a cry of triumph only just muzzled by the discipline of thirty years in service.

Across the passageway in Billy and Freddie's dusty broom cupboard, at the very nadir of despair in their sleuthing endeavours, about to abandon their post, circumstances took control. To their amazement, they saw the cabin door opposite fly open and their quarry shoot off down the corridor at tremendous speed, a streak of navy-blue serge.

They stared disbelievingly. First at the disappearing figure and then at the open cabin door.

With one move, the two boys were across the corridor and into the cabin, only to be brought up sharp by the muddle and mess. Bits of newspaper, old rags, a jumble of shoes and boots.

'Stand guard outside,' hissed Billy. He started to sweep aside newspaper and rags, peering all about with eagle-eyes until he recognised, amidst the mayhem, sitting neatly in the middle of the bunk-bed, the tin box with the word OXO written on it. He snapped open the lid.

'By gum. What've we here?'

Inside the tin, twinkling amongst various odds and ends,

sat a delicate diamond bracelet. The stolen item – of that he was sure. He'd found the culprit; the nurse *was* innocent after all.

Suddenly he heard Freddie screech from outside, 'Billy! The old biddy's coming back!'

Billy was under the bunk in a blink. He lay frozen-still. But no one entered.

Worse.

The key turned in the lock and Billy was prisoner…

The footsteps hurried away.

Billy held his breath.

Silence. And the clunking of the engines. Billy felt very sick. He started to burrow from under the bunk and heard, at the base of the door, a small scuffling sound. He scrambled across.

'You all right, Bill?' Freddie whispered through a low grill. 'Yeah.'

'What you going to do?' Freddie sounded very dismal and bleak.

Billy screwed up his eyes and tried to think his way through the maze of possibilities, all of which seemed to lead to Big Trouble. *But more important than me neck,* he thought, *there's this here bracelet. The captain's gotta be told.*

A decision made, he called out, 'Fred, go and get your gran. I need her to get me out of here. I've gotta see the captain.'

'But, Billy—'

'It's a matter of life and death, Fred. I've found the "swag"!'

'But—'

'Quick! Go!'

* * *

'This is our Anthea. Say "how do".'

In the tiny Valley cabin, Nellie was introducing her granddaughter to young Nicholas. Both children looked down at their shoes.

'Let's get you into this outfit, Nickie love.' Nellie bustled as best she could in the constricted space, and at the sight of his very own clown suit, saw the boy's shyness magically disappear.

'You've got green pom-poms,' Anthea said in a tiny voice. But no one answered for at that moment Mr Valley appeared in the doorway.

'No sign?' asked Nellie.

The man shook his head.

'Didn't you find Mummy?'

Nellie could see the boy was anxious; she pulled him round to face her. 'Now then, lad, stand still. We're nearly done.' With great sufferance, he allowed his green pom-poms to be fastened.

'Is Mummy still upstairs?'

'Next, make-up.' The boy's distraction was complete as out of her handbag Nellie produced her 'Outdoor Girl' Lip and Cheek rouge and a small box of face powder.

Mr Valley stood momentarily lost in the doorway. *His face could hold a day's rain, it's that lined with worry*, thought Nellie, looking up. Behind him, she could see Eastern potentates and policemen, wizards and witches, surging towards the third-class general room. Laughter and shouting, singing and dancing. But no sign of Mrs Valley.

'Now then.' Mr Valley firmly closed the door against the noise. 'When we're at the fancy-dress parade we're all to stick together. We're to keep hold of each other's hands so none of us gets lost, as there are lots and lots of people. Do you understand, you two?'

Both children nodded seriously, standing side by side, two little clowns with white faces and cherry noses and lips, only red and green pom-poms marking them apart.

'And may I say how very splendid you two look,' Mr Valley said with a smile.

The suspense as to their appearance proving too much, Nickie and Anthea shyly turned and saw the reflected glory in the other. Two Pierrots, no looking-glass required. Surprised and delighted, the little clowns began to twirl and bob, becoming giddier and giddier with excitement, the noise in the small cabin growing, the two youngsters injecting each other with great gusts of joy.

'Nickie!' Mrs Valley came through the cabin door. 'You and Anthea look splendid.'

'Lily—'

'Oh, Mrs Valley!' *Thank the Lord*, thought Nellie.

'Sorry to be so long. Thought it wise to disrobe in your cabin first, Mrs Webb. I've left the uniform there for Barney to collect.' The woman's face was gleaming.

'We're all to stick together at the fancy-dress party, Mummy,' said Nicholas.

'And we 'ave to 'old each other's 'ands,' added Anthea, in her tiny voice. Nellie smiled down at her and the little girl's hand crept into hers.

'Well, here we go. Everybody ready at last?' asked Mr Valley. Relief made him sound cross, and Nellie saw Mrs Valley whisper, 'Sorry.' He nodded curtly.

The five of them set off from the cabin, and it was only as they were jostling along the passageway that Mr Valley asked,

'I presume everything went all right up there?' There was a decided edge to his voice.

'Splendid,' beamed Mrs Valley. 'Couldn't have gone better.'

She looks that bonny when she's happy, thought Nellie, and saw at the same moment Mr Valley's anger vanish. Good, peace was restored between her new friends. 'You remembered to give Nurse Grossman the letter?' she asked.

All three grown-ups ducked into a huddle above the turbans, halos and helmets.

'Yes, *and* I also made absolutely clear that I had to remain anonymous. Because of the letter's contents.'

'But the nurse'll see it gets delivered proper, like?'

Mrs Valley nodded.

'And did she tell you what happened to her? How she got accused and that?' Nellie wanted the detail, the full story.

'Yes, poor lamb. Lavinia appears to have behaved even more poisonously than usual. Dear God, I had forgotten how dangerous she can be.' Nellie saw the woman caught off-guard by the terrible fear and, reaching forward, quickly put a hand on her son's bouncing shoulder. 'She must never, ever know we're down here.'

'And we won't ever let her know,' stated Nellie forcefully.

Around them swirled the jolly crowd, intent on moving forward.

'Mummy, Mummy. Look!' Nickie grabbed his mother's hand and was pulling her onward. No more dawdling. They all surged through the big double doors into the third-class general room.

Down at one end of the large room, rows of chairs faced a newly erected stage, framed and decorated with twirling strips of bunting and little paper flags. To one side, various passengers had got together to make up a small band, the sight of this motley crew adding to the festive air though any actual music was drowned out by the noise of the crowd.

The big room was packed and most of the seats had already been taken. But, with an efficiency that highly impressed her, Nellie watched Mr Valley cut through the crowd and find a trestle–table, upon which he placed a couple of orange boxes. Onto these he installed the children whilst, with much laughter, the two ladies perched side by side on the wooden table.

They all now found themselves sitting above most of the audience and having a splendidly clear view.

In the luxurious hush of Suite 1018, Miss Timms, with ghost-like quiet, placed the breakfast tray before Lady Slocombe, smoothed the ivory satin covers, slotted a fifth pillow between her Ladyship and the bed-head, and then gently pulled back the thick curtains to reveal a distinctly grey day.

Standing at the end of the bed as Lady Slocombe removed her eye-mask, Miss Timms' face held no expression. She watched her mistress turn her attention to two lightly boiled eggs. And waited.

'What in the name of—' Her ladyship stopped short, her eye caught by the front page of the day's *Poseidon Post*.

'Oh my lady—' Miss Timms began. For the first time in thirty years, the maid's voice held a tremor of excitement.

Lady Slocombe's head came up; she held her maid in a gimlet stare. '*Well?*'

'Early this morning, I took the liberty of furnishing the editor of the ship's newspaper with a photograph in my possession.

It was of the Sutton boy.' The maid could restrain herself no longer. 'They have placed it in today's paper. I thought it might help to "flush" Lady Sutton out, so to speak.'

Her ladyship was very still. She put out a hand to her bedside table, found a lorgnette and, bringing it carefully to her face, stared down at the photograph of the little boy in a cowboy hat.

The noise level in the third-class general room was deafening. The master of ceremonies, a very harassed and hoarse purser, was resorting to the use of a large gong as a means of getting attention.

'And now, ladies and gentlemen, the winners.'

An uncertain hush fell.

On the little stage stood an awkward row of wiggling children, these, the finalists, gazed on by anxious parents and friends, bursting with pride. But Lily only had eyes for Nickie and Anthea, standing at one end of the line, holding hands but pretending not to.

'They'd better get a place at least,' muttered Johnnie. 'I've got half a crown each way on our two. And a tanner on the Chinese mandarin.'

The gong sounded. 'And in third position is James for his very life-like Mr Charlie Chaplin.'

A storm of applause.

'Well, I don't think it matters either way.' Lily nudged Mrs Webb. 'Just see how much happier Anthea looks.'

But Mrs Webb couldn't see anything. She sat in a huddle with her hands clamped over her eyes. 'I *can't* look. The suspense is killing me.'

'And the second prize goes to – wait for it...'

A half-hush descended.

'The two clowns, Nickie and Anthea!'

They were all on their feet.

'And that,' announced Johnnie, 'is a very tidy ten bob. Thank you very much, ladies, for your sterling work in assembling such splendid costumes.' He solemnly shook them both by the hand. 'I think this calls for a celebration. I'm going to splash out my winnings and treat us all to a glass of beer.'

Off he headed into the crowd leaving Lily and Nellie, with not a word to be said, both beaming with pride and happiness.

On the other side of the huge room, a little figure was jumping up and down.

Young Freddie in a far doorway, with a hundred people or so between him and his family, was trying to attract their attention and going mad with frustration. Having found the family's cabin empty, he'd at last tracked down his gran, here. He could see her, over the other side of the room. Sat up on a table with the posh woman. But he couldn't get to her. Nobody would let him through.

He stood on the edge of the fancy-dress room and re-thought his plan. *I'll go round t'other side.*

Off he set once more down the corridor, turning right and right again. And became completely lost; he didn't recognise anything. He stood turning every which way, the sounds of the fancy dress far, far away. But he was determined; he was on a mission. It was a matter of life and death, Billy had found the 'swag' and he had to be rescued. Freddie was the man to do it.

Trying not to despair, he started back the way he'd come.

Then – blow me! – there he was walking along behind the old Timms biddy and an officer. And all three of them seemed to be heading for the fancy-dress room together.

Don't panic – keep your distance, Freddie thought. He'd read about jungle-stalking in *The Ranger*.

He tucked in behind a young couple, their arms all round each other, and dodging about behind them, managed to keep his prey in sight. Then, to his horror, his 'hiding-place' stopped in the middle of the corridor and began kissing.

Disgusted, Freddie stepped away and nearly found himself tumbling into Miss Timms and the officer, who were now hovering in the doorway of the fancy-dress room. Freddie ducked back behind the kissing couple and watched.

The old biddy was stretching up on her tiptoes and searching the horizon. *What's she looking for?* And for no reason he rightly knew, Freddie felt fear in his heart. He stood very still.

The officer asked, 'Any luck, mum?' Whereupon the woman let out a long low moan and, so strange was the sound, everybody nearby turned and looked.

The moan turned into a strangled sob. 'Yes! That's the woman. There! There! In brown…' She was jabbing and pointing, and then her body went all stiff and trembly. 'There's the child! I can't believe it! There's the child!' she managed to cry.

'Which one?' the officer asked.

It was when she answered, 'The one dressed like a clown, next to the fat woman,' that Freddie knew something was really wrong. He couldn't see anything but he knew, just *knew*, it had to be his gran and Anthea. Through fright and confusion, he heard the officer say, 'Thank you, ma'am, I can take it from here.'

It was too much; he couldn't take any more. He had to

find out what was happening, to see what danger was about to befall his family. He pushed and shoved his way into the room, but all around it was too dark to see amongst the people. He ducked down onto all fours and peered through trousers and skirts. By the nearest wall, he saw the legs of a table. 'Oi! Watch it, young man! Less of a rough-house.' Ignoring a clutching hand, he scrambled through, his life depending on it; he had to save his family.

He pulled himself up onto the table, cups and saucers spilling off, and frantically looked around, his head swivelling left and right. And with so much relief he nearly fell off, he saw Mr Valley pouring beer at the next table.

'Mr Valley, Mr Valley!' he called with all his might. But the man didn't seem to hear for he picked up his glasses of beer and, moving away, disappeared back into the crowd.

'Look, Gran, we won a yo-yo. One each!'

'Mummy, Mummy, we came second!'

'Excuse me, madam, I wonder if you and your child would come with me?'

At the sound of this new voice, Nellie spun round and saw Mrs Valley hesitate and then stand upright. She appeared to be smiling at the man at their side. It was a very serious-looking petty officer.

Half questioningly, Mrs Valley said, 'Certainly, Officer, I hope there's no trouble?' Nellie heard the woman's voice sounded quite firm.

'We have been asked to follow up certain inquiries. It's been suggested that you may be able to help.'

'But my husband isn't here at the moment—' Mrs Valley was looking around.

'His presence won't be necessary, madam. It's just a few routine questions. Perhaps not here?' Heads were beginning to turn in interest.

Mrs Valley ducked down and quietly said to Nickie, 'Be brave, darling.'

She stood back up and the two women exchanged the briefest look, Nellie giving what she hoped was a nod of encouragement. Mrs Valley took the child's hand.

'Madam?' The petty officer held out his arm and signalled the way for mother and child to follow.

'Of course. Um, Mrs Webb, would you be so kind as to tell my husband?' Again the woman sounded quite calm.

Nellie nodded. She put a reassuring hand on the woman's arm and stood helpless as the little group disappeared into the crowd.

Later she would remember that, for all her seeming calm, Mrs Valley was shaking like a leaf.

Lady Lavinia Slocombe had made the extremely unwise choice of Schiaparelli pink. Under cover of various documents, Captain Henshaw was surveying her carefully and, it must be said, with no little fascination, as she sat across the wide desk from him.

There was no doubt that the colour was far too bright but he was aware that her ladyship was mistakenly convinced of its youth-giving properties. What is more, she had chosen the colour not only for her three-quarter length coat with its standing collar of shaved lamb but also for her snugly-fitting cloche hat, which, no doubt, she hoped enhanced the face it framed. *This morning*, he thought, *it resembles an old white-washed wall with all its pits and pocks, not helped by that gash of purple lipstick.* Lady Slocombe was dressed to kill. She was in an especially buoyant mood and thoroughly enjoying her own conversation. Captain Henshaw was finding the interview very wearying, the Schiaparelli pink and the purple lipstick, as a colour combination, heavily jarring on the eye.

'It would have been 1922. After that my dear husband, Sir Charteris,' the woman flagged up the name with all the delicacy of a pirate prince unfurling the skull and crossbones, 'never considered travelling with any other line. Indeed, he has become one of its major shareholders, such is the faith he puts in Silver Star.' She paused briefly to allow the full monetary implication of her presence to sink in. 'Which is why I knew I could turn to you, Captain, at our little tête à tête this morning and share this – not to put too fine a point on it – this particular burden.' She paused once more.

The captain placed his elbows on his desk and rested his chin on his clasped hands, his expression impenetrable. He glanced down once again at the sheet of newspaper before him and looked at the picture of the little boy.

He'd hoped to keep the 'tête à tête' to a bare minimum having decided to dismiss the 'theft' of Lady Slocombe's bracelet as a most unfortunate mishap. He had, however, been out-manoeuvred by her ladyship, who had sailed into his office, her maid in her wake, and docked across the desk from him. 'I have a matter of grave importance to discuss with you, Captain.'

The woman had then launched into a lurid tale of child abandonment and, having dispatched her maid to identify a possible suspect, from the moment of her arrival twenty minutes earlier, had barely drawn breath. The matter of the unfortunate bracelet remained unmentioned.

'I have always believed discretion to be the better part of

valour and, although it saddens me to say I may actually know the perpetrator of this particular crime – terribly upsetting when one is so fearful for the safety of an innocent child.' A lace handkerchief appeared from the cuff of her glove accompanied by a tremulous intake of breath. 'I have decided not to take the matter into my own hands but to lay all before you as our captain.' So saying, she drenched him with a dazzling smile.

Much to Captain Henshaw's relief, at that moment there was a sharp tap at the door. It was opened from outside by a member of the crew to reveal Miss Timms hovering in the doorway in some agitation.

'Ah, Timms!' said Lady Slocombe excitedly, who, upon turning back to the captain, asked with sweet and unexpected deference, 'May my maid join us once again, Captain?'

He waved the woman into the office but before he could say anything, her mistress snapped, '*Well?*'

'She is on her way with the officer, I believe, your ladyship. And there is a further development.'

'Yes?'

'The boy appears to be with her. The officer will be bringing him as well. I was sent on ahead. They were attending a fancy-dress parade—' Miss Timms giddily shared this information but, such was her eagerness, she found her breath out-ran her and she couldn't continue.

'I knew it!' cried Lady Slocombe, clapping her hands like an excited child. 'She has abducted the boy!'

Fearing the two women's excitement was about to spiral out of control, the captain spoke up in a calm and even voice. 'In that case, your ladyship, may I suggest we have some coffee whilst we await the arrival of the party?'

* * *

Lily quietly followed Petty Officer Staps, the little clown at her side. They didn't speak but tightly held hands, both terrified.

Her mind chaotic with fear, Lily prayed that the walk from third to first class would calm her so that she could be mentally clear and alert for the unknown encounter ahead. For the second time that morning she arrived at the electric service lift, her mood so different to the optimism she had felt for her encounter with Nurse Grossman.

She looked down and asked as brightly as she could, 'All right, Nickie darling?' The little pointed hat barely moved.

Along the corridor, two maids appeared balancing high towers of towels. 'Good morning, Mr Staps.' There was a spiral of laughter and a dimply pink face appeared atop the pile of towelling. They all stood as a group in front of the lift.

''Morning, Florence, 'morning, Mabel.' The young man, all formality.

A shared look between the girls and then one of them winked a cornflower-blue eye.

'Stop it, Florence.' The young man's voice was serious. 'I'm on Captain's duty.'

'Oh!' said Florence, high spirits unquenched, and, leaning against him, she chucked a jaunty nudge of the hips. Towels tumbled.

In the ensuing disorder, Lily dropped to tie the little shoe. 'Not one word, darling. Remember.'

Mrs Webb was play-acting though she'd never been more deadly earnest in all her born days. As she had listened to Freddie's garbled tale, she had realised at once, if she could get Billy Bottle out of the cabin with the 'swag', it might be the very thing to distract the captain from Mrs Valley.

She had rushed from the general room and, falling upon a passing steward, thrown herself at his mercy. '…And then, Officer, I lock th' door of me cabin, not thinking, like, go for a walk and cack-handedly drop me key over t'side.'

Urging the steward towards Miss Timms' cabin, the minutes ticking away, Mrs Webb cajoled the poor man for all she was worth. And such was her desperation, her performance enriched by the tension of the morning, she even managed to convince herself. Which probably accounted for the unexpected tears, the arrival of which finally persuaded the dubious steward.

Standing outside Timms' cabin door, Mrs Webb's tears trickling, he slowly started to sort through his keys on a ring which he unclipped, with care, from his belt. Mrs Webb sneaked a look at her watch. Eighteen minutes since Mrs Valley had been taken away. She let out a fresh wail.

'Now, now, missus, don't take on so.' The steward appeared to fractionally hasten his efforts and at last the cabin door swung wide. No doubt concerned that further tears might appear, the man all but pushed Nellie inside and swiftly left her to it.

'Billy Bottle, you get upstairs as quick as yer legs can carry yer!'

The bellboy needed no such urging. With the OXO tin under his arm, he streaked from Miss Timms' cabin. Nellie sagged, emotionally exhausted, onto the untidy bunk-bed.

As the minutes ticked by in the captain's suite, the increasing tension was such that Lady Slocombe ceased to talk altogether. She had drawn off one glove and was making her presence felt by drumming a set of manicured fingernails upon the desk. It was the only sound in the room. A cup of coffee sat untouched in front of her. Timms stood silently to attention at her side, rigid with anticipation.

In the far corner of the room, the captain, having excused himself from further conversation, was taking advantage of the lull and checking through a cargo manifest with First Officer Hodder.

Since the captain's cocktail party four days earlier, when he had met Lady Slocombe for the very first time, Henshaw had attempted to avoid the woman, having found her tiresome and opinionated. He had been surprised, for he knew her good-humoured husband well and had only continued to invite her ladyship to his dinner table out of a fondness for Sir Charteris. The two men had enjoyed many an Atlantic crossing together, each respecting the other as having made an upward journey through life's many hazards. Now Captain Henshaw realised why Sir Charteris always travelled alone. In so doing, the man spared himself the undiluted challenge of his wife's conversation, leaving others, not so well prepared, to make the discovery for themselves.

Casting his eye down the cargo manifest, all Captain Henshaw wanted more than life was to be left in peace to enjoy the final chapters of his Walter Scott with a nice glass of malt whisky.

The electric lift deposited the little party on B deck. They climbed the great sweeping staircase to level A and followed Petty Officer Staps out through a swing door into the open air. A blast of freezing March wind and an arc of fizzing spray made Lily gasp out loud.

'Sorry, ma'am, nearly there.'

Even in her state of terror Lily looked about amazed; the ocean was so much further away than what she had become used to in third class.

Suddenly, there was a twanging ring behind them. She jumped and turned to see a clay pigeon released into the air. A shot was fired true and a small burst of clay fireworked against the smoky sky.

'Clay pigeon shoot,' said young Staps nonchalantly. 'Now then, this way.' They followed him carefully along the slippery deck. 'In there's a Palm Court Orchestra and over there, that's what they call the Verandah Café, where you'll find an ice cream soda fountain.' An affable young man, Petty Officer Staps was taking great pride in affording these two a glimpse of the high life. Lily was torn between courteously acknowledging her guide and carefully averting her face for fear of being recognised by a strolling passenger.

'Oh my! You should be in a magazine,' declared an American voice. Lily spun round.

Behind them stood a young woman holding up a camera. 'Aren't you the darlingest thing.' There was the sturdy click of a shutter closing and the woman dropped to the child's level.

'May I take a couple of photographs?'

Aware that Petty Officer Staps was watching intently, Lily bent and gathered the child into her. (*Please, please, darling, don't say anything*, she prayed.) Straightening up, she looked the young woman in the eye. 'That would be such fun but not today, thank you.' Her voice sounded strangely light but at least it hadn't wavered.

'Excuse me, ma'am, I didn't mean to startle you.' The American woman briefly rested a hand on Lily's arm. 'It's just your kid looked such a honey, I wanted to capture the image. Forgive me for troubling you.' She gave Lily a warm smile and walked away along the deck.

'Mrs Valley?' Staps discreetly cleared his throat. 'The captain will be waiting.' He unclipped a rope from which hung a sign declaring 'No Entry', and herded them up a gangway. 'Captain's quarters, this way. Further along's the bridge.'

They ducked through a door into a lino-clad corridor, mercifully out of the winds. Lily stood numb, her eyes streaming, her ears ringing. Was it fear or cold? She didn't know and she didn't care, for up ahead stood the door with a sign saying 'Captain'.

'Here we are,' said Officer Staps cheerfully and knocked.

The three of them stood huddled in the doorway before a firm voice called out, 'Come.' Officer Staps opened the door and held it for the mother and child.

As they stepped into the captain's office, Lily saw the room was unexpectedly full of people. She glanced from one to the other and then her eyes locked on the one sight she feared above all others. In the middle of the room, swathed in vicious pink, sat Lavinia Slocombe. Swung round in her chair to observe their arrival, the woman was smiling at them, a most terrible smile.

The shock caused Lily to lose all breath and it was only fear of discovery that kept her conscious, preventing her from swaying to the ground. Far away, she heard Petty Officer Staps announce, 'Mrs Valley, Captain. And Nickie.'

Her heart was beating so strongly, she felt an extraordinary, unaccountable surge of energy and was appalled that fear might make her cry out. She frantically tried to make herself concentrate; she was no use to Nickie unless she was calm, focused. But her thoughts scattered and raced. She stared at the tall man, the captain, standing easily to one side of his desk, and tried to re-group her thoughts, tried to grasp at some element of calm. For no reason, she found her eye held by his lopsided shoulders, upon which was a spattering of dandruff. He moved forward and her eyes lifted to his face. He smiled at her and the unexpected warmth nearly made her lose all resolve. She felt her step falter and made herself stand still.

The captain looked away. 'Thank you, Mr Staps, you may step outside for the moment.'

It was in this brief moment, the captain's attention from her, a tough clarity entered her mind. She made herself think of Nickie, only of Nickie. With so much danger encircling them, she knew she had to do everything she could to protect her helpless child.

The captain turned back. 'Please won't you have a seat.' He motioned to an empty chair beside Lady Slocombe. As they moved forward into the room, Lady Slocombe turned her gaze away to face the captain, who now resumed his own seat across the desk. There was a look of childish expectancy on Lavinia's heavily made-up face and Lily saw the captain choose to ignore it. Instead, he looked intently down at a newspaper on the desk in front of him. He seemed to be the only person in the room at any ease.

Suddenly he looked up at her. She felt herself glance hastily away. She sensed his gaze moving slowly to the little clown pulled close to her side.

A tense silence held, the only sound the sturdy ticking of a clock. And as she sat there, Lily became aware of the swell of pent-up emotion, the ill-disguised hatred emanating from the woman beside her. She could hear Lavinia breathing heavily and hoarsely through her teeth. *Dear God, to have this as my enemy.*

The captain pushed the paper from him and began. 'Mrs Valley, do you know why we have asked you here this morning?'

Lavinia exploded, 'This woman is no more Mrs Valley than I am!'

'Your ladyship, *please!*' The captain's authority rang round the cabin. It was so impressive that Lady Slocombe's mouth slammed shut.

There was complete silence.

Captain Henshaw started again. 'Now, Mrs Valley?'

'Captain?' Her voice sounded strained but she held the captain's eye.

'Before we begin I think it only fair to explain why I have asked you here this morning. I don't know if you are aware but there have been reports in the newspaper of a missing woman, a Lady Sutton.' Through the kick of the shock, Lily struggled to hold her face immobile. But her mind was chaos. How did they know, here on the ship, she was missing?

Slowly, she focused. The captain was holding up the newspaper he had been reading. Under the words *Poseidon Post* was a headline stating in bold, 'Aristocrat's Wife Still Missing', and beside it a picture of Nickie in his cowboy hat.

The shock was so great she instinctively pulled the child into her, ducking her head in an attempt not to cry out loud. But to her dismay, the sudden movement caused a gasp, which rapidly turned into the scratchy sound of crying and, looking down, she saw large teary globs making wide pink tracks through the white clown make-up.

'Oh, darling, don't—'

'I'm afraid I really do have to get to the bottom of this, Mrs Valley.'

She scrabbled for her handkerchief and tried to mop the tears but the crying wouldn't stop. And all the while, at her side, she could feel Lavinia Slocombe gazing at the pair of them, the power and stillness of the woman frightening and malevolent. She looked hopelessly back at the Captain.

He put down the newspaper and lifted a sheet of lists. No, oh no, the passenger lists. Lily braced herself for the blow.

'Our lists say here you are travelling third class, with your husband, Mr John Valley, and your daughter, Miss Nickie Valley. This is Nickie, I take it?'

Lily closed her eyes and nodded.

The captain's eyes travelled once more down his lists. 'And you are ten years old, I see. Yes?'

With the question, Lily heard the crying quieten. 'I'm afraid she's very shy, Captain,' she said quickly.

But the captain was insistent. 'Please, Nickie, can you tell me how old you are?'

There was a silence.

The little clown raised its face, all streaky and blotchy. Looking first at Lily and then at the big man behind the desk, Anthea said, 'I'm ten.'

'You see how shy she is,' said Lily hastily. She snuggled the little girl into her arms and Anthea's thumb disappeared into her mouth. The crying had stopped.

'Well, Lady Slocombe?'

But before her ladyship could say anything, the cry of a small trapped animal issued from the thin woman standing at Lady Slocombe's side. All stared as this tiny mewing changed pitch to that of a faintly whistling kettle, and the colour leaked from the woman's pinched face as her eyes held Lily's in a violent stare.

'Be quiet, Timms!' Such was the force of Lady Slocombe's command that the thin woman fell back and was only just caught by the quick-thinking Mr Hodder.

'May I ask everyone in this room for the moment to say and do absolutely nothing.' The authority in the captain's voice brought all to attention. 'Mr Hodder, find the lady a chair.' He turned towards the moaning woman. 'Madam, are you in need of medical assistance?' The woman sat with an indecorous bump, a further whimper emitting from her. She weakly shook her head.

The captain watched for a moment, then, satisfied that another 'turn' was not about to occur, said, 'I hope this satisfies you, Lady Slocombe. This little girl is quite obviously not the little boy in the newspaper photograph—'

'Lily Sutton, don't you dare play games with me!' Lavinia's voice was coarse and snarling, the intent electric. Anthea burst into new and terrified tears.

'Lady Slocombe, I really must ask you—' the captain started.

But Lavinia Slocombe was on her feet, pointing at Lily. 'This woman is Lady Sutton! Her husband is Sir Charles Sutton, for God's sake! This is not her child—'

She lunged forward, greedily snatching at the little girl, ripping her away from Lily's arms. The captain was out of his chair but not before Lavinia's fingers had dug into Anthea, and as he pulled the child away, the long nails tore through the thin clown-suit and a livid scratch rose up on the pudgy little arm.

Lily was upon the woman, hauling at the pink coat. At the same moment, First Officer Hodder leapt forward and interposed himself between the two women.

'For God's sake, your ladyship, have you lost your mind!' Captain Henshaw exploded, carefully cradling the child away from danger. Everyone held their ground, the shock of the violence paralysing them all. Very gently, the captain handed Anthea back into Lily's arms; the child's fear was trembling out of her in wrenching sobs.

Lily rocked her, the scratch puffing up, red and raw, through the freckles. 'Hush, hush now, I'll kiss it better.' She carried Anthea to the corner of the room, far from Lavinia.

Lavinia Slocombe reluctantly resumed her chair.

'Now, Lady Slocombe, please be so good as to explain what you mean by "Not her child".'

As the woman went to open her mouth there came a loud insistent knocking on the captain's door. He chose to ignore it. 'Lady Slocombe?'

Lily felt ice-fear spill through her. Anthea started to whimper.

'This child does not belong to this woman, Captain,' Lady Slocombe spat out the charge in a heavy untidy voice. 'She is Lady Sutton and—'

Again there was a loud knocking.

But the captain appeared not to hear; he was intent on an answer. 'Lady Slocombe, do you have any reason to believe that this woman may have abducted this child?' He gestured briefly towards the little girl, his voice sharp; he would take no further nonsense.

'Not this child, Captain!' snapped the woman. 'Nicholas. Nicholas Sutton, the boy in the newspaper.' Lily felt the little girl start to shiver violently in her arms.

For a third time the knocking came again. Lady Slocombe let out a wail of irritation at the noise, her prey so nearly trapped.

Equally irritated, the captain submitted to the knocking and called out sharply, 'Come.'

Petty Officer Staps entered.

'What is it, Mr Staps?' The captain's eye never left Lady Slocombe.

'Sorry to disturb you, Captain, but Mr Bottle insists on seeing you at once.'

'Good heavens, man, can't you see I'm busy?' the captain snapped in fury.

But young Staps persevered. 'Says he has some very important information, relevant to the present inquiry, Captain.'

Such was the urgency in the young man's voice, the Captain looked at him fully. 'Does he indeed? Well, to be honest, I would welcome the distraction.' He cast a disgusted look around the room. 'Show him in.'

As Staps disappeared, he commanded, 'Ladies, if there is any further disturbance, I shall be forced to take extreme measures.' He addressed the remark solely to Lady Slocombe.

'Hang on, darling,' Lily whispered to Anthea. The little girl's shivering had ceased; she had gone strangely still.

Billy Bottle entered, saluted. He stood heaving breaths.

'Been in a race, Mr Bottle?'

'Sorry, Cap'n,' the lad gasped, his face, bright red. 'Had to run to get here – something to show you, Cap'n. Thought it might be useful to the present inquiry.'

'Continue,' nodded the captain curtly.

'This, sir.' From behind his back, Billy brought forth the

dented OXO tin and, opening it, took out the diamond bracelet and placed it on the blotter.

With a screech, Miss Timms started forward, making to snatch at the bracelet and crying at the same time, 'She made me do it! She made me do it!' She was pointing wildly at her mistress.

'Keep your mouth shut, Timms!' Lady Slocombe snarled at her maid.

Surprisingly, the woman hushed immediately. Everything went unnaturally quiet.

Captain Henshaw rose from his desk. Out of the silence, he said in a careful even voice, 'I am warning you all, I am not prepared to put up with any more of this hysterical behaviour.'

He stood, waited. His authority held; no one moved.

'First things first. Let us deal with the matter at hand. Lady Slocombe.' He turned. The big woman had sunk back down into her chair. 'Once and for all, will you tell me why you think this woman is implicated in the abduction of this child?'

Lily held her breath. She made herself look into her mortal enemy's face. The hatred she found there was palpable and she clung to Anthea with every ounce of love she had, as if for her own child. She held the look and waited for the woman to speak out against her. But as she watched, she saw the fury in Lavinia's look wither and slip away, the terrible gaze dying. Lavinia no longer appeared to fill the vast shocking-pink costume but sat, diminished, as she stared with a resigned and aged air at the diamond bracelet in the middle of the captain's desk. With a slight swagger, she raised her head, and Lily realised the face had lost its adder-puff of fury and looked folded and withered, the smudged purple lipstick lifting the mouth into an absurdly childish grin. Staring into the middle distance, the woman baldly stated, 'Now I meet her face to face, I realise I do not know this woman. Nor her daughter.'

This pronouncement over, she ducked back down into a large handbag and started rummaging amongst the contents, eventually withdrawing a compact. Very slowly and with great concentration, she started to re-gild her mouth, all the while keeping her face averted from the company.

Lily watched amazed, the relief not to be trusted.

The captain nodded. 'Very well.' He turned to Lily. 'Mrs Valley, I think we should let you and your little girl get back to the fancy-dress party.'

He walked around the desk to join them and, dropping to Anthea's level, smiled into the blotchy face. 'It's a very splendid outfit.'

Anthea leant towards him and whispered, 'We won a yo-yo.'

'Good for you.' He straightened up. 'Mr Staps, please be so good as to take Mrs Valley and Nickie back below.' Stepping forward, he held the door and, with the smallest of bows, said, 'I am so sorry to have disturbed your morning, Mrs Valley.'

Lily gave a nod and, with her arm around the little girl's shoulders, she quickly left the captain's quarters.

CHAPTER SIXTEEN

SS *Etoile*. Saturday afternoon

Mrs Webb was extremely partial to a bit of brawn. She sat in her cabin with a tray on her knees tucking into a plateful.

At her feet, Nickie and Anthea played silently and with great concentration. The little girl, tears all gone, the long scratch on her arm a badge of honour marking her bravery that morning, was strangely fascinated by the game Nickie was teaching her. And the little boy, happy at last to have a pal to play with, even a girl, was fully prepared to share some of the secrets on how to win card-cricket. Mrs Webb nodded approvingly – oh, the peace.

She closed her eyes. *What a terrible, terrible morning.* For the moment, food forgotten, she mulled over the events of the last few hours. Mind, she'd even impressed herself in gulling that steward. But then the long awful wait for Mrs Valley to come back from the captain, Mr Valley all silent and jumpy, neither of them knowing if Billy Bottle had reached the captain in time. And she'd only had to take one look at the poor woman's face when she'd come at last to know something was very wrong.

'Mrs Webb, please have the children for a little while, I must talk to my husband alone.' With Anthea at her side, white and silent, the woman added, 'Your little one has been wonderfully brave. But you got a little scratch, didn't you, darling?' At this point, emotions so overwhelmed the woman she couldn't speak.

'Don't you worry, dear,' Nellie'd replied. 'You stay 'ere with Mr Valley and 'ave a rest. You look fair done in.' She had hurriedly turned to usher the little ones away but Mrs Valley had caught her wrist and said in a frantic whisper, 'Keep Nickie hidden. *All* the time.'

Well, the little ones were safe as pie now, all tucked up in her cabin. She was mad to know what had happened, Anthea's side of things being a little hazy, but she'd have to wait. The child was upset, she could see that; she didn't want to push her further. No, she'd just have to bide her time for the full story.

She stretched and smiled. A bit of jam sponge for 'afters', the children playing nicely, Freddie up there with his dogs, and the latest copy of *Picturegoer* that she'd been saving as a treat. That would keep her going this rainy afternoon and take her mind off everything.

Lily was in despair. As the cabin door closed behind Mrs Webb and the children, she fell into Johnnie's arms and sobbed uncontrollably.

'Nickie's – says Aristocrat's Wife – front's a big picture—' She kept gulping up words. 'She – spitefully – so horrible – and the danger—'

Johnnie held her, saying nothing, letting the horror spill

out. As best he could, he tried to piece together the story whilst gently rubbing her back. Like a child, she allowed herself to be soothed, the tears slowly stopping.

But her fear couldn't be contained. 'Charles must have found us. Why else is our story in the newspaper?'

'If Charles had discovered your whereabouts, Lily, he would have wired the ship and the Captain would have known your true identity.'

'Yes, but Lavinia does—'

'The captain – and that's who's important in this case – called you Mrs Valley.'

'But Nickie's picture's in the paper—'

'Which doesn't mean anyone knows that you, Lily Sutton, are here on board. Now, tell me exactly what happened. From the beginning.'

On the blotter in the middle of Captain Henshaw's desk lay the diamond bracelet. Beside it sat the open OXO tin, inside the lid of which was written in a large clear hand:

This is the property of Enid Mary Timms, 1911
23 Manor Lane
Woolwich
London SE
Great Britain
The Empire
The World
The Universe

Emptied of the bracelet, the OXO tin now appeared to contain a small bottle of green ink, a pen with a couple of detachable nibs, a lock of pale hair bound by a delicate strand of pink thread, a small notebook and two or three stubs of white chalk. Wedged at the bottom was an old envelope marked 'Private'.

'Does this bracelet belong to you, Lady Slocombe?' The captain picked up the dainty jewellery from the blotter. He turned it over, on the clasp was engraved '*LS from CS on our wedding-day, 7th May 1921.*'

'Indeed it does, Captain, a wedding present from dear Charteris. Oh, Timms.' The hefty woman turned to her maid. The thin woman sat still as a statue, staring down at the floor.

Lady Slocombe turned back to the captain and, in a lowered voice, requested, 'May I have a brief word with you in private, Captain?'

With little ceremony, Enid Timms was bundled outside to be guarded by a naval rating. As the door closed, Captain Henshaw looked at his watch; he was determined to keep this tête-à-tête as brief as possible.

In a voice weary with grief, Lady Slocombe began. 'I am devastated. I had so hoped this – this *thievery* had ceased. Timms has always had, shall we say, a weakness for being light-fingered. "Kleptomania", I believe it is called. I know Sir Charteris will be as appalled as I am.'

In his desire to be rid of the woman, Captain Henshaw nodded curtly. 'I shall wire Scotland Yard immediately—'

He stopped. For the second time that morning Lady Slocombe's face had gone grey. In a whisper, she gasped, 'Oh no, you mustn't call the police!'

'But why on earth not, Lady Slocombe?'

The big woman floundered. She opened her mouth to

speak then thought better of it.

'Lady Slocombe, I should have thought you of all people would wish to see justice done. And done properly.'

'Indeed I do, Captain.' He watched as the woman drew her large handbag onto her lap and, in so doing, appear to rally. Her voice stronger, she confided, 'There are certain aspects to this affair that I feel should remain private, that I would prefer not to discuss.' She ducked her head towards the captain, lowering her voice to a remorseful whisper. 'Mental instability and so on. Very upsetting if you get my meaning. I trust I need say no more?'

The question was hypothetical as she did not wait for a reply but steamed on regardless. 'I would be obliged if you would leave me to handle this extremely delicate matter. Timms has been a family servant for over thirty years and I would not wish to publicly press charges.' Her smile was all bountiful. *Dear God,* thought Henshaw, *the woman is going to beg for mercy.* And indeed she did.

'I beg you, Captain – as the Bard himself has it – 'the quality of mercy'?'

Unable to stomach the woman's ill-disguised hypocrisy further and aware that whatever punishment he meted out would probably be out-done by any walking the plank she could devise, he nodded agreement. Though he feared there were the pair of them in it, he sadly had no proof to corroborate his misgivings; the stolen item had been found in the maid's possession.

'Under the circumstances, I think an apology to Miss Grossman would be suitable?' He held the woman's eye.

'Indeed, Captain, I will be going to her cabin straight away,' her ladyship replied smoothly. She rose from her chair.

He gave her a curt nod and she left.

Alone, he swiftly ran through the happenings of the morning, trying to sift fact from fiction. A curiosity had begun to niggle at the back of his mind all through these last minutes with Lady Slocombe. Why had the well-spoken Mrs Valley been dressed as a chambermaid, carrying a breakfast tray, when he'd first met her during morning inspection? And she'd used the oddest alias, he remembered. What was it? A racecourse, that was it. Aintree. And why did her child speak with such a strong North Country accent?

He rang down on his intercom to the wireless room.

'Contact Scotland Yard. I want details concerning a young boy. Name: Nicholas Sutton. Age: about ten years old.' He looked down at the newspaper article on his desk. 'He appears to be the son of a Sir Charles Sutton. Treat it as a matter of some urgency.'

He rose to leave his office; he needed to clear his head. There was something extremely unsettling about the whole affair that he couldn't put his finger on. *I am a man of the sea*, he thought wearily, *I fancy myself neither as politician nor policeman.*

Full speed maintained, 519 miles covered in the last twenty-four hours, they would be docking in New York on time at ten o'clock the next morning. God willing and the weather remaining fair.

He stepped out of his office and, turning into the wind, headed towards the bridge.

At midday exactly, Lord Clairmont and his nurse entered the Paris Lounge. A shaft of primrose sunlight pierced the dreary clouds and glanced through the long windows as from the nearby Palm Court the gentle strains of 'It's Just the Time For Dancing' started up; the lunchtime concert had commenced.

Billy watched as the couple made their way to their table. Miss Grossman certainly looked perkier than she had the night before and he had to admit she looked right dapper in her little hat with its pom-pom on the side. Quite the business! As for m'lord, well, all he was good for was gazing and gazing at the nurse as though his heart would burst with pride.

Billy checked the room – he had a letter to deliver to Lady Slocombe – and noticed most of the guests smiling and nodding at the young couple. *Hmm, that's a bit late,* he thought, *the pair of 'em could have done with a spot of that last night.*

Lady Slocombe was sitting in the far corner of the room. As he made towards her, he was brought up short by her expression. She was sitting in a fury staring at m'lord and his nurse whilst commenting loudly to her companion, 'I don't think I have ever witnessed such barefaced cheek, Dora. When I think of that Grossman girl's behaviour last evening—'

Billy's arrival silenced her. She stared haughtily at the bellboy, who proffered the letter on a tray. 'Your ladyship.'

Snatching it, she began greedily tearing at the envelope. 'Give him a coin, Dora. I expect it's from the captain.' Unfolding the page, she held her lorgnette to it. But as she read, much to Billy's amazement, the woman's energy appeared to leak away until she sat trembling like a hunted animal, flicking tiny glances all about her. Suddenly she let out a gasp and the lorgnette clattered from her fingers. Frozen, she stared across the lounge, something holding her gaze in a vice-like grip.

There, on the other side of the room, Lord Clairmont and

his nurse sat calmly and boldly regarding the woman.

So startling seemingly was this challenge that Lady Slocombe forcefully hauled herself to her feet and made to move off at speed, but she stumbled at once, nearly falling, this giddy progress bringing every eye to her. Her exit was rendered even more ridiculous by her tubby little companion frantically padding after her, calling out, 'Lavinia, wait for me. Oh, Lavinia, are you not well?'

As the two women passed out of sight, Billy turned back and saw Lord Clairmont raise the nurse's gloved hand to his lips. Kissing it, he held it tenderly against his face for all the world to see.

'If the captain's doing his job properly, he'd want to get to the bottom of Lavinia's allegation.' Lily's voice was sullen. She sat huddled and wretched on the bunk, Johnnie standing only inches away by the door. Both felt trapped by the tiny cabin.

'For God's sake, Lily, we've been over and over this. The captain will dismiss the entire rumpus as a troublesome piece of meddling.' He didn't believe what he said, not for one minute, but he was sick of the whole bloody affair and he couldn't see any way forward.

'Don't shout at me, Johnnie! Just because you don't know what to do.'

He sank down onto the bunk beside her; he could feel the terrible misery of the morning threatening to consume them. He'd been terrified from the outset that they'd drop their guard, some petty error betraying them. Added to which he could feel his own personal terrors welling up, the stress baiting his illness back into life.

He closed his eyes, hearing as he did so the wretched insistence continuing in Lily's voice. 'Do you seriously think the captain believes Lavinia doesn't know this third-class passenger she's accusing! We should never have come.' Her tone sulky and shut, he could hear her kicking at fate. *Dear God, what wouldn't she do now?*

He felt a surge of panic and desperately reached for her hands. 'Lily, *we* mustn't fight. What chance do we have if we become enemies?' He clung to her, frantic that circumstances were about to tear them apart. And the choking fear, for so long unspoken, welled up between them both, driving away the sullen rage that threatened to drown them. They found themselves huddling together, desperate for comfort. Their love, so great and so new, would make them, *must* make them survive and, without warning, he started to cry. To hide the stupid ridiculous tears, he found her mouth, kissing her desperately. He mustn't lose her, this woman who'd unlocked his heart.

Lily clung to him, suddenly sensing the desperation between them, and the life, the daring leaping within her, she started to tear at his tie and the buttons on his shirt – 'Oh, hell's bells, these clothes!' – her other arm clinging round his neck as she passionately returned his kiss.

They fell back, gasping, their knees and elbows knocking and banging against the wooden confines of the bunk, the kiss between them rough. And Johnnie, feeling his neurasthenic panic pass, helped push up her skirt and together, untidily wrapped, they fell back, panting and laughing onto the bunk.

Now so great was his need of her, he roughly climbed on top and, with Lily helping him, tore aside her underclothing.

She wrapped her legs, her arms around him and fought the desire to close her eyes, to succumb to her own longing. She must see him, she must watch the weary beauty of him. And astonished by his great desire, so different from anything she had ever shared with Charles, she felt an extraordinary love as Johnnie came with a shout, the joy of which Lily was never to forget.

CHAPTER SEVENTEEN

Scotland Yard, London. Saturday afternoon

'Sir, sir!'

Young PC Battle could hardly contain his excitement. He hared along the highly polished corridor and skidded to a stop in Superintendent Outwood's doorway.

'Is there a fire, Battle?' asked Outwood in measured tones.

'Sir, we may have had a breakthrough! A cable from the captain of the SS *Etoile*'s just come through. Concerning the whereabouts of Nicholas Sutton.'

Outwood jumped up and, pulling on his jacket, pushed Battle out of the door. 'Where's the vessel now?'

'En route for New York, sir. Docks ten o'clock tomorrow morning.'

The children were by now playing Lotto and Anthea was proving a master of the game. With supreme joy at this new-found skill, she kept yelling at the top of her voice, 'Got yer! Got yer!' leaving Nickie giggling and pop-eyed at the enormous noise his new friend could make.

'She's found her voice then,' Mr Valley remarked.

'Thank the Lord,' muttered Nellie, polishing off a second jam sponge and sitting back. '"Ding-ding, full up," as my gran used to say. And very nice too.'

'And this pea and ham soup is extremely tasty as well,' remarked Mrs Valley, scraping her bowl, clean as clean.

'You've got a bit of an appetite, I'm glad to see,' said Nellie, ever-comforted by life's small gifts.

'I think I'll take these trays back, it's getting rather crowded in here. Anything further I can get you, ladies?' Mr Valley asked.

'A cup o' tea would be very nice, thank you,' replied Nellie.

As he left the cabin, she said, 'I'd forgotten how pleasant it is to have a man about the place. My Davy could be that bloody-minded, pardon my French, neither use nor ornament, but he could charm't birds off trees.'

A fleeting memory made her smile. Davy serenading her outside Sheffield General, one dark morning as she'd left the night shift. Down on one knee, in front of all her girl-friends too. He hadn't cared what anyone'd thought. Nor had she. Best-looking lad of the lot of 'em, her Davy. Always fit as a butcher's dog.

Before the memory took hold and turned sour, she shook it away. 'Enough of all that,' she said briskly and, gathering her work-basket to her, started to unravel a holey sock. 'Now, what I'm wanting to know, if it's not an impertinent question, is 'ow do you and Mr Valley intend making your money in this 'ere America?'

'Johnnie's cousin, Howard, lives in Connecticut. He runs a small school there. So we're hoping he might take us in until we get settled. I can always do my sewing and there's nothing about pigs that Johnnie doesn't know.'

'Well, I never,' said Nellie, 'but good luck to yer both, I say.' She held her sock to the light and considered the darn for a minute. 'Hard work, mind,' she added, unable to squash the cluck in her voice. Well, better the devil you know than the devil you don't. After all, the woman had never had to work for a living.

'We're not afraid of that, Mrs Webb. We'll work as hard as we can.' Nellie caught the passion in the woman's voice. 'We simply have to make enough to deal with Charles, for whenever he catches up with us. Pray God it's later rather than sooner.' She glanced down at her child, dropping her voice. 'We have to make enough so that we can all stay together.'

The child took no notice; Nellie could see that grown-ups talking was boring beside a game of Lotto. She looked across at little Anthea and smiled; her grandbabbie was talking nineteen t'dozen to her new friend.

'So you'll start off with this Howard then?'

'Yes, we're hoping to get Nickie properly settled there. It's rather a good school, I believe.'

Nellie watched the woman's hopes for the future momentarily blot out her fears for the present. *She's a lovely fresh complexion,* she thought, *and that orange hair's right pretty on her, too. Though not on some!* The image of Davy's plain sister, Bertha, swam into her mind. Poor Bertha, with her whey face and curly carrotty hair…

There was a knock, both women swung round.

'Only me,' Mr Valley called out and entered with a tray of teacups and glasses of lemon squash. 'I've just heard there's a bit of a "show fight" up there tonight with a 50 guinea purse. "The Bermondsey Bomber v The Townsend Terror". Should be worth a look.'

'I'm afraid you'll have to make do wi' fancy-dress parade down here, Mr Valley. The other's for nobs up top!'

All light drained out of the afternoon sky, leaving it the colour of smoke.

In her darkened cabin, Enid Timms sat very still amid the chaos of newspaper and shoes. On her lap, the OXO tin lay open.

The bracelet had, of course, been kept by the captain and, no doubt, returned to her mistress. But when he handed her back the tin, how could she be sure everything was present and correct, all the valuables she kept in it accounted for? She felt invaded, her world pillaged.

Carefully, Miss Timms started to make an inventory of her little possessions. She took out the green ink-bottle, the pieces of chalk, the small notebook, the little lock of hair and, most precious of all, tucked away at the bottom, the old envelope.

She unfolded it and drew out the frail document from which fell a tiny photograph. As always, she turned it over and read the fading pencil marks. 'Amy 9 months February 1916.' She opened the document. She did not need her spectacles; she knew what was written. 'Thirty-first May 1915. Chobham Hall. Amy Frances – Girl. Father: Unknown. Mother: Enid Mary Timms. Occupation of Father: Unknown.'

In utter misery, she curled up in the chaos of her little bunk. Who had found this in her cabin? Who had read this? Who now knew her secrets?

Lady Slocombe sat frozen in an armchair in her palatial suite staring across at the letter that lay open on the Louis XVI mahogany desk. Beside it, as though standing guard, a heavy silver-framed photograph of her husband, Charteris. As usual, she hadn't given him a moment's thought until now, when disaster loomed, her husband's wrath being the only thing in the world that truly frightened her. What was she to do? She had read that damned letter so many times since its delivery in the Paris Lounge, the phrases wouldn't stop whistling round her mind...

Madam,

Certain matters have come to our attention concerning your past and the acquisition of a criminal record. Silence regarding these matters will only be considered if a full and public apology is made to Miss Matilda Grossman for the inconvenience caused by your false accusation of her. It is to be hoped that this may be the last time such mischief is perpetrated through your thievery. We will be watching.

She closed her eyes and, as she did so, a wave of terror made her feel alarmingly sick and dizzy.

Why did no one understand there was an order to the world? An order which, if it was not adhered to, allowed chaos to reign. She, Lavinia, knew the order of things, had always known the order. Power and order. Power was given to so very few; it was a God-given right, as unassailable as the divine right of kings. Not to be ignored but used, in the creation of order.

That power Lavinia knew to be her right. Her birthright. To be carefully administered, often with secrecy, so that she always had control. Control over chaos. Control to guide thoughtless creatures, creatures so often indulging in selfish pleasures and joy. She had watched them, crudely demonstrating their enjoyment. Laughing, always laughing. Heedless, hateful laughter. How she hated the sound, the spectacle. Heads thrown back, bodies doubled forward. No control.

Control must be brought to chaos. This truth, Lavinia had realised long ago, was her duty to impose. This duty was her path through life; its course marked out by, of all people, her stupid little cousin Harriet. Thirty years along, Lavinia could still freshly savour the incident and the girl's insolence. Harriet on her tiny opera chair, smirking, making Grandmama and that hateful Lily Sutton laugh and giggle. Lavinia closed her eyes; she could see the wretched girl and her cohorts, all three turned towards her, sharing the same silly joke.

As always with these thoughts, Lavinia felt the consoling, boiling rage swelling through her and, as the anger burned, it felt glorious. How had the pathetic child so dared to overstep the mark? Cousin Harriet, revolting in her poverty, childish in her needs. But dangerous, too, turning the social order upside down, this impoverished relation insinuating herself where she had no right to be.

Just as the ghastly Grossman girl was doing now, her and her Jewish brethren. Just as so many threatened, everywhere. They had to be stopped before some dreary revolution took place. All of them. She, Lavinia, had to bring order to chaos…

Alone in her palatial suite, she thought, *No one understands that this has been my path through life, my Calvary.*

Now, in this difficult moment, when no one understood her desire to bring order to the chaos, she thought lovingly of her birthright and, in cherishing it, hoped it would bring the comfort she so desperately craved. But tonight as she sat alone, the comfort was joyless.

'Pooh, promise me you won't forget about me, ever. Not even when I am a hundred.'

Pooh thought for a little. 'How old shall I be then?'

'Ninety-nine.'

Pooh nodded. 'I promise,' he said.

Anthea and Nickie were curled up, a tangle of pyjamas, pillows and blankets – even Freddie, the day's dog-duties behind him, was more than happy to be one of the bunch – three scrubbed faces, turned towards Lily, silent and rapt.

Mrs Webb put her head round the cabin door and called, 'My turn.'

'Read it again! Read it again!' The three, having all snuggled down, suddenly were toppling around, pillows flying.

'*Quiet!*' roared Mrs Webb, frightening even herself, and for a moment she looked quite put out. There was a nervous pause. Then they all burst out laughing.

The youngsters were snuggled down again, lulled by the wondrous sleeping draught of sea-air and excitement, and after a brief, whispered conversation, Lily tiptoed away, leaving Mrs Webb contentedly sewing under the shaded light amidst the gentle dreaming snuffles of the children.

Chapter Eighteen

SS *Etoile*. Saturday evening

The Starlight Room is aglow. At each corner, the famed Lalique columns of light softly bathe the cocktail lounge in a seductive glow. All around, this evening, the crystalline chatter and fizzing laughter rises and falls as the pearly light catches the twist and turn of lustrous marcelled heads and the sheen of powdered arms and shoulders. Drinks before dinner, this last night at sea.

Lord Clairmont and his nurse sit in the middle of the room. He, this evening, dapper in white tie and tails; the young woman, at his side, blooming in a slender gown of peach velour. Billy, on evening duty, watches from his post by the door as m'lord carefully explains a game of baseball to the young nurse, using a bowl of pistachio nuts, two champagne flutes and an ice-bucket. *Jiminy Cricket, they're sweethearts,* he realises. *They ain't got eyes for no one else.*

Indeed, so concentrated are the young couple that they're completely unaware of oncoming danger. Towards them, making portly progress, comes Lady Slocombe, dressed this evening in a upholstered gown of maroon velvet. She is proceeding hatchet-faced through the cocktail crowd, a purser in attendance. *Oh jeepers*, thinks Billy, and braces himself on the young couple's behalf.

All around conversation drizzles to a halt, well-bred ears and eyes intent upon the encounter to come. A complete hush descends on the room.

'Lord Clairmont.' Lady Slocombe's usually loud splashy voice this evening is strangely high and tight, her face a mask.

M'lord looks up, his smiling expression vanishing. 'Lady Slocombe.' Reluctantly, he gets to his feet.

Jutting her chin and looking into the middle distance, Lady Lavinia starts. 'I believe I owe you – and your nurse—'

But Lord Henry has raised a hand. 'Excuse me, Lady Slocombe, *whom* did you say?' The cocktail lounge is completely still.

'Your nurse.' There is a discernible quaver in the big woman's voice though her jaw is still jutted. Never once does she drop her glance to the subject under discussion.

'Lady Slocombe,' says the young man, his voice cheerful and easy. 'I am afraid you are under a misapprehension.' He looks down; the young nurse is staring up at him, wide-eyed. 'I think you must mean my *wife*, Matilda Clairmont.'

There is a sudden rustle of wind through wheat as this nugget of information is hungrily devoured by the passengers. Lady Slocombe stands stock-still.

Very slowly, still staring into the middle-distance, never allowing her eyes to glance down, she turns her maroon bulk towards the younger woman. 'I believe I owe you an apology, Lady Clairmont, for, as you see, my bracelet has been recovered.' Limply, she proffers a pudgy wrist from which peeps the delicate bracelet.

But the young couple do not reply, they say nothing. Unwillingly, the weight of the silence nudges the big woman on.

'I'm very sorry for whatever inconvenience…' Whereupon she falters and gives up entirely this terrible duty. Then, before she can stop herself, she gabbles incredulously, 'Your *wife* you say, Lord Clairmont?'

'Yes, indeed.' With infinite tenderness, Lord Henry takes up his young bride's hand and looks at her with shining eyes. 'You see, Lady Slocombe, it would have been especially cruel if such an error were to have spoilt our honeymoon.'

'Quite, um…' All command has left the woman. 'May I congratulate you – both – um… If you'll excuse me, I must go in to dine.'

At this moment, the purser standing at her ladyship's side steps forward and delays her exit. 'Excuse me, my lady. I've been asked to inform you that the captain has had to make certain adjustments to his table tonight. I think you'll find you're dining at table 23.' Startled, Lady Slocombe ducks her head as she absorbs this information. 'Perhaps I may show you to your table—'

But the woman has already sped off, released.

Smartly, the purser turns back to the young couple and, speaking in a voice loud enough for all to hear, says, 'The captain is very much looking forward to your company at dinner.' And with great solemnity, he bows to young Lady Clairmont.

* * *

Beneath glimpses of the cloud-streaked moon, Lily stood alone on the poop deck. She pulled Mary's old woollen coat tightly around her. The end of this terrible day had brought no solace; the fears for the morrow still overwhelmed her. She stared up at the moon.

'The odds is gone
And there is nothing left remarkable
Beneath the visiting moon.'

If only it were so; if only nothing more could be remarkable. Her brain hurt and the backs of her legs tingled with the constant strain. She hung over the rail and looked out to sea, out into the darkness, and tried to make herself fear no more. After all, for the moment, Nickie was safe in Mrs Webb's cabin.

Above, the ship's flag flapped in the wind, the high cracking the only noise surmounting the huge roar of the heavy wash. After a time, gazing at the treacle ocean, Lily found she could think of nothing. She turned and put her back to the wind.

Johnnie was walking towards her, the ship producing a drunken roll in his stride.

'One tartan travelling rug, madam, as requested. And a surprise.'

'Oh God, Johnnie, now what?' Her hand was at her mouth, the terror instant.

'No, no, my love, this is a lovely surprise.' From behind his back, he produced a bottle of champagne.

'No! Where did you get it? You didn't nick it?' She felt a flick of the ruffian.

'Certainly not. I found it in our cabin when I went for the rug. There's a card, you read it, I'll do the honours.' Out of his pocket, he produced a tooth mug with a flourish. 'A loving-cup.'

She read out, '"Thank you for the perfect plan. It has helped to make our honeymoon so special. With all our best wishes, Matilda and Henry Clairmont." So our plan worked after all.' She sank back but felt no joy, weary once again. 'Even so, it does seem such a wretchedly big risk to have taken.' Johnnie said nothing. The champagne frothed into the tooth mug.

They sat huddled together, the rug about their knees, sheltered from the wind by a lifeboat, both with their thoughts tucked away from the other.

'And they're married. I did wonder,' she said into the darkness. She took Johnnie's hand under the rug, she hated even the glimmer of his disapproval. Had she really been so dangerously foolish in helping the Grossman Girl? Johnnie sat saying nothing. 'Do you know, I would have given anything to have seen Lavinia's face when she received my letter. It's the only thing I really regret about being down here.'

'I think it was mad for you to have gone aloft,' Johnnie said, the subject to be addressed and dealt with. 'But it did work, my love. And it has probably made that young woman's life much happier. As to your meeting Slocombe, actually no harm was done.'

'But how did Lavinia know I was on board? Oh, Johnnie, I have this awful feeling that we're being secretly watched.' She hung her head; she felt such bone-tiredness and a slackness through her body, usually so upright, the straightness of her back a grandmother's inheritance.

'No, my love, nobody is watching us. And tomorrow, to get us through disembarkation, we'll once again accept Mrs Webb's loan of little Anthea. And Barney'll slip Nicholas on land along with young Freddie.' He was smiling at her. 'Thank God, children don't need their photograph in a passport.'

She nodded mutely. Then sensing his concern for her, she pushed away her brooding fears. 'I've got a present for us as well. Hold out your hand.' She dropped five coins into Johnnie's gloved hand. 'My first ever wages.'

'How? Where from?' He stared, amazed.

'The sewing,' she smiled. 'They're from Madame.'

'Who?'

'The needlework woman. She paid Mrs Webb, who said it was only fair to share. I know it's not exactly a fortune—'

'But it's a start.' He sat back and sighed. 'Thank goodness you're a working woman at last. Now you can keep me in the style to which I hope to become accustomed.' He topped up the mug.

They sat silent, staring up at the stars and the racing moon, sipping in tandem.

Enid Timms never looked in a mirror. Since her early years in service as the lowliest maid at Chobham Hall, she had learnt to rise at 5.30 a.m. and, in the dark, twist and pin her long thick hair, bundling it neatly under her cap. She had always washed her face with household soap and water; she had no need of fancy creams. Except once, that long, hot summer, the last of peacetime, she had secretly sent away for a V&H Parisian Beauty Box to be returned 'post free in a perfectly plain cover'. But when it had arrived, 'Twelve of the finest toilet aids to beauty you can get *anywhere* for 6d', there was no longer need of it. He was dead, killed in the first battle of the war, and she was left with an OXO tin full of his fishing-flies and bait. And a child in her belly.

Willie Harrap. A poor simpleton who went to war for a drunken bet – and to avoid the promise of marriage. She hadn't really even liked him but she was nineteen and had no sweetheart. How drunk he'd become that afternoon after their fumble in a hedge, a fumble given only in return for that marriage-promise. More fool her.

And when the child came it was not as if she'd felt anything for it, that bright pink knot of messy baby. Not then…

She looked down at the little photograph. Where is my Amy now? Eighteen years of age, almost a grown woman. And here am I, her mother and an old maid. And this terrible secret of her birth that has been my eternal jail-sentence, manacling me to an all-knowing mistress who is herself a thief. A thief!

Firmly resolved, Enid Timms took from her bedside shelf a newly written letter and placed it in an envelope. But she hesitated to address it.

She checked her watch, twenty minutes before she was needed by her ladyship.

Carefully she put away the little photograph, safely nestling it beside the lock of baby hair. At the same time she removed from the tin a length of white chalk, which she wrapped in a handkerchief and placed in her pocket.

But the fury of injustice still poured through her. She, Enid Timms, was *not* a thief nor would she let herself be wrongly accused of a crime that was not even of her own devising. She had been hoodwinked by her mistress into being used as a 'fence'. And *not* for the first time. But after today, surely the last. No, the world had to know it was her mistress – and not her – who had the police record.

Without hesitation, she turned over the envelope. She

dipped her pen into the little bottle of green ink and wrote: *The Federal Bureau of Investigation, New York City.*

The letter inside remained unsigned.

'I give you, ladies and gentlemen, the newlyweds.'

Around the captain's table, champagne glasses were held high. 'The newlyweds!' 'Matilda and Henry!' 'Happy days!'

Matty couldn't stop smiling; she felt wonderful. It was public, at last. After four long secret months, the world was going to know that she and Henry were married.

Across the table, the world-famous Irish tenor Donald O'Dea caught her eye and raised his glass. '*Slainté*, my dear. Long and happy days.' He smiled widely, his fame distilled into an easy air. Matty could have hugged herself. Aunt Hilda would be so excited – Donald O'Dea himself had toasted her!

At her side, the captain leant towards her. 'Mr O'Dea's one of our most faithful passengers, Lady Clairmont. Very nice man. I thought it might be fun to ask him and his wife to join us this evening. I'm glad he agreed; often when travelling he wishes to remain more private.' But such was the enormity of the man's stature and girth that, even without his international fame, thought Matty, he drew the eye, however private he might attempt to be.

'Oh, indeed, Captain, it's wonderful. He was telling me before dinner he's en route to the highest-ever paid concert tour of America. Coast to coast.'

'Quite something, eh? And his wife is very entertaining too.'

Matty looked across at the woman whose gaunt, sepulchral aspect she'd already discovered belied enormous energy, bubbling fun and a deep devotion to porter, which she was drinking with her meal. '... Now Gaelic football is a different matter altogether,' Maud O'Dea was telling the table. 'A family sport, y'know, a real country sport. In Killkenny, when Donald and I were first courting, we followed the team. And grand was the day we came up to Dublin and saw them play at Croke Park; it was our first time away from home, y'know.' The memory painted a beguiling softness over the woman's gaunt features and, looking round at her audience, she caught Matty's eye and winked.

'A delightful couple, I think you'll agree,' said the captain. 'And tell me, have you ever heard Mr O'Dea sing in the flesh, so to speak?'

'Do you know, I have. My Uncle Maurice and my Aunt Hilda are big fans and they took me to see him at the Golders Green Hippodrome. They're going to be so excited that I've actually met the great man! But is it true that Mr O'Dea might grace us with a couple of songs later this evening?'

'He usually can be persuaded on the last night, Lady Clairmont. The cabaret's a benefit for the seamen's charities – a cause close to Mr O'Dea's heart.'

That's me, she thought, *Lady Clairmont*. On her other side, she felt Henry reach for her hand and squeeze it. She turned and grinned at him. He'd done it; he'd told the world they were married. 'I can't believe the secret's out. I'm so proud of you,' she whispered. 'I just hope your mother understands why we let the cat out of the bag before telling her first.'

'She'll understand,' Henry purred. 'In fact, knowing Mama, she'll cheer from the rooftops. She's been waiting for years to put that Slocombe woman in her place!'

'I notice she hasn't taken up the offer of table 23.' They

both started to giggle, such relief at the vanquishing of the enemy, and then suddenly the young man's face went still. 'There's something else. Last night, the ship's doctor—'

'Oh, Henry, the doctor's told you?'

He nodded.

'Isn't it wonderful?' She grinned at him.

But Henry carried on anxiously. 'The doc's concerned – after last night – your terrible anguish, perhaps it harmed you – you *and* the baby – because it's such early days.'

'He needn't worry, all's well.' She cheerfully took his hand. 'After all, I should know, I'm not a nurse for nothing.'

She longed to embrace him but for decorum's sake only stroked his hand. 'All's well, I promise. But, oh dear, Henry,' she whispered. 'Now we're going to have to tell your mother – on top of everything else – she's about to be a grandmother!'

Before her the waiter set down a delicate glass dish. It held a swirl of palest lavender cream and was exquisitely decorated with little purple flowers and tiny green leaves.

'Our soufflé of violets,' said the captain proudly. 'It is one of the great specialities of Monsieur Tavernier – our esteemed master chef.'

'Oh, it looks so beautiful, I hardly dare eat it.'

'Please do. The taste is even more wonderful than its appearance, I promise you.'

She gently pierced the soufflé with the tip of her spoon. The sweet smell of violets rose up.

At that moment, the first officer appeared. 'Excuse me, Captain.'

'Yes, what is it?'

'I'm sorry to interrupt, sir, but we've just received the wire from Scotland Yard.'

Captain Henshaw nodded. He turned back to Matty. 'You'll have to excuse me, Lady Clairmont. Duty calls.' Rising to his feet, he gave a courteous nod to the assembled table and departed.

When the steward went to collect Lady Slocombe's supper tray, he thought at first there was no one in the palatial suite of rooms for they lay silent and in semi-darkness. However, as his eyes grew accustomed to the gloom, he realised that her ladyship was sitting in a large armchair, motionless, Sphinx-like; not even stirring at his hurried apology.

He, therefore, quietly picked up the tray upon which a light supper of congealed coddled eggs sat untouched, and withdrew.

Outside in the corridor, he stared once more at the door of the suite. Scrawled across it in white chalk was one word: *thief.*

Mayfair, London. Saturday evening

Thelma Duttine stood in the bathroom doorway staring at the prone figure of Charles Sutton.

He lay on her bed submerged in a swirl of oyster satin coverlet, snoring softly, his head thrown back and his mouth wide. *For such a big man*, she thought, *his snores are surprisingly girlie.*

He looked ridiculous, of course, stretched along the bed, his top-half still formally attired in black tie, his bottom-half naked. Except for his socks and suspenders. Above his head, his arms were raised as if in submission, each prettily tied to a bedpost with a scarf of rainbow colours.

Carefully she watched the whale-smooth belly rise and fall, the tiny flaccid penis all but hidden within the folds of his thighs, and judged that she needn't untie him quite yet. Just a few more moments of peace then she would rouse him again.

She smiled; how right her friend Dolores had been, all those war years ago. 'Find the most secret desire of a man in bed,' she'd counselled, 'perform it successfully, and that man is yours for life.'

To that end, Thelma had set out to learn much. So much so, nothing now ever shocked her. Though nothing ever aroused her either.

Tant pis! Sexual ecstasy was for simpletons and innocents. What did it matter when she had such a prize at stake? On this man, Sir Charles Sutton, she'd banked all. And her business sense had never failed her to date. Tonight, after three years, she was out to get what she wanted: his wealth, his title, Melsham…

She looked back down at Charles and quickly crossed to the bedside table, an excitement growing within her. Snapping open her little black and red lacquer box, she withdrew a phial of cocaine powder and emptied it into his brandy glass.

With one hand she untied her negligee, which fell wide exposing her nakedness, the skin powdered pearly-pale, the nipples, red-rouged. She picked up the glass and, leaning forward to hold it to his lips, she softly started to croon, 'Charlie is my darling, my darling, my darling.'

CHAPTER NINETEEN

SS *Etoile*. Early Sunday morning

When Mrs Webb and Freddie emerged onto the first-class promenade, they were both nearly blown off their feet by the unexpected gustiness of the wind. The sky was still dark as they staggered and swayed along the shadowed slippery deck. Their eyes ran and their noses streamed, *But*, thought Mrs Webb, *I feel grand!* She steadied herself against the railings and dug deep for a couple of handkerchiefs. Blowing their noses, the pair of them gingerly looked over the rail and stared down. Far below they could glimpse through the gloom the sea rolling, heavy and grey. 'Eh, my lad, look at that.'

A porthole opened and a fountain of waste arched into the navy sky. There was an instant string of silver gulls swooping and flocking, their high cries peppering the deep roar of the wash.

Facing away from the wind, Mrs Webb carefully unfolded the map of the ship Barney had given her. 'Now, where are them kennels?'

'Gran, they're there,' said Freddie pointing. High above them, a vast funnel soared into the darkness.

Mrs Webb laughed. 'Aye, well them things are that big, you can't see 'em for looking.'

When she put her head round the canvas-flap of Mr Degas's office, she had only to take one look at the poor man and she was ordering, 'Freddie, fetch up Mr Degas a nice cup o' tea. And get couple o' cloves put in from kitchen while you're about it.'

'But—'

'Go on, lad. Me and Mr Degas are going to have a chat.'

She looked at the pale man as he sat in his kennels.

'Forgive me, madame, I do not get up. Last night a party; too much absinthe.' He gingerly shook his head.

'Don't worry, dear, soon have you sorted. Cup o' freshly made tea with two cloves'll do't trick. My Davy – him that was me late 'usband – used to tie ribbon on once in a while. I know all't signs only too well.'

Degas only nodded, his usual good manners absent.

Mrs Webb hovered, unsure, in the doorway.

'Now then, Mr Degas, I 'ave to ask, what's all this about? I know it concerns young Freddie. What's 'e been up to? You can tell me. He's only a young lad, mind, so whatever 'e's done—'

Mr Degas was waving at her. 'Stop, madame, stop. It is nothing like this. I would like to offer M'sieur Freddie a job.'

Nellie stared.

'He is very good with the dogs. He has – how d'you say? Natural aptitude.' He placed an unseen 'h' in front of the last word.

Nellie looked down, silent.

'Forgive me if I surprise you, madame. *Mal de tête.*' He nervously touched his head.

When at last she spoke, Nellie said, 'His mam would've been right proud of the lad...' but her relief and joy proved too much, she couldn't continue.

'M'sieur Fred has told me about his uncle, Barney – and that Billy Bottle is also a friend. So I wish you, as his *grandmére*, not to worry; we will look after him well.'

Nellie nodded.

'*Bon.* I would like to apprentice him to me. I will talk to the chief steward about his money and his berth. D'you think this is well, madame?'

Mrs Webb finally gathered herself together. She threw her hands towards the Frenchman and, clasping both of his in an enthusiastic shaking, cried, 'Oh! Yes, Mr Degas, very well indeed. With Mersewer Fred's say-so, of course.'

Through the little port-hole, Lily watched as the dusty light slowly flooded to the edges of the ocean, the young morning gently pushing its primrose rays up the slate sky. There, across the dark sea, stood the New York skyline, clustered vague and uncertain along the horizon.

'Oh, Johnnie, look.'

They knelt side by side on the bunk, peering out.

'When Charles and I came in '23, we watched from up on deck as New York appeared through the morning mist. It was dawn then, too. And I remember this Italian woman sobbing beside me. She thought the high buildings were a range of mountains, you see, and that the ship had brought her to the wrong country.' She turned to Johnnie. 'We've not come to the wrong country, have we?'

He gathered her up in his arms. 'It's not called the New World for nothing. And so we will find it.' He kissed her briefly on the nose. 'Come on, enough of all this lovey-dovey business, let's go and take those youngsters off Mrs Webb's hands for a bit.'

All was silent in the Webb cabin. Lily could see the children crouched on the floor in their pyjamas, playing a very complicated version of Pop the Beacon completely of their own devising, so complicated, in fact, that even Anthea was hushed. Mrs Webb was nowhere to be seen.

'Gran's gone to see t'doggie man,' said the little girl without looking up.

Barney rolled over on the top bunk. 'Morning, folks.' He waggled a *Winning Post* in greeting.

'Let's get some grub, eh, Barney?' Johnnie was never his best with crowds first thing.

'Aye, aye, mate.'

Alone with the two children, Lily sat down on the edge of Mrs Webb's bunk. She absentmindedly started to fold a pile of clothes. Strangely, for all her mental turmoil of the night before, she felt clear and hopeful. She had slept a good sleep, the champagne and sea air having finally laid her flat. She let hope suffuse her heart. *All shall be well and all shall be well and all manner of things shall be well*, she prayed to a jumble of pants, vests and socks.

When she heard Johnnie knock on the door, she leapt up, eager for her steaming cup of coffee. She stepped over the rapt Nickie and Anthea and opened the cabin door.

Johnnie stood in the corridor, coffeeless. She took one look at his still, stern face and knew the worst.

'The captain wants to see us.' His voice was colourless. At his side stood First Officer Hodder. Barney was nowhere to be seen. She felt her throat constrict, dry and tight.

Johnnie held her elbow and leant into the cabin. 'Now, you two, be good until Mrs Webb gets back. Tell her we've gone to see the captain.'

'The big man?' asked Anthea. 'Can I come?'

'Not today,' said Johnnie firmly and closed the door.

With Mr Hodder leading the way, they followed silently up through the ship. Lily clutched Johnnie's arm, her resolve finally spent.

'Come!'

First Officer Hodder opened the office door. They stepped into the low morning sunlight and stood momentarily blinded.

Through the dazzle, she became aware of the tall figure of Captain Henshaw as he rounded his desk. 'Mrs Valley, I'm so sorry to bother you once again.' He firmly shook her hand. 'Won't you sit down? And is this your husband? Good morning to you. Some coffee, I think, Mr Hodder, please.'

Lily sat rigid, her every sense ready for the trap. Johnnie stood just behind her, his hand lightly resting on her shoulder. She looked across the desk to the captain; she could discern no expression, he was sitting against the March sun, his face shadowed.

'I wanted to thank you once again for helping us sort out that messy business of the stolen bracelet,' said the captain. 'Young Lady Clairmont, though most discreet, I may say even secretive, intimated that you'd assisted her in some way. As you may or may not know, a culprit has been apprehended.'

Johnnie and Lily said nothing.

'It's a most satisfactory outcome as the Clairmonts are on their honeymoon,' the captain smiled. 'It would have been so unfortunate, I'm sure you'll agree, if they had had it blighted in any way.'

He moved back in his chair and out of the shadow. At last his face was in clear view. 'Now, this is what I really wanted to see you about.' He opened his desk. 'I've received a cable from Scotland Yard.'

Lily felt Johnnie's grip tighten on her shoulder. She lowered her head and closed her eyes.

'I thought you might be interested to read it.'

With a mechanical lift of her head, she looked at the captain; he was pushing a telegram across the desk. She glanced up at Johnnie. He gave her an infinitesimal nod.

Very slowly, she picked up the cable.

'INQUIRY INTO DISAPPEARANCE OF LADY SUTTON AND SON DROPPED AT REQUEST OF FATHER STOP NO FURTHER DETAILS'

'You see, Mr Valley,' she could hear the captain's voice; it seemed far, far away. 'I don't know if your wife told you but Lady Slocombe seems to have been under the misapprehension that your little girl was a little boy.' Lily raised her eyes, Captain Henshaw was looking straight at her. 'It appears, Mrs Valley, to have been a case of mistaken identity all round.'

He paused. 'I just thought you would like to be put in the picture before we arrived in New York.'

CHAPTER TWENTY

SS *Etoile*. Sunday morning

Mrs Webb was sitting resplendent on a steamer trunk. She was wearing a voluminous cloth coat which was tied at the waist with a shawl and had a jaunty straw hat perched on her head. Sitting in the centre of many leaning towers of luggage, she was keeping an eye on the children playing 'tag' in and out of the leather jungle.

Making towards the group, Lily saw that the loudest noise was being made by Johnnie playing 'tag' too. He had abandoned his jacket despite the sharp March wind, and was tearing around the deck causing the children to squeal with joy and the other passengers to frown their disapproval as they patiently waited in rows to disembark.

Mrs Webb waved a welcome. 'Barney's told us all to wait quiet for a bit, he's got to finish down below. Then he'll give us an 'and.'

'I'm glad that's what Johnnie thinks "waiting quiet" means,' replied Lily.

'Yes but look at your Nickie. Talk about flying the coop. Little lamb,' the big woman smiled.

'I think he's mainly relieved he doesn't have to wear the tartan skirt he came on board in.'

Mrs Webb patted the spot beside her on the trunk. 'Here. Take the weight off your feet. I reckon we're not going to be gettin' off for hours.'

Lily sat. 'I found this when I was checking to see if we'd left anything in the cabin. Under Nickie's pillow.' She held up a little lead soldier. 'He always sleeps with it. Says it's to look after him if a bad man comes in the night. He means Charles, of course.' She stared at the swollen crowd of people unsuccessfully trying to squash down the narrow gangplank.

'Well,' said Nellie. 'He's in good 'ands now. Your Johnnie seems to have a natural aptitude.' Lily heard an unseen 'h' in front of the last word.

From behind the two women, a voice enquired, 'Lady Sutton?'

'Yes,' said Lily, turning round.

There stood Miss Timms, holding a small suitcase, a triumphant smile on her face. 'I thought as much.'

Lily froze. Mrs Webb grabbed her hand.

'You see, my lady,' the maid said evenly, 'I have this remarkable memory, though I say it myself. I never forget a face.' She was staring at Lily, her thin white face relieved only by a fierce redness that coloured her bony nose. 'Oh, don't worry, Lady Sutton, I won't say a word about your son.' She flicked a satisfied look to where Nickie were playing. 'I just wanted to be sure. For my own peace of mind.' She moved off through the crowds at speed and disappeared.

'She just wanted last word, more like. 'Orrible old bag,'
burst out Mrs Webb. She looked extremely agitated and started
to pat Lily's hand vigorously. 'You all right, my love? You've
gone that pale.'

Lily dropped her head; she felt sick. 'Just as I'd relaxed.
How could I be so stupid?'

'Now, now, don't take on so. All's well. I'll wager she'll
say nowt to no one.'

'That wretched title of Charles's. Dear God, how I hate
it.'

They sat saying nothing. The swollen crowd pushed on,
its size never changing.

After a bit Mrs Webb asked, 'So you and your Johnnie are
not going back to Blighty? Now the hunt's off.'

'No fear, Mrs Webb. Do you know, this trip's made me
realise just how much of my old life I hated. It's time to
start anew.'

'Well, this America's the right place to do it, so I'm told.'
She looked at Lily. 'Before I forget in all the goodbyes, I just
want to thank you good folks. Me and the children have had
a grand time. Joining in your adventures and that.'

'Well, we couldn't have done it without you.'

Mrs Webb gave a dismissive little laugh.

'No, I'm serious,' said Lily. 'You've been a very good friend
to us. To me, especially. I shall always be eternally grateful.
You, more than any one, have made our new life possible.'

And Mrs Webb sat, rosy and beaming.

'Your mug of tea, Cap'n.'

'Thank you, Mr Staps. And who are we sharing our berth
with today?'

'*Berengaria* and *Olympic*, sir, as far as I can make out. But word is the *Ile de France* is also tied up alongside.'

'Very good, Mr Staps. That'll be all for the minute.'

Henshaw took a sip of his tea. He still found a thrill in navigating his ship, flanked by little tugs and the occasional fireboat, past the Statue of Liberty and up the Hudson River into the busiest port in the world. The SS *Etoile* was a safe, solid liner, perhaps not as glamorous as some but she was certainly magnificent enough to bring the passengers crowding onto the decks as they entered the harbour, the fireboats letting off a triple blast.

From his view on high, he watched the passengers cramming all three decks. Even from up here in the wheelhouse with the doors closed, he could hear the wild cries of excitement, the cacophony of sounds that always heralded the arrival in port. And he knew, hidden from the passengers' view, the turn-around was well under way. Tucked out of sight, a line of lorries would be collecting the mountains of laundry whilst all over the ship inventories would be being taken, the food and liquor stocks in need of replenishing. A tight turn-around was to be encouraged; yearly the huge port fees escalated.

He finished his tea and stepped out onto the bridge. There was a fresh south-easterly and a clear sky, the dusty glass roof of the long immigration hall running alongside the ship surprisingly sparkling up at him this March morning.

Down on the dockside, he saw a small area roped off at the bottom of the first-class gangway, a clutch of newsreel cameras pointing towards the disembarking guests. The 'world famous' Donald O'Dea appeared to be giving an interview, his wife at his side, her hat today, the captain noted, a particularly eye-catching royal-blue toque. *Nice couple*, he thought, *not grand*

at all. In fact, they'd been a real asset last evening at dinner.
He could see, down below, everyone laughing at something
the big man had just said.

Looking along the landing platform, he watched a stream
of white-capped porters tailing their way through the crowds.
Though noisy, the general atmosphere was one of goodwill, the
hundreds of passengers cheerfully queuing their way down the
many gangplanks. And in the midst of this melee sat a policeman
on horseback, his gleaming chestnut mount completely at ease
with the human chaos all around. A Rolls Royce swung past
Henshaw's eyeline and he watched as the ship's crane hoisted
it high into the air and on towards land.

He turned away and stared straight ahead to the prow
of his ship, but the horizon was no longer filled with a vast
ocean. In front lay a highway, with large bulbous motor cars
trundling on their way, seemingly oblivious to the mighty liners
moored alongside the road. A vast roadside sign announced,
'Western Union'.

He smiled. It'd been a good trip; no major dramas, as far
as he was aware. He'd have a final talk with Billy Bottle before
they both disembarked, just to check all was ship-shape, then
ten days' leave. He was quite looking forward to it.

Epilogue

Freston, England. April 1943

Lily lay on her back, staring up through the apple trees. Beyond the puffs of blossom, she could see the sky was streaked with iron-grey slashes. There had been a dog-fight. At the first wasp-like drone of the engines, the children had rushed out into the orchard, hopping and dancing, madly tearing round in circles, stopping only to shake their fists at the two little planes whirling about the sky above. Eventually both aeroplanes had spiralled down somewhere near Salisbury Plain, leaving two thick black plumes of smoke. Giant exclamation marks down the sky. The children had run off in search of another game.

There're no survivors, Lily thought. *No parachutes swaying to earth.* She rolled onto her front. It was too beautiful a day to have death written all over the skies.

She lay spread-eagled on the old car-rug, feeling the warmth of the sun all along her back. What luxury. Squinting at her watch, she saw it was still only ten past twelve. She had another hour; the train wasn't arriving until two o'clock. She'd walk to the station in good time. Not that the train would be punctual.

Everything was ready, nothing else to prepare. She knew Mary had baked a cake; the last of the margarine ration – and no doubt all the eggs. How lovely, a party. And Anthea's room was waiting. At the top of the house, under the eaves. The little crooked room with many corners.

Lily jumped to her feet. She was too nervous to keep lolling about. Brushing the grass from her trousers, she crossed to the edge of the orchard but still hovered in the shade under the bent apple trees. She looked across the courtyard to where the big old farmhouse stood solid. Recently it had struck her that the place had taken on the wistful appearance of one of the war-wounded itself, the glass criss-crossed with pasted strips of linen and the windows dankly framed in black-out material.

'When I returned from the first war, this old place was dead,' Johnnie had said when they'd first moved back from America five years before. 'It had always been the hub of life but as every single farmhand had been killed, not surprisingly their mothers and sweethearts weren't very keen on hanging round any longer.'

But it's full of life now, thought Lily. *Once again*. How she loved this house; it was home in a way Melsham had never been. She remembered the first time she'd been brought here by Sam and Mary. Battered and broken. Running away from Charles. And she'd woken in a strange narrow bed, in a room full of a musty dusty smell. A crooked little room under the eaves. A room full of many corners. How long had she hidden here that first time? Three days? Four? She couldn't recall.

Now ten years on, she smiled as she thought of Johnnie, awkward and distant during that first stay, all the charm of Sam and Mary's wedding day totally absent. 'I didn't want you here,' he'd admitted. 'It felt like an intrusion, a demand. I was trying to push you away.'

Though at the time, she hadn't really noticed his mood nor minded. Life had been too dark; too dark to look around, let alone to look forward, to glimpse another possibility, a new future. The endless pain inflicted by Charles had become a drug, a habit. Inescapable. Even now, thinking back, she could feel her whole body sicken at the memory, the very thought of Charles bringing cold numbness to her veins, blankness to her mind and 'absence' to her heart. 'Only nursemaids have pain, Lily.' The old family training; Mother had taught her well. Her survival kit. No feelings...

And yet here in this very orchard, she had started to feel again, to come back to life. Lily shaded her eyes. Dotted through the long grass, clumps of orange-snouted daffodils swayed and danced round the base of the old fruit trees, yellow balloons of forsythia billowing from the hedges. How lovely it was, so peaceful. No one would ever guess at the misery of war so close at hand.

There was a clatter as Mary crossed the yard. Dressed in a floral printed overall, she came into the orchard, waggling a colander full of carrots. 'I'm doing these out here, take advantage of this weather. I've laid out something cold for us, salad and that – you can have it before you walk down to the station.'

She sat on the car-rug. 'Mind, when the war's over I'll be that pleased never to look a beetroot in the face again. Nice bit of steak and kidney, that's what Sam dreams of, with dumplings. I told him, "You'll have to wait till Doomsday, Mr Garnet's that mean with his suet." And you'd think kidneys were more precious than rubies, the carry-on that was going on at the butcher's yesterday.'

Three children, a boy and two girls, roared out of the house and into the orchard. They made straight for the two women and started playing 'tag' around them.

'Annie,' cried Mary, 'I'll not tell you again – leave be!'

The smallest girl, Annie, her pig-tails flying, stopped beside her mother and snatched a carrot from the colander.

'Urgh,' said the scrawny boy, and Annie, hurling herself forward, pushed the carrot up the boy's nose. The boy ducked; Annie was after him. The third child, a small thin girl, pattered, bored, along in their wake. They all disappeared round the front of the house.

The two women watched them go. Mary sighed loudly.

'You're not going to stop her,' said Lily. 'She's so pleased to have those two to play with. And I must say, it's heaven to have their noise even though the house is now fit to bursting.'

She sat back down on the rug. 'Come on, give me some of those, I'll help.' She reached into her trouser pocket for a penknife.

The noise of the children echoed up and round; they were playing at being dive-bombing aeroplanes. 'They seem happy enough, don't they? After London, those two little ones must feel safer here.'

'They don't know how lucky they are, little blighters. Mind, Sam was telling me some of the billets round here for these evacuees are disgusting. Government shouldn't allow it.' Mary nodded towards the noise of the children. 'They've got something planned later. In honour of our American guest! I could hear the three of them last night up in the attic.' She slipped a handkerchief from her sleeve and mopped her brow. 'Phew, it's that hot.'

Lily looked towards the outer edge of the orchard; there was a distant sound of water. 'I might go for a swim in the stream later on. First of the year.'

'Well, mind you wrap up after. I'm not having you in bed with pneumonia. What would Johnnie say if he gets back and you've caught a fever?'

'I hardly think a quick dip's going to kill me!'

'Well, I don't want any of those children going in – it'll be mud-cakes and all sorts before you can say "blink".' She started to swiftly slice the carrots into the colander.

Lily watched her out of the corner of her eye. In the last few years her friend had put on weight, despite the strictures of food rationing. Now she sat, a comfortably round middle-aged woman and Lily smiled, remembering how once she'd worn Mary's clothes to escape. Sam, on the other hand, seemed daily to get thinner and thinner. 'Jack Spratt and his wife,' he'd announced only last week, coming in from the pigs. 'She's after a bit o' fat and he a bit o' lean.' Mary had nudged him. 'I'd like to see where I could lay my hands on "a bit o' fat" these days.'

'Right here, my lass,' her husband had chuckled and pulled her to him.

Lily put down her knife and checked her watch again. 'I hope Johnnie and Anthea met up all right in London. They should be well on their way by now.'

'Stop fretting. The train'll not be on time anyhow. Good thing too, Johnnie and her coming down together. At least she'll know where to get off. Unlike my sister. Remember that time she came? Wandering about the countryside half the night before she found us.' Mary made a little clucking sound and shook her head. 'Taking away all the station names! I'd like to know what the Government's thinking of.' A favourite theme of Mary's, Lily left her to it. 'I don't know about them Nazi invaders but it's certainly left us all baffled. And then the name painted out on the church noticeboard. I mean, I ask you.'

By the time the train pulled into Freston Station, the platform was crowded. Soldiers spilled from the station buffet, a khaki sea thankfully obscuring the sign, 'Is Your Journey Really Necessary?', an admonition that had always got Lily's infrequent journeys to see Johnnie in London off to a bad start. As the engine wheezed to a long sighing halt, Lily turned and turned about trying to catch the window from which Anthea or Johnnie's head would emerge. Suddenly she saw a buxomly-built young woman throw open a carriage door and start to descend onto the platform. Lily pushed through the crowds towards her.

'Aunt Lily. Aunt Lily!' She became aware that the shout was coming not from in front of her but behind. 'Aunt Lily. Here!'

She turned to find herself confronting a slim young woman in a well-cut grey suit, no hat but short glossy brown hair, deep red lips and matching nails. A gas-mask, in its box, was slung over her shoulder.

'Anthea?' she said in disbelief, and saw Johnnie standing at the young woman's side, beaming for ear to ear. 'Is it really you?'

The young woman nodded seriously and then her face, too, broke into a smile.

'My goodness, how smart you look.' Lily felt tears spring into her eyes. 'Oh, forgive me. How stupid.'

But Anthea wasn't listening; she threw her arms around her neck. 'Oh, Aunt Lily.' And Lily hugged her back with all her might.

'We got seats all the way,' Johnnie chuckled. 'Thanks to this young lady looking such a smasher. I think they thought I was her elderly father and gave me one out of sympathy!'

Slowly the khaki sea was sucked into the train and with only a scattering of passengers left on the platform, the engine gave a piercing whistle followed by a deep groan. The train sturdily started to pull out of the station. Through one of the windows, Lily could see a bunch of soldiers tussling with the leather strap. As the window finally lurched down, the soldiers crammed through, blowing kisses towards the three of them. 'See you again, sweetheart.' 'Ta-ta, my lovely!'

Anthea waved back happily. 'Thanks for the ride, boys!' Lily instantly caught the American twang, the girl's North Country accent, seemingly no more.

And where had all the puppy-fat gone? Trim, that was the word for her now. A real stunner. Mr Suggs, the porter who never stirred for anyone without a six-pence, rushed to the young woman's side, swept up her case and whistled off down the platform, handing it back to her with a flourish at the barrier.

They set off up into the village, the three of them walking arm in arm, each chatting, each with their own thoughts.

She's gotten older, Anthea was thinking. *Her hair's faded to pale yellow, no more 'carrots' as Gran used to call it. Mind, it suits her better cut short, shows her face. Her face isn't the same either, so brown and freckly; looks like a schoolgirl. But her voice is the same; that hasn't changed. Posh but not scary, that's what me and Freddie reckoned, soft and posh. And Johnnie? Bald, completely bald! And that beard and tash make him look like the picture of the King we had at school. Nice eyes though, he's still got those.*

'I can't tell you how my standing will have gone up at the War Office,' Johnnie was saying. 'Crofty's eyes were out on stalks when he went to collect Anthea from the reception desk. Didn't believe his boss could know such a glamour-puss.'

As they passed along the High Street, Lily saw it all through Anthea's eyes. Most of the cottages needed a coat of paint, the windows criss-crossed with paper-strips, a few even boarded up, glass being in short supply. The Crown Hotel looked drab and not particularly welcoming, and the church, as always, stood sturdy, square and Norman. But people were friendly enough: bicycle bells ringing, Mrs Dauncey reminding Lily about a WVS meeting and the doctor's wife asking Johnnie to re-join the choir.

'No such chance, Pamela, I'm afraid. I've only managed to scrounge a forty-eight-hour leave this time.'

They cut through the churchyard, rooks cawing in the high dark trees, and made their way between higgledy-piggledy gravestones, which stuck out like old teeth. They reached an iron kissing-gate in the far corner. 'You do realise you're being treated to the scenic route,' said Johnnie, squeezing his way through after them.

'Gee, it's all so ancient. I'd forgotten how old everything is.' There was wonder in the girl's voice. 'At home, we've got nothing older than ten years.'

So 'home' is America, thought Lily.

'Did your gran know it was today you were coming down?'

'You bet. She'll be hanging over her calendar. My suitcase is stuffed with presents from her.'

'Oh, Nellie shouldn't have, she's so naughty.'

'Just try stopping her, she's been planning this trip for me for months.'

Later that afternoon, Anthea presented various wrapped parcels. 'Ooh, nylons! Oh Johnnie, look, how marvellous. But I'm going to keep them for best! *And* my favourite scent.'

'Lucky Strikes, I say.' Johnnie waved his present with delight. 'And I'm *not* going to keep them for best.' He lit up.

'And this is chocolate for Sam and Mary, and chewing-gum for the kids. Gran says she hopes you won't be cross with her if it gets stuck to the furniture! And, finally, there's these.' The girl handed across a paper wallet. 'Gran's wedding photos!'

'No!'

And indeed there was Nellie, resplendent, swathed in a gown of pale blue silk, a tiny hat like a white pie perched on the side of her head, a slip of veil hiding one eye. She looked wonderfully jaunty and radiant, standing with her arm wrapped through her new husband's, the two of them grinning at the camera, both round as barrels.

'He's called Lee Spencer Junior – he's still called "Junior" even though he's fifty-six – and he owns an automobile tyre business. And because of the war, it's made him a rich man, so Gran's got herself a gold-mine in her old age!'

'Marvellous!'

'And that makes him – let me see – your step-granddad?' guessed Johnnie.

'Yup, though we still call him "Uncle Lee". He's a real nice old guy.'

'Not so much of the old, if you don't mind,' said Johnnie.

'Hey, shucks, I don't mean you folks.' Anthea looked crestfallen, and at that moment Lily glimpsed the serious pudgy little girl who had been so important on their journey to America.

'Don't worry, he's only teasing,' she said. 'Go on with what you were saying.'

'Freddie's working in the business an' all – he just loves cars, any sorts. And Uncle Lee also has a son. He's called Frank and he's joined up even though he's thirty. Not that that's old,' she added hastily. 'Anyways, Frank's been sent over here to serve. Some camp near Winchester.' She pronounced the name in three even stresses.

'You've become a real American "gal". I can't believe it.' Lily shook her head. 'Where's that North Country accent I remember so well?'

'Gran's still got one. Uncle Lee and Frank tease her about it all the time.'

Tea was a treat, with Mary's cake gobbled up almost before it had left the larder and jam tarts made with 'our raspberries from the garden'.

'Lily's pride and joy,' said Johnnie. 'No doubt you'll be given a tour to see her goats and her kitchen garden tomorrow.'

Lily pulled a face at him. 'I'm just doing my bit. Digging for victory and making my cheese.' The success of her vegetables and home-made cheese had come as a surprise to everyone. She was now growing all their own produce and also helping to supply the local greengrocers.

'Well, as long as you don't mention Doctor Carrot and Potato Pete,' grumbled Mary. 'We're all heartily sick of them – and that Lord Woolton's Pie. Bet he's never had to eat it.' She went off muttering. Sounds of the washing-up could be heard.

'I can't believe I've met her at last,' said Anthea. 'Her and Sam always seemed like characters in a movie.'

Johnnie took out his pipe. 'Well, I've a bit of news. Come back, Mary,' he called through the kitchen door. 'I want you to hear this as well.'

She came in wiping her hands on her overall. 'That washing-up won't get done by leaving it in the sink, you know.'

'I'll do it later.'

She looked askance at him. 'Promise?'

He grinned and pulled out her chair; he waited for her to sit down.

'Now then. Some news came through last week "in the bag" from New York. I thought it'd be fun to tell you all together.' He paused and pulled his tobacco pouch from his pocket.

'Oh Johnnie, for goodness sake, what?'

'The Slocombes have been arrested for fiddling war bonds.'

'No!' 'When?' 'Serves them right.'

He sat back letting their reactions come thick and fast, packing his pipe, until eventually Lily cried, 'Shhh, the lot of you. Let Johnnie speak, I want to know more. *Is* there any more?'

He nodded. 'It seems their downfall came through an anonymous letter to the FBI.' He held a match to his pipe. 'It just surprises me, given Lavinia Slocombe's record, the authorities took so long to catch up with them.'

'Arrested by the FBI, it's like the pictures – oh, I can't wait to tell Sam.' Mary looked overjoyed.

'After all this time – horrible old bag.' Anthea's cheeks had gone bright pink and Lily saw the girl unconsciously rub the arm that had been scratched all those years ago.

She reached across and took Anthea's hand. 'Yes, I have to say I fully agree with you there. She *is* a horrible old bag.' She jumped to her feet. 'We must tell your gran. Oh dear, if only we could use the telephone. I'll write in the next couple of days and we can post it off at once.'

The next morning, Lily asked Anthea, 'Do you think you can face my vegetable garden?'

They made their way through the yard and round to the side of the big old house, both carrying forks and buckets. The side lawn had been turned over to vegetables and along the far stone wall, which served as a windbreak, a cold frame had been constructed. The kitchen garden itself was laid out in strict rows, and although it was only spring, Anthea could see hardy rows of green appearing. At the edge of the planting ran the original path of flagstones.

'I cleared all this two years ago. This is what saved my life,' said Lily evenly. 'After Nickie was killed.' She looked at Anthea.

The girl stood stranded, staring down at the ground. Tears began to flow down her face. She did nothing to stop them.

Lily put her arms around the girl. 'Oh, my dear. I know. Some days the pain is so extraordinary I think I won't be able to breathe.'

Anthea stood sobbing onto Lily's shoulder, the fork and bucket still in her hands. The sobs came in hard short blasts.

'Come on, come and sit down.' She led the girl to the wall, sat them on a couple of wooden boxes and pulled out her handkerchief. 'Here, have a big blow.'

'I'm sorry, so sorry—'

'Hush,' said Lily. 'No "sorrys". Not allowed.'

The girl tried to smile and began to cry even harder. 'It's why I had to come,' she sobbed. 'I miss him so much.'

'I know,' was all Lily said.

Later they sat, Anthea all cried-out, both of them smoking. 'It's why I've come to England also. I want to become a Wren.'

'Does Nellie know?'

Anthea nodded. 'She's not happy about it. But it's what Nickie would have wanted. I think.' She turned to Lily. 'I'm sorry I cried.'

'No "sorrys". We made that a house rule two years ago.'

'When the war started,' Anthea said, 'I always knew that if Nickie joined up, it would be the Navy. He was so mad about the sea, wasn't he? I think it started after our trip all together.'

Lily stared ahead.

'Me and Nickie, we wrote each other so much when you left the States. Silly letters and stuff. I remember he was so excited to be on that boat going back to England!'

'How did you hear? About Nickie, I mean. Nellie and I write all the time but I wasn't the one who told her he'd been killed. I always wondered how she knew. And so quickly.' Lily braced herself. Could she bear the pain of an unknown detail? But it had to be faced, whatever. She crushed the cigarette beneath her gumboot and crossed her arms over her knees.

'Johnnie put through a trunk-call to Gran. He told her the news.'

Lily sat silent, looking straight ahead.

'He said he thought it important she knew as soon as

possible.' The girl turned, unsure whether to continue.

'Go on,' said Lily, still looking ahead.

'On the day Gran got the call from Johnnie, she came to find me at work. They took me into the manager's office. Gran told me Nickie had been serving aboard HMS *Ramses* and that the ship had gone down and that he had been "killed in action".' The girl said the phrase very carefully. 'Gran was so worried about you. Johnnie said, when you were told—'

Lily grasped Anthea's hand. The girl stopped speaking.

When I was told. Lily stared up at the big dark trees and thought about that moment. *The moment when the world went silent, the moment there was no sound. Except for me screaming. The scream that I wanted to go on and on. The scream that would block out all sound. All sound that would tell me again and again my son was dead...*

But the scream hadn't saved her. The pain had hit her and gone on and on and on – and with it always the thought, *Why was I not with him? To protect him. My son. Why did I not die instead of him?*

Always these same thoughts.

'And yet,' said Lily quietly, 'somehow I have survived.' She turned to Anthea. 'It's a mystery to me how it is so. But it is so.'

They sat and, out of her bucket, Lily drew a Thermos flask. She poured some tea into the plastic cup and gave it to Anthea. High above them, the rooks cawed. Lily lit another cigarette.

She said, 'I keep looking for him. I can't stop myself. I'll be in the kitchen – or down by the stream, he loved it there from the first time he came to visit the farm as a little boy and Sam and Johnnie and him played mud-cakes. And I'll be by the stream, and I think, *If I swing round quickly enough, he'll be there. I'll catch him.*' She felt Anthea shiver. 'Go on, drink your tea. I've put some sugar in as a treat.'

The girl drank.

'Perhaps on Nickie's ship they were allowed a tot of rum in their tea,' Lily said. It was a new idea, a new piece of the jigsaw to hold over the puzzle that had so many gaps. And trivial as it was, the idea warmed her.

For weeks after the news had come through, she hadn't been able to keep still, so much was unknown and she had become desperate for facts. 'Plain facts, that's what I wanted. Eventually I went to the Admiralty – Johnnie wangled it – to see what I could find out. Where the ship was when it went down. Where Nickie was on the ship. How he was killed. I thought, if I *knew*, it would help me to think about him. You see,' she turned to Anthea, 'I dream about him all the time. Or rather, I dream that I can't find him. It's always the same dream. I'm walking through a hospital ward trying to find him. He's there somewhere, I know it, in one of the beds. Alive still.' She stopped. Sometimes the strength of the pain amazed her. Not so much its strength but the fact that she could live through it. Survive it. Now she waited as the well-known surge lurched through her. *Breathe, Lily, breathe.*

Silently Anthea handed her the cup and she made herself drink. She made herself think about the new idea; the warmth of a tot of rum. A tot of rum before a battle. It encouraged her. She took another sip of tea and, tasting it for the first time, made a face. 'Why does Thermos tea always taste of plastic? I thought the sugar might disguise it.'

'Tea does you good, though. When I was a babbie, Gran'd make us drink tea if we were upset. Sometimes she'd give it us as a treat an' all. With bread and marge and sugar. Me and Freddie'd spread spoons and spoons on't bread.' Lily heard marvelling in her voice. 'Spoons and spoons. Later, I realised she couldn't afford nowt else. It were a way to stop us children being hungry, like.'

At last, Lily heard the North Country accent clearly. 'I miss your gran,' she said. 'I wish she were here now. She'd talk some sense into us, eh?'

Anthea nodded.

The sun climbed the sky and, slowly, as it reached over the kitchen wall, Lily felt the spring warmth ease up the length of her body. 'I'm told dreams of looking for someone who's died are quite common. If there hasn't been a funeral. Or if you haven't seen the body.' She clutched Anthea's hand. No, no, that thought hadn't been dealt with yet, his body…

She closed her eyes; the sunshine spangled her eyelids.

After a bit, she heard Anthea say, 'When Mam died, 'cos it was a fire, nothing was left – no building, no people. So me and Freddie didn't know where Mam'd gone. Gran told us she'd gone into the air, like, in the flames and the smoke – and 'cos of that, she was all around us. Always. In the air and the clouds. So me and Freddie used to pretend we could wrap ourselves up in her, in her air. That way she would look after us.' She turned to Lily. 'There was a fire on his ship, wasn't there?'

For a moment, Lily couldn't speak, then she nodded.

Eventually she said, 'You're very wise, you know that? Just like your gran. I remember Nellie telling me, when we were on the *Etoile* how she'd had to learn to live with all that had happened to her. Losing her husband and then her children. I couldn't understand how she'd managed to survive such terrible loss. "You've got to look after the living, lass," she said, "And that means yourself as well."'

'Aye, well she were right,' said her granddaughter stoutly.

My dear Nellie,

It's early in the morning here, very still and peaceful, so I thought I would quickly write this and catch the first post.

Out of the study window I can see Sam going off to muck out the pigs and Mary's banging about lighting the range in the kitchen. She'll be out with the ash in a minute to put around her beloved roses. (By the by, she's as strict as you are: no fires laid once the spring cleaning has been done!) And upstairs, fast asleep under the eaves, is Anthea. I can't tell you how lovely it is to have her here. What a honey! She's turning quite a few heads in our little town, I can tell you. It's so strange how, one minute, she reminds me of you and then the next of Freddie. But for the most part I can't see sight nor sound of that plump silent sad little girl I first met. You must be so proud of her; she's grown into such a lovely young woman. Very much her own person — and for that, I know exactly who she takes after!

Thank you, dearest Nellie, for all our marvellous presents. They are glorious. My nylons will only be for 'best' but Johnnie lit up one of his Lucky Strikes immediately. I think he still secretly fancies himself in a Cadillac! And my scent — and the chocolates. Such goodies at such a time…

And what about your wedding photographs? You look so glamorous! As does your Lee; you make a perfect couple. I am so very pleased for you — I always felt he was the right man ever since you mentioned him in your letters last year. The minute this horrid war has ended we are going to be straight over to celebrate. God willing it will be soon.

Now, I have two bits of news. Firstly, the Slocombes have been caught fiddling war bonds – and, what's more, Johnnie was told at the War Office that they are going to have to stand trial in New York! Frankly, from what we all knew about Lavinia, it doesn't surprise me one bit, just that it took so long for the authorities to catch up with her. I almost wondered whether Matilda and Henry Clairmont had anything to do with 'turning them in' but my brother, Hugh, ran into them in Cape Town (where he's now living), and seemingly they have been tucked away 'up country' doing their good works for years, so I very much doubt it.

Secondly, I have seen Charles. I had to go to a funeral of an old friend, Dolly Barton, and he and Thelma were there. I must confess I got a terrible shock seeing him for the first time in years – he looked so very frail and thin, walking with the aid of a stick. I felt absurdly upset at one point but then I only had to think of how he cut Nickie off without a bean after the divorce – and then the awful silence after Nickie was killed – and my customary rage returned. Thelma looked very expensive, all in black Shantung silk and an enormous veil. Very 'lady of the manor'. But I mustn't be bitchy. I suppose, indirectly, I have her to thank for the fact Johnnie and I were able to get married and come home to England.

I have told Anthea to come and stay any time. I don't think I realised how close she and Nickie were, almost like brother and sister. We sat in the kitchen-garden and talked and talked of him. I felt it was a relief for her even though it has been over two years now. But the pain never ceases, does it? Every day, every moment. She also told me how worried they all were about you with Barney in that POW camp. But do not lose hope, I beg. I just wish I could be there with you.

I pray for us all every night. For an agnostic, I seem to do an awful lot of praying at the moment! Strangely, I realise the worst of times have often turned out to be a prelude to the best of times. We just mustn't give up hope; we must believe in that hidden dance around the corner...

To you all we send much love. And from me to you, a special hug.

Lily

She dropped the letter into the post-box and, after only a second's hesitation, turned her bike away from home. She pushed it along the lane until she reached an old gate, here leaving the bike against a hedge. She entered a newly planted field and carefully made her way round the edge. Clambering over a stile at the far corner, she took a path that began to rise. Climbing, climbing, she reached the crest of the hill and stood, her breath coming heavily, gazing down at the bright countryside rolling away all around her.

At last, calmed, she looked up at the sky.

Fat white clouds, billowing and free, sailed swiftly along to the east. And Lily, all alone, high on the hill, held out her arms and let the air and the clouds wrap around her.